The Forgotten Daughter

ALSO BY JOANNA GOODMAN

The Home for Unwanted Girls

The Finishing School

Harmony

You Made Me Love You

The Forgotten Daughter

A Novel

Joanna Goodman

HARPER LARGE PRINT

An Imprint of HarperCollinsPublishers

HarperCollins books may be purchased for educational, business, or sales promotional use. For information, please e-mail the Special Markets Department at SPsales@harpercollins.com.

FIRST HARPER LARGE PRINT EDITION

ISBN: 978-0-06-302976-7

Library of Congress Cataloging-in-Publication Data is available upon request.

20 21 22 23 24   LSC   10 9 8 7 6 5 4 3 2 1

To my family, Mig, Jessie & Luke

Down in the angle at Montreal, on the island about which the two rivers join, there is little of this sense of new and endless space. Two old races and religions meet here and live their separate legends, side by side. If this sprawling half-continent has a heart, here it is. Its pulse throbs out along the rivers and railroads; slow, reluctant and rarely simple, a double beat, a self-moved reciprocation.

—HUGH MACLENNAN,
TWO SOLITUDES

1982

To live outside the law you must be honest.
—BOB DYLAN

Véronique and Pierre are sitting outside on the fire escape. They're twelve. It's a cool, sunless day in April, and they're missing school because her father is getting out of prison today.

Pierre is smoking, which is new for him. The cigarette looks absurd in his little boy's hand. Even the way he puts it to his lips and inhales—squinting his eyes, holding the smoke in his lungs like his dad does—is contrived.

"You look like an idiot," she says.

He shrugs.

"You're going to get addicted."

"I already am," he says, thinking he's cool. "My dad started smoking at nine."

"That doesn't make it smart."

Pierre doesn't say anything. Her thoughts return to her father, his impending return. Inside, the apartment is decorated with balloons and streamers. Véronique painted a sign that says, WELCOME HOME!

Her mother made a venison stew and chocolate cake, his favorites. Camil brought the venison, fresh from a recent hunting expedition with Pierre. The fridge is stocked with beer and Pepsi. His sisters—Véronique's aunts—are bustling around, getting everything ready. Pierre's little brother, Marc, is napping in her room so he can stay up late tonight. It's going to be a big party— that's what the grown-ups keep saying. The excitement is a current in the air, vibrating.

Véronique is quietly apprehensive. She's lived alone with her mother for as long as she can remember. They have a routine, a familiar, well-established system with its own rules and rituals. Her father's arrival will surely disrupt—if not completely upheave—their world. What if he's strict? Lisette is not. What if he's a slob? Lisette keeps a spotless house. What if he steals Lisette from her, monopolizes her mother's time and energy? What if her mother loves him more than she loves Véronique? What if her father doesn't like her? What if she doesn't like him?

All this is running through her head as she gazes out

past the trees into the back alley, where two tabbies are hissing at each other.

"You happy he's coming home?" Pierre asks her, sensing she's not as thrilled as the rest of them.

Véronique shrugs. "I guess so."

"It's going to be weird."

"Yeah."

"When's the last time you saw him?"

"September," she says. "His birthday."

That's been the sum total of their relationship since she was one, sporadic visits to the Cowansville Penitentiary—Christmas, Easter, his birthday. Lisette didn't want Véronique anywhere near that environment on a regular basis, so she limited their visits to special occasions. Véronique was happy with that arrangement. She hated going there, started dreading it weeks in advance. It was a terrible, demoralizing place. The prison guards intimidated her, the inmates terrified her, the building was bleak. She much preferred talking to him on the phone once a week.

But that's all in the past now. She'll never, ever have to go back to that place.

"I guess you don't really know him," Pierre says, not looking at her.

"I sort of do."

"I mean you don't know what it's like to live with him," he says. "It's not like me and my dad."

"Obviously," she mutters, annoyed.

"I'm just saying I can understand why you're not jumping for joy."

Right on cue, Pierre's father sticks his head out the back door. "They're here!" Uncle Camil says. "Put that goddamn cigarette out, Pierre."

The door flies open to a burst of cheering and clapping, and her parents enter the apartment. Lisette is flushed, beaming ear to ear. She keeps leaning her head on Léo's arm, holding his hand, touching him like she can't believe he's real. Véronique has never seen her mother like this before, and her initial reaction is jealousy. Already he's infringing.

And there is Léo, her father, tall and skinny but sturdy. His hair is buzzed, he's clean-shaven, his brown eyes are glistening with tears. He rushes over to Véronique and pulls her into his arms, pressing her tight against him. She awkwardly wraps her arms around his waist. She can feel his ribs through his jacket.

"My little girl," he says, the words muffled in her hair. He folds her into himself and holds her there, his body convulsing while he sobs. Everyone is crying; she is aware of a cacophony of sniffles behind her. She locks eyes with her mother across the room, and Lisette smiles at her through her tears.

Finally he releases her and stands back to look at her. "I can't believe I'm home," he says, choking up. "I'm home with my wife and my daughter!"

More clapping. Someone puts on the music—one of his old Jimi Hendrix albums, which no one has touched since he went to jail. Lisette joins them, and they all embrace, Véronique smothered between them.

"Someone get me a beer!" Léo cries out. They disperse and Véronique slips away.

She finds Pierre in the kitchen, drinking a 50 straight from the can. Marc is lying on his tummy on the linoleum, pushing a toy police car around. Véronique sits down beside him. He's four, eight years younger than Pierre, with a different mother who left right after she had Marc, making Uncle Camil a single father of two boys. They've all grown up more like siblings than cousins. She thinks of Pierre and Marc as her brothers—especially Pierre, who's the same age as her. Lisette and Camil have each filled a void in the other's life. Together, they make up a complete family.

"You're lucky," Pierre says.

"I am?"

"At least you're getting your dad back."

Véronique is quiet. She doesn't consider herself lucky.

"I'll never get my mom back," he says, surprising her. He never talks about his mom.

Marc looks up at his big brother. "You have me," he says. "And I have you."

Véronique scoops Marc into her lap and smothers his fat cheek with kisses. "You sweet boy," she says. "You sweet, smart boy."

Pierre holds out his can of beer, offering her some.

"Don't be stupid," she says.

As a joke, he offers his little brother the beer. Marc reaches for the can with his pudgy hand, eager to please, but Véronique stops him.

"Let him have a sip," Pierre says.

Véronique ignores him. "Your brother is a bad influence," she tells Marc, smoothing his fine brown hair, which is as soft as feathers. She runs his toy police car up and down his little sausage leg, and he giggles, burrowing his head against her. She knows she will always have to protect him from his older brother.

Much later, when the party is winding down and most of the people have gone home, her father pulls her down onto his lap. She can tell he's very drunk. His lids are heavy, and he's slurring his words. "You're so beautiful," he weeps, tears sliding down his cheeks. "You look just like your mother."

"People say I look like you."

This pleases him. He kisses her forehead. He smells of body odor, cigarettes, and beer, but it's somehow fatherly and wonderful.

"I'm home now," he says. "For good."

She's staring down at the floor, a little uncomfortable.

"I'm going to make it up to you," he goes on, his breath warm in her ear. "I'm going to be the father you should have had all these years. I promise, I'm going to make up for lost time."

She nods, not knowing what to say. He seems to be waiting for something, a cue, an acknowledgment. He's watching her expectantly.

She wraps her arms around his neck and says, "Okay."

This seems to do the trick because he cries even harder and strokes her back and squeezes her, a little too hard, she thinks. "We're going to go places and do all kinds of things together," he says. "I'm going to teach you things."

He doesn't say what sort of things they're going to do together, or what he's going to teach her, but she's willing to have an open mind. Her big concern right now is how he's going to fit inside her life with her mother.

Uncle Camil and the boys leave around midnight. They're the last ones to go, and as Véronique watches them stumble out the door, she worries vaguely about their long drive back to Ste. Barbe. Camil is drunk, but refuses to spend the night here. "I'm fine to drive," he mumbles. "I need to sleep in my own bed."

Neither of her parents protest.

When the three of them are finally alone, Léo looks around the room as though he's seeing it for the first time. "I can't believe I'm home," he says. "With my girls."

He tugs them both brusquely into his arms. "This is the most beautiful apartment I've ever seen."

"Just wait a few weeks," Lisette mutters.

"I love you both so much."

Lisette kisses his neck, and then they kiss on the mouth. At first it's just a peck, but it quickly turns more passionate. When their tongues make an appearance, Véronique flees, disgusted.

A little while later, lying in her bed, she can hear them having sex through her bedroom wall. It starts with her mother moaning, her father grunting, the bed creaking rhythmically. She listens, sickened and fascinated at the same time. The noises get louder, more violent. Their four-poster bed is scraping the wall so forcefully it feels like *her* bed is rumbling. Her mother starts yelping like an animal; her father is swearing and calling out her mother's name over and over again: "Lisette! Lisette! *Câlice!* Lisette! *Câlice!*"

They don't seem the least bit concerned about Véronique in the next room. Pierre warned her. He said, "You know they're going to screw like crazy tonight."

"Shut up. That's gross."

"He hasn't done it in over ten years! My dad says he's going to erupt like a goddamn volcano."

Véronique reaches for a cassette and pops *London Calling* into her ghetto-blaster. She turns up the volume. "Clampdown" mercifully drowns out her parents' sex noises, and she tries to sleep.

But long after they pass out and the apartment falls silent, Véronique is still awake. All she can think about is what tomorrow and the day after and the day after that will look like. Will her mother still make her toast with butter and maple syrup, or will her father request something else? Eggs? French toast? Will his dirty underwear and socks and razors and manly deodorant clutter their only bathroom?

Will he be here when she gets home from school, invading her space? She likes having the place to herself after school, when her mother is at work.

Will they still watch their favorite shows together on

the couch every night—*Edgar Allan, Détective*; *Chez Denise*; *Boogie-Woogie 47*; *Peau de Banane*—or will Léo take over the TV with hockey and politics?

She closes her eyes, her chest knotted with apprehension. Everything is about to change.

A few weeks later, on a Friday night, Léo takes Véronique to McDonald's. He's been dying to go ever since he got out. The first Montreal McDonald's opened after he'd gone to jail, so he's never even had a Big Mac before. Maybe this is what he meant when he said he was going to take her places.

They drive all the way to Atwater, which is closer to downtown than she ever goes, and that in itself is exciting. Being with Léo is also exciting. She didn't realize how good it would feel to be out in the world with him. For the first time ever, she feels like she belongs to that rarefied caste of girls who have fathers. She never realized how much of a void it left until he filled it. Léo is so self-assured and charming, so eager to protect and take care of her. Sometimes his eagerness borders on cloying—even at twelve she is aware how much he needs her to accept him, to return his affections. His guilt is constant and unabashed, but she feels safe with him, adored.

It happened quickly, her falling in love with the idea

of him. He does take over the TV every night, watching the news and sports and dumb comedy shows; his stuff is everywhere, driving her and Lisette crazy. He doesn't wash his dishes, doesn't put the lid down on the toilet. He's loud and opinionated, and he fills every bit of space in their once quiet lives. He's at home waiting for her every day when she walks through the door after school with a million annoying questions. And yet none of that matters. Lisette and Véronique are smitten, both constantly absolving him of all his minor transgressions.

They get in line at McDonald's behind a tall man in a belted trench coat the color of pale sand. The fabric is so smooth it looks like velvet. Léo looks up and studies the menu.

"What are you getting?" she asks her father.

"You tell me," he says, lighting a smoke.

The man in front of them steps up to the counter and orders his meal in English. The girl serving him is French. She doesn't understand him and asks him in French to repeat his order.

"You don't understand 'Big Mac with no sauce'?" he says impatiently.

The girl looks flustered; her cheeks are turning red.

"Large fry and a medium orange drink?"

The girl shakes her head. The man sighs and looks around for some solidarity. "Can you believe this?"

The girl interrupts her coworker and asks for help.

"You need to learn English," the man says, raising his voice. "How hard can it be? Big Mac? French fries?"

Véronique looks over at her father. Léo's expression is inscrutable. He takes a long drag off his cigarette and exhales into the man's back. She wonders if he's going to say something and embarrass her.

Léo does not say a word. Instead, he leans in a little closer and nonchalantly presses the tip of his cigarette against the man's trench coat, burning a hole in the beautiful fabric.

Véronique looks up at her father in shock, but he pretends not to notice. When Léo finally pulls his hand away and the guy shuffles off to wait for his food, there is a perfect black sphere in the coat.

Léo approaches the counter and orders in French. He winks at the girl, and she smiles, relieved.

"Don't worry about assholes like him," Léo says. "Things are going to change in this province. The time is going to come when guys like him won't be able to order in English."

"*Merci*," she says.

The English guy in the fancy coat is oblivious. Either he didn't hear or he doesn't understand French. Léo smiles pleasantly at him.

When they sit down across from each other at one of

the little tables, with their Big Macs and their French fries spread out on the brown tray, Véronique says, "You shouldn't have burned his coat."

"I wanted to punch him in the face, but I didn't want to wind up back in jail."

"Pa, I'm serious."

"It was gabardine," Léo says. "That coat must have cost a fortune."

"You can't just do things like that in the real world."

"Did you hear how he spoke to her, Véro? Like she was some piece of garbage. That's how rich Anglos treat us. That's what they think of us. You think that's okay?"

"No, but—"

"No. It's not okay. He wasn't just speaking to her that way. Do you understand? He was speaking to *us* that way. Me and you. I can't believe how little has changed in this city since I went away. We're still second-class citizens!"

"You could have told him to be more respectful," Véronique says. "You still could have defended her."

"Sure," Léo says, chuckling. "That would have gone well. He would have laughed in my face and driven off in his BMW."

"So instead you burned a hole in his coat?"

"It's okay to stand up for what you believe in, Véro.

I did it for that poor girl. What was her crime? She doesn't speak English. This is *her* goddamn province!"

Véronique sweeps a handful of fries through a mound of ketchup.

"We have to stick together," Léo goes on. "We have to stand up to assholes like him who think they own this province. They think they own *us*. Sometimes it's okay to cross the line. Sometimes you *have* to cross the line."

Obviously her father has crossed the line before, but he almost never speaks of his crime. It's simply not discussed at home.

"The system is corrupt," Léo continues. "It's screwed up, my girl. Broken. I learned the hard way that if you want anything to change you have to operate *outside* the system."

Véronique is trying to align her father's actions—burning the coat—with his logic.

"You can't politely effect change," he says, waving his Big Mac around in the air. "It's about agitation, re-taliation."

"But you didn't teach him a lesson," Véronique points out.

"Don't you get it? You can't teach bastards like him a lesson. Trust me. I tried. You can only *retaliate*."

Véronique looks around the McDonald's for the

man with the cigarette burn in his coat. She doesn't see him. She imagines him getting home, removing his coat, and hanging it up on one of those ornate antique coat-stands in his vestibule, and noticing the burn. Who will he blame?

"I rejected this system a long time ago," Léo says, sinking his teeth into the soft sesame seed bun. "What is this pink sauce?"

"It's the special sauce."

"Listen, you can try to maneuver around inside the system if you want," he says, with his mouth full. "But if you're smart, Véronique, you'll reject it, just like I did."

He finishes chewing and nods his head approvingly. "*Tabarnak*," he says. "This is a damn good burger."

PART I
1992–1995

1

August 1992

Véronique slows the boat down, easily maneuvering it around a small island—purely by instinct, she can't see a thing—and then speeds up again, heading straight for the marina. The boat roars and jerks nose up into the air, and then they're slapping against the water at forty-five miles an hour again. There are islands and swamps all over the lake, but at night they're almost invisible.

Pierre is at the back of the boat, crouched down with his shotgun between his legs, keeping a lookout for other boats. The lake is a dark void, indistinguishable from the sky, but it doesn't matter. She doesn't need daylight to see where she's going. She knows the precise route from habit and intuition. She's done it every night for the past four months.

The sky is matte black, the stars and moon obscured by a low-hanging fog. The lake is swarming with other boats, motorized cockroaches scurrying in all directions. Her hearing is on high alert, hyper-attuned to the noise. Out here on the lake, Véronique is blind. So much could go wrong—cops, thieves, crashes. It's a miracle they survive night after night.

She pulls up to Billy's Marina and turns off the boat. The marina is right near the Canada–US border, on an Indian reservation they call the Triangle that covers part of Ontario, Quebec, and New York State. Tug is already there, standing on the dock. His cap is pulled down low over his eyes, and his long black hair is loose, falling to the middle of his back. Normally it's tied back in a braid. It looks freshly washed in the thin light of the dock lamp. Tug is tall and thick, intimidating. He barely looks up from under the rim of his cap as he helps them load twenty-four cases of cigarettes from his pickup truck onto their boat. No one speaks. Out of habit, Véronique keeps looking out to the lake, checking for other boats that may be lurking in the dark, waiting for them.

When they're finished, Tug jumps on his speedboat

and chaperones them out of the reservation, back into Quebec waters. Exactly seven minutes in, he holds up his arm, turns his boat around, and heads back to the marina. This is the scariest part, the moment her heart starts to hammer in her chest, pulsating through her life vest and camouflage jacket. She speeds the boat up to fifty-five miles an hour, knowing that any of the dark masses she can see idling on the water out of the corner of her eyes could be cops or potential thieves. She guns it all the way back to Ste. Barbe, holding her breath the entire way. They've got tens of thousands of dollars' worth of contraband in their possession now, and they're extremely vulnerable. Even Pierre—when she turns around to make sure he hasn't fallen overboard—is serious and still, the gun gripped solidly between his prayer hands.

When they approach Camil's dock and she can finally see his aluminum-sided house at the edge of the water, her breathing slowly starts to return to normal. Her heart rate settles down; her muscles unclench. They've made it through another night.

Camil starts unloading the cases, moving quickly in the dark. They're used to working in the middle of the night; they're comfortable in silence. They move with purpose and precision, a well-tuned machine.

———

It all started last summer when she was at their place for a barbecue and her cousin Pierre took her around back to the boathouse. He opened the door, and it was filled to the ceiling with cases of Du Maurier, Export, and Player's. There was no room for the boat. The septic tank was in there, too, so the cigarettes had a foul smell.

"Holy shit!" she gasped, stepping inside.

"This is it, cousin. A new life."

"What are you talking about? You're selling cigarettes?"

"How would you like to make an easy twenty grand this summer, Véro?"

She eyed him suspiciously. She had no problem doing something illegal, but this sounded too good to be true. "How?" she asked him.

"I need help running the cigarettes from the reservation."

"Why me? Why not your dad?"

"You speak English," he said. "I don't. Problem is the Indians don't speak French. We're having trouble communicating with them. It's been hard to build up trust."

She almost laughed out loud. The first opportunity of her life to make some real money, and it was entirely contingent on her being able to speak the very language she despised.

"I'm talking about thousands of dollars a week for all of us," Pierre went on. "Just for a short ride on the boat. And in the winter, we can use snowmobiles. We could be millionaires."

Uncle Camil's house was on the Quebec side of the lake, just outside the reservation, perfectly situated to run a smuggling operation. Cigarettes had gone up to eight bucks a pack by then, and the Triangle was becoming a mecca for smuggling tobacco from the reservation into Quebec, tax-free.

"All we have to do is load up our boat at Billy's Marina on the reservation and bring the cases back into Quebec," Pierre explained. "It's only a fifteen-minute ride out there, another fifteen back. It's the easiest cash you'll ever make."

There was never a question of conscience for Véronique. She considered the danger, but not the criminal aspect. That was of no concern. Pulling one over on the government—the greedy bastards who had hiked the taxes in the first place—would please her dad. They had it coming, he'd say. And money was money. It would benefit them all, especially her parents.

That night, Camil and Pierre explained to her how the whole operation worked. The Indians bought the cigarettes directly from the tobacco companies; they were at the top of the pyramid, making the most money without taking any risks. As long as they were on the reservation, everything was legal. Below them were guys like Billy, who sold directly to the smugglers from his marina. They were small-time operators compared to the Indians at the very top, but they weren't taking any risks either. Then you had the smugglers who ran operations like Uncle Camil and Pierre. They made good money but risked heavy fines and possible jail time. They were mostly the French people who lived on the lake, had boats, and weren't afraid of breaking the law or endangering their lives—none of which was a problem for Camil. He'd already been to jail twice for aggravated assault, and whisperings about his connection to the Hells Angels still persisted. While he consistently refuted those claims, he did admit to having some close friends in the outlaw biker gang.

Next there were the transporters, who loaded a few cases into the trunks of their cars and took them out to sell in various cities. Finally, at the very bottom of the pyramid, were the small-time salespeople who sold cartons to friends and neighbors out of their own homes or college dorms. As Pierre promised, it was easy money for everyone involved, no matter how low on the pyramid. Véronique would be multilevel, Pierre explained; she would smuggle, transport, and sell.

A few nights later, she smuggled cigarettes for the first time. Pierre took her out to the garage just as it was getting dark. "Here," he said, tossing her a pair of army fatigues and a life jacket.

"Are you kidding?"

"Put it on," he said. "And the boots and face mask, too."

"Seriously?"

"This isn't a joke, Véro."

She put on the gear without saying a word. He pulled a shotgun out of the gun safe, the kind her uncle used for duck hunting.

"*Sacrément*," she breathed. "I don't know how—"

"Don't worry," he said as they headed to the boat. "You're driving."

Pierre's job was to crouch down at the back of the boat and aim the gun behind them. If he saw or heard anyone suspicious, he was to shoot.

"Who's considered suspicious?" she asked him, starting to feel a little nervous.

"Other smugglers out to steal our cigarettes. Don't worry about it. That's my problem."

They climbed into the boat. Pierre went to the back and stretched his legs. He lit a cigarette. He was calm and relaxed. Véronique was shaking as she turned the key in the ignition.

She was an experienced boat driver, but not in the dark, not with someone holding a shotgun behind her. The lake was crawling with other smugglers, and none of them could turn on their lights; the point was not to be seen. She wanted to ask Pierre if he was afraid of dying like that, but it was the kind of question a girl would ask and she didn't want to be that girl.

By the time she eased the boat up to Billy's Marina, she was soaking wet. Pierre left his gun on the floor and got out of the boat first. He stood on the dock, waiting. Lit another cigarette from a pack of Export A green. "We're meeting Tug here," he said.

"Who's Tug?"

"Billy's brother."

Pierre explained that payment for the cigarettes was made during the day. Pierre would ride out to the reservation in the afternoon and pay Billy in advance. He never carried cash on the night runs. It was too dangerous. Besides, Billy didn't trust them enough to front them the product. It had to be paid for in advance, in broad daylight. "You'll come with me in the afternoons from now on," Pierre said. "It'll be easier with someone who speaks English."

Véronique was trying to take it all in, at the same time keeping an eye out for this Tug guy.

After about fifteen minutes, someone pulled up to the marina in a pickup truck and backed it right up to the edge of the dock.

"Who's this?" the guy mumbled, getting out of his truck and jerking his chin at Véronique.

"I'm Pierre's cousin Véronique," she said in English. "I'll be riding with him from now on." Her English was a bit rusty, but Tug understood her.

He thrust out his arm, and they shook hands. They loaded the cases onto the boat that night without uttering a word. When they were done, Pierre and Véronique got back in their boat and she started the engine. Tug got into the speedboat that was tied to the dock, and together they pulled out of the marina. "Is he coming with us?" she asked Pierre.

"He escorts us out of the reservation. No one fucks with Tug."

Tug followed them until they were about halfway home. Véronique was timing the ride with her Indiglo stopwatch. At the seven-minute mark, he held up his arm and turned back. Pierre waved.

Uncle Camil was waiting on the dock when they got back. His arms were folded across his bare chest, resting on the shelf of his beer belly. His expression was stern, menacing.

He seemed so different from the uncle of her childhood that night. When she was little, he used to let her put on his yellow hard hat, and he would knock on it with his fist and tell her knock-knock jokes until she keeled over laughing. He was the one who dressed up as Santa Claus every Christmas—except for that one year he got really drunk and threw the Christmas tree onto the frozen lake and disappeared. That was the only side of him she knew, and she wasn't afraid of him. But that night on the dock, she could see the man who got into bar fights and hung out with Hells Angels.

They unloaded the cases into the boathouse, and then Véronique pulled off her camouflage gear and life jacket. She was sweating. Pierre made a joke about Véronique driving like a girl, and Camil laughed. Véronique laughed with them, out of nervousness. She was relieved, giddy. They ran down to the lake, and Pierre pushed her into the water and then dove in after her. They splashed around; the water was warm and glorious. It was a clear night.

Camil went inside the house while they were swimming, and then he came back outside with a handful of cash. It was a thick wad, all twenties. She'd never forget the first time she saw that much cash. Her eyes bulged. Her heart was racing from the adrenaline. Playing the system and getting away with it was a rush. People like her weren't used to that kind of money, certainly not for a half hour of work.

Véronique jumped out of the water, and Camil counted out $240 into her wet hand. "You get ten dollars a case," he said.

She did the math, calculating up to December, when the lake would freeze and they wouldn't be able to continue by boat. If she were to go out four or five times a week over the course of the summer, she could make as much as thirty grand.

Next, Camil doled out $360 to Pierre. Pierre got fifteen bucks a case. Véronique didn't complain about that until about a month later, when she threatened to quit if Camil didn't pay her the same as Pierre. She'd only been bluffing, but Camil agreed. What did he care? He was making hundreds of thousands by then. He'd already added an extension to the house—a living room with glass walls so you could look out onto the lake if you were eating supper or relaxing on the couch. He'd also put in a Jacuzzi and renovated the kitchen with shiny white appliances. He'd bought a sound system, a big-screen TV, a Jet Ski, a new speedboat, and a shiny black Harley-Davidson.

Their market expanded quickly. In the pharmacies and *dépanneurs*, cigarette cartons were up to forty bucks. If customers bought contraband, they only paid twenty-five. Véronique felt like she was doing her people a favor. They all smoked. Why not help them out a bit?

She put her first thousand bucks in an envelope and gave it to her uncle to keep in his safe. She's been doing that for exactly a year now. After a while, she lost track of how many envelopes were in the safe, but Camil keeps track. Right down to the last dollar.

She's just trying to make as much cash as she can before the whole thing blows up. And it will. The government will eventually catch on and slash taxes, rendering their business obsolete, or they'll have the RCMP bust the entire Triangle and put them all in jail.

For now, it's a windfall. She's twenty-two years old and rolling in cash. What a part-time job! Her mother thinks she's always in Ste. Barbe because she's painting houses with Pierre. It's the same routine every day. She drives up in the afternoons, music cranked, hair blowing out the window. There's no stress during the day, just fun and relaxation by the lake. Sometimes they bike over to the butcher in town and splurge on expensive cuts of meat and slabs of cheese. After, they feast; they swim and jet-ski and play cards on the dock while Uncle Camil takes cigarette orders, writing names down in the customer book, totaling up exactly how many cases they'll need. At some point in the afternoon, Pierre and Véronique will go out to Billy's Marina with about twenty grand in a money belt.

Billy is always there, sitting on his dock with his feet dangling over the edge. He'll fill their boat with gas, without a smile or any kind of acknowledgment. His face is wide and coarse, his features smudged into deeply tanned, pockmarked skin. His black hair is short, not like his brother's, and he always wears tinted shades and a blue-and-white trucker cap that says BILLY'S MARINA. They'll hand over the cash—twenty grand for a tank of gas—but no one is ever there to question them. Véronique has to make small talk—that's her job. She's always polite, thanks Billy, tells him to have a good day. It's important that he likes her. She's trying to establish a relationship, build *trust*—that's what she's there for.

When it's all done, she'll typically pack about five cases in her beat-up old Pontiac Acadian to sell to customers in Montreal, Quebec City, and Valleyfield. She tries never to drive more than two hours for a delivery, and she always makes sure she's got other business wherever she goes—usually politics. She can afford not to work, but she bores easily and doesn't want to waste her time lazing around and getting high every day like Pierre.

After they're done stashing the cigarettes in the boathouse, Véronique and Pierre run back to the lake for a swim. She dips her head below the surface of the water and pops up, exhaling deeply. The water is still warm, even without the sun. It envelopes her, calms her nerves. It's a quiet night on the lake tonight.

Pierre holds her head underwater, and she retaliates by pulling his boxer shorts down to his knees and then teasing him about his shriveled dick.

They're still close. Twin cousins, Lisette calls them. With Marc being eight years younger, it was always just Pierre and Véronique at the Christmas parties, Easter egg hunts, weddings, First Communions, and confirmations. How many games of hide-and-seek and tag and 500 did they play together? How many shows did they put on for the grown-ups, pranks did they pull, punishments did they incur? Mischief makers, shit disturbers, partners in crime. They were inseparable. Véronique spent a lot of time in Ste. Barbe in the years before her dad got out of prison. Her mother wanted her to have a father figure in her life, and Camil fit the bill—Hells Angels connections notwithstanding. The boys liked the infusion of Véronique and Lisette into their world, with their feminine wisdom and perspectives, of which they were sorely in need. Pierre was always getting into trouble. Véronique was supposed to be the good influence, Lisette the grounding mother figure. What usually ended up happening though was that Pierre would drag Véronique into whatever escapade he had concocted and they both would wind up in trouble.

Pierre hoists himself onto the dock, and Véronique joins him. They lie side by side, shivering.

"How much have you saved?" she asks him.

"What do I have to save for?" he says. "I'm making three grand a week."

"The future?"

He laughs, pulling a fist-sized chunk of hash from the pocket of his shorts, which are lying next to him in a heap. He rolls a fat joint and lights it. "I'm living my life now," he says. "As it comes."

"What about when this ends?"

"Why would I think about that now?" he says, sucking long and hard on the joint. "Things are good. I'm enjoying it."

Véronique takes a haul. She doesn't know whether to be pissed off or feel sorry for Pierre. She worries about him. He thinks too small; he's an underachiever. She wants him to *want* to be more than what he is. Pierre is lazy and lacks ambition. He grabs whatever is put in front of him, greedily and without forethought. Véronique is different. She's no less a criminal, but she's cautious and thoughtful; she has principles. She doesn't squander the money she makes.

She's already saved $15,000 by her uncle's accounting—that's with paying rent, buying a car, and splurging on a few things she couldn't resist: a necklace for her mom, a new TV with a built-in DVD player, a pager. Pierre has saved nothing. He's too busy buying dope and booze and fireworks, which he sets off over the lake every weekend. Camil and Pierre are always throwing wild parties, buying expensive booze—wine and cognac and enough beer to get the whole town loaded—and thick slabs of meat, all of which cost literally hundreds of dollars a day. They're rich. Why not?

Véronique has a longer vision than drugs and parties and fireworks. She knows there's a lot more to life than unfettered, instant gratification. She has brains and passion, like her father did at her age. She cares about politics and protecting the French language in Quebec. She cares about her people. She's just waiting for the right cause. Her father had the FLQ. Hers is on the horizon.

"Don't you ever worry about anything?" she asks him, handing him back the joint.

"Yeah," he says, tousling her damp hair. "I worry about keeping you safe, cousin. That's it."

The next morning, she sleeps in until eleven. It's the best part of smuggling—her freedom. She can come and go as she pleases. Most people her age work crappy jobs in factories or retail stores; they have to answer to asshole bosses and have almost no free time, which is particularly miserable in the summer.

She puts on a pot of coffee and pops a slice of bread into the toaster. Adds peanut butter and honey to the toast, milk and cinnamon to the coffee. She takes it outside to eat on the balcony. The sun is already white-hot, and the black iron steps burn her bare thighs when she sits. She's wearing boxer shorts and a T-shirt. Her hair is matted, starting to form little dreadlocks.

St. Urbain Street is quiet this morning. She lives on the Plateau, around the corner from the mountain and just a few blocks north of the bar scene on St. Laurent Boulevard. She's been living here ever since she moved out at eighteen. It's a nice place, with high ceilings and hardwood floors and lots of sunlight coming in through the old windows, and the rent is reasonable. Not that money is a concern anymore. The concern now is that it's not going to last forever. Smuggling contraband is not a career; it's a gift. She'll be lucky to get two more years out of it.

"Excuse me?"

Véronique looks down from her second-floor balcony. Balconville, they used to call it. All the wrought iron balconies lined up in rows. There's a guy standing on the sidewalk, squinting up at her. "Are you Véronique Fortin?" he asks. He's an older guy, late twenties or early thirties. Dirty-blond hair, slim. Looks good in those jeans.

"Who's asking?" she says.

"Me."

"And you are?"

He climbs a few steps, meeting her halfway. "J. G. Phénix."

"J. G.? That's your name?"

"James Gabriel," he says.

"James. That's English."

"My grandfather was English," he says in perfect French. No hint of an English accent.

"And how do you know who I am?" she wants to know.

"I'm doing a story—"

"Ah. A reporter. So this is an ambush." She's used to this sort of thing. They always crawl out of the woodwork every time there's an anniversary or a related death.

"Not at all," he says. "You're listed in the white pages, and I live in the neighborhood. You probably know that François Tremblay died last week. I'm doing a piece on the October Crisis—"

"How original. You and every other reporter in the country."

He laughs. "You're right. We're not very original. But people are always interested in the FLQ."

"Are they?"

"They are. Especially your father."

It always comes back to her father. Two years ago, on the twentieth anniversary of the October Crisis, the press came beating down her parents' door. Now they're coming after her. The daughter of the infamous FLQ terrorist . . .

"I'm a reporter for the Canadian News Association."

Véronique roars with laughter. "Goodbye," she says, immediately dismissing him. *Too bad, though*, she thinks. There's something a little seductive about him. Not just his looks, but the way he's looking at her. He's sexy. She likes a man with charisma, a little brashness. But he's a traitor to his own people. What kind of Québécois journalist works for the enemy? The Canadian News Association is the biggest English news agency in the country, feeding stories to all the Anglo papers.

"Why not tell your story to an English journalist?" he says.

"No thank you," she responds. "And it's not my story."

"Do you stand behind what your father did? Do you support Quebec independence?"

She seethes quietly for a few seconds, annoyed by his arrogance and sense of entitlement. Who the hell does he think he is showing up at her apartment to harass her about her father? And for an *English* newspaper? "Get lost," she says. "Let me eat my breakfast in peace."

"I don't represent Anglophones," he tells her. "I'm French. I just happen to write for an English news agency, that's all. My father was *pure laine*. He worked at Vickers. He was a nationalist long before October 1970."

Véronique's interest is piqued. Vickers was a well-known airplane factory; it became one of the symbols of Québécois oppression back in the sixties.

"He came from a family of farmers," the reporter goes on, his voice turning emotional. "He drove a cab. He was no better and no worse than your father. You don't know me at all."

"So why do you work at CNA? It's almost worse, given where you come from."

"I was raised to understand and respect both sides equally."

Véronique rolls her eyes. "In other words, you were educated in English and you grew up middle or upper class and you've had all kinds of opportunities and *choices*, but you think because your daddy worked at Vickers thirty years ago you can claim to understand us . . . but only as a means to an end."

"Means to what end?"

"Pretending you're a separatist to get your story."

"I never said I'm a separatist," he says. "I said I'm *French*. Last I checked those aren't the same thing."

"I'm going inside," she says, standing up. "Don't come back or I'll call the police."

"What could you possibly be so angry about?" he asks her. "You haven't even lived long enough to be this angry!"

"It's none of your goddamn business."

She slams the door behind her, his question still drumming in her head. That same goddamn question her entire life: *Do you stand behind what your father did?*

As if she could ever begin to answer that, for him or his readers. For herself.

2

October 1992

James Phénix is huddled in a scrum outside the National Assembly in Quebec City, with his tape recorder in one hand and the mic in the other, ready to shove it in one of the politicians' faces. It's the day before yet another vote on yet another round of proposed constitutional changes. James ostensibly made the two-hour drive to get a quote for his column, but the truth is he wanted to get out of the city on a road trip. Everyone knows this vote is futile. Trying to get all ten provinces to agree on constitutional amendments—let alone compromise or meet in the middle—is doomed to fail. It's all bullshit. It's Quebec versus the rest of the country like warring siblings. It always has been. The proposed changes don't go nearly far enough to appease the separatists in Quebec. Nothing short of total independence from Canada will make them happy. James is fairly certain the outcome of tomorrow's referendum will be all too familiar—a big *SCREW YOU, CANADA* from Quebec and a *SCREW YOURSELF RIGHT BACK, QUEBEC* from the rest of Canada.

Which brings them here again, to another political circus, which is really just an excuse for both sides to squabble and picket and rant. James couldn't be more bored of the whole cycle.

Quebec's premier, Bourassa, is the first one out, looking gaunt and exhausted. The scrum rushes at him, closing around him like wild dogs on an antelope. James thrusts his microphone forward and yells above the crowd, "What makes you think this referendum in Charlottetown will succeed where the last one failed?"

"These new proposed amendments were determined by public opinion, not by a small elite. We listened to the people this time," Bourassa states. *How novel,* James thinks.

"It's time to put an end to these interminable constitutional talks and focus on the economy," Bourassa goes on. "So far, 1992 has been one of the worst years for us since the Depression."

"Are you satisfied with the treatment of Quebec in this new accord? Is Quebec getting enough?"

"Yes, I believe Canada is finally willing to formally recognize our language, our culture, and our distinctiveness. As we all know, having two official languages and cultures is an asset to the country, not a detriment."

The usual rehearsed bullshit. When his opponent steps out of the National Assembly, the mob of wild dogs abandons Bourassa and turns their greedy attention to the beleaguered PQ leader. "M. Parizeau, what's your prediction for tomorrow?"

"I've said all I can say about this ad nauseum," Parizeau responds. "I predict a resounding rejection of this pathetic 'accord.' We will never endorse it."

"We *who*?"

"We the Parti Québécois *and* the French people of Quebec."

Decent quote, James thinks. Having gotten what he needs, he heads outside, where a cluster of protesters has collected on the front steps of the Parliament Building. They're milling around and chanting, a little lackadaisically, if you ask him, with their signs pumping in the air. VOTE NO TO CHARLOTTETOWN! NO TO A DISTINCT SOCIETY! YES TO AN INDEPENDENT QUEBEC! SAY NO TO MULRONEY'S DEAL!

James recognizes Véronique Fortin right away. Her face—delicate but hard—is not easily forgotten; he's not above finding her beautiful. Back in the summer, he saw her from a distance, half blinded by the sun. Today, up close, he's a little stunned by her. Pale skin, warm brown eyes, a tiny doll's nose, the curve of her upper lip like a butterfly's wing. Her hair is dark auburn, almost red, a little unkempt and wild. She's wearing a plaid shirt and jean shorts with scuffed combat boots. Her legs, long and milky white, move up the front steps. He can't look away.

He must be about ten years older than she. He knows she was an infant during the October Crisis, which makes her about twenty-two. There's nine years between them. Reasonable, he thinks. He considers himself a young, slightly immature thirty-one. He can't resist approaching her. "Mam'selle Fortin?"

She stops marching and eyes him with an expression somewhere between suspicion and disdain. And then, to his surprise, her face relaxes into a smile. "J. G. Phénix," she says, which pleases him immensely.

"You remember me."

"James Gabriel Phénix. How could I forget?"

"So you've traveled all the way to Quebec City to protest the referendum?" he asks her.

"I believe in the cause."

"I know last time we met you threatened to call the

cops on me," he says, "but I'm heading over to the old town to grab a beer. Why don't you join me and we can argue about the Charlottetown Accord?"

He's sure she's going to say no, rebuff him on all counts—personal and professional. But she hesitates. "I'll even carry your sign," he adds, trying to be playful.

Without a word, she hands him the sign. MEECH LAKE NO! CHARLOTTETOWN NO! SOVEREIGNTY YES!

He takes it from her and tucks it under his arm.

"You have to carry it," she says, "and wave it around as we walk."

He's willing to do this for her—he's not sure why. He holds it up like he's picketing, and she smiles triumphantly as they set off along Rue Joly de Lotbinière toward the old town.

He realizes as he's walking alongside her that, in spite of the separatist sign she's forcing him to carry and the fact that she told him to piss off the first time they met, he's in a great mood. The sun feels warmer; the fall foliage seems more vibrant, the cobblestone streets more enchanting.

"This part of Quebec City always reminds me of those miniature Christmas villages," he says. "You know, with a train going through and the old Dickensian buildings? Like it should be Christmas here twelve months a year."

She looks at him but doesn't say anything. Her silence makes him feel like a blathering idiot. What the hell is she thinking? She's young to be so poised, so confident.

When they turn onto Rue St. Jean, a group of young French guys catch sight of his sign and start high-fiving him in solidarity, shouting, "*Quebec libre! Quebec libre!*"

Véronique is laughing.

"*Quebec libre!*" he says back to them, fist-bumping one of the guys. Why not? She seems to like it. She's having a good time at his expense.

"It suits you," she tells him. "Being a nationalist."

They come to the Pub St. Alexandre, and James stops. "I used to come here when it was still the Taverne Coloniale," he says. "I was the National Assembly reporter in the mid-eighties."

He can hear himself trying to impress her and realizes it just makes him sound old. She would have been thirteen or fourteen back then. "I know I'm old," he admits, not bothering to mention the stints he did in Tehran in '88 and Panama in '89.

He holds the door open for her and they enter the pub. It's exactly what you'd expect of a tavern in the old town—exposed brick walls, leather banquettes, carved pillars, and wooden tables. The only touch of modernity is the wall of international beers behind the dark mahogany bar.

They grab a seat in the banquette. He orders a Guinness, and she orders St-Ambroise.

"So what do you do?" he asks her. "You're here on a weekday."

"I do bookkeeping for my uncle. The hours are flexible."

There's a hint of a smile playing on her lips.

"A bookkeeper? Really?"

She folds her arms on the table and cocks her head. She's playing with him, like he's one of those annoying jingly balls that cats push around with their paws.

A Pearl Jam song comes on, and Véronique's eyes light up. "I love this song," she says, sounding more her age. "Do you know Pearl Jam?"

"I'm thirty-one," he reminds her. "Not seventy."

She jumps up and asks the bartender to make it louder. He does. Smitten, no doubt. Back at the table, she sings along in terrible English. "'Son, she said, 'ave I got a little story for you . . .'"

She's adorable. Those lips.

"Do you play pool?" she asks him.

"I play." He waits a beat. "Is that a challenge?"

The pool table is on the second floor. She breaks, impressively. He's suddenly nervous. His palms feel sticky. He imagines taking such a bad shot that the ball bounces off the table and rolls.

He takes his turn and sinks a few, including a bank shot. *Nice one*, he tells himself. He sneaks a sideways glance at her, to see if she looks impressed. He can't tell with her.

When it's her turn, she takes off her plaid shirt and ties it around her narrow waist. She's wearing a black tank top underneath. When she bends over the table, he notices a fresh tattoo on her back, right between her shoulder blades. The ink is still black, the skin around it swollen and puckered, red. It's a fleur-de-lis.

"You just got a tattoo," he says, a bit choked up. He's usually not the least bit open-minded about fate or destiny, but *this*—it's hard to dismiss as mere coincidence and not at least consider that her tattoo might be a sign. *Sign of what?* he thinks. Before he finishes the thought, he stops himself. It's embarrassing, even if it's only in his head.

"I got it last week," she says.

"A fleur-de-lis."

"Naturally."

"My father had the same one," he says, lowering his eyes, staring at the eight ball until it blurs. Why can't he look at her?

"He did? Really?"

"Yeah. On his arm." He touches his biceps, remembering.

"You said 'had'?"

When he finally lifts his eyes, her expression has softened. She looks absolutely angelic without her edge. "He died a few years ago," James says.

He doesn't elaborate, just goes back to playing pool. He takes a shot, sinks it. Goes on an impressive run. She doesn't press him about his father. She seems to understand a person's pain points. She obviously has her own.

He beats her twice in a row, much to his relief. They return to their table, and he orders another round. Talking to her is easy, fun.

"Did you see your father when you were growing up?" he ventures. He's opened up about his father; now it's her turn.

"Of course."

"So you went out to the penitentiary?"

"How else would I have seen him?"

"And now? He's in your life?"

"He's my dad."

"Is he sorry for what he did?"

"Are you interviewing me?" she asks him, her tone changing.

"No, I'm just curious. I know you believe in his cause."

"It's not just *his* cause," she interrupts. "It's Quebec's cause. It's the French working-class cause. It was and still is so much bigger than the FLQ."

"He brainwashed you from jail."

"I think for myself."

"So you're okay with what he did?"

She sighs. "You don't understand."

"I understand that an innocent man died," he says. "And you haven't had a father for most of your life. How can you possibly agree with what they did?"

"I never said I agreed with it. You can't stop being a journalist, can you?"

"I'm inquisitive, yes," he admits. "But I'm not asking for my job. I genuinely want to know."

"I'm sure you do," she says, her eyes darkening. "But it's none of your business."

"Do you ever lighten up?"

"You tricked me."

"Tricked you? How?"

"I would never have come here if I thought you were going to interrogate me about my father."

"I'm just trying to get to know you," he scrambles. "I thought we were . . . connecting."

"Why? Because your father had a fleur-de-lis tattoo?"

"You said the exact same thing to me in August," he reminds her. "You said, 'You think just because your dad worked at Vickers . . .' You've got some serious trust issues, Miss Fortin."

Before he finishes his sentence, she gets up out of her seat, calm and cool, pulls a handful of cash out of her back pocket, and tosses a twenty onto the table. Without uttering a word, she's out the door, leaving him alone with her abandoned protest sign and her half-full beer.

Screw her. He doesn't need this adolescent drama in his life.

He drives back to Montreal in a bad mood. He pops a Pearl Jam CD in the player and cranks it up, but it only makes him grumpier. Now she's ruined the band for him. He'll never listen to them again and not think of her, not see those big brown eyes staring at him or that lovely white back with the fleur-de-lis carved into the hollow between her shoulder blades.

Was he out of line? Did he ambush her? He couldn't stop himself from asking her about the infamous Léo Fortin. That doesn't mean he doesn't want her as much as he wants the story. Now he's messed up both opportunities.

3

It's late October, a cold night with a sharp wind pushing the tree branches against her building. Elodie keeps the window open because she likes to feel and smell the outdoors at all times, no matter how cold it gets. It reminds her that she is free. She likes the distinct smell of every season, each one with its own sensory memories. She will never forget her first autumn after seventeen years of being locked up; the way the leaves felt beneath her shoes when she walked, the ashy breath of chimneys coming to life, the bite of air in her nostrils and the smell of damp earth decaying. This is October for her.

Elodie is having her dinner in front of the TV, which she does every night. She doesn't like to eat alone, and TV is a good companion. She's watching the news.

The results of the referendum on this recent constitutional accord have come in, and it was rejected. Voted down, just like the last one. It doesn't surprise Elodie. Quebec is not the compromising type, and the rest of the country is sick of it. A young woman on TV is raging at the camera. "This accord was a waste of time and energy," she says, the microphone right up to her mouth. "Hopefully this is the end of all constitutional talks for a long time. It's a joke.'"

This girl should be happy, Elodie thinks. Someone as smart and well-spoken as her, someone so young and beautiful. The world is hers for the taking, and yet she seems so full of rage. When Elodie was her age, she was afraid to breathe, let alone scream into a TV camera about the government.

When Elodie first got out of the asylum and discovered this tension between the French and English, she was absolutely baffled. How could speaking a different language be enough to make someone an enemy? The real enemies were the doctors and the nuns, the monsters who put you in the mental hospital, the ones who labeled you crazy when you weren't and abused the hell out of you, the government that profited from it all. *Those* were formidable enemies. But an English person? A Francophone? For no other reason than the language they spoke? This ongoing animosity between both sides has always annoyed Elodie. There are far more serious matters to get angry about in this province.

"This country has never shown Quebec the respect it deserves," the girl on TV is saying. "This referendum result proves that Quebec independence is the only way forward!"

Quebec throws a referendum like it's a birthday party. Elodie doesn't understand it. She remembers the first referendum in 1980—the big one, the one that would decide whether or not Quebec would separate from Canada and become its own country. Her daughter, Nancy, was nine at the time. She came home from school one day, in the midst of all the political propaganda, and she was crying.

"What's wrong?" Elodie asked her, pulling the little girl into her arms. She always made a point of being affectionate with Nancy; a hug or a caress was like a salve to a child—she knew that.

"They called me a stupid frog and a separatist," Nancy sobbed, her face pressed into Elodie's sweater.

"Who did?"

"The English kids from the English school."

"What English school?"

Nancy went to a French school. She'd only ever spoken French.

"It was pen pal day," Nancy explained. "Our English

pen pals came to our class for the day, and they started writing *NO* on the blackboard, and then we started writing *OUI*, and then they started calling us frogs and peppers and separatists."

Nine years old and already the divisiveness had been wholly absorbed by a new generation. It was generally understood that if you were English, you would vote No in the referendum; and if you were French, you would vote Yes. The campaign exploded around those two simple words; they became symbolic, iconic. There were stickers, signs, placards on front lawns. You were either No or Oui; everything was understood about you based on that. Of course it was much more complicated than that. Not all the French wanted to separate. Many were afraid of the financial uncertainty that would follow; others thought it was extreme. But the separatists, as they were known, were longtime French nationalists, mainly blue collar. They were the *pure laine* and they fiercely wanted their own country. They had for decades.

In the end, the No side won. Sixty percent of Quebeckers voted against separation. That put the separation question to rest. Until now.

Elodie wonders if the failure of this new proposed accord will resurrect it. Those nine-year-olds from

Nancy's fourth grade class are twenty-one now, and if their generation is anything like this girl on TV, they're angry and ready for battle.

Just as Elodie is about to change the channel, the news anchor says two words that stop her cold.

Duplessis. Orphans.

Elodie turns up the volume, barely breathing.

"In the fifties, the Duplessis government made a shocking decision to convert the province's orphanages into mental institutions to gain larger subsidies from the federal government. Seemingly overnight, thousands of Quebec orphans were reclassified as mental patients—"

Reclassified, Elodie thinks, disgusted. It almost makes it sound humane.

"The Bédard report of 1962 revealed that about one-third of the province's twenty thousand mental patients did not belong in the institutions, and it put an end to the monstrous practice. Many of the orphans who had reached adulthood were released from these institutions. Today, they are grown up and they are angry. They call themselves the Duplessis Orphans Committee."

Cut to a group of men and women marching in front of Cardinal Turcotte's office at the Archdiocese of Montreal. "They want justice," the announcer continues, in voice-over. "Louise Tremblay was sent to Mont Providence Hospital in 1950, when she was just six years old."

A woman about fifty, a little older than Elodie, appears on screen. She's crying as she tells her story to the reporter. "They told me I was mentally challenged. One day I was in school, an orphan. The next day, bars went up on the windows and mental patients were shipped in. That was it. From that day on, the nuns and the doctors spent the next two decades convincing me I was crazy."

Elodie closes her eyes, reliving her own experience of Change of Vocation Day. She remembers Mother Superior standing before them in the classroom and announcing that the orphanage was to become a mental hospital. Some of the other nuns were crying as Mother Superior went on to say there would be no more school. "From this day forward," she told them, "you are all mentally deficient."

The orphanage, Ste. Sulpice, was the only home Elodie had ever known. She'd always been happy there, but everything changed quickly after the Change of Vocation. The children now had to take care of real mental patients, who had arrived by bus one day from a mental hospital in the city. Elodie's job was to bathe them. One of the crazies bit her. Soon, new nuns began arriving—mean ones, always yelling at them. And then, without warning, Elodie was taken away in the middle of the night.

"I want an apology!" Louise Tremblay cries on TV.

She's got those sad eyes, Elodie thinks. That's what Nancy's father said to Elodie, lying in bed the only time they were ever together, right before he went off to Vietnam. *You have such sad eyes for someone so young.*

"I want compensation," Louise Tremblay rails. "I'm on welfare, I can't read or write. I can't work because of a back injury from all the beatings I endured."

On TV, the announcer is wrapping up her story. "The Duplessis orphans are rallying together and speaking up," she says. "They want to be heard. They won't be ignored anymore. They want everyone to know what was done to them and why."

I am one of them, Elodie thinks. What she lived through has a name. *Duplessis orphan.*

She goes to her bedroom and retrieves her notebook and the book proposal her mother wrote not long after they'd found each other. The book no one would touch. Maybe now it's time to tell her story.

Maybe now someone is finally willing to hear it.

The phone rings, right on cue. Her mother.

"Are you watching the news?" Maggie asks her.

"Yes."

"Are you okay?"

"Yes."

"You're going to fight now, aren't you?"

"Yes."

4

November 1992

Outside the Verdun metro station, an Arctic wind pummels Véronique's face, and she has to pull the hood of her parka down over her eyes. She probably thinks the same thing every year, but this feels like the coldest November she can remember. Head down, she passes a parked car and notices a brand-new Le Château bag on the passenger seat. The door is unlocked, and she could easily swipe the bag. Not that she would ever steal from one of her own, but the carelessness of it annoys her. It's not always a bad thing to think like a criminal.

She continues walking quickly toward Rue Rielle, where her parents have lived in the same beige-brick duplex with the S-shaped balcony for the past nine years. This afternoon the sky is matte gray, dull, giving the neighborhood a depressed feeling. She opens the door without knocking. "*Allo?* M'ma? Papa?"

It's Sunday dinner, and the foyer smells of cigarette smoke and roast chicken. Her father is in his recliner, beer in one hand, cigarette in the other, with a Montreal Canadiens ashtray balancing on the arm of the chair. His shaggy hair is completely gray on the sides, but it's still a full head. He's got his own teeth—impressive for a French Canadian pushing fifty—and only a slight beer pooch above his belt buckle. A thick moustache covers most of the lower half of his face. He barely looks up from the TV to greet her, but his voice is warm, fond. "*Allo, ma belle fille.*"

"Hi, Pa," she says, unwinding her scarf. "How was your week?"

"Same as always," he complains.

There's an undercurrent of disappointment that vibrates around Léo. Even he acknowledges on a regular basis how much jail changed him. "A man gets broken in prison," he'll say. "That's what it's designed to do: tear you down, destroy your spirit, take away all your passions, one by one. First you forget what music sounds like. Then you forget how to sing, how to laugh, even how to cry. They take away every single thing that's precious to you. It's damn hard to get the joie de vivre back."

When he first got out, he still had some fire in him. He probably thought he could pick up where he'd left off with his crusade, but he soon realized that the eighties were very different from the sixties. He tried to reestablish himself as a prominent nationalist. He saw himself as a hero, and although he'd always had a cult-like following of admirers and hard-core separatists, his attempts at repurposing a career in the nationalist political milieu went nowhere. His supporters were, and always had been, the marginalized and disparate minority. Léo wrote a few articles for a leftist Quebec magazine that advocated sovereignty and democratic socialism, but when the magazine folded, so did Léo. He talked briefly about running for leadership in the Parti de la Démocratie Socialiste, but his talk had a delusional undertone, as though even he knew he was living in a fantasy world. The separatists had lost their first big referendum in 1980, and people were sick of thinking, hearing, and talking about it.

After his first few exhilarating months out of jail, the high began to wear off and the promise of everything he would accomplish with his newfound freedom began to fade. He settled back into life on the outside, and Véronique watched as the fight slowly began to seep out of him, replaced by an unhappy resignation. He went back to work, operating a forklift at a plastics factory, and bought the small house on Rue Rielle; Lisette continued to clean houses.

The only thing that remained stalwart was their marriage. Prison, at least, had not managed to diminish Léo and Lisette's love for each other. Together, they quietly continued to pit themselves against the unjust world, the Goliath that had always oppressed them. The only difference between now and then—youth and middle age, pre- and post-jail—was that their battle was now waged from the couch or kitchen table, not through bold action or violence.

"I pulled my back again," he mutters, still staring at the TV. "Goddamn factory work. Promise me you won't let this happen to you"—"this" being a regular job, working for the man. "Don't let my twelve years in the slammer be for nothing."

She can see he's in one of his moods. She leans over and kisses his forehead. He has his usual smell of tobacco and hair gel. "I won't," she says, appeasing him.

It hasn't always been easy with Léo. Even though she no longer lives at home, his erratic temperament still rattles her.

When he first got out of jail, he barged into their

lives with his big personality and his dark moods, his unrealistic expectations for everyone and everything around him. As his expectations began to topple, he grew even more sullen. Véronique, who was used to Lisette's steady pragmatism, was unnerved by him. But he tried to be a good father. He genuinely adored her, always wanted to spend time with her. Too much, she sometimes thought. He didn't discipline her; he left that to Lisette. His domain was imparting life lessons: *The French are as exploited as they've always been. Nothing has changed. The rich are evil. The Anglos are the enemy. The government is corrupt. The system is fixed against us. You have to stand up for what you believe in, no matter what. Lines are made for crossing. True freedom is living outside the law.*

He put great effort into making up for lost time. His generosity was overwrought, slightly smothering. He wanted things from her, too—forgiveness, approval, absolution. Even at twelve, Véronique understood this and knew what was expected of her. It was a lot of pressure, the responsibility for mending his broken spirit and grouting his unfulfilled cracks with her potential.

Around the age of fourteen, assailed by puberty, she became angry with him. Angry that he'd missed her entire childhood, frustrated with the burden of having to make up for a decade of lost time, of having to carry the torch of all his failed ambitions and dreams. *Who the hell did he think he was?* He'd homed in on *her* territory, and all she wanted was some privacy. They began to bump up against each other. They fought often. She used to tell him he wasn't a real father. She was fond of saying, "*You don't belong here.*" About his crime, Léo said very little. This was unspoken in their house; they were all complicit in the shroud of silence. But one day, in the midst of those turbulent teen years, Véronique said, "Are you the one who murdered Pierre Laporte?"

They were outside washing his car. "It was all of us," he said, not looking up from the windshield he was scrubbing. "We acted as one."

"Why did you do it?"

"So you'd grow up in a better world than I did."

He'd said as much to the cameras, too, the night they captured him hiding in the Townships: "I did it for my baby girl!" It was all over the news, her father declaring that a man's life had been sacrificed for his child's.

"Well, I don't want someone's murder on my conscience," she said.

Léo looked slapped. He didn't say another word. He rinsed off the suds with a hose as she stood watching. "Besides, how could all of you have killed him together?" she said, feeling suddenly emboldened. She'd always wanted to know, but had never had the courage to ask. "It doesn't make sense."

He set the hose down and stared at her meaningfully. "A man has nothing if not his word," he said, silencing her.

That was the last he spoke of it. If Lisette knew the truth, she was equally tight-lipped. She clearly accepted and loved him no matter what. It didn't seem to matter to her, the depth of his involvement in ending another man's life. Véronique was not quite so blasé about it. One time she actually went to the library and looked up Pierre Laporte in the encyclopedia. She also read about the October Crisis on microfiche for hours. Reading about Laporte's family—his son, Jean; his daughter, Claire; his wife, Françoise—gave her a sick feeling deep in the pit of her stomach. She couldn't reconcile the man she loved—her father—with the man who had taken away someone else's father and husband. She's never stopped grappling with it, but she has mastered the strategy of compartmentalizing.

Over time, as her hormones began to settle, so did their relationship. They eventually arrived at something fairly normal, much less contentious and volatile. Léo's charm and charisma, which he could turn on and off as he pleased, won her heart. One day she realized she loved him.

It helped that her friends thought he was cool. She was still vulnerable, impressionable; their opinions mattered. And she could do no wrong in Léo's eyes. His only disappointment in Véronique was that she could speak English. He felt her bilingualism was a betrayal. It meant she'd "caved to the elite," which was absurd since she was only four years old at the time.

She learned English when her mother was cleaning houses in Westmount. Lisette never had childcare, so she used to drag Véronique along with her to work. One of the families had a nanny for their three kids, and Véronique spent three mornings a week with them— playing, watching English TV, reading their books, absorbing the language without even realizing it. By the time she started kindergarten, she was fluently bilingual, a skill that has served her well in her current profession, about which her father knows nothing.

"Turn the volume up, will you?" he says. "The batteries in my remote are dead."

She finds her mother in the kitchen, pulling a chicken out of the oven. Lisette is still pretty, in a slightly fatigued way. Her dark hair is cut short with filaments of silver woven throughout, and she wears glasses now, but her skin is smooth and she's long-legged and slim. Véronique kisses her cheek and hoists herself up onto the counter, long legs dangling. A cigarette is burning in the ashtray, an open Labatt 50 beside it. "The house reeks of smoke," she says. "When are you guys going to quit?"

"When we're in the ground."

Véronique sighs. "What's new?"

"I got the new Roch Voisine CD," Lisette says. "It's the greatest hits from his European concerts."

"Did you vote?"

"Of course. You?"

"Obviously."

Lisette turns on the mixer and starts whipping the potatoes into a creamy mash. She adds a half stick of butter, heavy cream, and a generous amount of salt. "Put this on the table," she says. Véronique slides off the counter and places the bowl of potatoes in the center. The small round table is already set for three. "Léo!" her mother shouts.

Moments later, Léo shuffles in and they all sit. Lisette transfers the roast chicken from the stove to the table, followed by the peas and carrots, gravy, and a plate of white bread and butter.

"Go put on my new Roch Voisine CD," she tells Léo, and he gets up obediently and disappears for a few minutes, and then they can hear Roch's deep voice from the living room.

"Have you found a job yet?" Lisette asks her as Léo returns to the table. He pinches his wife's ass before sitting back down, and she playfully slaps his arm.

"Not yet," Véronique responds, not looking at her mother. She still hasn't told them she's been smuggling cigarettes, has no plans to. They would object not to the illegality, but to the danger. "I will, though."

"Ginette's daughter works at that big record store downtown," Lisette says. "I could speak to her. She gets a good discount on CDs."

"Sure."

Lisette grabs two more beers from the fridge, opens both, and hands one to Léo. She doesn't offer one to Véronique. Véronique knows it's not on principle; it's because her mother doesn't want to share. She's probably counted out exactly how many she'll need for tonight. Lisette is a heavy drinker. When can you call a person an alcoholic? Véronique has no idea. She knows her mother occasionally has a beer in the morning; knows she drinks every single day, though that doesn't necessarily mean much. Most people she knows do. She wishes she'd known them before he went to jail, that she hadn't been born on the cusp of the end of their best selves.

"The chicken's good," Véronique says.

"You don't think it's dry? It was juicier last week."

"I think it's juicy."

"Next week I'm going to start my holiday baking," Lisette announces. "How many *tourtières* do you want?"

"I don't know," Véronique says. "One is fine, I guess."

"You can freeze them and keep them until spring."

"Who wants *tourtière* in the spring?" Léo says.

"It's just a meat pie," Lisette points out. "Why the hell can't she eat a meat pie in the spring? There's no law that says *tourtière* can only be eaten at Christmas."

"What did you think of the referendum?" Véronique asks her father, desperate to change the subject.

"It was a good outcome," he says, drowning his plate in gravy. "Not surprising, but positive. Now that the goddamn accord is dead, we can move on."

"To what?"

"What do you think?" he says. "Separation. Now we know what the rest of the country thinks of us. We don't have to be polite anymore."

"Were we ever polite?"

"The Liberals are too polite," Lisette says.

"Two more years," Léo states. "And then the PQ will get back in and we'll have our own country. We've all had enough of being second-class citizens when *we're* the goddamn majority. We need a place to call our own, like Palestine."

Lisette is smiling, her faith in him unwavering. She can't hide her delight at this rare glimpse of the old, determined Léo. This is when she loves him best—even Véronique can see that.

After supper, Léo offers to drive Véronique home so he can try out his new car starter. He points the little gizmo at the window, aiming it down at his '89 Tempo, and presses the button until the exhaust puffs to life and the car starts. "A miracle of technology!" he cries. "No more freezing my ass off in the morning!"

They wait ten minutes for the car to warm up, and then they dash out and jump in, and it really is a miracle. Inside, the heater is blowing on high and it's toasty warm. "Revolutionary," she says.

As soon as they pull onto De l'Église, Léo lowers the volume on the radio and says, "I know you're smuggling cigarettes, Véro. Your uncle told me."

"So?"

"It's dangerous."

"Coming from the man who threw bombs into buildings and kidnapped an innocent man at gunpoint."

"I'm still a parent."

"You were then, too."

"This is different," he says. "It's *you* who's in danger now."

"I'm making good money," she tells him. "And I'm really careful."

He doesn't say anything for a while. The roads are deserted, typical for a Sunday night in the middle of winter. As they wind through the streets of Verdun and then into St. Henri, past the row houses and duplexes and apartment buildings, Véronique imagines other families inside them, huddled in their kitchens, eating roasts and buttery mashed potatoes, discussing the aftermath of the referendum and what will come next; bickering over *tourtière*. She imagines them all like her family, with one glaring difference: their fathers and husbands are probably not notorious FLQ members from the October Crisis, ex-cons who lived more than a decade in prison. But then the people in those row houses, enduring the daily grind like sheep, will never know the freedom of living life on one's own terms. She will never settle for such a mediocre existence.

"You saving your money?" Léo asks. She detects a tinge of pride in his voice.

"Of course."

"Good," he says. "The government deserves to get fucked. They're a bunch of greedy pigs, taxing the shit out of our cigarettes. It's us, the working class, who smoke. They know that. You know how much I paid for this pack?" He points to the Player's on his dashboard. "Eight goddamn bucks. The motherfuckers."

Véronique is pleased to have his endorsement. It's exactly the way she feels.

"Just don't get caught," Léo says, winking. "I won't tell your mother."

5

December 1992

Elodie's father, Gabriel Phénix, is buried in the East-Dunham Cemetery in the town where he grew up, the same town where he fell in love with Elodie's mother, Maggie. He rests next to his parents and two of his siblings, all of whom had died in a car crash when he was young. On the other side of the cemetery, Maggie's parents—Elodie's grandparents—are buried side by side.

Gabriel had been in Elodie's life exactly ten years when he died, not nearly enough time to get to know him. Today would have been his sixtieth birthday. They're all here today at her mother's request. Later, they will go back to Maggie's house in Cowansville for what she is calling a celebration of his life.

Stephanie crouches down on all fours and lays a bouquet of winterberry at the foot of his headstone. Maggie brought copies of the *Brome County News* and the *Quebec Farmers' Advocate*, which she sets down in the snow next to Stephanie's berries. Elodie doesn't understand why she brings these sorts of things. He's dead. He can't read the papers.

She looks over at her brother, James, who is stone-faced and stoic. He hasn't brought anything either. He's wearing sunglasses and a tuque, as though trying to go unnoticed. The only ones missing are Clémentine and Nancy. Clémentine moved to Rimouski with her husband and daughter, Georgette, about a year after Gabriel's death. Gabriel was more like a son to her than a little brother, and she couldn't bear to be in Dunham after he was gone. The cornfield, the farm, the cottage where they'd always lived, all were saturated with her memories of him. Everywhere she looked, she'd complain mournfully, she could feel him, smell him, *see him*. Her daily life was so fraught with grief, her husband put the cottage up for sale and moved them to his hometown of Rimouski for a fresh start.

She still writes to them. She's found her footing again. She's a grandmother now and works part-time at a local bakery. She's never returned to the Townships.

Nancy is also gone. Moved away to start a new life.

She lives in Bouctouche, New Brunswick, of all places. She never gave a proper reason for leaving other than to say she liked the beach and wanted to explore "different places."

Elodie is the one who always encouraged Nancy to be independent and self-confident, so she can only blame herself for Nancy leaving. She wanted her child to live a life free of fear and insecurity. She wanted her child to grow up and be *in* the world, not cowering on the sidelines of it. In spite of her own inadequacies, Elodie somehow managed to foster a healthy self-reliance in Nancy. It's been her greatest gift to her daughter: freedom. Nancy lives her life with gusto; she doesn't even know to know to be afraid of the world.

Elodie's been a good mother. She can say that with certainty. She never raised a hand to Nancy, never screamed, never intimidated her. She was affectionate—no small feat given where she came from. She had to teach herself how to hold another human being, how to be tender and gentle and loving. It never came easy, and it certainly wasn't natural, but she tried until it *became* natural. My God, she tried. Besides that, there was always food on the table, heat and hot water, even some extras so that Nancy never felt different from any of her peers—a VCR, a Sony Walkman, whatever running shoes all the kids were wearing at the time.

You can hide a lot from a young child, and that's exactly what she did. She kept her secrets to herself, concealed the horrors of her childhood, and pretended to know what she was doing, even when she didn't. Nancy knows her mother grew up in an "orphanage" and only reunited with her parents at twenty-four, but that's about the extent of what she knows.

There was only one time when Elodie was made aware of just how perceptive Nancy was and how careful she had to be. They were watching a documentary about the deadly London fogs of the nineteenth century, those dense, foul-smelling blankets of soot that smothered the city, obscuring it in murk. "That's what happens to you, M'ma," Nancy said, precocious beyond her years. "You get the dark fog sometimes."

After that, Elodie doubled her efforts to shield Nancy from her "dark fog." And it's paid off. She's created a stable life for them, a life she would even go as far as to call normal.

In spite of the late-afternoon sun flooding the cemetery, the mid-December air is frigid. Elodie is grateful when Maggie and Stephanie step away from Gabriel's headstone and look at everyone as though to say, *I guess that's it.*

What else is one to do at the cemetery? Elodie has

always found these visits to be awkward. Sometimes Maggie kisses his stone. Other times, she kisses her fingers and then touches the stone. She's been known to converse with the stone, or simply to sit there in front of it in meditation, as though it helps her to conjure Gabriel back into the world. Elodie understands; he was the love of her life.

Maggie lives in an old farmhouse on the edge of the lake, the same one where Elodie first met her birth parents eighteen years ago. Elodie will never forget arriving at their front door in 1974. At that time, thanks to Sister Ignatia's monstrous lie, Elodie still believed her real mother was dead. She remembers thinking how beautiful Maggie was, standing there in the living room with her thick black hair and lovely cream skin. As a couple, Maggie and Gabriel were perfect; the life they had created was a fairy tale, with their good looks and their two well-adjusted kids and their warm, welcoming farmhouse.

The reunion was charged with emotion. After the initial shock of discovering that her mother wasn't dead and that she was actually face-to-face with her real parents, they got down to the business of explaining how she'd wound up in an orphanage. In some ways, it was everything Elodie had always wanted to hear.

Maggie had been fifteen when she'd gotten pregnant; her parents had made the decision for her. It was like that back then, in the fifties. Good Catholic girls did not get to keep their illegitimate babies. *Maggie hadn't had a choice.*

It buoyed Elodie to know that they had at least come looking for her. They told her they'd tried to find her numerous times over the years, even getting as close as the mental ward of St. Nazarius Hospital, where Elodie had been locked on the other side of the metal doors.

That night, Maggie asked her if she could ever forgive her. Elodie remembers wanting to, desperately. She said, "What else could you have done back then? Everyone knows it's a sin to have a baby out of wedlock."

She said those things to let Maggie off the hook. But the sincerity behind the words took much longer to catch up. It would be years before she truly felt any peace with Maggie's choices.

She slept in her parents' guest room that night. She remembers her mind swirling with angry, vindictive thoughts; her chest clenched with hatred for little Stephanie—Maggie's other daughter, the one who was born *after* her—and rage at God. And then Maggie was there, standing over her, asking if she could stay. Elodie said yes, and Maggie lay down beside her. She sang her a song, or told her a poem—Elodie can't quite remember. Something about seeds. She held Elodie all night.

Maggie wanted Elodie to move in with them right away back in '74, but Elodie felt it was too much. She needed space and she was scared. She didn't want to fall headfirst into a relationship that could just as easily be taken from her. So she visited them on weekends, and they got to know each other slowly, on her terms. Maggie frequently came to see her in the city, and they would spend hours in the diner on Wellington, interviewing each other about their lives and working on the manuscript of her memoir. Elodie recounted a story about St. Nazarius while Maggie sobbed and swore, overcome with guilt. She blamed herself. Elodie felt this was reasonable and did not try to talk her out of it.

About two years after they'd found each other, something happened that very nearly severed their embryonic relationship. Maggie and Gabriel decided to take the family to Old Orchard Beach for the construction holiday, but they did not invite Elodie. When Maggie told her about their plans, Elodie burst into tears.

"I didn't think you'd want to go!" Maggie said, her face collapsing.

"You could have asked."

They were at Paul Patates in Pointe St. Charles, having coffee and sharing a plate of French fries.

"I know you work weekends, Elo."

"You still could have asked," Elodie said. "Nancy would love the beach. We've never been."

"I'm sorry. It's just—"

"What?"

Maggie reached for her hands and clasped them in her own. Elodie would never get tired of Maggie's gestures of affection. Over the two years, she had become reliant on them, needy. That's what made her exclusion from their vacation so painful. She almost felt entitled to be included, as though they owed her. And didn't they?

"It's just the kids . . ." Maggie fumbled. "We haven't really done anything with them, just the four of us, in so long."

Oh, how that cut deep. *Just the four of us.* Elodie could feel the rejection coagulating into rage. She retracted her hands and stood up.

She left the diner, vowing never to see them again. Let them go to Old Orchard just the four of them. Let them swim in the ocean and eat lobster and build sandcastles without her, the way they used be before she crashed their cozy little family.

She could hear Maggie calling after her as she fled, but she did not turn back. She neither saw nor spoke to Maggie and Gabriel for over a year.

Today, as she watches Maggie turn the sausages over in the pan, humming her favorite Edith Piaf song, Elodie can't quite believe she ever had the nerve to sever ties with this beautiful woman, her mother. But she had lost so much in her years at St. Nazarius, and the one thing the nuns and doctors had not managed to destroy was her stubbornness. That stubbornness, bolstered by profound hurt, propelled her in her isolation. She was determined to punish her parents for their indifference and insensitivity, no matter how hard it was. And it *was* hard, especially with Nancy asking all the time, "Where are Grand-maman and Grand-père? How come we never see them anymore?"

When Maggie called her after their trip to Maine, Elodie said, "Please don't call me anymore. Having you in my life is more painful than not having you."

"Elo—"

She hung up on her mother, and again on her father when he called back later. The next day when she got home from work, there was a plastic bag outside her door. Inside were two hooded Old Orchard Beach sweatshirts—one for her, one for Nancy—and a small white box of saltwater taffy. Elodie threw all of it in the trash and cried.

Maggie and Gabriel did not respect her wish to be left alone. Maggie wrote her letters and called regularly. Elodie stopped answering the phone, but often came home to messages like *We're here when you're ready. We're not going anywhere.*

A couple of times, Elodie spotted them in their car, parked across the street, watching her house. She did not relent and invite them in. She couldn't. She would not put herself at risk again. Her parents were damn persistent, though. Eventually, over the course of that year, Elodie's anger began to subside. Perhaps she'd been testing them to see how long they would hang in before giving up on her. Some part of her thought they'd be relieved to be rid of her, but that didn't seem to be the case.

One morning she woke up and felt no more animosity toward them. The grudge she'd been hanging onto over the Old Orchard vacation suddenly seemed absurd. She felt light, cleansed. She missed them both terribly. Who the hell was she to kick them out of her life after she'd spent her first twenty-four years conjuring them and longing for them and wishing she'd had them?

She got in her car and drove directly to Maggie's seed store in Cowansville. She remembers the bell jangling when she walked in, Maggie looking up from serving a customer, their eyes locking. Maggie's face broke into a wide smile. She didn't even finish serving the customer. She just ran to Elodie and pulled her into her arms and held her.

"I miss you," she murmured.

"Me, too," Elodie said.

"I'm sorry, *cocotte*."

"*I'm* sorry," Elodie said.

"Don't be sorry, Elo. You have every right to your anger. We handled this poorly. And you need to know, we are never going anywhere."

Elodie has had a mother for eighteen years, almost as long as she didn't have one. Having Maggie in her life doesn't completely erase her pain or blot out the memories or stave off the anxiety that can twist inside her chest, but Maggie makes everything infinitely better.

Looking at them all now, bustling around the warm, sunlit kitchen, passing plates to one another and chatting in familial shorthand, no one would guess that Elodie grew up apart and came to them as a complete stranger, fully grown. Sometimes even *she* forgets, and that's the beautiful thing about family.

Maggie is trying valiantly to keep the mood upbeat in spite of this being a birthday party for someone who is dead. She's made baked spaghetti with sausages and roast potatoes, and James has brought baguettes from Duc de Lorraine—Gabriel's favorite—and there's even a chocolate cake for dessert. The kitchen smells like heaven.

Maggie wanted to have a party. No one begrudged her, though James and Elodie did discuss how strange it was, maybe even a little unnerving. But everyone agreed to be here because it was for Maggie, and, of course, to honor Gabriel.

"As long as you're not hanging streamers and putting sixty birthday candles in a cake," James said when Maggie first brought up the idea at one of their Sunday family dinners. "That would just be creepy."

It's nothing like that today, but there is still a feeling of it being a little forced, as though Gabriel is merely upstairs showering and will be downstairs soon to join them. The feigning of joy is something Elodie is not only well practiced at, but also can easily detect.

Maggie brings the food to the table, and everyone sits down. James opens a bottle of Chianti, fills their glasses. "Happy birthday, Pa," he says, holding up his glass.

"Happy sixtieth, my love," Maggie says, her eyes shining. "You should be here."

"He's here with us, Maman," Stephanie reassures her.

"No, he's not," James mutters.

"You don't know that," Stephanie argues. She's twenty-one and thinks she knows everything. She goes to university in Sherbrooke, and every time she comes home for a visit, Elodie is convinced she's a little more self-centered. Elodie hasn't always gotten along with Stephanie; she finds her spoiled and entitled, like most kids her age. Maybe Elodie is just jealous that Stephanie was here first. Regardless, there's been a rivalry between them since the day Elodie showed up to claim a piece of their mother.

"You don't know what happens after we die," Stephanie is saying. "How can you be so sure Daddy isn't here?"

"I don't see him at the table, do you?"

"James," Maggie says, silencing him.

"I mean his spirit," Stephanie clarifies.

"You've got to stop watching *Oprah*, sis."

"James," Maggie repeats, more sternly this time. James and Stephanie still bicker like children, even though they are twenty-one and thirty-one.

Maggie serves them each a generous helping of baked spaghetti, sausage, and potatoes, and then tears the baguette into pieces. Elodie's mouth is watering. She will never forget the first time Maggie made her her famous baked spaghetti, the way the top layer was charred and crispy and underneath the noodles were creamy and rich, full of fresh tomatoes and a whole block of melted Velveeta cheese. Maggie tried to teach Elodie how to make it—she's been trying to teach her how to cook for years—but Elodie has no talent for it, and even less interest. She'd rather eat Maggie's food.

"Did you see the *Journal de Montreal* the other day?" Stephanie says, to no one in particular. "There was a story about the Duplessis orphans."

"It's horrific," Maggie says, looking across the table at Elodie. "The stories that are coming out."

"Not that we didn't already know," James adds.

"Are you going to sue?" Stephanie asks her. "That's what they're talking about on the news."

"Sue who?" Elodie says. "The government? The nuns? The doctor who had me locked up?"

"All of them."

"I'm going to call the Duplessis Orphans Committee in the new year," she says. "But I don't see how a bunch of poor, uneducated mental patients can possibly stand up to the government, let alone the church."

"You're not a mental patient," Maggie says.

"I *was* for ten years. The fact that I wasn't crazy doesn't change that."

"It's still worth trying," James adds.

Elodie nods, savoring a mouthful of spaghetti. Part of her is eager for the chance to fight for some kind of restitution—money, criminal charges, and an apology from all who were complicit—but another part of her is terrified to dredge up the past. She's managed to string an impressive number of good days together, days that have quietly morphed into solid chunks of time without despair, anxiety, or grief. Does she dare even consider tampering with such a fragile accord?

"I was thinking," Maggie says. "With everything coming out in the news lately and so many orphans coming forward, maybe now's the time for us to update your memoir, Elo. Try to get a publisher."

"I could help," James offers.

"Do you think someone would publish it now?"

"Absolutely. And I don't think yours will be the only one. I'd like it to be the first."

"You should find that nun," Stephanie says. "Don't you want to confront her?"

Elodie looks away. She hasn't had any desire to find Sister Ignatia.

Elodie was barely twelve when Gabriel and Maggie

showed up at St. Nazarius looking for her. Had they found her that day, they would have brought her home right then. Instead, Sister Ignatia told them she was dead. And then, for no other reason than inexplicable evil, she went and told Elodie that her mother was dead, purposely keeping them apart for twelve years longer than necessary.

Not long after Elodie came into their lives, Gabriel went back to St. Nazarius to find Sister Ignatia, but she'd already retired from the hospital by then. He was denied access to the convent's residence where she was living. Maggie always said it was a good thing because he probably would have killed her with his bare hands.

"When Elodie is ready," Maggie says, "she will do whatever she needs to do for *herself.* This isn't about revenge—"

"Yes, it is," Elodie says.

"Well, fine," Maggie concedes. "But it's also about getting some closure."

"If that's even possible."

"I hope it is."

"I prefer revenge," Elodie says, not meaning to be funny, but the others laugh. "I would like the world to know what she did to us. I'd like people to know that she murdered Emmeline and little Agathe, and told me that you were dead when you came to take me home. I don't think closure is realistic, but I'll feel a lot better when Sister Ignatia and the doctor who put me in that place are exposed for the monsters they are."

Elodie can already feel the dark fog beginning to rise up inside her, so she does what she always does. She smiles. She breathes. She silently acknowledges everything she has—health, family, home, food. "Let's change the subject," she says. "Pass me the cheese, please."

"I met someone," James announces.

"Really?" Maggie says, brightening. "What's her name? Is it serious?"

"Her name is Véronique Fortin. The relationship is purely one-sided. She actually hates me."

"I'm almost sixty, you know. Time is running out."

"She's the daughter of a convicted FLQ terrorist."

"Not Léo Fortin?" Maggie cries.

"The very one."

"You're kidding."

"I wish I was," he says. "She's a bad idea, I know. But I can't stop thinking about her."

"Is she a separatist?"

"Of course. Hard-core."

Maggie rolls her eyes. "What is it with us? First my father fell for one, then I did. Now you . . ."

"The heart wants what the heart wants," Stephanie says.

"Why the hell do we always want angry French Canadian nationalists?"

"It must be a gene," Elodie says, and they all laugh.

After dessert, when the dishes are done and the kitchen is sparkling and smells of Fantastik, Stephanie takes off to meet friends and James announces he's heading out.

"Sleep here," Maggie says to James, a little slurry from the wine. "Don't drive back tonight. It's snowing."

"I have to," he says, hugging both of them. Maggie hands him a large chunk of cake wrapped in tinfoil and a Tupperware of spaghetti.

Elodie knows he probably wants to be alone for a while on his father's birthday. Probably needs to get drunk and punch a wall or get in a fight.

When they're alone, Maggie opens another bottle of wine, and the two of them settle in the den. Maggie has a new couch, navy blue corduroy, with an absurd amount of plaid and floral toss cushions that leave very little room for sitting. Maggie throws a handful of them on the floor to make room. "I wanted it to look like a Ralph Lauren room," she explains.

"It's nice," Elodie says. "I like it."

Maggie replenishes their wine, and they touch glasses. Maggie says, "To Gabriel."

"To Gabriel," Elodie echoes.

"I miss him."

"Me, too."

"I feel very sad tonight," Maggie admits, her eyes filling with tears. Elodie doesn't know what to say. "We were supposed to get old together," Maggie goes on. "I'm just so glad you were all here with me. It means a lot. He would have been so proud of you, Elo."

"Why?"

"Oh, Elo. You don't give yourself enough credit." Maggie takes her by the hand and pulls her into the hallway. They stand side by side, looking into the carved oval mirror on the wall, just as they did the very first time they met. Elodie has changed so much since that day, both inside and out. She still has the physical scars on her face, but she's able to see beyond them now. She can see Gabriel in her full brow and blue eyes, Maggie in the shape of them. She wears her dirty-blond hair in a blunt cut to her chin, an improvement over the long drape of hair she used to hide behind. She has color in her cheeks, meat on her bones. They tell her she looks a lot like Clémentine, who is beautiful.

"Look at the woman you've become," Maggie says.

"You paid for my teeth to be fixed."

"I'm not talking about your teeth. I'm talking about your strength. You've raised a wonderful daughter, you've supported her for twenty years at the same job, you've overcome so much."

"I'm a waitress—"

"Are you kidding me?" Maggie says, her voice rising. Elodie can tell she's quite drunk. "Holding down a job for two decades after what you've been through, Elo? Do you know how many orphans like you are probably on welfare? Or back in institutions? Or dead? Your father would be proud of you for *surviving*."

"It's all because of you and Pa."

"It's because of *you*. You are the person I admire most in the world, Elodie Phénix. I've never known anyone as resilient as you are. Do you hear me?"

Elodie nods, moved beyond words.

"You are nothing short of a miracle," Maggie says, pulling her into her arms and holding her against her breast. "God took Gabriel from me," she says, her mouth in Elodie's hair, "but He gave me *you*. And I love you so much, my girl."

Elodie relaxes, allowing the good feelings to course through her body. In her mother's arms, all is right with the world, as she always imagined it would be.

6

The roads aren't bad until James gets to Granby, and then he hits a whiteout. He slows the car down to a crawl, flicks on his high beams, and turns up the volume on disc one of the Led Zeppelin box set, settling in and singing along.

He got into Zeppelin when they released the box set a couple of years ago. Forget grunge music, he thinks. Give him seventies rock any day. *Forget Véronique* is what he really means.

He just wants to get back to the city and drink. Not a polite Chianti with his mother and sisters, but a tsunami of booze to drown out the shitty feelings and fill the hole in his heart. This is what he does every year on his father's birthday. He blacks out.

By the time he reaches the Champlain Bridge, the

snowstorm has relented and just a few plump flakes are dancing in front of his windshield. Zeppelin is nearing the end of disc two—"D'yer Mak'er," a classic—and all he wants to do is get the hell out of the car—and out of his head—and surround himself with people.

He parks in front of his apartment on Ste. Famille and heads over to the Bifteck, an unpretentious bar on a shabby strip of the Main whose mission is appealingly straightforward: offer cheap beer, stale popcorn, and pool. The place is long and dark, cramped and smoke-filled, with round tables that face the sidewalk and a couple of pool tables at the very back. When you walk down the narrow length of the bar, spilled draft beer sticks to your shoes.

In spite of it being your basic crappy drinking hole, the Bifteck has recently become a Scene. Everywhere you look, there are musicians from cool local bands like GrimSkunk or Groovy Aardvark; beautiful girls in secondhand jeans and suede miniskirts, with their flat milk-white tummies and their nose rings and their Montreal Plateau attitudes on display; Concordia communications students discussing their short films, artists discussing their latest installations. Combat boots, tattoos, dreadlocks, and Jane's Addiction T-shirts. Never mind the filthy toilet or the stench of poorly cleaned vomit. This is the place to be.

James orders a pitcher and spends the next couple of hours drinking warm draft and shooting pool. He feels old. He *is* old. Everyone else here looks to be in their early twenties. He should be at Winnie's on Crescent Street, with his middle-aged colleagues. He should be drinking cold pints with other journalists, talking politics.

Not tonight. Tonight is about obliteration.

He's not the first guy to lose his father, won't be the last. People tell him he should be grateful he had his dad for twenty-three years—the most "formative" years, apparently. No. He's not grateful that his dad had a heart attack at fifty-two, standing in the middle of his beloved cornfield. James would have preferred his father to be at his wedding—should there ever be one—and to meet his future children. He would have preferred his father to be there for his mother, to take care of her into their old age. Would have preferred to keep fishing with him, hunting, having their long father-son talks in the cornfield while they examined corn tassels and swelling cobs. He does not feel grateful for having lost his best friend and mentor a year after graduating college.

Gabriel was not a perfect father by any means. He had a temper and could hold a grudge well beyond what was reasonable or rational. One time, when James was sixteen, he borrowed his father's pickup truck without asking and accidentally backed it up into a parked trailer. Gabriel grounded him for a month, but also didn't speak to him for the same amount of time. He felt betrayed by James in a way that was strikingly disproportionate to the actual misdemeanor; really, it was nothing more than a teenage boy's poor judgment and impulsivity, but Gabriel took it personally. Maggie kept telling him the grounding was punishment enough, and that the silent treatment was overkill, but Gabriel had to let his grudges burn off, however long it took. He had similar cold wars with his sisters at various times, the neighbors, even Maggie. He was infuriatingly stubborn. Maggie used to joke that he kept a collection of grievances and resentments in a notebook, referring to it frequently to maintain and update them, like a stamp or a coin collector. He could not forgive easily.

But that heart of his was as expansive as it was sensitive, and full of passion. He loved ferociously, protected fiercely. He was loyal and magnanimous. While Maggie was the backbone of their family, the provider of stability and calm, Gabriel was the heart of it. He loved the outdoors and was the one who taught them to fish and hunt, farm and pick wildflowers, eat blueberries off the bushes. He encouraged them to live off the land.

He was a good father to a son. He was not the type of man to hide his feelings and keep things bottled up, the way a lot of men do. He was open and straightforward, never held back an opinion. When James started hanging out with a group of potheads in high school, his father brought him out on the boat and gave him a serious talking-to. This was usually how he gave his lectures, out on the boat with a fishing rod in his hand.

"That crowd you're hanging with," he said, casting his line. "You think they're a good influence?"

James shrugged. He was deep in a shrugging, eye-rolling, insolent phase at that time. He wanted to be anywhere but on that boat with his dad.

"Your mother put you in English school so you'd have a better future," Gabriel said, not without some bitterness. He'd been against it—he'd wanted James educated in French—but Maggie had felt strongly that if the kids were fluently bilingual, they would have far more opportunities in the future. Because they only spoke French at home, the only way for the kids to learn English was at school. It was the same agreement Maggie's parents had made for Maggie and her siblings.

"You're at an age now," Gabriel went on, "where your choices and decisions actually matter. They affect your future. You talk about wanting to be a journalist? You need to be thinking about that now."

"I'm only in grade nine," James sulked. "Why are we talking about my future?"

"I was working full-time at a factory when I was your age," Gabriel reminded him. "I wish I'd had the luxury of staying in school."

"I'm not quitting school."

"This isn't about quitting school," Gabriel said. "It's about what you do with the opportunity while you're there."

"School isn't an opportunity. It's not like I have a choice."

Gabriel was quiet for a while. James will never forget the discomfort of that silence. He never knew how Gabriel was going to react to something, especially when James was being a smart-ass. He might have tossed James overboard and let him swim back home to teach him a lesson.

At last, Gabriel spoke. "I can't tell you who to hang around with," he said. "But I'm your father and I'm sure as hell going to tell you my opinion. The guys you're hanging around are losers and I don't like them. They don't look your mother or me in the eye when they're at our house, and they're high all the time. Half of them won't finish school. Their futures are going to happen by default. Do you understand what I mean?"

"No."

"It means if they continue on like this, they won't have any say in what they do. They'll wind up working at some factory or farming—not because they *want* to, but because it's all they can do—or they'll be on welfare."

James rolled his eyes skyward.

"Roll your eyes," Gabriel continued. "I get it. I was an asshole at your age, too. Just remember this conversation. You hear me? You're better than those guys."

"You don't even know them."

"I know *you*. And I know you're better than this. You're not too young to start thinking about your values."

That was the end of the conversation. Gabriel caught some perch while James sulked, and then they went back home. Gabriel didn't bring it up again, but his words had penetrated. James started to think about that word a lot. *Values.* What did it even mean?

Gabriel's opinion mattered a great deal to him. He wanted his father's respect and approval, even though he wouldn't let that be known. The next fall, James grew bored with that group of stoners and they fell away. He started hanging around Frank Pouliot, a football player for Cowansville High, a good student and a stand-up guy. They were best friends until they graduated high school. Frank went on to Bishop's to study law—he's a lawyer now in Sherbrooke—and James went to Concordia for journalism. Maybe it would have turned out that way anyway, even if Gabriel hadn't spoken to him that day, but maybe not. Though he never told him back then, later on, he appreciated that his father had interfered in his life, had cared enough to speak his mind.

That was Gabriel. The way he wore his heart on his sleeve gave them all permission to express themselves, good and bad. There was a lot of laughter and slammed doors and drama and tears, but there was always honesty.

After his death, it was like a heavy curtain had fallen. When James would come home to visit his mother, it felt like all the vibrancy and conviviality had been sucked out of the house. Although it has improved over the past eight years, and they've managed to recover some of the spirit they used to have, it's never been quite the same.

At twenty-three years old, James left his internship at the *Montreal Gazette* and took off to Europe. It was 1984. He did the backpack thing for a while, and eventually wound up in Greece, living in a tent on the island of Páros. He stayed there for a couple of months, drinking all night, sleeping all day. Forgetting. When the summer wound down and the tourists fled, James headed over to London, where he worked at the Hard Rock Cafe, selling T-shirts to tourists. He quickly established a similar routine—working all day, drinking all night. Oblivion, he discovered, made for an efficient travel companion.

After a while, he started to get bored again. It was becoming his MO, but he could hear his father's voice in his head getting louder: *You're better than this.* And so he returned home and got the job at CNA, first as their Parliament Hill reporter in Ottawa, and then covering the National Assembly in Quebec City.

By '87, he'd landed the job at the Montreal bureau, covering news and politics, with the occasional plum international assignment. Much to his relief, oblivion was available everywhere he went. He worked by day— he was always a damn good reporter—and drank all night. He'd also picked up a hash habit along the way, as well as a sleeping-around habit. All of it—the drinking, working, drugs, and sex—did what they were supposed to do: keep him numb.

He never spoke of his father, rarely went home to Cowansville—seeing his mother had become too painful—and tried not to form any serious relationships or attachments. It worked until it didn't. It worked until AIDS scared the living shit out of him.

The summer James turned twenty-six, there was a headline in the papers that profoundly shook him: "Quarantine Plan for AIDS."

AIDS had been in the news for a couple of years. It wasn't new; certainly it had been in the media throughout James's travels across Europe. He'd simply ignored it. But for some reason, early in the summer of '87, he started to worry. He'd been wildly promiscuous in his early twenties.

He was too scared to get tested. Instead, he became celibate. Stopped sleeping around cold turkey. He continued to drink and get high, occasionally experiencing intense paranoia. Aside from his job, which he managed to hang on to through a combination of talent and youth, he became something of a shut-in, drinking and smoking up in his apartment alone every night.

He suffered his first real panic attack on July 14 of that summer. He remembers the exact date because there was a massive flood in Montreal that day and the city was immobilized. He remembers the rain falling in heavy sheets against his window and water rising on his street like a river. On the news, there were images of school buses and trucks floating on flooded highways, people abandoning their cars and trudging knee-deep in water.

James was on his couch, high as a kite. His heart started pounding really fast. His first thought was, *I'm having a heart attack like Dad.*

He tried to calm himself, but the palpitations intensified. It felt like his heart was going to break free of his chest. Was this how his father had felt right before he died? He knew he couldn't call 9-1-1. There was no point; the roads were flooded. He couldn't call his mother either; it would have killed her, especially because there was nothing she could do from the Townships. First her husband, now her son. He realized that his life had become so small. There was no one he could call.

He considered it was probably better to die of a heart attack than from AIDS. Less stigma attached. At least a heart attack would spare him quarantine and shame.

He closed his eyes and waited to die. There was nothing else to do. His heart was racing; his breath was shallow. And then he remembered. There was Elodie. She lived in the Pointe, so he knew she wouldn't be able to get to him, but he thought hearing her voice might be comforting.

He called her. She answered on the first ring.

"I think I'm having a heart attack," he said, and he started to cry.

He realized the burden he was putting on her. She was so fragile, but then he was desperate.

"Did you call 9-1-1?" she asked him calmly.

"Have you looked outside?" he sobbed. "It's a fucking deluge."

She was quiet.

"I'm scared I have AIDS," he said.

"Do you have AIDS, or are you having a heart attack?" He wasn't sure if she was trying to make light of it or be funny, which wasn't her way.

"Both," he said. "I never use condoms and now I'm having a heart attack . . ."

He was slurring.

"Are you drunk?" she asked him.

"No. Yes. A little."

"I'm coming over."

"How?"

"It isn't too badly flooded over here. I'll drive north as far as I can go and walk the rest of the way."

"You don't have to—"

"I'm leaving now."

She hung up. An hour and a half later, she was there. He was living on Monkland at the time, in NDG. It had to have been a trek. Her jeans were soaking wet up to her knees. His heart was still racing. He didn't know what was happening to him.

She silently took in the dozen or so empty beer bottles, the half-smoked joint in the ashtray. She then sat down beside him and let him rest his head on her lap. She stroked his hair, the way his mother would have done. They couldn't get to a hospital, so he was prepared to die in her arms like that. AIDS or a heart attack, it didn't even matter anymore. He would be reunited with his father, at least. There was that.

"I miss my dad," he told her.

"I know." She kept stroking his hair. "How's your heart?"

"Pounding. Fast. It won't slow down."

"Is there pain?"

"No."

"I called 9-1-1 before I left. Hopefully they're going to be here soon."

"What if I have AIDS?"

"James, it's going to be okay."

"I think I'm dying, Elo. I really do."

He wasn't dying. An ambulance finally came after two hours and was able to get him to the Montreal General. Elodie went with him and they did all sorts of tests, but his heart was fine. It was a panic attack. The doctor told him to stop smoking drugs, warned him it was making him paranoid. Elodie convinced him to have an HIV test while he was there, to settle his mind.

James waited two weeks for those goddamn results. The worst fourteen days of his life. He didn't get high during that time, but he drank a hell of a lot and had more panic attacks. They were less scary now that he knew what they were. But he always thought about his father dying of a heart attack. When he finally went back to the hospital for his follow-up appointment after the HIV test, the results were negative.

When he called Elodie to share the good news, she did something she had never done before: offered him some advice. "I've tried doing what you're doing," she said. "And it doesn't work."

"What am I doing?"

"Trying to drink enough to not feel bad anymore."

"Is that right?"

"I tried a lot of things to make my pain go away," she confessed. "Drinking, weed. You know why I stopped? Because it didn't work."

"Is that supposed to cheer me up?"

"No. It's just the truth. Maybe it's okay to let yourself feel sad."

"Do you? Let yourself feel sad?"

"I have a daughter. It's different."

"I'm afraid those feelings will kill me."

"I know," she said. "But they don't. Or I'd have been dead a long time ago."

He didn't do anything radical after that. Didn't go to grief counseling or therapy or AA. He didn't go to the cemetery and sob openly at the foot of his father's grave. There was no one symbolic gesture that made the difference, but there was a new awareness that everything he'd been doing to avoid his pain had failed. And if he didn't make a change, he was going to fail at life, or die. And that would have been the most devastating disappointment to his father.

He gave up smoking dope and never went back to it. He cut back on the drinking and threw himself into work. Black Monday happened that October and the stock markets crashed, which turned out to be a great opportunity for James. His bureau chief sent him to Hong Kong. His life began to take shape. He even started dating someone—an Anglo from the Ottawa bureau. It was a long-distance relationship, which suited him. It was a way for him to ease back into the world at his own pace. And he always, always uses a condom now.

When James is thoroughly wasted, the bartender cuts him off. "I think you've had enough, Dad," she says. She's about nineteen. He mutters something and leaves the bar.

Outside on the street, he bums a cigarette and looks for another drinking hole. He decides on the Double Deuce, but just as he's about to head up the stairs, he feels that familiar flutter of his heart. Panic. He leans against the wall and draws a breath, then another. The palpitations gain momentum. *No, no, no. Please, no.*

He goes back outside and starts walking up St. Laurent Boulevard, with no clear destination in mind. He's breathing deeply, his hand on his heart. After a few blocks, he turns off onto Rachel and then over to St. Urbain, all the way up to Mont Royal, until he finds himself standing in front of Véronique's apartment. Imagine that.

He climbs the stairs. It's one o'clock in the morning. He pounds on the door. His heart is still racing.

To his surprise, she answers. She's wearing a tank top and boxer shorts, exactly what she was wearing last summer when he showed up uninvited. Her hair, a pile of dreadlocks now, is tied on top of her head.

She doesn't say anything.

"Hey," he says.

"Hey."

He runs a hand through his hair. "I can't stop thinking about you."

"You're drunk."

"Yes, I am. I'm celebrating."

"What?"

"My dad's birthday."

She cocks her head, that way she does. She understands.

"I just wanted to, uh, apologize," he says. "For what happened in Quebec City."

"It's one in the morning."

"I was a complete dick."

"Yes, you were."

"I don't agree with anything you stand for," he says, "but . . ." He groans. "Why can't I get you out of my head?"

She steps aside, allowing him to come in. He hesitates, not sure he isn't dreaming.

"You coming in?" she says.

He stumbles inside. She's listening to the Beastie Boys. *Check Your Head.* He loves this album. "I do agree with your taste in music."

"I'm so glad," she says, deadpan.

"You let me in."

"I did."

"Does this mean you forgive me?"

She takes a step toward him, pressing her body against his so his back is up against the wall. "No," she says.

"So . . ."

"So, that doesn't mean I don't want you here."

He reaches for her hand, brings it up to his heart, which has started to settle. It smells like vanilla hand cream. He lets out a little moan.

What the hell is happening to him? He's managed to go thirty-one years without ever feeling this way. He's made a point of it, in fact.

"You've got balls showing up here," she murmurs.

Their faces are so close. He debates his next move—she is a bad idea—and then he thinks, *Screw it,* and he places his hands on either side of her lovely face and kisses her. The grief subsides instantly, along with his racing heartbeat. Everything goes quiet inside. When they finally pull apart, she takes him by the hand and leads him to her bedroom.

7

"I have to go," Véronique says, not convincingly.

"Why? It's Sunday." They're lying in her bed, bodies entangled. They've been dozing and talking and having sex since he showed up last night.

"My cousin just paged me."

"And?"

"It's warm out," she explains. "It's probably the last weekend to take the boat out before the lake freezes."

"You're serious?"

"It's my job."

She told him what she does for a living, which she knows was a risk. The things they were sharing in the middle of the night were so honest and raw, it just came out. Maybe she was trying to shock him or impress him; maybe she wants him to know who she is before they get any deeper.

"How do you rationalize it?" he asked her.

"What?"

"Selling cigarettes to kids. Breaking the law."

"I don't rationalize it," she said. "Why should I have to?"

"Let me guess. You're entitled to do it because you grew up poor and oppressed by the evil, rich elite."

"Something like that," she said. "My parents used to rob banks for the FLQ. This is much less illegal."

James laughed. "Less illegal. I like that." Then he asked her if he could write a story about it. She said no and, for a flicker, regretted having divulged what she does.

She attempts to roll away, but he grabs her by the wrist. "Please stay."

"I can't." She'd like to, but she doesn't let on. She kisses him and he tries to pull her down on top of him, but she wriggles free and escapes. She walks over to her window and pulls open the blind, letting sunshine flood the room.

"You're so beautiful," he says, squinting in the bright light.

She grabs underwear and a bra from her dresser drawer and starts to dress.

"Don't," he says. "Just stand there for a bit."

"I can't. I've got at least an hour's drive and I need to get there before it gets dark." She pulls on her jeans and a gray sweater that's hanging on the back of her chair. "You can sleep a bit longer and let yourself out. Just make sure the door is locked when you go."

"How about your number?" he says, looking up at her with his sleepy, dark-blue eyes. His blond hair is disheveled, falling over one side of his face; his bare shoulders, smooth and broad, are peeking out from under the tangle of sheets. She looks away.

"Can you leave it for me so I don't have to keep showing up on your doorstep?"

She scribbles her number on a scrap of paper and leaves it on her dresser for him.

"We're not going to discuss last night?" he says.

"What's to discuss?"

"I don't know. What happened, I guess."

"What happened?"

"You're not making this easy. I'm trying to say that although I was quite inebriated—"

"Quite."

"—I meant what I said."

"What did you say?" she teases. "I don't remember."

"I said I can't stop thinking about you."

She doesn't tell him it's been the same for her, even though it has. She would never admit it.

"It wasn't just drunken bullshit," he says. "It's . . . it's actually a problem."

She smiles. He's adorable, but again, she won't let on that she thinks so. It's not even a game for her; it's self-preservation.

"Can I get a goodbye kiss?"

She climbs back on the bed and straddles him, her legs locked tightly on either side of his hips. She feels him get hard right away.

He pulls her head down and kisses her, tries to flip her around so he's on top. They wrestle playfully on the bed, and although she would like to stay, Pierre and her uncle are waiting for her.

"I have to go," she says.

James reluctantly gives up and lets her go. She slides off the bed.

"I'll call you," he tells her.

She doesn't say anything as she leaves the room to go into the bathroom. When she comes back, James hasn't moved. She's relieved. She likes the idea of him in her bed, even when she's gone.

She stands above him, watching him. He's watching her, too. He reaches for her hand. They stand like that, fingers entwined, for a minute, and then she leans over him and kisses him. A tender kiss, less fervent than last night, but a kiss that leaves her wanting more.

Camil, Pierre, and Marc are waiting for her in the garage when she gets to Ste. Barbe. Marc is on his Game Boy and barely looks up when she walks in. He's fourteen now, a handsomer, smarter version of Pierre. She's always had a soft spot for him, an inclination to look out for him.

Pierre is already in his camouflage gear and a heavy parka, the shotgun leaning against his truck. "We were about to send Marc out," Camil says.

"Marc can't do a run. He's just a kid—"

"What took you so long?"

"The roads are icy," she lies. Really, she's in a post-sex daze, distracted, thinking about last night, about James.

"*Allo?*" Camil says, interrupting her thoughts. "Did you hear what I said?"

"What?"

"Billy and Tug's mother died yesterday. She had cancer. You need to give condolences on our behalf."

Véronique pulls on her camouflage pants. "What am I supposed to say?"

"Tell him we're sorry for his loss," Camil says. "And another thing. I just lost my only bilingual transporter. He's in jail for assault."

"And?"

"He does the universities in Ottawa and Kingston. I need you to take over for him."

"My English isn't good enough."

"The money is good. One of my best customers is in Ottawa. Name's Callahan. He's a stoner, but steady. Decent guy. Always pays. He buys shitloads of smokes for the dorms on campus. Runs a thriving business. It's an opportunity for you, Véronique."

That's how he always spins it when he's trying to get her to do something she doesn't want to do. It's an "opportunity."

She finishes dressing—tonight she needs a parka, tuque, and thick gloves—and follows Pierre down to the dock. "This'll be our last boat run till spring," he says, crouching down in his usual spot, shotgun across his knees.

She loves this moment, right before they head out on a run—the tension in her body, the fear prickling her skin, the knowledge she is brazenly living her life outside the law.

The sky is already dark as they set off, with the temperature rapidly dropping. She can see her breath in the air, and the wind out on the lake is violent. By the time they reach Billy's marina, her face is numb and chafed.

Billy is the one who's waiting for them tonight. The moment he spots them approaching, he starts unloading cases of cigarettes onto the dock.

Véronique climbs out of the boat first to pay her respects.

"Sorry about your mudder," she says, in thickly accented English.

Billy doesn't say anything. Doesn't even stop what he's doing.

"My uncle send his condolence," she adds.

Still nothing. She looks at Pierre, who shrugs and starts tossing the cases on his boat. Véronique helps him, embarrassed. No one says anything else. When they're done, Billy says, "Tug's not here to escort you out of the reservation."

Pierre and Véronique nod silently, and then Billy turns and gets in his truck.

"I'll drive back," Pierre says when they're alone on the dock.

"Why?"

"We don't have Tug. I need to get us out as fast as possible. People on the reservation probably know about their mother. We're vulnerable."

"I can drive fast."

"Not as fast as I can."

Véronique's heart is pounding. She has a bad feeling.

"You know how to use the gun?" he asks her.

"I'll figure it out."

"Rest the butt really snug inside your shoulder and point it at your target," he says. "Don't forget to flip the safety off, and then squeeze the trigger like you're shaking someone's hand. Don't jerk the gun up when you fire. Just be smooth. You want to keep both your eyes open. The kick of the gun is pretty powerful, so be ready."

They get in the boat and Pierre starts the engine. Véronique sits down cross-legged on one of the cases, holding the shotgun. She examines it, placing one hand on the stock and the other midway up the grip.

"You won't need to use it," Pierre says, watching her.

She nods and he pulls away from the dock. Her heart is still pounding. There's a feeling of powerlessness, being the passenger, especially as Pierre is picking up speed. She prefers being the driver. The lake is a black hole; she can't see a thing in any direction. She tells herself that there are fewer boaters out than there typically are in the summer, but that doesn't mean thieves aren't lurking in the dark corners somewhere, hiding behind one of the islands or idling in their path, waiting for them to pass without an escort.

Pierre speeds up some more, and Véronique is sure he must be pushing sixty miles an hour, about the max the boat will go. "Slow down!" she screams, but the motor swallows her voice and he doesn't hear her. "*Pierre!*"

She's terrified, totally at the mercy of her cousin, who, at the best of times, is reckless and rash. He's also high. He's always high. She should never have let him drive. The boat is moving like a rocket in the dark. The wind is whipping her face, water spraying her like a hose. She's gripping the edge of the boat with her gloved hands while the shotgun bobs around in her lap. She's hasn't exhaled a breath since they took off. "*Tabarnak*, Pierre, slow down!"

He glances back, laughing. He's enjoying himself. Véronique checks her watch; it's been six minutes. They're out of the reservation. He can slow down, but of course, he doesn't. He's going to take them home like this, pushing the boat to its limits. She wonders sometimes if he doesn't care about dying.

She closes her eyes and continues to hold her breath. The wind shapes the water into high, choppy waves; the boat slams against each one with such force her head is thrown forward and she goes flying into the air, landing hard on her coccyx bone. She's never been a neurotic person, but in this moment, she's certain death is imminent. By the time they finally reach Camil's place, she's soaking wet, freezing, and every muscle in her body aches.

Pierre brings the boat in, backing it in carefully, and then hops out to tie it up. Véronique stands up, her lower back throbbing. She can hardly turn her head.

"Hand me the gun."

She bends down, wincing as she does, and grabs the gun. She hands it to him without a word. Her uncle joins them, and they start unloading the cases. "Did you give him our condolences?" Camil asks, handing over her share of cash.

She nods, too angry to speak.

"You okay?"

Another nod. She won't look at him; she's worried she might cry. She's so wound up—so tense and taut—she doesn't know what will spill out of her if she opens her mouth.

When all the cigarettes are safely locked inside the boathouse, Pierre offers her a joint. She's tempted to say yes, just to stop the shaking, but all she wants is to get out of this wet parka and away from him. "I have to go," she says, turning away.

"We'll call you in January," Camil says. "The next run will be by snowmobile. And then you'll deliver the smokes to Kingston and Ottawa."

Véronique doesn't answer. She's already on her way back up to the garage.

"Merry Christmas!" he calls after her.

She drives back to the city more slowly than usual, with the heat on high. She can't get comfortable sitting—her tailbone must be badly bruised. She can't stop shaking, can't warm up. Her clothes are damp, her teeth chattering. The roar of the boat's motor is still echoing inside her head, which also hurts. She doesn't even bother to turn on the music.

It's just after nine when she gets home. There's a light snow falling, and it's much milder here than it was in Ste. Barbe. She leaves the car on the street, not caring if she gets a ticket. All she can think about is a shower and her bed. She climbs the balcony with great difficulty. Her limbs are so stiff she has to pull herself up by the railing. When she finally lets herself inside, she exhales a long breath. It may be the first full breath she's expelled since climbing into that boat.

The first thing she notices is the light still on in her bedroom, its warm syrupy glow spilling onto the hardwood floor. She hears music, too, also coming from her room. And then she remembers. James must have left everything on when he left this morning. She closes the door behind her and kicks off her wet boots.

"*Allo?*" he calls out.

"James?"

"In here."

Her mood soars at the sound of his voice. She goes down the hall in her wet socks, her body tingling, feeling happier than she would have thought possible. And there he is, lying on her bed, reading *La Belle Bête*.

"Hope you don't mind," he says, looking up at her. "Once I started reading it, I couldn't put it down."

"You like Marie-Claire Blais?"

"Never read her before."

"You've never read Blais?" She frowns. "She's one of my favorite writers."

"I can see why."

"So that's why you're still here?"

"It's the only reason," he says, putting the book down beside him, grinning.

She sits down on the edge of her bed, which he's made, and he reaches out to touch her hair. "You're soaking wet," he says.

"You've been here all day?"

"All day."

"Why?"

"Why do you think? I wanted to see you. I couldn't

stand the thought of leaving here and having to wait."
He sits up. "Is that okay?"

"I guess so."

"You sure you don't want to be alone?"

She shakes her head, no. She didn't realize how much she didn't want to be alone until just now.

"I ate some of your food," he confesses. "You don't have much, but I managed. The cheese had a funny smell—"

All of a sudden she starts to cry.

"Hey, hey," he says gently. "What's wrong?"

He takes her in his arms, and she melts against him. Even as the tension eases in her body, the emotional hangover remains. The more James strokes her back, asking what's wrong in his tender voice, the harder she cries.

"Véronique? What is it? Did something happen?"

She doesn't tell him anything. Doesn't tell him that her heart won't stop racing or how angry she is with Pierre for his callousness with their lives. She doesn't tell him that this is how she lives, perpetually on the cusp of danger, and that if he wants to be with her, he's going to have to get used to it.

8

January 1993

Véronique glides toward him like a professional speed skater, body low to the ice, legs bent, arms swinging out behind her. *Shk shk shk.* Just as she's about to crash into him, she comes to a sudden flamboyant stop, spraying ice at his feet. Not surprisingly, she's a good skater. She's good at everything. She consistently beats him at cards and Trivial Pursuit—the Quebec edition—and *Jeopardy!*, which they watch in French on TVA almost every night. She can run 5K at the same clip as him. Winter sports—forget about it. She snowboards, cross-country skis, can hold her own in hockey, and can obviously handle a snowmobile. She's a natural athlete, among all her other abilities, not the least of which is her impressive intellect. She reads a lot, knows her politics, doesn't back down from an argument—he's not sure if that's a pro or a con yet—and has a quick wit that keeps him captivated. She can even cook.

Did he mention she's also gorgeous? Even today, when she's wearing her pompom tuque, puffy winter jacket, and clunky black men's skates, he can't take his eyes off her. Her cheeks are pink and her dark eyes shining; her beauty is effortless. When she smiles in his direction or laughs at something he says or does, his heart ricochets. He is completely spellbound.

This weekend they're in the Townships to visit his mother. Elodie is also planning to come, and it will be the first time Véronique meets his family. He hasn't brought a girlfriend home in years, so they know Véronique is special.

He's planned a full weekend, starting with what he hoped would be a romantic skate on Lac Brome in Knowlton, and so far, it has not disappointed. His mother is working until five today, and Elodie won't be up until suppertime, so he figured they could spend some time together alone, doing something fun and outdoorsy to alleviate their nerves. Well, *his* nerves. He's not sure if Véronique is nervous. She doesn't say, doesn't reveal. She rarely talks about how she's feeling, something he finds both frustrating and mysterious.

He wants his mother to like her. And if it weren't for her father's past, he wouldn't be the least bit concerned about it. He knows all Maggie wants is for him to be happy, but a separatist/murderer father-in-law is a definite drawback. Neither Maggie nor Véronique is good at standing down when they believe in something; if their values and opinions don't align, it will be disastrous. The X factor then becomes how much both women are willing to bend for *him*.

"Show-off," he says, skating around her. "Is there anything you're not good at?"

She cocks her head, thinking.

"Come on. There must be something."

"Relationships."

His mother always says, *People tell you who they are right away.*

"You've been pretty good at this one so far," he says.

She grabs his hands and pulls him along the ice. They've been seeing each other for almost two months, and he's sure he loves her. He can actually see himself with her in the future—their wedding, their children, their old age. He's never been a romantic before, but he's also thirty-two. There's a restlessness inside him now, a sudden urge to settle down and be with one person. With *her.*

The sun is shining, the sky is bright blue, the air is

crisp but not too cold, and James is in a marvelous mood. He almost says, *I love you*, but stops himself. It's definitely too soon. She's only twenty-three and it's pretty obvious she has commitment issues. "I love being with you," he says, settling for that right now.

She looks away. He's noticed she has a hard time with compliments—giving them, receiving them. She attempts to skate away, but he grabs her mitten. "Don't skate off," he says, pulling her back. "Did you hear what I said?"

"Me, too," she says as though she's just conceded a victory. She jerks her hand free and races off.

They do a few more loops on the lake, racing against each other—she's extremely competitive—and then seeing who can skate backwards faster. (She can.)

"Do you want to see my mom's store?" he asks when the sun starts to wane and they're unlacing their skates. "It used to be my grandfather's."

She turns her head to look at him. There's something in her eyes, a shadow that wasn't there a moment ago. She's quiet.

"We don't have to," he says.

"No, of course I want to."

"What's wrong?"

"Nothing."

She slips on her boots and stands up. "Let's go."

As they approach Rue Principale in Cowansville en route to the seed store, Véronique places her hand on James's forearm and says, "Can we take a detour?"

"Where to?"

"Get on Rue de la Rivière and stay on it until Fordyce."

He does as she asks, and they drive in silence on the familiar country road, which is bordered on both sides by endless white farmland stretching out toward the sky. This will always be home, he thinks, with a bittersweet tug of nostalgia. The Townships are rich with memories of his childhood and the father he lost. This was Gabriel's world, from the cornfields to the lake and everything in between.

He looks over at Véronique, following her gaze out the window. He knows exactly where he's taking her and understands why she got so quiet all of a sudden. He grew up fifteen minutes away, after all.

"Did you used to visit him often?" he asks her.

"Only on special occasions."

"What were the visits like?"

"I hated it," she says. "It was the most depressing place in the world. Have you ever been inside a prison?"

"No."

"I always dreaded coming. It was awful."

She doesn't talk about her father very often, and almost never about his time in jail. He's glad she's opening up now, quietly honored that she's having him take her to the penitentiary.

They continue in silence until they turn onto Chemin Fordyce. The landscape is a blanket of white, lovely and serene, the trees fluffy with fresh snow. If not for the orange cones flanking the entrance and the government sign announcing the Cowansville Penitentiary, you could forget where you were.

"You okay?"

"This is far enough," she says. "Can we just sit here a minute?"

James pulls the car to the side of the road, puts it in park.

"This road," she says. "I can't tell you how much I dreaded this drive."

"What was it like, seeing him inside?"

"You have to understand," she says. "I didn't know him. I'd never known him. He went to jail when I was a baby, so he was just this stranger I had to visit in this terrifying place. We'd sit across from each other at a table, and he'd ask me questions. I'd have to sit on his lap. He'd hold me and sob. It was so awkward. I'd cry the whole way home."

"Your mother waited for him, though. She didn't leave him."

"She loved him."

James nods, pretending to understand.

"I only got to know him when he came home," she says. "He would talk to me about his upbringing, his struggles, how he became interested in politics. The more he explained to me about the struggle, the more I was able to understand why he wound up in the FLQ. Why he did what he did."

"But what he did—"

"He's my dad, James. I was happy to have him home, to be able to get to know him, to actually have a father. He's a great guy. He really is. You just don't understand where he came from, what he lived through."

James holds back, bites his tongue. This is not the time for one of their arguments. She's finally opening up to him, and he doesn't want to risk losing her trust. He doesn't agree with her, but he doesn't have to win this one. Doesn't have to prove he's right and she's wrong and convince her that her father is a villain.

"Will you introduce me to him?" he asks her. The journalist in him would love a crack at Léo Fortin.

"Let's just get through your mother," she says.

The seed store is on the main street in Cowansville. His mother's been running Semences Supérieures/ Superior Seeds since her father died in the early sixties. She started working for him as a little girl, weighing seeds up in the attic, some fifty years ago. It still blows his mind. She loves that store as much as she loves her kids, and she's never fussed about trying to convince them otherwise. "It's my passion," she always says. She plans to work there until they put her in the grave, just like her father did.

The bell jingles when James opens the door. Whenever he visits, he's always surprised by how little has changed over the years. Even the sign out front— written in both French and English—has never been updated. His mother's marketing strategy in the face of the American big-box store invasion has been to dig in and do what she and her father before her had always done: offer personalized "Mom and Pop" service, build lasting relationships with their loyal customers, and preserve the authentic feel of a charming seed shop from days gone by, which is why she's kept her father's antique bank counter and oak filing cabinets for the seeds. She's got three things over her competitors: rare seeds, expertise, and heart. "You won't find any of those at Seed Depot or Garden World," she likes to say. "My store smells like things are *growing*."

To her credit, her store has managed to flourish in the good times and survive the bad; right now is one of the bad. The economy is grim and business has been slow, but she's pulled through before, and frankly, she secretly loves the challenge of having to "save the business." It's a free pass for her to work even harder than usual. James and his sisters all recognize that Maggie is a workaholic—even more so since Gabriel died—but it also helped her get through one of the darkest periods of her life. Besides, it's not like any of them could talk her out of it. Maggie is a force.

They find her in her office, which is not unusual for a winter Saturday. This is the time of year where her work shifts to budgeting, marketing, and stocking up for spring.

"Ma?"

Maggie looks up from her work, and James sees her as Véronique must be seeing her for the first time. Her hair is still thick and black—dyed now, but no less striking—and for someone just a year shy of sixty, she looks damn good. She'll tell you the work keeps her young, but good genes don't hurt either.

"Ma, this is Véronique."

Maggie stands up and comes around the desk. She

embraces Véronique and says, "He's been talking about you since October. It's nice to finally meet you."

"I love your store," Véronique says. "It has such a happy feeling when you walk in."

"It was my father's," she says proudly. "I've tried not to change too much."

James realizes his palms are sweaty. He's relieved that Véronique cut off her dreadlocks and now has a sexy bob of soft auburn waves. Maggie wouldn't have liked the dreadlocks, but then she was never one to choose her boyfriends by what might please *her* parents. "I met James's father here," Maggie is saying. "He came in one day with his sister, and I was hiding on the stairs over there, spying on the shop floor. I loved all the action down here. Anyway, Gabriel came in—he must have been about fifteen or sixteen. My God, he was gorgeous. He looked exactly like James, only rougher around the edges."

Maggie smiles, remembering. "That was it," she says. "The moment I saw him, I was infatuated. I loved him until the day he died."

"Well, Ma," James says, "this is a lot for the first five minutes."

Maggie and Véronique both laugh, and James starts to relax.

"We'll have lots to talk about tonight," Maggie

says. "I'll be home by five thirty. I made a shepherd's pie."

Véronique and Maggie exchange two kisses on either cheek, and then Maggie wraps her arms around James and holds tight. "You look happy," she whispers. *T'as l'air b'ein content.*

"She can hear you, Ma," he says, but he doesn't mind. He is happy.

Back at the house, he takes Véronique upstairs to his former room, which is now the guest room. His mother has always loved decorating—much like Véronique, she does almost everything well—and this season the house is an homage to her current idol, Ralph Lauren. Each room is a tasteful blend of stripes and checks and bold floral patterns in navy blues and hunter greens; the walls are papered in classic ticking stripes, the pine floors are laden with dark floral rugs, and the curtains are gingham. Couches are buried under throw pillows, bookshelves are overflowing, dark mahogany antiques are decorated with candles and family pictures. Every room strikes a confounding balance between overdone and understated, the overall effect being one of warmth and hominess.

His bed—now the guest bed—is layered with a brown plaid duvet cover, wool blanket, and cable-knit throw, as well as about a half dozen decorative pillows in a variety of leather and suede and flannel.

"Your mom likes pillows," Véronique says, falling back into a pile of them.

James climbs on top of her and starts kissing her. They can't get each other's clothes off fast enough. They're in that glorious early stage when every touch is electric, when it's all exploratory and new. She likes to be on top, isn't shy about telling him what to do. It's such a turn-on the way she places her hands on his chest and says his name over and over again—a whimper almost, like she's pleading with him, her beautiful body rocking back and forth—and then that final arch of her slender back, the way her body shudders and quivers against him when she collapses.

"How many girls have you slept with in this bed?" she asks him when they've finished.

"Not that many," he says. "My parents were in the room next door."

She's got her head on the flat of his stomach, her arm draped across him. "I need to shower before your sister and mom get here."

"I'll join you, in case there's parts you can't reach."

"I'm a little anxious."

"About what?"

"The dinner conversation."

"Why? My mom and Elodie are harmless."

Véronique doesn't look convinced. "My father is always the elephant in the room."

"Don't worry," he says. "We have our own elephants."

After dinner, which is jovial and relaxed—helped along by a couple of excellent bottles of Barolo—the four of them move into the den for a round of cards. Turns out they all play 500, and to make things more interesting, it's Elodie and Véronique against Maggie and James. Not surprisingly, Véronique is a formidable opponent, even against Maggie, whose competitiveness is matched only by James's. Maggie and James take the first win, at which point Maggie goes out to the liquor cabinet in the dining room to retrieve a bottle of cognac. Things are going well.

"So what's the age difference between you two?" Véronique asks James and Elodie as she deals the next hand.

James looks over at Elodie. He hasn't told Véronique anything about Elodie's past, which is the family's unspoken rule. Elodie prefers not to discuss her past with anyone, and out of respect for her wishes, they all keep it within the family. But Véronique is not blind; she can plainly see that Elodie is a good decade older than

James, and that Maggie must have had her when she was a teenager.

"I'm eleven years older," Elodie says.

"She got the ball rolling for my parents," James adds, making light.

"I was definitely a surprise."

"Your mom must have been so young when she had you," Véronique says.

Elodie doesn't respond. James shoots Véronique a look, and it silences her right away. She seems to register that this conversation is off-limits. "All right, Elo," she says lightly. "Let's destroy them this round."

Elodie smiles and visibly relaxes. James can tell she likes Véronique, which is no small achievement. Elodie is typically very shy around strangers, but tonight he's observing an ease with Véronique that pleases him.

"No more mercy," Véronique warns, winking at her partner. "We were just warming up, right, Elo?"

Lying in bed later on, Véronique curls up inside the nook of his arm. They're both a little drunk—maybe more than a little—and all he wants to do is have sex with her.

"Your parents weren't married when your mom got pregnant, were they?" she asks him.

"No."

"How old was she?"

"Fifteen."

He doesn't want to keep anything from her—not even Elodie's story. This feels like the right moment to deepen their connection, and although he doesn't want to betray his sister—Elodie deserves her dignity—everything about not telling Véronique the truth feels wrong.

"You're not the only one with a dark family secret," he says softly.

"You know mine, though, so you've got an advantage over me."

"It's not really my secret to tell, though."

Véronique nods, understanding. "Elodie has a sadness about her," she says. "You can see it in her eyes."

"She's had a hard life."

"But not growing up here with you."

"My grandfather wasn't a bad guy, he just did what was expected. He took her to an orphanage."

Véronique props herself up on one elbow, listening with her full attention.

"I don't know if you know this, but in the early fifties, Duplessis converted all the orphanages in the province into mental hospitals."

"I saw something on the news, but I didn't pay much attention."

"Elodie was sent to an asylum when she was seven. She spent ten years there. It was brutal. She wasn't educated, she was violently abused."

"How did your parents find her?"

James explains about the ad his grandfather ran for years in the classified section of all the French papers, looking for Elodie. Eventually—miraculously—Elodie saw the notice and called Maggie.

James will never forget the first time he was introduced to his older sister. He was thirteen, Elodie twenty-four. He remembers thinking she looked like a scared animal. She hid behind a long curtain of hair, but still he could see the sorrow in her face. She was badly damaged, you knew at once.

He didn't learn the details of her story until much later, at about eighteen. His father told him one afternoon when they were out fishing. He'd known her five years by then, and he cried as Gabriel unspooled all the horrific details of what she'd endured. He already loved her; she was kind to him, and they'd become friends. Because she had learned so little to that point—both in school and in life—they were more like the same age. He introduced her to music—Stevie Wonder, CCR, the

Beatles, the Stones—and the best rock station, CHOM; his favorite TV shows and Kentucky Fried Chicken. He taught her how to play cards and how to ride a bike. Gabriel taught her to fish, grow corn, and drive a car; Maggie taught her high school math and grammar, and tried to teach her how to cook—she's not a natural—and slowly, they managed to get her caught up to the rest of the world.

"You should write a book," Véronique says. "Why haven't you already?"

"Elodie and my mother actually wrote a memoir years ago," he says. "Nobody wanted it. But now that the orphans are starting to come forward and speak out, we're going to try again. I'm going to do it, update it with all the journalistic context."

"And Elodie doesn't mind?"

"It's what she wants."

James waits until Véronique is snoring softly beside him, and then he slips out of the bed and creeps downstairs. He knows Maggie will be awake, working on her spring marketing, balancing the books, fretting about the winter sales.

Sure enough, he finds her at the kitchen table, surrounded by papers and sketches for a new catalogue, her mug of cold tea, and some half-eaten cookies on a plate.

"Hey, love," she says, looking up from her type-writer and removing her glasses. She still refuses to get a desktop computer for the house.

"Still typing, eh?" he says, sitting down and reaching for a cookie.

"I can't set up a computer at the kitchen table," she says. "Besides, I like typing. It reminds me of my dad."

"What do you think of her?" he asks.

"You stayed up this late so you could ask me that?"

"Yeah."

"Your father would have loved her."

"And you?"

"I can see she's intelligent and obviously beautiful. And she's in love with you. And I get why you're in love with her."

"But?"

"No 'but.'"

"*But?*"

"I've been where you are, my love. My father forbade me to see Gabriel, but he couldn't change how I felt about him. For a while, he made me doubt my feelings, but love prevailed, so to speak."

"What are you saying?"

"I'm saying I know better than to give my opinion."

"But you have one."

"I always have one," Maggie says dryly. "I think

she's wonderful, don't get me wrong. I'm a little concerned that she doesn't have a college degree. What can she really do without one?"

"She'll figure it out," he says. "She's so young. Steph's age. But she's brilliant, and she's ambitious."

"I also have reservations about her family," Maggie says. "How can she be okay, James? Her father is a convicted murderer."

"Véronique isn't. She's totally innocent." Not exactly the truth, but white lies are required here.

"As in-laws go, they wouldn't be my first choice."

"What her father did has nothing to do with her," James says, his voice rising. "How can you hold that against her? That would be like her family holding your teenage pregnancy against you."

"I'm not holding anything against her, James. You asked my opinion, and all I'm saying is I worry about her parents' history. It's not just about what her father did—although he did murder an innocent man—it's about her beliefs and her principles. You said she's a separatist. You work for the most prominent English news agency. You can't stand the separatists. Will that be an issue down the road? That's all I'm saying."

"I'm in love with her," James says. "The last thing that would ever be an issue for me is our politics. We're able to disagree."

"Well, good then," Maggie says, and he's annoyed with her.

"I'm in love with her," he repeats.

"I know you are, my love. And you have my blessing and I support you, always. I just can't pretend I don't have concerns about your future together."

"Your father had reservations about Dad, and you guys worked out."

"You're right. Which is why my mind is open."

9

March 1993

Elodie parks in the lot of the Beaudry Community Center, staying in her car a few extra minutes. The building looks like a small institution—a rectangular, light-colored brick box with multiple rows of dormer windows—made all the more grim by the gray sky, dirty snowbanks, and puddles of slush. She wonders about the people inside, the Duplessis orphans. She isn't sure how many of them will be there, but even a handful will be something. Maybe she'll recognize someone from St. Nazarius. It's been twenty-five years, but she could never forget those haunted faces. How strange it is to sit here now, about to have everything she's fought so hard to forget thrust back into the forefront of her life. This time, though, it's by choice.

She draws a breath and gets out of the car, feeling extremely nervous. The meeting is in the basement, and she follows the hand-written signs that say DUPLESSIS ORPHANS COMMITTEE MEETING. When she gets to the room, the meeting is already underway.

She stands by the door, taking it all in. There are about fifty men and women in the room, seated on folding chairs, which are lined up in rows. At the front, there's a long banquet-style table where one man—the leader, presumably—is facing the audience. There are pitchers of water on the table, with Styrofoam cups and ashtrays. A large banner hangs behind him: DUPLESSIS ORPHANS COMMITTEE—SOUTHEAST REGION.

Elodie immediately starts scanning the women, row by row, searching for familiar faces. She doesn't recognize anyone from St. Nazarius, and yet she recognizes *something* in all of them—a shared sadness. There are the obvious signs of physical abuse—one man is missing an eye, another has a scar traversing his skull like a river on a map, several have canes, most have facial scars and missing teeth. But what she sees in all of them is the evidence of an upbringing barren of love, nurturing, and hope; the dead stare of a wasted life, the ossification of grief. She quickly realizes she has fared much better than they have.

A woman on one of the aisle seats notices Elodie hovering by the door and beckons her over to the empty seat beside her. Elodie quietly takes the seat. The woman's name tag says HUGUETTE.

Huguette smiles warmly. She looks about forty-five.

"Here is what you all have in common," the man up at the front is saying. "You all came from orphanages. You were never adopted, you were all institutionalized."

The man's name tag says BRUNO. He's heavyset with a round face and a full, silver-flecked beard. He wears glasses and a snug tweed jacket over his sweater. When he speaks, a respectful hush falls over the room.

"You were deprived of an education," he continues. "You were sexually abused, physically abused, et cetera, et cetera. And you were financially exploited, forced to work every day of your lives for *nothing*!"

The crowd comes to life, yelling, "Yes! Yes!"

"But there's more, my friends. There's more," roars Bruno, riling them up. "Let's continue with this portrait of the Duplessis orphan—"

"*Oui! Oui!*"

"Marginalized from society. Poverty. Mental disorders—and not ones that you were born with, but which were the result of everything you suffered in those institutions! To conclude, you've had extremely hard lives, to say the least. Lives that were absolutely destroyed by Premier Duplessis."

Bruno's speech is met with whistles and wild applause. He talks like an educated man. He can't possibly be one of them. Even Elodie is clapping, her eyes filled with tears. *Yes!* she thinks. *Yes. That's me.*

The woman beside her, Huguette, suddenly reaches for her hand and squeezes. Elodie squeezes back.

"You learned not to dream," Bruno goes on. "You learned not to speak up, or have desires. You gave up your illusions and your hopes, until, finally, they turned you into zombies."

He pauses and looks around the room, acknowledging as many of them as he can. Elodie also looks around the room again. Bodies ravaged by hard lives, addiction, and poverty. Minds destroyed by medication, operations. Elodie has to remind herself that, like her, they're still only in their forties. She understands now just how fortunate she was to have been rescued by her parents at twenty-four, when she was still young enough for their care to make a difference in her life. Their love restored her while it was still possible for at least part of her to be restored. They gave her a chance. They gave her the practical things—dentists, doctors, healthy food, siblings, Christmas presents, decent clothes. They taught her to read and do simple math. They loved her and loved her and loved her until she began to love herself, even just a little bit. She was only twenty-four.

"What now?" Bruno asks them.

"Now we fight!" someone cries out.

"Now we fight," Bruno repeats. "Now we have each other. We're stronger together. They can't put us in straitjackets and throw us in locked cells anymore! We will continue to meet, and to protest, and to hold press conferences, and to tell our stories to whoever will listen. Call the media. They love a good story. We have a lawyer now, and we're going to file a class action lawsuit!"

"Against who?"

"Against the College of Physicians for their misdiagnoses, the religious orders for their crimes against humanity—"

Elodie cheers along with the others, feeling as hopeful and excited as she's ever felt in her life.

"Please, friends," Bruno says. "Please, stand up one by one and say your name and the institution where you were confined."

One by one, they stand.

"Gilles Galipeau, Hôtel de Dieu."

"Hubert Tremblay, St. Julien."

"Honoré Lagasse, Mont Providence."

"Huguette Lalonde, Mont Providence."

"Francine Dion, Mont Providence."

"Elodie Phénix, St. Nazarius."

After the meeting, Huguette invites Elodie to join her and her friend Francine for a coffee at a diner down the street. They sit at a booth, with Elodie facing the two women. She orders her usual. Coffee and French fries.

"Is Bruno a Duplessis orphan?" she asks them.

"Sort of," Huguette says. "He was at one of the psychiatric hospitals—I can't remember which—but one of the nuns there took him under her wing. She protected him and took care of him, gave him lessons. She recognized he was smart. She managed to get him out and placed with a foster family when he was still young."

"He missed out on a lot of the abuse," Francine explains.

"He's the only one I know of who got a college education," Huguette says. "That's why we asked him to be our spokesperson. We needed someone like him. The rest of us, we're helpless."

"He's the reason we have a lawyer now," Francine says.

"And we're allowed to sue the church and the doctors?"

Both women shrug. "Who knows?" Huguette says. "It's worth a try. I don't think Bruno would let us down."

"It's not up to him," Francine mutters. She has heavy lids and speaks very slowly, like someone who is still medicated.

"Were you both at Mont Providence together?" Elodie asks them.

"We were," Francine says. "Same ward. We were released at the same time, too. We lived together until Huguette got married."

"Remember that club we started at Mont Providence?" Huguette says. "We called it the Club for Not Crazies." *Le Club des Pas Folles.*

Francine laughs, a melancholic sound.

"We used to say over and over to each other, 'We're not crazy, we're not crazy.' And then one of us would say, 'Are you sure? Maybe we are?' And then someone else had to reassure the rest, 'We're not crazy. *They're* crazy.' That was our club."

"I wish I'd had a club like that," Elodie says.

"Usually we were in the common room," Francine says. "There was nothing else to do."

"Sundays were the worst," Huguette reminisces. "We'd sit and vegetate all day on those goddamn chairs, staring at the walls, listening to the real crazies scream all day. Nothing to do. I used to prefer working."

Elodie nods, remembering. It was the same at St. Nazarius. They called it the Big Room. Time crawled; your mind played tricks on you. Those times, she thought she really was going crazy.

"Did you ever have the shock treatment?" Francine asks her.

"No. Did you?"

They both nod. "We were lucky we didn't get lobotomized. She had a mouth on her, this one," Huguette says of Francine. "She was always in trouble."

"They kept me tranquilized the last four years I was there."

"She was basically in a coma."

"I'm not much better now. I never really got back to normal."

"*Normal*," Huguette scoffs. "Imagine?"

"I didn't think it was possible that there could be another place as bad as St. Nazarius," Elodie says.

"You heard it in that meeting. They were all bad."

"We're lucky we're alive," Huguette says. "Not like the ones who were killed and tossed down the incinerator, or out in the fields behind the hospitals. Apparently there's a whole cemetery of dead orphans behind St. Nazarius."

Huguette has used that word twice now. *Lucky.* Lucky by the lowest possible standard.

"I found my real parents when I was twenty-four," Elodie says. "I really do feel fortunate compared to everyone else."

"That's a miracle," Francine says. "How did you find them?"

Elodie tells them her story, including the part about Sister Ignatia keeping them apart, and when she's finished, both Francine and Huguette are dabbing their eyes with a napkin. "You should write a book," Francine says. "Can you write?"

"Not well, but my mother does. We wrote a first draft a long time ago, but she thinks there might be more interest now."

"What a story," Huguette says. "Not many of us got a happy ending."

It's such a relief to talk to these women, to be regarded as the one with the happy ending. Never in the real world has Elodie ever been the "fortunate" one or the least damaged one. She's always had to pretend. Here, she can be completely herself.

Thinking back on it, that was the most challenging

part of integrating into the world when she first got out of St. Nazarius—having to act her way into normalcy. She was always self-conscious, always doubting herself. There wasn't a moment in public when she wasn't studying how to behave like a normal person, carefully observing people and emulating them. She could never be herself. For years she faked it—not just for Nancy, but for everyone, everywhere. She always worried people could tell that something wasn't quite right with her. *Maybe they know,* she would think. *Maybe I am crazy and I'm not fooling them.*

And although it became easier over time and with a great deal of practice, especially with Nancy, there's still a certain amount of pretending that has to happen. She's so used to it now, it hardly takes any effort to play her role. These days, she's mostly able to let go in public and not monitor herself so carefully, but she's never completely rid of that voice.

Being with other Duplessis orphans for the first time in decades has emphasized the chasm between where she came from and who she is today. It's a good reminder that while she's healed a great deal, it's actually a relief to be able to let that wounded little orphan be herself for a while. *You can come out now. You can speak your truth with these women. You can be you here. It's safe.* What a revelation.

"You mentioned Sister Ignatia," Huguette says, turning to Francine. "Didn't Lucille from St. Nazarius used to talk about a Sister Ignatia?"

Elodie's blood goes cold.

"I wouldn't remember," Francine says.

"She did," Huguette says. "I remember. She said she was as terrifying as her ugly name."

10

October 1993

It's his turn to meet Véronique's parents. He's had to wait almost a year for the privilege. He's been patient with her, understands her reservations. It would be hard to introduce any boyfriend to your convicted-murderer father, let alone a reporter for the Canadian News Association.

So he hasn't pushed. He knows it's a big move for her, and big relationship moves are not her strong suit. But here's the thing about her timing. The federal election just happened on Monday, and now, Friday, he's on his way to meet her parents. He can't help but think she was motivated by Quebec's recent political victory— small but significant—to give her father some leverage.

She's denied any ulterior motives, simply stating, "I'm just ready."

"You mean I've passed the test?"

"Meeting them will be the test."

He's sworn an oath not to interrogate Léo about the October Crisis or his time in prison. The name Pierre Laporte is never to be uttered. She's given him permission to state his opinions about separatism and the constitutional debacle and the Bloc Québécois, but all conversation must stay in the present. The Past—capital *P*—is off-limits.

"It's just a normal family dinner," she said.

"With a terrorist who was at the center of the infamous October Crisis," he quipped. "One of the most violent periods in Quebec history. Yes, a normal family dinner."

At least they've been together long enough to be able to have that sort of dialogue. In the beginning, such conversations were a landmine; a joke like that would have set her off in a rage and ended in a terrible fight. Not that they don't still fight. They do, just less frequently.

"You got the beer?" he asks her.

"Shit."

She gets out of the car and runs back up to her apartment, returning five minutes later with a case of Labatt

Ice. James would have opted for wine or at least craft beer, but Véronique said the Labatt Ice would impress them more.

The ride to Verdun is quiet. He can only imagine what's going through Véronique's head, but he assumes she wants everything to go smoothly, wants her parents to approve of him, wants him to like them and maybe even come away from tonight a little less judgmental about her father's past. At the moment, James has nothing but contempt for Léo Fortin. What can the man possibly do over dinner to sway his opinion?

He loves Véronique. Wants to spend the rest of his life with her, except for that one nagging fear that she will turn out to be just like her father. He worries that the writing may already be on the wall. She is a professional criminal who shows no sign of contrition, nor any outward desire to change. She's young, sure, and he hopes she'll find her calling and leave the criminal life behind, but whether she absorbed the trade through osmosis or simply because she wants to please her father, this is what she chooses to be right now.

Lisette has made beef stew and potatoes. She's tall and statuesque, with the same dark auburn hair as her daughter, and as she ladles out the stew, it's easy to see where Véronique gets her looks. Léo has been polite and restrained so far, and is less gregarious than James was expecting. He finds himself wishing he didn't know about Léo's past; otherwise he could actually like the man, who seems intelligent and thoughtful, clearly adores his wife and daughter. He looks at them fawningly and is easy with his praise and affection.

The awkwardness is unavoidable as they sit across from each other at the kitchen table. They've covered a lot of the usual small talk—the warm fall weather they've been having, the shitty economy, his mother's seed store and how impressive it is that she runs her own business, the still fresh Stanley Cup victory and the upcoming hockey season.

"Patrick Roy better earn that sixteen million dollar contract he signed," Léo says, dousing his stew with salt and pepper. "Grab me another beer while you're up, Lise."

Lisette brings him a beer, asks James if he needs another. No, he's still working on his first.

"I don't know if the city can handle another Stanley Cup win," James says, referring to the riot that erupted on Ste. Catherine Street after the final game.

"Never mind the city," Léo says. "What about my heart? Ten straight overtime victories. I can't go through that again."

James nods in agreement.

"Did you vote?" Léo asks him, switching gears.

"I did," he says. *Here we go.*

"The best thing for us was the resounding failure of those goddamn constitutional talks," Léo says. "Support for separation has never been higher."

At last, they've come around to the conversation James thought they'd be having as soon as he got through the front door.

"You can feel the tide changing again in our favor," Léo effuses.

"You think Canada is going to take care of Quebec after a separation?" James asks him.

"We don't need Canada," Léo responds. "That's the whole point. We've been exploited by the English for long enough, threatened with assimilation every step of the way. This has been the source of all our problems. Now it's time for total independence."

Véronique is watching James, waiting to see what he does next.

"I understand you're not a separatist," Léo says magnanimously. "And even though you work for the enemy, you're still French."

"I am," James acknowledges, not sure if Léo is teasing him. "And proud of it."

"Good. And your father worked at Vickers, and he was a nationalist."

"I see Véronique has filled you in on the key points about my background."

"I had to tell him something to redeem your politics and your job at the Canadian News Association," she says, pouring her beer into a glass. Her father and mother drink from the bottle.

"Did you know that the CNA is owned by the *Globe and Mail*?" Léo says, not bothering to hide his disgust. "And based in Toronto?" He spits out the word *Toronto*.

"Yes, I know."

Léo sighs. "Did your father ever talk to you about his job at the factory?"

"He did actually. He liked it."

"Did he? Are you sure? Who likes working in a factory?"

James isn't really so sure anymore. Gabriel used to say that when he was really young, thirteen or fourteen, he was proud of the fact that he was one of the people making the aircrafts for the Royal Canadian Air Force. But he eventually quit factory life and returned to farming, where he was happiest.

"You have no idea, do you?" Léo says. "Let me tell you, it's slave labor, that's what it is."

James has to work hard to hold back a snide comeback.

"My mother used to work in an underwear factory," Léo says, clearly enjoying the sound of his own voice. "She worked twelve hours a day, six days a week. She was paid by the piece, sticking panties on a metal form one at a time, so she couldn't ever stop for a break. There were no unions. It was mostly women working there, and every night, the foreman would take one of the young ones up to his office and have sex with her. My mother was one of them. She never quit. She couldn't. She needed the paycheck to pay for the room she shared with six other girls from the factory."

"And that's the fault of the English?" James says.

"Absolutely! They're the goddamn *minority*, using *our* people—*les habitants*—for cheap labor. Does that remind you of anything?"

James doesn't respond, can't imagine where Léo is going.

"The blacks in America?" he says. "The slaves?"

"Oh, please," James groans. "For Christ's sake."

"You're young," Lisette says, in a lecturing tone. "Why do you think you know better than we do? We lived it."

"Your complaints date back to the Plains of Abraham!" James cries, frustrated. "And you can't compare the Québécois to the slaves!"

"You tell that to my mother," Léo says, lowering his voice. "You don't know what slave labor is. You think it means only chains? It doesn't. Our chains are symbolic."

James sighs emphatically. Lisette gets two more beers for her and Léo. James has barely touched his.

"Don't you drink?" Lisette asks him, noticing his still full beer. Her tone is accusatory.

"I'm driving," he says, and Léo and Lisette both turn to Véronique with looks of unspoken disdain.

You could have taken my side at some point tonight," James says quietly. They're in the car, driving back to the Plateau.

"But I don't agree with you," she says. "You're wrong."

"About everything?"

"We just see the world differently. You've never experienced what they lived through, so you can't understand."

"Neither have you. They've brainwashed you."

"I have a mind of my own."

"Do you?"

"Take me home."

"Why? Because we're having an argument? Every time we fight you're going to bolt?"

Silence.

"Baby, I don't want to fight about politics," he says. "I want to sleep beside you tonight. This is ridiculous."

"We fight a lot," she says, staring out the window.

"It's your fault."

She cracks a smile. "You were rude to my father."

"He's arrogant."

"So are you."

"But I'm not a—"

"What? Say it."

"No."

"Just take me home."

He's too tired to fight with her, so he takes her home.

11

In spite of it being the capital city, Ottawa has a certain small-town charm that Véronique likes. There's a wholesomeness about it that Montreal does not have, a lack of attention to status and hipness that is a relief. When she thinks of Ottawa, she thinks of rosy cheeks and healthy hearts and outdoorsy people who bike-ride or ice-skate as their primary means of transportation. Maybe it's because the heart of the city is the Rideau Canal, and depending on the season, you can either skate on or jog alongside it from one end of the city to the other.

She likes Carleton, with its sprawling campus and shabby residence buildings and its maze of tunnels, where students rush to their classes wearing pajamas and slippers, so that no one ever has to set foot outside when it's cold. Her impression of college life is that it's a bit cultish and self-involved; the campus is very much an island unto itself, completely disconnected from the rest of the world, moving to its own circadian rhythms, beholden to its strange customs and rituals—the Breeze on Tuesdays, Rooster's on Wednesdays, the Market on Saturdays, frosh week, Panda, Midwinter Ball, Kosmic.

Callahan talks about these things as though everyone knows what they mean. All Véronique knows is Callahan sells tons of cigarettes around campus, and she in turn makes shitloads of money off him, just like her uncle promised. Callahan will page her and say, "Kosmic is this weekend, bring a few extra cases." Or, "Double my usual order for frosh week." Kosmic, frosh week—who knows what any of those are? She doesn't care. All she knows is she makes tons of cash off them.

Once, he took her around campus. They went to the dorms first, delivering the cartons of cigarettes, where everyone greeted him like he was Santa Claus.

"The Marlboro Man is here!" they cheered, inviting him in, offering him weed or hash or mushrooms, asking him to join in a round of euchre.

Afterwards, the two of them shared a pitcher of beer at Rooster's in the University Centre—he called it the Unicentre—and then they walked around the entire campus, ending up in the quad, where they got high.

She could see the appeal of college life, the coddled, insular cocoon of safety and inclusion it fostered, but she wouldn't trade her freedom for the experience. Not now, not at this point in her life. In the end, these kids would graduate and have to trade in their precious freedom for a regular job and a slot on society's assembly line.

Callahan is in his fourth year, which means he'll be graduating this year and he'll have to pass the Marlboro Man torch on to another guy. Véronique is sorry to lose him as her point of contact and to have to start all over again with someone new, someone she might not like as much.

She can't imagine what Callahan will do with his life. He's not that intelligent. His best bet, Véronique thinks, would be to continue selling contraband.

When she shows up at his house on Glen Street, she can tell right away he's stoned. Aside from the glassy eyeballs, he talks really slowly when he's high. "Veronica," he drawls. "*Bienvenue!* You made it."

He helps her unload the cases from her trunk and invites her inside. Further evidence of his being high is spread all over his coffee table—a beer bottle with a hole in the bottom, tiny balls of tinfoil, broken cigarettes, sprinkles of hash that look like mouse shit, two burnt knives. The first time she saw the bottle with the hole, he had to explain to her it was a makeshift bong. Apparently, they like to use props in college—knives, bots, bongs. They get bored easily.

There's a Pizza Pizza box on the floor, which she steps over on her way to the couch, and a rancid smell in the room—sweat socks mixed with hash and the faint breeze of garbage. He's blasting Soundgarden. The place is a dump, which is to be expected from six twenty-something guys living together.

"You want?" he asks her, holding up the bottle bong.

"No thanks," she says. "I can't stay long." Her English is pretty terrible, but she's gotten better at understanding him.

"Why not?" he asks, lighting a half-smoked cigarette from the table. He's wearing a baggy Roots sweatshirt and matching sweatpants. He has pale skin and blue eyes and reddish-blond hair that looks orange in the sunlight. His body is soft and milky.

"I have plans with James," she says.

"How's he doing?"

They met once, James and Callahan. James had to drive her here because her car had broken down.

"He's fine."

Whenever she's with Callahan in his collegiate microcosm, she's always reminded of what a grown-up James is, and even though she can appreciate what Callahan and his friends enjoy about this utopian pit stop on their way to the real world, she's glad she's with a man who doesn't smoke hash from a Molson bottle.

"My roommate Perky's friend was up from Montreal last weekend," he says, over Chris Cornell's wailing. They're sitting side by side on the couch. "He told me something really fascinating."

"Oh, yeah. What's that?"

"I mentioned your name to him."

"Why?"

"I don't know," he says. "I was just talking about you. Probably in the context of him being from Montreal. As in, *Hey, I've got a friend from Montreal—*"

She's eyeing him.

"Dude, chill." Callahan laughs. "He's not a cop. Anyway, I mentioned your name—"

She doesn't like where this is going. She's been here before.

"And it turns out he knows you."

"Does he."

"Well, he doesn't *know you* know you. He knows of you."

She can feel her neck tensing, that familiar ripple of panic inside her chest.

"Your dad is, like, Léo Fortin, the FLQ guy who kidnapped that politician."

Véronique is quiet.

"You're famous," Callahan says, smiling stupidly.

"Hardly."

"Is your dad still in jail?"

"No," she says, quietly seething.

She doesn't want to overreact and make this a bigger deal than it is, but something feels broken now. She's always enjoyed her anonymity here; the way she could pretend, even just to herself, that she was a regular undergrad without any history.

"Did he actually murder the guy?" Callahan asks her, leaning forward on his knees. "Are you a separatist?"

When she used to get bullied as a kid, her mother would say to her, "This will always be your cross to bear."

She remembers in grade six, one of the boys in her class had found out about her father. She overheard him talking to his friends about it. "Her father is Léo Fortin, the FLQ murderer!"

It was 1981. Kids her age were old enough to know about the October Crisis; it was already lodged in their collective consciousness. But Véronique didn't really understand what her father had done; all she knew was she had to visit him in prison and tell people her parents were divorced.

When she overheard those boys talking about her father, she could feel her face getting hot, her hands curling into fists. She didn't turn around, but a cluster of kids soon surrounded her in the hall.

"Véronique's father is an FLQ murderer," one of them said.

Shock moved through the group in a wave. She watched their expressions change, from curiosity to surprise to disgust.

"He's still in jail, isn't he?"

"Did he also plant those bombs in the mailboxes?"

"They murdered a bunch of people," someone said. "They bombed factories and buildings."

Véronique was fighting back tears.

"I knew there was something sinister about you, Véronique."

She ran out of the building, humiliated. She never forgot that word. *Sinister.*

She was ostracized for a couple of weeks, but eventually, as with most gossip, her story lost its sheen and became old news. After a while, no one cared anymore. In fact, as she got older, it became more of a badge, something cool and differentiating at a time in their lives when everyone desperately wanted to be different. As the years went on, the separation movement started gaining momentum again and her father's story made her less of a pariah and more of a rock star. She was very popular in high school.

Still, she will never forget the first time her secret came out in public. How the word *sinister* had embedded itself inside her and remained there all through high school, no matter how popular she became. In the end, her father's crime would always impact her reputation, for good or bad. How could it not?

"I've got to go," she says, standing up. Callahan is watching her, bewildered.

"You just got here," he says, sounding disappointed.

"Can you get my money, please?"

"Sure, come on up."

She follows him upstairs, remembering the last time she was here. The house had been full of people—one of his roommates was having a keg party before the big Panda football game. Callahan told her he wasn't in the mood—he was over it, had been to enough of them—and he asked her if she wanted to listen to music in his room before she had to turn around and drive back to Montreal.

They'd known each other for a while at that point, and he'd never tried anything or given any indication of an attraction—she thought of him as a harmless mascot, the Marlboro Man gamboling across campus—and so after a split second's hesitation, she said, "Sure."

They listened to music. She sat in a chair, and he lay on his bed. He played her the Smashing Pumpkins and Radiohead. It was the first time she'd ever heard the song "Creep," and she loved it. It was a languid afternoon. They passed a joint around. She wasn't in a rush to jump back on the road. The drive to and from Ottawa is long and tedious, especially back-to-back.

"You're not pissed at me, are you?" he asks, obviously sensing he may have crossed a line talking about her father.

"No," she says, trying to sound neutral. He's a good customer. She can't be a bitch to him.

"Hey, let me play you something," he says, bending over a crate of CDs.

She looks at her watch. She wants to get home to James, but there's a certain amount of customer service involved in her job. She sits down on the chair next to his desk. She tries to imagine him doing homework here and can't. She can't figure out how he's managed to get to fourth year, let alone graduate soon.

"This song reminds me of you," he says, popping a Lemonheads disc out of its case.

He slides it into his deck and presses play, then lights a joint and hands it to her before flopping backwards on his bed. "It's called 'My Drug Buddy.'"

"Is that what I am?"

"Sort of. And my cigarette dealer, of course."

Callahan sings along. "'She's coming over. We'll go out walking. Make a call on the way . . .'"

"It's good," she says, humoring him. After a measured beat, she says, "I should really get going."

"You sure you can't hang for a while?" he asks, his voice slightly supplicating. He's looking at her with stoned, reverential eyes.

"I've got to go. I have another delivery."

"Sure," he says, disappointed. He pays her and gives her an awkward hug, and she lets herself out.

When she gets home, she finds James on her couch, tapping away on his laptop. They usually spend weekends at her place, weeknights at his. He looks up when she comes into the room and smiles, holds out his arm to her. She takes his hand and lets him pull her onto his lap.

"What are you working on?" she asks him.

"My column about the Duplessis orphans. Tell me what you think so far," he says, turning the laptop so she can read his piece. "It's an opinion column. Every once in a while they let me have some fun."

She settles in beside him on the couch and starts to read.

The Most Horrific Quebec Scandal
You've Never Heard About

J. G. Phénix, Canadian News Association

Elodie de Ste. Sulpice is only 44 years old, but she's resigned to the fact that she will never live a normal life, having grown up in one of Quebec's mental institutions. But Elodie is not mentally deficient in any way. She was born to an unwed teenage girl in 1950 and sent to the Ste. Sulpice Orphanage in the hope that she would soon be adopted. Instead, under Premier Maurice Duplessis's dark regime, all the orphanages in the province were "reclassified" as mental institutions, and little Elodie, along with thousands of other innocent orphans, was declared mentally deficient.

Why do such a thing? Because mental patients got more federal subsidy money than orphans did, so in collusion with the Catholic Church and the medical association, the provincial government concocted a scheme to effectively rob the orphans of their childhoods.

Elodie is my sister. I met her in 1974, when she showed up on our family's doorstep. "I was a perfectly normal little girl," she says. "But they declared me mentally deficient to line their pockets. It's hard to get over that."

Elodie has filed a criminal complaint with the Sûreté du Quebec, and is part of a class action lawsuit that was filed on behalf of the Duplessis Orphans Committee . . .

"What do you think?" he asks her.

"How can you write about your own sister like she's a fictional character?"

"It's called journalistic objectivity."

"Even I can't *not* think about the real Elodie when I read it. How do you separate out your emotion?"

"I'm a professional," he says, full of self-importance. "The five core values of journalism are accuracy, independence, humanity, accountability, and *impartiality*."

Véronique can't stand this side of him. "It's hard for me to read this," she says, aware she's being nasty, but annoyed that it's in English. Annoyed he works for an English news agency.

"We both know you understand English," he says.

"It's still hard for me to *read* it."

"You get the gist, though."

"It frustrates me that you have to write in English," she says. "You could be such an asset for our side."

"Our *side*? What side? We're on the same side, V.

I'm a working journalist. I write the news. I happen to do that for an English agency at the moment. Why're you in such a shit mood? Did something happen in Ottawa?"

"No."

"If you want to talk about hating what your partner does for a living, let's talk about your current vocation."

"Forget I said anything," she says, cutting him off. "It's brilliant. Your article is brilliant."

"If you're going to bitch and complain about my job," he goes on, "at least be willing to hear how I feel about yours."

Here comes the lecture.

"I hate that you smuggle cigarettes," he starts. "I hate how dangerous it is. I worry every second that you're in Ste. Barbe on a run. Worried you're going to get caught and thrown in jail. Worried someone's going to shoot you."

"Are you done?"

"No, I'm not. I hate that you hang out with college guys, partying with them and pretending to be friends with them."

"You're jealous?"

"Yeah! I'm fucking jealous!" he admits. "Frankly, I hate that my girlfriend is a professional criminal."

"So you wish I had a real job."

"Can you blame me?"

He's mentioned this to her before, though with more subtlety. He went so far as to suggest that journalism would be a good career path for her, given her enthusiasm for politics. He even looked up journalism programs in Montreal, which irritated her. She's of the opinion that journalists are sellouts. The constraint of having to report objectively on events that are meaningful to her, without being able to assert her opinion, holds absolutely no interest for her. Besides, she's only twenty-three. There's time for her cause to reveal itself. "It's not who I am," she says. "Being part of the grind."

She can feel herself rebelling against his desire for her to quit smuggling, to become an upstanding citizen. The more he presses, the more she resists. She's not asking for his approval, just some acceptance. *Take me or leave me.*

James throws his hands up, exasperated. "What the hell does that even mean, 'It's not who you are'?"

"You don't know who I am."

"All I know is I can't stand that you're part of that world."

"That world is my family!" she cries, getting up off the couch and facing him with her hands on her hips.

"Callahan is not your family," he counters. "The gangsters and smugglers on the lake are not your family. The guys on the reservation are not your family."

"You just don't get it."

"No," he says, shaking his head. "I don't get it. I want better for you. I want *you* to want better for yourself. Some integrity at least!"

His words sting, more than she could have imagined. Her face feels hot, and she turns away, not wanting him to see her tears. How dare he judge her, awash in his own self-righteousness, tossing out that word *integrity*. At least now she knows what he really thinks of her.

12

When two police officers show up at Elodie's door early in the morning, she isn't entirely surprised. At the urging of Bruno and Huguette, she filed a criminal complaint with the Sûreté du Quebec against St. Nazarius Hospital. They told her the police would show up to ask her questions. Under the Access to Information Act, she was able to obtain a single record of her transfer from the Ste. Sulpice Orphanage to St. Nazarius Hospital in 1957. She keeps a copy of it in her nightstand, taped inside her notebook, the one that contains sketches and journal entries immortalizing her decade of institutionalization.

She's memorized her record by now, each and every word. *Profound mental retardation. Danger to herself and others. Paranoid delusions. Violent outbursts and convulsions.* None of those things are true, but it made her question herself. It cast doubt about her own sanity. Reading that report for the first time, it was incomprehensible to her that a doctor could have made up such horrific things and signed her life away.

Bruno is the one who helped her write the complaint. Last year the Quebec government opened an inquiry into all the criminal complaints that had been lodged by Duplessis orphans. Bruno says the more complaints they file, the more credibility they'll have.

"Yes?" she says timidly, the door slightly ajar, just enough for them to see her face.

"We're with the Sûreté de Quebec," the taller cop says. "We're here to follow up on a complaint you made against St. Nazarius Hospital?"

She lets them inside her apartment. "Would you like coffee?" she asks them.

"No thank you."

They follow her to the kitchen, and she invites them to sit down at the small Formica table, which only seats three. The tall one has to turn his chair to fit his long legs underneath. The other one is shorter but overweight. He looks just as uncomfortable.

"You filed a complaint against St. Nazarius Hospital in June of this year?" the stocky one says. From his name tag, he's Lucien Gagnon. The other, Paul Drouin.

"Yes," she says.

"And you're alleging mistreatment by the nuns and wrongful classification as 'mentally deficient'?"

"Correct."

"How long were you there?"

"Ten years. From 1957 to 1967."

He writes it down.

"Will my case go to court?" she asks him, lighting a cigarette.

"We're investigating more than two hundred and fifty of these complaints," Drouin says. "When we're done, we'll make our deposition at the attorney general's office."

"And then what?"

"Trust me, all hell is going to break loose in Quebec when all these complaints come to light."

"What will I have to do?"

"Once you've had a response from the prosecutor, you would go to the Palais de Justice and make your criminal deposition."

"And then I get to go to court?"

"Yes."

She gets up and excuses herself, goes to her bedroom and retrieves her notebook. When she returns to the kitchen, she sits back down at the table and opens the notebook to the first page. Her record of transfer is taped to the inside front cover. She reads it out loud to them.

"You can see," she says, looking up at them, "I am not mentally deficient. I never have been. I was a normal little girl."

Drouin transcribes her record into his notepad.

"When I first got out," she explains, "I started this scrapbook so I'd never forget what they did to me. As sickening as my memories are, and as much as I wish I could forget, I also wanted to remember so that I'd be able to tell my story one day."

She turns the pages, showing them her drawings and descriptions.

"In your complaint, you mentioned sexual abuse," Gagnon says, not making eye contact. "That was with the orderlies?"

"And the nuns."

"Anything else?"

She lets out what is meant to be a laugh, but there is no humor in it. "It's all in here," she says, sliding the scrapbook across the table.

The cop stops taking notes and flips through it.

"It's all true," she says, stubbing out her cigarette. "And now I want justice. Do you think that will happen?"

Drouin and Gagnon look at each other, nodding. "I think so," Drouin says.

"I hope so," says the other.

After they leave, she brings her cigarettes and ashtray into the living room and calls Nancy. It's time to tell her everything.

"*Allo*, M'ma," she says, light, cheerful.

"I have to tell you something, Nance."

"That sounds ominous."

"I filed a criminal complaint."

"Against who? *What happened?*"

"Sweetheart, St. Nazarius wasn't an orphanage," she blurts. "It was a mental hospital. I was sent there when I was seven, after being falsely diagnosed."

She explains about Change of Vocation Day, the Duplessis orphans, and the pending class action suit. She gives a very abridged version of the abuse she endured at St. Nazarius.

Nancy is silent on the other end.

"I know it's a lot—"

"Why didn't you ever tell me?"

"I wanted you to have a normal mother, a normal life. I wanted to forget."

"And now?"

"Now I want justice," she says. "And you need to know because it's going to be in the news. It already has been over here."

"Who's your complaint against?"

"The Catholic Church, the provincial government, and the doctors who falsified our records."

"Holy shit. Is that realistic?"

"I don't know."

More silence.

"I have to do this," Elodie says. "It's important to me."

"It was such a long time ago," Nancy says gently. "Maybe it should be left in the past? You have a good life now, M'ma."

Elodie doesn't expect Nancy to understand. She doesn't know enough about what really happened to Elodie at St. Nazarius. Doesn't know about Sister Ignatia and the monstrous lie she told to keep Elodie from her parents. Besides, Nancy is wired differently. She's pragmatic and practical; she's never been overtly emotional, not even when she was a teenager. When Elodie told her that her father had fought in the Vietnam War, all she said was, "Was he a hero?"

"I don't know," Elodie responded. "I didn't know him very well."

"You didn't know my father?" she said, confused. She seemed more disturbed by that than by the fact that he might have been killed in Vietnam. "What was his name?"

"Dennis."

"Dennis what?"

"I don't know. He never said."

Nancy was dry-eyed, stoic. She had no other questions. Elodie wasn't about to go into details about that lost weekend, the prolonged one-night stand with a stranger from Boston. It was her first normal— *mutual*—sexual experience. It was special, maybe even more so because she didn't know him. He was going off to war, and there was no possibility of him ever discovering that she was uneducated, possibly crazy, damaged. In its own way, it was simple and perfect. And it produced Nancy, the best thing she's accomplished in her life. Nancy never asked about her father again. She just took it in stride and moved on.

"I wish I could shield you from all of this," Elodie says. "Like I always have."

"You don't have to protect me, M'ma. You never did."

But that's not true. Nancy did need protecting. It's no small feat that Nancy has no idea her mother keeps a scrapbook of all the abuses and transgressions that were ever done to her. All Nancy has are the mostly pleasant memories of her upbringing, a childhood that checked off all the appropriate milestones and included plenty of special family rituals—homemade gifts at Christmas, planting their small garden every spring, summer outings to La Ronde, the big amusement park on St. Helen's Island. Those were the best years, when Nancy was old enough to be interesting but still young enough to see her mother through a lens of pure unblighted adoration.

"Remember when we used to go to La Ronde?" Elodie says, out of the blue.

Elodie loved the scary rides best, which was strange, considering how skittish and anxious she was back then. Her favorite was the Wildcat, a plunging roller coaster that flipped upside down and hung suspended in the air above the city. It was a more straightforward kind of terror, physical not mental. She appreciated that. She remembers how Nancy would skip off ahead of her, wild with excitement, her T-shirt stained with purple slush and pink cotton candy, and Elodie would marvel, *She is so free.* It would fill her heart up like a balloon.

"You gave me a happy childhood," Nancy says. "But you don't need to shield me anymore. You need to take care of *yourself.*"

"That's exactly what I'm doing," Elodie says. "This is really about my future, not my past."

Stephanie once accused her of not wanting to close the chapter on her past. It was after a particularly contentious sisterly argument, and she called Elodie a "lifelong victim." She was wrong, though. Elodie's life mission has always been to keep moving forward, as far away from the past as she could get. But she's starting to realize that closing the chapter on her past will require much more than just willpower and tenacity. *Real* freedom, she is convinced, can only come from the triumph of justice.

13

January 1994

The delicatessen where Elodie works is a few blocks east of the record store, but with this insulting wind, it feels more like miles. When Véronique reaches Len's, with its famous window display of brisket slabs and Black Forest cakes, she opens the door and is immediately welcomed by the smell of smoked meat.

Elodie looks up from where she's reading behind the counter and waves.

"Sorry I'm late," Véronique says. "There was a problem on the metro."

Elodie is wearing the same beige uniform Len's waitresses have been wearing for decades. Elodie once told her that nothing really changes here, which is why she likes it. In fact, the only thing that has ever changed is Len himself, who died in '89 and was replaced by his son, Barry.

She pops her head into the back room, where her boss has a small office. "I'm taking lunch," she tells him.

Véronique can hear a muffled response, and then Elodie grabs a big plastic menu and hands it to her. Usually there's more of a lunch-hour bustle, but they have the place to themselves today. Véronique's gotten in the habit of stopping by for a weekly smoked meat sandwich or a coffee before the start of her shift at the record store.

"What would you like?"

"Just coffee."

"You sure? I can make you a smoked meat sandwich?"

"I'm fine. I'm not that hungry."

Elodie pours a cup of coffee for Véronique and a Pepsi for herself. They sit at one of the booths.

"What's happening with the criminal case?" Véronique asks her.

"I haven't heard yet, but Bruno says nothing ever happens over the holidays."

"How are you doing?"

"It's definitely bringing up a lot of the old memories," Elodie says.

"It'll be worth it, though, won't it? When you win your case?"

"If we win."

"You will," Véronique states. "How can you not? When the court hears all your stories? My God. They owe you."

"They sure as hell do." She pulls a pack of Du Mauriers out of her apron pocket and lights a cigarette. "I need more of these," she says, holding up the pack. "I'm getting low."

"I'm doing a run next week. I'll bring you a few cartons."

Elodie smiles appreciatively. This is exactly why Véronique smuggles—to help good, hardworking people like Elodie who can't afford to pay what the government charges them for smokes.

"How're you and James?" Elodie asks her.

"Good. Better."

"You sure?"

"It's been a lot better the last couple of months."

Elodie cocks her head, waiting for more. She exhales a straight line of smoke above Véronique's head.

"We were fighting a lot in the fall."

"About?"

"About these," Véronique says, holding up the pack of cigarettes.

Elodie nods, understanding immediately.

"He hates me smuggling," Véronique confides. "He's the reason I got the job at the record store."

"But you're still smuggling."

"I told James I would stop as soon as my uncle finds someone to replace me."

"Will you?"

"I don't know," Véronique admits. "It's such good money, it's easy. Plus, I can't just shaft my uncle. He needs me. I don't know what to do."

"James worries about you, that's why he wants you to stop."

"He's ashamed of me."

"No," Elodie says. "I know he worries. Even I worry about you. It's dangerous what you do."

"He wants me to go to school."

"That sounds like a good plan."

"It's James's plan," she says. "Not mine. I mean, I have nothing against school, but it just hasn't been necessary for me. I'm not sure it ever will be."

"Meaning you plan to continue smuggling."

"As long as I'm making good money, I plan to keep seizing the opportunities that come up," she says, thinking about the record store. As far as everyone knows, she's just a cashier there.

"James wants me to know exactly what I want to do

with my life," she goes on. "But I don't think that way. All I know is that I want to feel excited by what I do. I want to feel passion, the way my father was passionate about the FLQ, or the way your mother is passionate about her seed store. I'm willing to wait for it."

"How long?"

"My dad was in jail at my age, his life basically over. I'm just at the beginning of mine."

"I love your optimism," Elodie says. "Who says you need to have it all mapped out by your early twenties?"

"Your brother."

"You know he just wants you to be happy."

"Enough about my shit," Véronique says, taking a small sip of coffee. It tastes awful, bitter and watery. There are grounds floating on the surface, which stick on her tongue. "James mentioned you also filed your civil complaint?"

Elodie nods, not looking especially enthused.

"Do you ever think about taking matters into your own hands?"

"You mean like *revenge*?"

"I guess. I just wonder if winning your lawsuits will be enough."

"What's the alternative? Buying a gun and murdering them all? I wouldn't even know where to start. The nuns, the orderlies, the doctor who put me in St. Nazarius?"

Her uncle Camil probably knows someone who would gladly take out a few child abusers. She almost says, *You could hire someone*, but Elodie is from a different world. "This is probably the last thing you want to talk about."

"It's actually kind of cathartic. I'm so used to *not* talking about it."

Véronique is always struck by Elodie's pragmatism. She approaches her life without melodrama or mawkish grandstanding, never trying to call attention to herself. She's managed to raise a child, find her birth mother, support herself, share her story, and now seek justice in a system that wants to keep her silent and oppressed, and she does all of it with her dignity intact.

"You can't bury something that's still alive," Elodie says. "I'm just starting to figure that out now."

"That's how I feel about the October Crisis," Véronique admits, thinking about her father's legacy. "I can't seem to get out from under its shadow."

"Everyone has their own October," Elodie says, swirling the ice cubes around in her glass of Pepsi. "No one comes through life without experiencing something that changes who they were going to be."

"What about your daughter?"

"I've tried to shield Nancy from my past," Elodie says. "I'm not sure I succeeded. A parent leaves a legacy no matter what. She'll have her own October Crisis to deal with. I can't see how she won't."

"Does she come back to visit often?"

"Not really. She likes adventure."

"Where's her father, if you don't mind me asking?"

"Probably dead," Elodie says. "He was American, going off to Vietnam. He was spending his last weekend of freedom in Montreal. I never even knew his last name. He probably died over there."

"But you don't know for sure?"

"Most of them died," she says. "I just assume he did, too. I've just tried to move forward, not be defined by my past."

Véronique takes a sip of coffee, thinking about James's article. "I don't think you're defined by your past, for what it's worth."

"You asked me if I ever think about revenge," Elodie says. "I do secretly fantasize about smothering Sister Ignatia with a pillow or spitting in her face." She laughs nervously, embarrassed. "But if I become the monster they believed me to be—or *wanted* me to be—then they've won."

"Not if they're dead."

"Even if they're dead. The only power I ever had was in not letting them destroy me. I mean, I'm still here, aren't I? I got out and I made a life. I had a child. I'm not a terrible person."

"You're a beautiful person," Véronique says. She hasn't known Elodie very long, but she recognizes in her a kindred spirit, a surrogate big sister who understands her and never judges.

Elodie waves her hand in the air, shooing away the compliment. Véronique looks at her watch and frowns. "My shift starts in fifteen minutes."

"Talk to James," Elodie says. "Maybe he sees something in you that you don't even see in yourself yet."

Véronique considers Elodie's parting words as she heads the few blocks over to Stanley Records. Maybe she doesn't know who she is yet, but she knows she's her father's daughter. She will always be the woman Léo taught her to be, someone willing to cross the line when it's justified.

She loves James, but if he can't accept that about her, they won't make it. This is what worries her most, even during this current truce. Eventually he's going to figure out that her job at Stanley Records is a placation tactic, and that even if she were to give up smuggling, she will still and forever *be* a smuggler at the core. This is who she is.

When she arrives at work, the guy at the door greets her with a bored hello. It's a shit job, sitting there all day on a stool, greeting people and checking their bags when the alarm goes off. And in turn, he does a shitty, lackadaisical job. It's an empire run by teenagers, most of them lazy and uninterested. Someone scribbled *Smells like teen shit* on the bathroom wall, and it fits.

Stanley Records is an institution. It used to be a small record shop on Stanley Street when it first opened, but moved to this much bigger location in the late seventies. It's essentially a massive warehouse—garishly bright with industrial carpeting and serviceable fixtures— with the best selection of music anywhere in the city. The kids who work here are mostly between sixteen and twenty-five years old, and generally they're all into music.

She doesn't really mind the job, especially now that she's found a way to supplement her meager hourly wage. She's a cashier, so she's always busy, and the shifts tend to fly by. The music is good, she's always on the cutting edge of what's new, and her coworkers are okay—some more okay than others. Occasionally, famous people show up and everyone stops what they're doing and there's a festive vibe in the air. The other day, Weird Al Yankovic showed up to promote his

Alapalooza album—he brought Dunkin' Donuts for the staff—and when Iron Maiden dropped by in December, Bruce Dickinson gave her tickets to their show. (She sold them.) She can wear jeans to work and not comb her hair and mostly be herself, which is more than she can say for many other jobs of this ilk.

She walks through the security detection system and then downstairs to punch in for her shift. The break room is in the basement. There's a microwave, a TV, a wall of lockers, and a high-school-cafeteria-style table, around which the employees smoke and eat fast food or warmed-up leftovers in Tupperware.

Roger is there, smoking while eating his poutine. Roger works upstairs in the warehouse. He has shaggy blond hair, piercings in his eyebrow, nose, and lip, and a tattoo of one of the Teenage Mutant Ninja Turtles on his chest.

"Your food must taste like cigarettes," she says, disgusted.

He shrugs.

"You have hockey tonight?" she asks, sitting down across from him.

"Yep."

Someone else joins them—the beautiful Italian girl from International Music on the mezzanine—and Véronique turns toward the TV, where news is breaking on CNN about a figure skater being attacked by another figure skater.

Roger stubs out his cigarette in what's left of his poutine, gets up from the table noisily—pushing his chair back, burping—and dumps the container in the trash. He doesn't make eye contact with Véronique, doesn't acknowledge her when he leaves the break room.

This is mainly for show. They have an understanding—act polite with each another, but not too friendly. They're an unlikely pair—she's beautiful, intelligent, seemingly untouchable in all ways, while Roger is crude, ugly, not very bright. No one would associate them together, which is exactly how she planned it. This way no one will ever suspect they're business partners in a surprisingly lucrative CD-stealing operation.

She first got the idea when she saw Roger leaving the warehouse after work one day with a hockey bag over his shoulder. The warehouse is on the fourth floor, above the offices, with a freight elevator that goes directly down to the loading dock out back. No one checks the staff's bags at the loading dock door. The warehouse guys load and unload the stock completely unsupervised.

The following week, she saw Roger walk through the store again with his hockey bag over his shoulder.

She started to formulate a plan—both to challenge herself and to earn some extra cash. On a Friday night after work, Véronique joined the gang at the St. Regis pub for the usual gathering to bitch about their jobs, gossip about management, and mock the customers.

Someone asked me where to find the Traveling Blueberries. Some guy got pissed off when I removed the security box from his CD. He thought it was included in the price! She didn't have to tell the shift manager I was "anti-English" just because I didn't understand "Jeff Beck, Beck-Ola."

After a while, when everyone was pretty drunk, a few of them started pulling CDs out of their backpacks and comparing what they'd stolen. The new Alice in Chains. Jean Leloup. The Beatles' White Album.

Stealing music is like a rite of passage at Stan's. Everyone does it. First of all, no one likes the owners, Maury and Rosalie Zimmerman. They're much older, rich and aloof, and never interact with the staff. Maury is the son of the guy who opened Stanley Records, so he acts very self-important, like he's some kind of legend. If he ever has anything to say to any of the employees— usually a critique of some sort—it's relayed through the managers. The Zimmermans do not speak to anyone else other than to fire them or interrogate them when one of the tills doesn't balance.

Also, the security is really lax. If the alarm goes off when someone is leaving at the end of their shift, a manager will give his or her backpack a half-assed search. But the alarm rarely goes off because everyone demagnetizes the CDs before stealing them. Even the managers steal. It's part of the culture.

Véronique was never interested in stealing CDs. She had a much bigger vision. That night at the St. Regis, she recruited Roger into stealing an entire hockey bag full of CDs straight from the warehouse, which she would sell off. She proposed charging ten bucks a CD, and splitting the earnings evenly with Roger.

The first time they did it, it went off seamlessly. Roger loaded up his hockey bag with the CDs she thought Callahan would like—the Tragically Hip, Blue Rodeo, Grateful Dead—and then he left work via the loading dock. Véronique had rented a locker at the Centre Eaton a few streets away, where he stashed the bag. She picked it up later, shoved it in her trunk, and drove to Ottawa the next day.

Callahan bought her entire stash, sold it all right away, and asked for more. He started to put in orders. Smashing Pumpkins, Indigo Girls, Natalie Merchant, Nirvana.

That was two months ago. Now they're making more money than either of them thought possible at

Stanley Records, and it couldn't be easier. She's able to give her parents CDs whenever she sees them, which makes them happy. James is happy. Everyone is happy. The best part is Véronique doesn't feel like she's fully conceded to James by taking a "real" job; it's her way of compromising, staying true to herself while doing something to assuage him.

On the news, the injured figure skater is on the ground, swarmed by doctors. Her dark hair is pulled back in a ponytail, and she's wearing a lacy white figure skating outfit that looks like a doily. She's clutching her leg and wailing. Apparently her chance of winning gold at the Olympics may now be in jeopardy.

Véronique gets up and goes upstairs for her shift. She's in a good mood. The new Tribe Called Quest is playing, and her favorite manager is working tonight. After work, she's going to pick up Roger's hockey bag from the locker and dump it in her car, which is parked in an all-day lot on President Kennedy. James is taking her to see the Vilain Pingouin concert tonight and then tomorrow morning she heads to Ste. Barbe for a cigarette run, followed by a short trip to Ottawa the next day.

Money is rolling in; her relationship with James is in a calmer place. Occasionally, she experiences a pang of guilt about lying to him, which is usually followed by a deep-seated uncertainty about their future together, but she loves him and she wants to be with him. Some secrets and lies are necessary to keep the peace.

14

James pulls into his mother's driveway, kicking up snow as he comes to a stop. He decided to come home for a visit while Véronique is in Ste. Barbe, hopefully on her last smuggling expedition. She seems happy at the record store, working a normal job, and he's hoping he can convince her to go back to school. He doesn't want to come off as too controlling or invested, but he does want to see her fulfill her potential. She's brilliant and strong—so much like his mother; he knows she could do great things. In the absence of constructive paternal advice, she seems to need a mentor. James has stepped in to offer some guidance and help her navigate her future.

He gets out of the car and goes to the garage to get a shovel. It still breaks his heart, showing up at home and seeing such simple things that need doing—the walk shoveled, the eaves cleaned, the windows replaced. All things his father used to take care of that Maggie doesn't have the wherewithal or physical strength to do herself anymore. James keeps telling her to hire someone to shovel and snowplow all winter, but Maggie refuses. "I can do it myself" is her standard, stubborn response. But she doesn't.

When he's finished shoveling, he leans the shovel up against the side of the house and lets himself inside. "M'ma?" he calls out, kicking off his boots.

"Kitchen!"

He hangs his ski jacket on the *porte-manteau* and is brushing snow off his jeans when Maggie appears in the foyer. "Hi, darling," she says, standing on tiptoes to hug him. "Good timing. I just got home from work."

"How's business?"

"Oh, terrible. All we sell is salt and discounted Christmas crap in January."

"I shoveled," he says.

"Thanks, love. I was hoping you would."

"Anything else you need today?"

"I have a list," she says, clasping his hand and leading him to the kitchen. "I can't figure out how to program *Oprah* on my new DVD player, the light bulbs in my bedroom chandelier are all burnt out. My garburator is broken. One of the elements on the stove keeps flickering, and I'm afraid there's going to be a gas explosion."

"I'll take care of it," James says, grabbing a warm brownie from a pan on the counter. "I should've come sooner."

He hasn't been home since Christmas. His only excuse is love, which isn't a very good excuse at all. Now he feels guilty for having neglected his mother, and he makes a mental note to come more often, even just for the day. "Smells good in here," he says, sitting down at the long pine table. "It always does."

She prepares a plate of brownies and a glass of milk for him, and then sits down where her typewriter is set up at the center of a messy pile of notes—sketches, diagrams, typewritten blurbs about seeds and flowers. She's already working on the spring seed catalogue, something she's been doing herself, on that same typewriter, for as long as he can remember. She won't hire someone to do it, no matter how many times he tells her there are graphic designers who will do it for her, probably better. But no, the catalogue is her baby, and her work ethic has always bordered on compulsion—turning sixty hasn't changed a thing.

"I miss you," she says. His beautiful, ebony-haired mother is finally starting to look her age. Her roots are silver about two inches long, which is unusual for her. She's normally meticulous about dyeing it black. She looks thin to him, the lines on her face more pronounced.

"You okay, M'ma?"

"A little lonely," she admits. "It comes in waves. It always does."

James nods. It's the same for him.

"Some days I miss your dad more than others," she says. "It's been one of those weeks."

"It always happens after the holidays."

"I know," she concedes. "They've never been the same without him, have they?"

"Nothing has."

"I keep thinking about the first time he ever saw you," she says. "I don't know why, but my mind keeps going there."

James was not quite a year old when his father first laid eyes on him. His parents had been together as a couple when she conceived him, but then Gabriel discovered that Maggie had given Elodie away without telling him, and he left her. Disappeared for almost a year, not knowing Maggie was pregnant with James. When Gabriel turned up on her doorstep, he had no idea he had a son.

"I remember you spit up as I was handing you over

to Daddy," she reminisces, laughing. "But he took you in his arms as though he'd been doing it since the day you were born. I was amazed. He was so confident with you, so comfortable. Some men are terrified the first time they hold a baby, but your dad didn't hesitate a second. It's like he *knew* you. Like you belonged in his arms."

Maggie grabs a tissue from a nearby Kleenex box and touches the corners of her eyes. "He rubbed your little head and kissed your face. He was crying. He sang to you, '*Fais do-do, bébé à papa . . .*'"

"You always said it was love at first sight."

"It really was," she says. "For both of you. That was the same day my father died. Strange, isn't it? I lost my father the day yours came into your life?"

James gets up and goes around the table. He wraps his arms around her and she presses her cheek against his forearm. He can feel the wetness of her tears on his skin. "I'm sorry you're having a hard time."

"It's January," she says. "I should have seen it coming."

She pats his arm and sits up a little straighter. "Why don't you start tackling my list," she says. "Let me finish up this last part of my catalogue before I start dinner. I'm roasting duck."

"Do you ever take a day off?"

"The busier I am, the less time I have for feeling sorry for myself."

"You've always been this way."

"You mean a workaholic?"

"You said it, not me."

"I prefer to call it having a good work ethic."

"Dad was the same."

James grew up having those words instilled in him. *Work ethic. Values. Purpose.* Both his parents believed in hard work—work they loved, work that lined up with their values. His mother inherited her life's philosophy from her father. *Without hard work, nothing grows but weeds. Do the hard jobs first; the easy jobs will take care of themselves. You have to pay your dues.* This was a big one. *Everyone* had to pay their dues. His mother's office at the store is papered with those old-fashioned slogans, handed down from her father; her library is lined with his business and motivational books, written by his mentors and idols. Dale Carnegie, Napoleon Hill, Norman Vincent Peale, Gordon B. Hinckley. Maggie always said her father was way ahead of the self-help movement.

James grew up watching his mother work six days a week at the seed store, come home and toil all night over her catalogues or a translation. His father was the same. In spring, summer, and fall, he was up at dawn tending to his family's cornfield; in winter, he was working alongside Maggie at the seed store. Gabriel could have sold his family's land and they could have lived well enough off the seed store, but he loved that land. Loved it like it was his fourth child. The cornfield was where he met Maggie, where they hid from her mother and fooled around, where she lost her virginity to him—so goes the family lore. Gabriel was devoted to the Phénix property. For his father's name, for his sisters, for his own sake, he worked his ass off to keep it alive and thriving.

Clémentine sold the land about a year after Gabriel died. They grieved all over again, the wound reopened, fresh and harrowing. Gabriel was so intertwined with that cornfield, losing it was like a second death.

James eventually came to embrace his parents' values—hard work, an honest wage, the pursuit of truth and integrity. With its canons and codes and principles, journalism was the perfect fit for his burgeoning ideals. From that very first ethics class, he knew he'd found his calling.

His father was pleased with his choice. Gabriel's pride on the day James graduated with honors in journalism was unabashed. He cried all afternoon, pulling James into his arms after the ceremony. "My son is a college graduate," he kept saying, incredulous. He couldn't take his eyes off the diploma. He'd never seen one before.

They had a small celebration in their backyard, and Gabriel made a toast. "To my son the journalist!" he declared, tipsy and impassioned. He could not have been more impressed.

James gave his diploma to his father, which Gabriel framed and hung over the fireplace in the family room. He died a year later. He never got to read one of James's published articles; never even saw James's byline in the paper.

Maggie sets the steaming-hot duck in the center of the table, its skin crackling and golden, the juice still bubbling in the pan. The smell of rosemary fills the air as she brings platters of mashed potatoes, buttery carrots, Le Sueur baby peas. James opens a bottle of L'Orpailleur Blanc from the vineyard in Dunham and pours them each a glass.

"Cheers, my love," she says, when they're both sitting down.

"Looks great, M'ma."

"So how's Véronique?" Maggie asks. "She couldn't come this weekend?"

"She's in Ste. Barbe."

"She's still working for her uncle?"

"Yeah, but not for much longer."

Maggie thinks Véronique does the bookkeeping for Camil's construction business. The lie has held up well over the past year, but it will be a relief when he can actually tell his mother the truth about what his girl-friend does for a living.

"She got a job at a record store downtown," he says, reaching for the peas. "She may go back to school, too."

"That would be great," Maggie says. "Having a degree will be much better for her future."

James nods, feeling a little guilty. Véronique doesn't really want to go back to school; he knows that. Why does that make him so uncomfortable?

"Does she know what she wants to do?" Maggie asks him.

"Politics, maybe."

"Ah, yes. She's her father's daughter."

"Hardly," he says. "Can you please pass me the po-tatoes?"

Maggie hands over the glass platter of mash. "I have a confession to make," she says.

He looks up, curious.

"I went to the library in Granby," she says. "I looked up Léo Fortin."

"Why?"

"He could be your father-in-law one day," she says. "You're almost thirty-five. I know you're thinking about marriage."

Indeed, she knows him too well.

"I read everything I could find about him," she says.

"And?"

"He's a monster, James. He never apologized or showed any remorse for the murder."

"Véronique is not her father."

"Is Véronique close to him? I know it's none of my business, but you two are getting serious. I wasn't sure you guys would last this long, if I'm being honest. I know she's lovely . . . I just wonder how she's lived with it her whole life? Her father is a murderer. Do you talk about it?"

"He's her father," James says. "She loves him. Dad could have murdered someone and I would have loved him no matter what."

"Your father would never have been capable of taking someone's life," Maggie says, her tone rising.

"That's not what I said."

"You know what your father would have thought of them."

"Do I?"

"Remember when you started hanging around with those druggies and your grades started dropping? Remember how he took you out on the boat and gave you a talking-to?"

"You're comparing Véronique to those losers in high school?"

"No, of course not. But Daddy always used to say that the people closest to you are the best reflection of who you are."

"Are you saying that Véronique is like a murderer because of her father? Or that *I* am because I love her?"

Maggie replenishes her wine and stares into her glass for a few seconds before responding. "I'm just saying that the company you keep says a lot about *you*. And from a moral and ethical standpoint, I'm struggling with how she was raised and the people who raised her."

"She's a good person," James says. "She was raised by her mother. She works hard. And Léo isn't evil. He was just a kid himself when the kidnapping happened."

"The kidnapping didn't *happen*, son. Léo organized it and carried it out. He put a machine gun to Laporte's head and snatched him in broad daylight. And then he strangled him to make a political point. If that's not evil, what is? And frankly, even if I could chalk that up to a young man's political ideals leading to a moment of insanity, what I can't accept is that to this day, the guy has not shown a shred of remorse for what he did. This is the man you want me to welcome into my family?"

"I don't want you to welcome him to the family. Just his daughter."

"It's hard to separate them."

James puts his knife and fork down. He's lost his appetite.

"I know you don't like hearing this," Maggie says, more gently. "But I'm your mother and I have to say it. The Fortins trouble me."

James doesn't say anything. He knows his silence will make Maggie more uncomfortable than an argument. He doesn't know what to say anyway.

"I never told you this," Maggie says. "But your father was quite involved with the RIN for a very short time, when it was still very new."

James looks up, surprised. "Léo started off in the RIN," he says. "Before he joined the FLQ."

"Your dad always had an interest in politics," Maggie explains. "After he left me—when I was pregnant with you—he started going to RIN meetings. It would have been about 1960 or '61. He was very much on board with their ideals, but not always with their methods. A lot of them were too radical for him, so he left. That's when he moved out to the Gaspé."

"I had no idea."

"When we were back together and you were about three," she continues, "He read a book by Marcel

Chaput called *Why I Am a Separatist*. It really excited him. After that, he started reading *L'Indépendance*, which was an RIN magazine, and slowly getting back into the whole separatist movement."

"How did you feel about that?"

"Well, obviously I was completely on the other side. I've always been a Liberal. We argued plenty, but we respected each other's beliefs. It's not like either of us was ever going to bend or change our minds."

James laughs softly. It's not lost on him that he is living out the very same dynamic with Véronique. "Why don't I know any of this?" he asks her. "How come you never told me before?"

"There was nothing to tell. His involvement was very short-lived. As much as he loved the cause, the same radicals he couldn't stand before were getting even more agitated. When the FLQ bombed an English radio station and some military barracks in Westmount, your dad became really disillusioned. He decided he wanted no part of politics anymore. He was embarrassed by what they were doing," she says.

"He never stopped caring about Quebec's independence, but he was against the violence. He thought it diminished their cause, made them look like thugs. He wanted the cause to be taken seriously. Instead, the FLQ became exactly what the English expected of a gang of poor French Quebeckers. Your father walked away from all his nationalist affiliations and that was it."

"Okay. And?"

"My point in telling you all this," Maggie says, "is that your father had the same beliefs as Léo Fortin. He just made different choices. Violence wasn't the only option for them, you know."

"But Dad walked away from all of it."

"He walked away because of his morality, which is better than the road Léo Fortin and the FLQ went down. Had your father been more interested in politics and less interested in farming, maybe he would have continued to fight in a way that lined up with his belief system. Many politicians did. Not all of them turned to violence. That's why for Léo to say he did what he did for the province and for his people is complete bullshit. James, a man has to be *capable* of bombing a building. He has to be *capable* of putting a gun to a man's head. He has to be *capable* of murder."

"I don't disagree with that, M'ma. I'm no fan of Léo Fortin either, but Véronique is her own person. She can't help who her father is. I can't leave her because I don't like what her father did twenty-five years ago."

Maggie sighs.

"I mean, is that what you're suggesting I do?"

"I just want you to be sure you really know her."

"I do."

"I know you love her."

"I really do."

Maggie smiles wistfully. "It can be an affliction, though, can't it?"

Her words resonate, more than he cares to admit.

15

February 1994

Callahan's front door is unlocked, and Véronique lets herself in, as per his message on her phone. The house smells of weed, stale beer, and garbage, as usual. The front hallway is lined with empties—hundreds of them—because he can't be bothered to return them to the beer store. They just keep piling up, more of them every time she comes.

"I'm upstairs!" he calls down to her. "Come on up."

She leaves the hockey bags in the vestibule—two full of smokes, a third with CDs—and heads upstairs to collect her money.

"Hey, girl!" he says, coming out of the bathroom. He's wearing a Maple Leafs cap, an open plaid shirt over a stained T-shirt, pale jeans. He smells minty.

She follows him to his room but stays by the door. "I really can't stay today," she tells him.

"It looks like the government is going to slash the cigarette taxes any day," he says. "This could be our last time doing business together."

She's been discussing the situation with Pierre and Camil, trying to figure out what's next. The prime minister will most likely cut the taxes on cigarettes this month in an attempt to stamp out tobacco smuggling, effectively killing Camil's business. The price for a carton of cigarettes will be cut in half, and the demand for contraband will disappear. They've always known it would happen, but it's no less devastating. "My uncle will figure something out," she says.

Camil is already talking about switching to weed and booze. Pierre mentioned coke, but Véronique wants no part of that. She's still got the CDs.

"Like what?" Callahan wants to know.

"Weed, I guess. Cheap alcohol."

"I've got plenty of dealers already," he says, loading a CD into his player. "But if your prices are better, it could work." He turns to face her, lights a smoke. "You like Mudhoney?"

Véronique shrugs. She just wants to get her money and get back on the road. "I can't stay long," she says again. James is coming back from Cowansville, and she's eager to see him.

"How much do I owe you?" he asks her, reaching into his desk drawer and pulling out a fat roll of bills.

"Twenty-four hundred," she says. "Same as always."

He turns around, his mouth stretching into a smile. "How about two grand?"

"Heh?"

"Come on," he says. "You guys have made a fortune off me. How about a little more of the profit since this is probably our last deal?"

"Come on, Callahan."

"Twenty-two K?"

"It's not my decision," she says. "This is my uncle's price. You want to fuck with my uncle?"

Callahan considers this for a moment and then hands over the entire ball of cash. She takes off the elastic and starts counting.

"You don't trust me?" he says. "After all this time?"

"I always count the money."

Callahan takes off his Toronto Maple Leafs cap and sets it down on his desk. He runs a hand through his orange hair, which is flat and straight, and reaches into the pocket of his jeans. "Want to do 'shrooms?"

"I can't," she says impatiently, still counting. "I told you I have to head back."

"Come on." He holds out the palm of his hand, revealing an ample pile that looks like dirt.

She ignores him, continues counting.

"Let's do the 'shrooms and then go for a long walk on the canal."

"It's freezing outside."

Unfazed, he shoves all of them in his mouth. "I had this whole afternoon planned for us," he says, stepping closer to her. "You sure I can't convince you to stay?"

His face is uncomfortably close. She can count the freckles on his cheeks. She notices his eyelashes and brows are pale orange. She's never noticed before.

"We don't have to go out," he says, still chewing the mushrooms. "We can hang here, listen to music. My roommates are both away for the weekend."

"I have to go," she says, stuffing the money in her pocket. "I'll be in touch about next steps if the taxes do get cut—"

Before she can finish her sentence, he grabs both her wrists and holds her arms down by her side.

"Let go of me."

"What the hell's been going on the past few months?"

"What do you mean?"

"Skating on the canal. Hanging out in the quad. Listening to music in my room."

Shit.

"Don't tell me you weren't aware of the messages you've been sending me," he says. "No one is that stupid, especially you."

"I didn't realize . . ."

"The hell you didn't." He's still holding her wrists, hurting her. "Does your uncle make you do this?"

"Do what?"

"Flirt with the customers. Lead them on so they'll keep buying from you. Is that why he sends you—like you're some kind of prostitute?"

"He sends me because I speak English," she says angrily. "I don't need to sell you cigarettes. Someone else will buy them if you don't."

Even as she says it, she isn't certain it's true. He *is* a great client, one of her best until now. Maybe—inadvertently—she has been leading him on, but never intentionally.

"You've been playing with me, Veronica," he says, and she can see bits of mushroom on his tongue.

She's trying to break free of his grip, but he's deceptively strong. His bulk is not just baby fat. "Get off me!" she cries.

He slams her back against the wall and pins her arms above her head, holding them there with one hand. With his other hand, he rips the fly of her jeans open and attempts to pull them down.

THE FORGOTTEN DAUGHTER · 225

"Stop!" she screams. "Get the fuck off!"

He tugs at her panties, but she's squirming so violently, he has a hard time getting his hand underneath them. His knees are slightly bent, digging into her legs—pinning them against the wall so she can't kick him. His free hand is on her breasts now, over her sweater and then sliding under.

When she tries to scream for help, he puts his mouth on hers and bites her lip. She can feel blood on her chin, and she rolls her head wildly from side to side. "My uncle is going to kill you!"

"Murder runs in your family," Callahan says calmly, struggling to hold her still. "If you say anything, I'll go to the cops and tell them about your little family business."

"Callahan, please," she says, her voice pleading. "Why are you doing this? I know you. We're friends. Don't do this."

"You want this," he pants into her ear. "We both know you do. I don't know why you're being such a bitch all of a sudden."

"Callahan—"

With his free hand, he unzips his own jeans and shimmies them down to his knees, followed by his boxer shorts. She can feel his naked hard-on between her thighs, and she gags, then squeezes her legs together as tight as she can, closing her body off to him, fighting him with all her strength. He's still wrestling with her underwear, trying to get them off and get his dick inside her while keeping her arms pinned to the wall. "Calm down, you slut," he says. "Stop pretending you don't want this."

She stops fighting him and lets her body go limp. Encouraged, Callahan applies himself and succeeds in getting her panties down to her mid-thighs. "Attagirl," he whispers. "Just enjoy it."

But the moment he loosens the pressure on her legs, she raises her right knee and thrusts it hard into his groin. He lets out a loud cry and doubles over, collapsing to his knees and releasing her. It gives her enough time to step away from the wall, grab the purple lava lamp on his nightstand, and bash it against the side of his head before fleeing his room.

She pulls up her jeans as she's running down the stairs, stopping briefly at the bottom to make sure the money is still in her pocket. She grabs her jacket and, at the last minute, randomly throws his DVD player across the room.

She gets in her car and swerves away from the house, her hands white-knuckling the steering wheel. As she races toward the highway, she vows never to tell anyone about what just happened. Why did she go upstairs to his room? How could she have been so stupid? She sees now that the power she thought she had was only ever an illusion.

She's startled to find James on the couch when she gets home, reading and listening to music. He looks up when she comes in, and his face opens into a wide smile. "Hey, baby," he says, setting his book down on the coffee table. "I missed you."

She tries to force a smile but can't manage it. She wants to shower, wants to be alone.

"Come here," he says.

She goes to him, worried he'll smell Callahan's disgusting cologne on her. He pulls her down beside him and leans in to kiss her.

She pushes him away.

"What's wrong?"

"I'm tired," she says. "I need a shower."

"I'll join you."

"No."

"Are you okay?" he asks, reaching out to touch her hair.

"I'm fine," she says, moving his hand away.

"You sure?"

"I told you, I'm exhausted."

"Let me take care of you," he says, making another

attempt to embrace her. This time she lets him. She doesn't want to hurt him or rouse his suspicions.

She slumps against him, and he rubs her back, kisses the top of her head.

"You're so tense," he murmurs, and she's aware of how rigidly she's holding her body. His kisses and touches are making her faintly nauseated. She fights to keep back tears.

When his hand slides underneath her sweater, her back stiffens even more. "Stop it!" she cries.

"What the hell is going on?"

"I just don't feel like it."

"You sure?" he says playfully, grazing her nipple with his fingertips.

Something in her snaps, and she slaps him in the face, hard. "I said don't feel like being touched right now. Can't you just respect that?"

James looks stunned. For a moment, he doesn't move, doesn't speak.

"I'm sorry," she murmurs.

He doesn't say anything as he gets up. His hand is on his cheek, his expression incredulous.

"James, I'm sorry—"

She wants to tell him everything, but she can't. He'll be angry. He'll say, *I told you so.* She'll expose how vulnerable she is. Instead, she watches him disappear into her bedroom; hears drawers opening and closing, the closet door slam. He emerges with his overnight bag over his shoulder.

"Don't go," she says, panic constricting her throat. She doesn't want him to leave. She wants him to hold her, but she doesn't ask for that.

"I'm sorry!" she calls after him.

He doesn't say anything, just opens the front door and leaves. Elodie's words come back to her, pounding in her temples. *You can't bury something that's still alive.*

16

March 1994

Elodie is sitting at the back of the courtroom in the Palais de Justice, Véronique on one side of her, Maggie on the other. She's holding both of their hands for moral support, awaiting the judge's decision. Bruno is seated next to their lawyer in the row right in front of them, his back straight as a board, a nodule of sweat trickling down his thick neck. Huguette and Francine are in the row behind her.

"This case is very sensitive," the judge says. "The lawyers for the defendants have pointed out that the religious orders in question are elderly and have lived with great stress, anxiety, and shame since these petitions were filed. These troubling accusations call into question their very lives' work."

Elodie can feel her face getting hot. Her palms are damp.

"The Duplessis orphans are seeking group damages from three sources: the religious orders, the Quebec government, and the medical establishment," the judge explains. "Let's address the religious orders first. They are accused of falsifying records, making false diagnoses, illegally interning children in mental institutions, forcing them to work without remuneration, depriving them of a proper education, and subjecting them to corporal punishment and mental cruelty."

Elodie tunes out the judge, her mind wandering to Claire, her best friend from the orphanage. She's never seen her at any of the Duplessis Orphans Committee gatherings, which may mean she was never sent to one of the asylums. Elodie prays that to be the case. Still, she thinks of her constantly. Where is she? What does she look like now? She still imagines her as she was then: always with her hair in braids, missing her two front teeth. They'd been friends from the time Elodie could walk and talk. Other girls came and went, but Claire and Elodie remained, more inseparable as the years passed. They promised each other that whoever's mother came for them first, they would take the other with them.

Elodie remembers one of their last conversations

before she was sent away. They were coloring under Claire's bed. Elodie was drawing one of her families—a yellow-haired mother, plenty of brothers and sisters. Claire said, "I think I know why my parents gave me away."

"Why?"

"My thumbs. Look." She held out both her hands, revealing two bent thumbs. "They don't straighten."

Elodie was awestruck. She reached out and tried to straighten them for her, but Claire was right; they wouldn't budge. "Have they always been like this?"

"Yes. And also this." She pulled off her sock and thrust out her foot, as though proud of her abnormalities. "My fourth toe doesn't grow." The toe was just a nubbin, about an inch shorter than the others. "I'm deformed," she said, matter-of-factly. "And people always want perfect babies."

Elodie's wish for Claire is that she got out unscathed, without ever having seen the inside of an institution.

"The religious orders in question list the following points in their defense," the judge says, "which I will now read to the court."

Elodie tunes back to the proceeding.

"First, we cannot judge the past by today's values. All societies evolve over time. What was once considered normal and morally acceptable may seem cruel and unfair to a new generation." He glances up briefly to acknowledge the gallery and then resumes reading. "Corporal punishment and child labor were the norm back then."

"Bullshit," Francine says from behind her.

"Second," the judge continues, "the nuns were the only ones who would care for the abandoned children. No one else wanted them. They devoted themselves to this task with limited means and did the best they could based on the knowledge available to them at the time."

There's an outburst of angry twittering in the gallery behind Elodie. A couple of orphans are swearing in loud whispers. Elodie sneaks a glance behind her at Huguette. Her expression is stoic.

"Although some members of the religious orders have acknowledged that there may have been some isolated instances of abuse, they worry, as do I, that by proceeding with a class action suit, we will be setting a precedent that would put the church on trial and risk denigrating the entire Catholic faith."

"What about how they denigrated us?" someone cries out.

"Furthermore, progress in psychiatry is a recent phenomenon," the judge says, ignoring the heckling. "The distinctions made today between mental handicap and mental illness were much less clear in the fifties—"

"You're telling us they couldn't tell the difference between a normal kid and one who was *mentally challenged?*" someone yells. "This is a joke!"

"Please take your seat, sir," the judge instructs. "What we have here is an impossible situation. These orphans are looking for a scapegoat. Since they were abandoned and don't know who their biological parents are, it seems to me they're taking their frustrations out on the only parents they've ever known, the nuns who cared for them."

"He's calling those monsters *parents?*" Maggie mutters, rummaging in her bag for a Kleenex. She finds one and angrily blows her nose.

"Both the plaintiffs and defendants want desperately to be heard," the judge says, his tone dispassionate. "The former claim they were mistreated, the latter wish to explain their side of things. But the truth has become distorted over the last forty years, making it impossible for the judicial system to serve justice in this case."

A wave of disappointment travels through the gallery, and Elodie can feel the collective sagging of spirits in the room. Véronique puts her arm around Elodie's shoulders, as though holding her together.

"Regarding the claims against the religious orders," the judge concludes, "the Court of Quebec rejects the plaintiffs' applications to pursue a class action suit on behalf of the Duplessis Orphans Committee. It is simply not the appropriate avenue."

Elodie doesn't move. Bruno and the lawyer turn around to face them. "We're going to appeal," the lawyer says.

"And we still have the criminal cases," Bruno adds. "It's not over."

"It's just the beginning," the lawyer promises. "Don't be discouraged."

"As for the plaintiffs' claim against the government," the judge continues, "they accuse the government of failing to act as legal guardian for all the orphans and failing to ensure they were cared for and educated. The government has not responded to these charges, other than to reiterate the arguments of the religious orders, in which case the court must concur."

Elodie is on her feet, making her way to the exit. The judge is still delivering his verdict. "It is the medical association's position that it is not responsible for any decisions made by hospital management, particularly ones made more than thirty years ago, when all hospitals were run by the church. Again, the court concurs—"

Elodie bursts through the doors, Maggie and Véronique close on her heels. The moment she steps outside,

TV cameras surround her and a microphone is shoved in her face. "What's your reaction to the decision?" Radio-Canada.

She looks around for Bruno or the lawyer, someone equipped to speak on her behalf. Maggie is touching her elbow, steadying her. "You don't have to say anything," she says into her ear.

"Are you a Duplessis orphan, madame?" CKAC.

Elodie stares down at the microphones and takes a breath. Her heart is beating rapidly. "I'm disgusted by the judge's decision," she says, her voice shaky. "All we want is a public apology. Justice for our suffering and our stolen childhoods. I was diagnosed mentally deficient. Do I look mentally deficient to you? No, but that was how they got rid of us back then."

"What's next?"

"Our lawyer will appeal," Elodie says, realizing with some shock that she is actually speaking articulately in front of a camera and all these people are hanging onto her every word, as though she is some kind of an authority or expert. "We still have the criminal complaints," she says, her voice gaining confidence. "If they think we're going to give up and disappear, they're wrong."

The questions continue to come at her like bullets. *You're saying you've filed a criminal complaint against the church? For what? Can you tell us what crimes you believe were committed against you?*

"The first crime against me was failure to provide an education" Elodie says, looking over at Maggie and Véronique, who are watching her from the sidelines. Maggie is beaming, the proud mother. Véronique winks at her. "They deprived us not only of schooling, but of basic life skills," she continues, really finding her footing now. "I wasn't prepared for the real world when I got out. I had no way to cope with life. The nuns treated me as if I didn't exist, never gave me even the slightest bit of human affection. I was tortured in every way possible. It's unforgivable, and I won't rest until those crimes are acknowledged."

"Can you spell your name, please?"

"Elodie Phénix," she says, her voice stronger, more certain. She looks directly into the camera and spells her name. "E-l-o-d-i-e. P-h-é-n-i-x."

As she does so, her determination crystallizes. This *is* just the beginning, she thinks. She will continue to fight. She will do whatever she is called on to do until there is a satisfactory resolution—whatever the hell that looks like.

17

April 1994

The TV is on in the break room, and most of Stan's employees are huddled in front of it, watching coverage of Kurt Cobain's suicide. A couple of grunge girls are crying. It's always shocking when an icon dies young, especially in a culture like Stan's, where everyone is obsessed with music. Upstairs in the store, they're playing *Nevermind* on a loop. It's all anyone can talk about.

Véronique shoves a flat bag of popcorn in the microwave and watches it pop. Dinner. She's got the night shift tonight. She prefers the later shifts these days, can't stand being home alone at night. It's the loneliest time, where she feels James's absence most profoundly. They haven't officially ended things, but they haven't spoken in a couple of weeks. She's giving him space and giving herself time, too. The incident with Callahan is still fresh—in her mind, on her body. Some of the bruises haven't fully healed yet, and the thought of having sex still makes her uneasy.

She hasn't told anyone what Callahan did, including her uncle and Pierre. She was worried Callahan would retaliate and blow up her uncle's operation, get them all arrested and thrown in jail. Or that her uncle would simply murder Callahan—which wouldn't be so bad— but what if Camil got caught and spent the rest of his life in jail on account of her?

She did stop smuggling. In some ways, the timing worked out. At the end of February, the government slashed the taxes on cigarettes, basically putting the tobacco smugglers permanently out of business. Her uncle was prepared for it and switched seamlessly to smuggling marijuana and booze, but it gave Véronique a plausible excuse to take a break. She told Camil she wasn't sure she wanted to get involved with dope and that she needed time off to think about her future. In some ways, it's the truth. Not that she cares whether she's selling cigarettes or weed—she doesn't give two shits—but she does need time to regroup.

Pierre and Camil are not pleased with her. They want her back in the business, handling the Ottawa colleges—specifically Callahan's clientele. Callahan makes a ton of money for them, and they need her as much for her popularity with men as for her English. They don't understand her hesitation around selling weed.

"What's the difference?" Camil said, yelling at her over the phone. "Weed is probably better for them than tobacco anyway!"

She held her ground, and they haven't spoken to her since. It's the longest she hasn't spoken to Pierre since they were kids. They've never had a real falling-out before, but she figures time will heal both their resentments. Besides, Pierre has a short attention span.

What Callahan did scared her. It *scarred* her. She misjudged him, thought of him as a harmless frat boy. Worse, she trusted him, which has left her doubting herself.

"Hey, Véronique. Your parents are here."

She looks up from the microwave, where she's become entranced by the popping corn, the bag puffing up before her eyes like a self-inflating balloon. She turns to the stairwell, where Encino Man, the cashier manager, has thrust his head into the lunchroom, his wild black frizz of hair throwing lion shadows on the wall.

"My parents?"

Encino Man shrugs. Véronique lets her popcorn finish popping and removes it from the microwave. She opens it, the steam rising into her face, and reaches in for a handful. She goes upstairs, starving, wondering what the hell her parents are doing here. When she spots them standing by the front counter, her mother ever so slightly leaning on her father, she can tell right away something is wrong. They both look shell-shocked, their skin bleached. As she approaches, her mother's mouth is trembling.

"What's wrong?" she says. "What happened?"

"Let's go outside," her father says.

She follows them out wordlessly, heart rushing, cheeks hot. "What is it? What happened?"

"Are you cold?" her father asks her. "You don't have a jacket."

"Why are you here? What's happened?"

Her mother reaches for her hand. "It's Pierre," her mother says, her voice cracking. "He died in a boat accident this afternoon."

"No—"

Pierre dead? It can't be. Her mother tries to pull her into her arms, but Véronique pushes her away. "How?" she wants to know. "In broad daylight? It doesn't make sense."

"It was a collision with another boat. Everyone died."

Véronique is shaking her head. Her father pulls her into his arms, and she buries her face against his chest. He strokes her hair. Lisette is sobbing. They stay huddled together like that for a long time, ignoring the world rushing past. *Pierre is dead. Pierre is dead.* She repeats this to herself, to see if it will make it feel more real. It doesn't.

"How's *mon'onc* Camil?" she asks, lifting her face from her father's jacket.

"What do you think?" Lisette says. "He's devastated. He blames himself. We're going there now."

"I can't."

"Véro . . . You have to come."

"I can't. Not today. I just . . . I can't go there today. I'll drive up tomorrow."

Lisette purses her lips.

"You shouldn't drive," Léo says. "Come with us."

"I want to be alone. Can you just take me home?"

Her father nods, and she goes back into the store to get her jacket and backpack, and to let Encino Man know she won't be back for a few days. "My cousin died," she tells him, and it comes out as a question, as though she isn't sure. She goes downstairs to the lunchroom in a trance, her limbs moving as slowly as if she were underwater. Kurt Cobain is still on the news. No one even looks up at her.

At home, she opens a bottle of wine, puts on R.E.M., and curls up on the couch. She should have been driving the boat. She should never have walked away. Pierre would be alive. He handled the shotgun and kept lookout; she drove. She let them down. How will she ever make peace with that? Who will take his place in her life? He was her brother. Her twin cousin.

The more she drinks, the more the memories come. When they were eleven, their parents—her mother and his father—decided to send them to sleepaway camp just outside the reservation. It was meant to be a sort of boot camp to keep them out of trouble for the summer, but it had no effect whatsoever on Pierre. The camp was housed in a convent off the highway, set back on the edge of the woods. They did archery, rope courses, pellet gun shooting, and pottery. Every night, around the campfire, Véronique earned a green feather for good behavior, which all the green-feather kids would tuck into their headbands. Pierre always got yellow, as a warning. He never wore his in his headband. At the end of two weeks, Véronique earned an eagle feather and Pierre nothing.

The ceremony to become a warrior was the grand finale. Only the boys were allowed to participate. Girls could not become "braves," which outraged Véronique, especially after she'd worked so hard for all those green feathers. She challenged the "elders," who were only about sixteen, pointing out the unfairness of their sexist rule, the infuriating lopsidedness of it, but they just said that was the way it had always been done. Instead, the girls had to spend the night in a tepee, and for this, they earned another measly eagle feather. The boys, on the other hand, were dropped in the middle of the forest by themselves, and had to find their way back to camp in the pitch-black dark.

Pierre, facing the forest alone, looked uncertain. Véronique had never seen him scared before. She gave him a nod of encouragement and watched as one of the counselors wrapped a blindfold around his head and led him behind the convent into a different part of the woods. They had flashlights to guide them in, but the boys would be left deep, deep in the woods with no light at all.

Véronique lay awake most of the night in her tepee, worrying about him. As the sun began to rise, she peered outside. That's when she heard a loud whoop from the woods and recognized Pierre's voice. He came charging through the trees, his arms above his head, waving a stick. Everyone started clapping. Véronique's body relaxed. He looked exhilarated. She was proud of him. Two of the counselors picked him up, one by the feet and the other under the armpits, and they passed his body over the flames of the fire, chanting their traditional chants. And then they gave him a beautiful eagle feather and declared him a brave.

She thought he would be different after that, thought he would be more mature, maybe straighten out and get into less trouble, but nothing changed. The eagle feather was lost, and his pride over surviving the night alone in the woods was first exploited, and then quickly forgotten.

Véronique curls up into a tight ball, thinking about the time they ran over a raccoon in Camil's truck and Pierre insisted on burying it instead of leaving it on the road. Or the time they put scoops of flour on every blade of Lisette's kitchen ceiling fan because Pierre wanted to understand the air-circulation pattern by creating a wind tunnel effect. Another time, Pierre had the idea to trap a skunk with a hot dog and a milk crate, but when the crate fell on the skunk's back, it sprayed them both in the face.

She can't believe he's gone. It's surreal. She pours

more wine, rolls a joint. Impulsively, she reaches for the phone and calls James. Screw being tough and prideful and shutting him out. He answers on the second ring. "V," he says, and she can hear the relief in his voice.

"Pierre's dead," she tells him, and starts to cry.

Within fifteen minutes he's at her place, holding her. He feels so good. They stay like that for a long time, hours. He says nothing, no mention of what happened between them last time. She loves him for that.

Around midnight, he gently tugs her off the couch and walks her to her bedroom. She's drunk, grief-stricken, hollow. He lies down beside her and holds her until she falls asleep. The next morning, she wakes up in his arms. Her head is pounding, there's a moment of confusion—a split second of oblivion—and then she remembers.

"I'm so glad you quit smuggling," James says, when she's still half asleep. "Promise me you'll never go back to it. Please, V. You see now how dangerous it is."

He's probably been waiting all night to say that to her.

"It was an accident," she says, rolling over. "A collision in broad daylight. He wasn't smuggling."

"We both know that's not true. If it happened during the day, then he was bringing the cash to the reservation or he was on his way back—"

"It was a random accident," she says, raising her voice. And if she had been there to rein him in, to drive the boat responsibly, Pierre would be alive. He didn't die because he was trying to outrun bandits on the lake. He died because he was reckless and cocky, probably high, and because Véronique had abandoned him. "He'd be alive if I had been there," she says.

"V, that's not true." He grips her by the shoulders and gives her a firm shake. "Do you hear me? It's not true."

She looks away, thinking about Callahan. If it hadn't been for him, she would have been on the boat with Pierre. Callahan is the reason Pierre is dead.

"V, if Pierre hadn't been killed on that boat, he would have wound up in jail. I don't want to sound harsh, but there is no happy ending to this story. I don't want you to be next."

They've been locked in this battle since the beginning. She lives by her principles, he by his morals. When does one outweigh the other? she wonders. When you get caught? When a life is lost?

"I know you, V. I know you feel guilty right now and you probably think you should go back to smuggling to help out your uncle—"

"He's going to need me."

"*I* need you," James says. "I see you grappling with this—"

"I'm not the one grappling with it, you are."

Léo always says you have to be willing to cross the line, that there shouldn't even be a line. Pierre is dead. How far is too far?

18

When she called him after two weeks of radio silence, he was relieved. Whatever grudge he'd been holding onto after she slapped him was quickly forgotten in the face of her cousin's death. It was just good to hear her voice. He found her on the couch in fetal position, wine and weed spread all over the coffee table, blaming herself because she wasn't the one driving the boat. He scooped her into his arms and held her while she cried, and he hasn't left her side since.

"I've lost everything," she murmurs, her eyes an explosion of pink blood vessels. "My cousin, my livelihood."

"You haven't lost everything."

She's shaking her head, inconsolable. "I almost lost you."

"I'm right here," he says.

"You don't understand."

"I do, though," he says. "My dad had a heart attack while he was out working in the cornfield. I was supposed to have been home visiting that weekend, but I canceled at the last minute to go up north with friends."

He's never talked about this with anyone before. He's always been too ashamed. "If I'd been home," he says, "if I'd been out in the field with him like I was supposed to be, maybe I could have gotten him help faster. He might have lived."

He sees something happen in Véronique's face—a shift, an opening.

"It's taken me a long time to accept that it wasn't my fault," he tells her. "A hell of a long time. But it wasn't my fault he had a heart attack, V. And it's not your fault Pierre crashed."

She reaches for a half-smoked joint in the ashtray, lights it, takes a long steadying inhalation. "It's Callahan's fault," she says, a little wild-eyed.

"The Marlboro Man? What's he got to do with Pierre?"

"He's a rapist."

James sits up and faces her. Puzzle pieces sliding into place. "V?" he says shakily. "Did he rape you? Is that why you slapped me when I touched you?"

"He tried," she confesses, breaking down. "I was doing a delivery. He had a weird edge that day. We were in his room—"

"Why the hell would you go up to his room?"

"That's where he kept his cash. I had no reason not to trust him," she says. "We'd hung out before. I thought he was harmless!"

"What happened?"

"He attacked me. Pushed me against the wall, put his hand up my shirt, pulled my pants down—"

"That fucking bastard."

"He got his pants down, too, but I managed to knee him in the balls before he could . . ." She shudders, remembering. "He was so high—he wasn't able to recover. I hit him with a lamp and ran out."

James wraps his arms around her and touches her hair, trying to keep his anger in check for the moment. "Why didn't you tell me?" he asks her.

"I wanted to," she says, her sobs muffled by his chest.

"Is that why you quit smuggling?" he asks her, putting it all together now, beginning to understand. She didn't quit for him, as he'd thought. She quit because she was almost raped.

She nods wordlessly.

"And you haven't told anyone?"

"I couldn't."

"Not even your uncle?"

"Callahan threatened to go to the police about my uncle's operation. I didn't know what to do."

"You could have told me, V. How can you not have known that?"

"I don't know. I don't know how to do this, obviously. I figured you'd say you told me so."

"What happened with Callahan has nothing to do with Pierre's death."

She shakes her head violently, pushing his hands away. "It does, though. If I hadn't quit—"

"Véronique, if you hadn't quit, you would also be dead."

"Not if I had been driving."

"How do you know it wasn't the other driver's fault? Do you hear me? Pierre's death *is not on you.*"

"He drove high, he drove too fast. He was so reckless, James. He almost killed us both one time. I knew better. I should have warned my uncle!"

"Stop. Please." He takes the joint from her fingers and stubs it out. "You need some sleep."

"I can't sleep."

He reaches into the drawer of her nightstand and pulls out a bottle of sleeping pills. "You will. Take one."

He goes to the bathroom and pours her a glass of

water, places the pill on her tongue, and lies back down beside her. She nestles under his arm, resting her hand on his stomach. He breathes in the smell of her hair and waits for her to fall asleep, still thinking about Callahan.

It's a straightforward two-hour drive to Ottawa. He left Véronique sleeping soundly this morning at six, and he's just now pulling into Ottawa, right before the morning rush hour. It's taken him the entire two hours to calm himself down and rein in his still-smoldering anger. He's here to meet a former colleague for a story on Somalia, so he's got to put the situation with Véronique on ice for the moment and act like a professional.

When he shows up at the Elgin Street Diner, Ed is already in a booth reading the paper. James sits down across from him.

"What brings you to the capital, Phénix?"

"You, my friend."

Ed chuckles. "Right."

Ed Moody used to be a political columnist for the *Citizen* when James was working on the Hill. He became a mentor to James, which James desperately needed in his twenties. He's the dean of journalism at Carleton now, but they've stayed in touch.

"I want to pick your brain about Somalia."

"Can I order breakfast first?"

"My treat."

They order a round of fried eggs and poutine, a side of sausage, coffee, and juice. James has been up all night with Véronique; he's wired and starving. They talk about Ed's job at Carleton, his grown kids, the senators, the usual shit. But James is too tired for small talk and quickly gets to the point.

"What are you hearing about Somalia?" he asks, pulling out his notebook. "You think there's going to be an inquiry?"

"That's the word on the Hill," Ed says. "When a Somali teenager is murdered by a couple of Canadian soldiers, there's got to be an inquiry."

"But one of the them was already convicted and the other one hung himself."

"Those soldiers beat a *kid* to death. People want to know what happened. That shit doesn't happen in a vacuum."

"Is it true their captain offered a case of beer to any of his men who killed a Somali?"

"He's denying it," Ed says, dragging his toast through a puddle of oozing yolk. "Claims he was just telling his men to work hard."

"Will there be more convictions, you think?"

"Nah. The military already has its two lower-rank scapegoats. One's in jail and the other is in a coma. It's perfect. More convictions would only expose the rampant racism in our military."

"There have always been rumors of a white supremacist problem at the base in Petawawa," James says, flagging down the waitress for more coffee.

"So you're covering international politics now?" Ed says, letting out a soft burp.

"I'm doing a piece on the captain of the Airborne Regiment. He's a Quebecker. I'm going to head over to Petawawa later."

"The Airborne Regiment was trained for combat, not peacekeeping," Ed says. "They never should have been in Somalia in the first place."

With the seeds of a good feature planted, James pays for breakfast and gives his old friend a slap on the back. He's got one more stop before he visits the military base at Petawawa.

He knows where Callahan lives because he accompanied Véronique on one of her tobacco deliveries. Her car had broken down, and he offered to drive her. The stupid shit you do for love. They'd loaded his trunk with cases of cigarettes, and off they'd gone, on a romantic little contraband-smuggling holiday. He remembers Callahan as a smug, orange-haired douchebag. He'd thought so then, even before this happened.

He parks around the corner from the dilapidated semidetached house, pulls his hoodie over his head, and jogs up the three front steps to Callahan's door. He can see the blue light of the TV in the window. He's not sure how he's going to handle the roommates if they're home, but he takes his chances. Pounds on the door. A few minutes later, Callahan is standing in the doorway, staring at him with glassy eyes and a questioning look. He obviously has no clue who the hell James is. "What's up, man?" he says.

"You got any weed?"

"Sure, dude. Come on in."

James follows him inside. The place reeks. *Jerry Springer* is on TV. "Your roommates home?" he asks.

Callahan turns around, gives him a quizzical look. "No, man. School's over. They've all gone back to Toronto."

"You're staying for the summer?"

"Yeah, I'm sticking around another year. I make so much money during the school year, I'm not ready to give it up yet."

"Even without the contraband smokes?"

"Hell, yeah. Shrooms and hash are always steady, and now I've got the CDs."

"The CDs?"

"My new side business," he says, opening the closet and pulling out a duffel bag. "How much you need?"

"An ounce."

"I've got some smokes left from my last shipment," he says. "You want? I'll give you a good price."

"Sure. Du Mauriers."

Callahan hands him a carton. "One seventy-five for all of it," he says. "You a TA? You look a little old, dude. No offense."

"None taken, man."

"Have you bought from me before?" Callahan asks, trying to place him. He's not very sharp.

"No," James says. "I haven't. Actually, I *sold* you some, though."

Callahan looks confused. He's too stoned to remember. James can see him sifting through all the dead brain cells.

"Actually, it was my girlfriend who sold them to you," James says calmly.

Now he sees the light go on in Callahan's head. His eyes stretch open, and he takes a step back. "I don't know what she told you—"

In one swift movement, James drops the carton of

cigarettes and grabs Callahan's flabby neck, pushing him back against the closet door. "She told me you tried to rape her, you son of a bitch."

"She wanted it, man. I swear. It was mutual. She—"

James's fist smashes into Callahan's mouth before he can finish his next sentence. "No, she didn't want it," James says, keeping his voice low. "Is this how you had her pinned against the wall?"

"Dude, I swear—"

James punches him again, this time knocking out his tooth. Callahan moans. He's got no fight in him. It's almost too easy. He's stoned and out of shape, no match for James.

"Get the fuck out of my house!" Callahan manages, and James thumps him again, connecting with the bridge of his nose. Blood spurts everywhere, running down Callahan's face and sweatshirt, seeping between the cracks of James's fingers. James is going on pure adrenaline now, his mind blank. He's lost control, can't stop throwing punches. Even as he feels himself going over the edge, his fists keep flying into Callahan's bloody face.

"You tried to rape my girlfriend," James grunts, with a hard punch to Callahan's gut. His hand sinks into Callahan's belly, the impact dulled by a padding of fat. He does it again and again until Callahan doubles over, collapsing on the floor, at which point James grabs him by the neck of his Champion sweatshirt. Callahan is on his knees, gasping for breath. "Please stop," he begs.

James lets go of his collar, and Callahan's head falls back. James stands over him for a few seconds, trying to catch his breath. He'd like to finish him off with a boot to the nuts, but he's starting to regain some self-control.

Callahan lets out a couple of pitiful moans, his head lolling to the side. James kneels down and puts his mouth right up against Callahan's ear. "If you say a word to anyone about their operation, her uncle will kill you. You understand me? You're lucky I'm the one who came to talk to you. If it had been Camil—if he knew that you tried to rape his niece—he'd murder you. He's a Hells Angel, dude, and he would fucking murder you."

He crawls back into bed with Véronique around five in the evening, not even bothering to remove his clothes. She stirs beside him and turns to face him. Without a word, she pulls him on top of her and hurriedly removes his shirt, his pants. She's already naked beneath him. He's hard and eager and penetrates right away. She cries out his name when he enters her, arching her back. She feels so good after all this time. He pushes himself deeper inside her, and she lowers her spine, slowly like a strand of pearls, her nails digging into the back of his neck. "Don't leave me again," she moans.

When they finish, they collapse next to each other, panting, damp. She looks at him, her eyes glistening with tears. Grief sex, he realizes. He did plenty of it after his father died.

"Where'd you go?"

"Ottawa."

She props herself up on one elbow.

"I met with Ed about my Somalia piece."

"Your knuckles are bloody," she says. "You went to see Callahan."

"I had to go to Ottawa at some point to visit Ed. I decided to kill two birds with one stone."

"You didn't kill him, did you?"

He's watching her face, and nothing about her expression suggests she isn't serious. "Of course not."

She's quiet for a long time. "I don't need you to fight my battles."

"I know. I did it for me."

She reaches for his hand and examines the dried blood, his bruised knuckles, kissing each one. She rolls against him, straddling her leg over his body. "Thank you," she says, softening. "I hope you beat the shit out of him."

"He mentioned you're selling him stolen CDs now," James says, unable to stop himself.

She doesn't say anything.

"Is that true?"

"It's none of your business."

"We're in a relationship," he says. "Your criminal life is definitely my business."

"I was just trying to make a little extra cash," she says. "For our future."

"Don't bullshit me. Your income took a hit when cigarette prices went down. A contraband-CD ring was your backup plan, am I right?"

"So? What's wrong with a backup plan?"

"Have you considered just having your regular job like the rest of us? Taking home an honest paycheck?"

"You mean the shitty minimum wage salary I earn at Stan's that wouldn't even cover my rent and utilities if it was my only source of income?"

"I mean any job that's safe and respectable, that won't land you in jail."

"And what? Become an upstanding citizen like you?"

"Your job is being a thief."

"I'd rather be a thief than a poor sanctimonious *cog*."

"I'm hardly a cog. I disseminate information to the public. I'm a truth-seeker."

Véronique laughs at him. "And I steal from the rich to give to the poor. That doesn't make you better than me."

"It makes me *honest*."

"I'm honest," she says. "To the ones who matter."

"You don't have to be like your father, you know. You don't have to live up to his legacy."

"Please, not another sermon."

"You should aspire to more."

"I do aspire to much more," she says. "For myself, my people, this province."

"*Your people*," he scoffs.

"It's easy for you," she says. "With your college education and your English mother and your affluent upbringing."

"And where has crime gotten you?" he asks her. "Where did it get your cousin Pierre?"

He regrets it the moment the words are out. Véronique falls silent, doesn't move.

His mother's words come back to him, and he realizes, locked beneath her long smooth leg, that he has no idea who she really is or how strong her father's blood runs in her veins.

He also knows she's in a lot of pain right now, and

this wasn't the time to discuss her career aspirations. Her grief is still so raw. He should never have brought up the CD smuggling. He has no goddamn self-control. "I'm sorry," he says softly. "V? Baby, I'm so sorry." He pulls her into his arms and holds her, scratching her back.

Her body lies limply against his, but she stays there and eventually falls asleep. As he listens to her jagged breathing late into the night, he vows to keep her safe, whatever he has to do. She needs saving—mostly from herself—and he's got to be the one to do it.

19

February 1995

Huguette picks Elodie up in front of her apartment with an Egg McMuffin and a thermos of coffee. She's wearing dark burgundy lipstick and chewing Clorets gum. Véronique—who's coming along for extra moral support—is already in the back seat with a box of Dunkin' Donuts on her lap.

"Have you seen your brother's article?" Huguette says, handing Elodie the newspaper along with the McDonald's bag. "He wrote about what happened with the attorney general."

"No," Elodie says, barely inside the car. She felt bad last night when James called to ask her if she'd read it. He was excited that it had been picked up by the French papers and translated. She could tell he was looking for her approval, but she couldn't fake it. She didn't have the stamina. Not after what happened this week.

The attorney general announced that no charges would be laid in the 240 criminal complaints made against the Catholic Church and the Quebec medical association. After the Duplessis Orphans Committee failed to push forward the class action suit in the Quebec Court last year, all their hopes had been pinned to the criminal case. And now, after more than a year of waiting, it's come to nothing.

She didn't feel like sharing any of that with her family. She's been spending more time with Huguette and Francine lately, which is easier. There's no effort with them; they just get it. She's come to regard these protests and meetings and court dates as her *real* vocation—the truly meaningful work of her life. Losses notwithstanding, this work continues to invigorate her.

"Read the article now," Huguette says. "Your brother is really on our side. It's good for us to have an ally in the media."

Elodie opens the *Journal de Montreal* and skims the article, skipping most of it. A few sentences leap off the page, mostly for how much they aggravate her.

One wonders how the attorney general can rationalize dismissing so many similar complaints, but this is just one more injustice in a long history of injustices suffered by the now-grown Duplessis orphans. Today, they still struggle to find a place in the society that rejected them years ago. Many of them are battling a number of chronic medical, developmental, and emotional problems, most of which are irreversible. So how does a society begin to compensate for the lost freedom of its own children?

The attorney general doesn't seem to want to risk hurting the nuns' feelings by holding the religious orders accountable for their actions, nor does he want to set a precedent for condemning Catholicism. Instead, he concluded that there was insufficient proof to pursue any of the orphans' complaints in criminal court. Their memories were failing, he said. They'd exceeded the statute of limitations, he said. There was contradictory testimony, he said. As a result, *all* the complainants' statements to the police have been dismissed.

Elodie folds up the paper and tosses it on the floor. She felt differently when she read James's first article about her, a profile piece that made her feel heard one of the few times in her life. Although he cast her very

much as a victim, at least someone was publicly advo-
cating for the Duplessis orphans. She remembers feeling quite hopeful when she read it, like something good
could actually come of its publication. Reading today's
story merely has the effect of pissing her off.

The drive to Granby in the Eastern Townships
usually takes an hour on the Autoroute, but a nasty
clump of traffic on the Champlain Bridge delays them
about twenty minutes. When they arrive at the house
on Terrace Groulx—a new red-brick two-story with
a white portico and white windows—a small crowd
of about two dozen people has already gathered on
the front lawn, picket signs in hand. I AM NOT CRAZY!
APOLOGIZE NOW! DR. DUCEPPE IS A LIAR!

Huguette, Véronique, and Elodie climb out of the
car and grab their signs from the trunk. Elodie's sign
says I AM NOT MENTALLY RETARDED! in dark blue
paint. Huguette's says, ACKNOWLEDGE THE CONSPIRACY
OF LIES! Véronique's says, JUSTICE FOR THE DUPLESSIS
ORPHANS!

The sky is white and clear, the air frigid. Elodie is
bundled in a heavy parka, tuque, scarf, and snowmobile
mittens. The thermos of coffee and the Dunkin' Donuts
are for sustenance. They are prepared to be here all day,
protesting outside the home of Dr. Guillaume Duceppe,
the doctor who sent Elodie to St. Nazarius almost thirty-

five years ago. With a few simple questions she was ill-equipped to answer—could she identify keys, a stove, a wallet?—he determined, with a satisfied swirl of his pen, that she was mentally deficient. So much power he wielded with that pen, enough to alter the course of her entire life. She will never forget his face—his pale beige skin, like a pan of solid bacon fat, his curling moustache and chilling indifference. If only she'd answered differently. Keys, a stove, a wallet. If he dares step outside today, she doesn't know what she'll do.

She marches back and forth alongside Huguette and Véronique, her sisters in solidarity. She isn't sure how Véronique fits in; she only knows she loves the girl. Her youth and vigor motivate Elodie when her own energy lags, and her empathy over the last year has been like a balm.

"Is he inside?" Huguette asks a woman wearing a hand-knit brown hat and silver parka.

"No," she says. "It's just the wife inside."

The woman has aged much the same way many of them have—quickly and unkindly. She looks much older than her forties. Her skin is sallow, pocked.

"How do you know?" Huguette asks her.

"We knocked on their door when we got here," the woman says. "He was already gone. She's probably called him by now and told him to stay away."

"He can't stay away forever," Elodie says.

The woman holds out a gloved hand. "Danielle Daoust."

"I'm Huguette. This is Elodie."

The woman's hand freezes around Elodie's, her grip tightening. Her lower jaw drops as though to say something, but nothing comes out. Her eyes instantly fill with tears, and Elodie isn't sure if it's from the cold wind.

"Elodie from Ste. Sulpice?" the woman says.

"Yes. Do I know you? Were you at St. Nazarius?"

"I was at St. Julien with your friend Claire."

Elodie's free hand drops to her side. *Claire.*

"She always talked about you," Danielle says. "She said you were her only family. There can't be another Elodie, can there?"

"She was my best friend," Elodie says, choking up. "She wound up at St. Julien? Do you remember what year?"

"Same as me, summer of 1958."

"When did she get out? Where is she now? Are you still in touch?"

Danielle rests a hand on Elodie's shoulder. "Claire died," she says softly. "She didn't make it."

Didn't make it.

People with picket signs are still circling purposefully

around them. Elodie realizes she's stopped moving. Her sign is resting on her shoulder, forgotten. Huguette's arm is lightly touching one elbow, Véronique's the other.

"She died at St. Julien?" Elodie manages, trying to keep the uprising of grief locked down.

"No, we both left in '71," Danielle explains. "We were twenty-two. We got an apartment together and started working at the Café Cléopâtre. Another girl from St. Julien got us jobs as go-go dancers. It was all we knew how to do besides clean toilets, and we weren't about to do that ever again."

Elodie shakes her head in disbelief. Her beloved Claire wound up as a stripper. The braids, the missing front teeth. It's not possible. "How did she die?"

"It was an overdose," Danielle says. "She was only twenty-four."

"An accident, or . . ."

Danielle shrugs. "We'll never know."

Elodie hugs her, as though they've known each other all their lives. In some ways they have; they both loved Claire.

"She was a good soul."

"Even when we were little, she had such a big heart," Elodie says. "She was only a year older than me, but she took care of me."

"She talked about you all the time."

"We had no one else but each other."

"She loved you."

"Do you remember her thumbs?" Elodie says, through tears.

"They didn't straighten!"

"She thought that was why no one wanted to adopt her."

"And her deformed toe."

They both laugh and cry at the same time. They hug again like old friends, and then Danielle shuffles off, her picket sign in the air.

"Those nuns deserve to be punished for what they did," Véronique says, putting her arm around Elodie.

Not all the nuns were cruel, though. When Claire and Elodie used to hide under the bed together, Sister Tata would spy them and call them the Little Mice. *Les 'Tis Souris.* But she would leave them be, let them play. Once, she even told one of the newer nuns, "Leave them alone. They're just children having fun."

We will have justice, she silently vows. *We will have justice, Claire.*

20

September 1995

"The first poll shows the No side leading by a landslide," James says with satisfaction, showing Véronique the article in the *Gazette*.

"Get that thing away from me," Véronique responds, unfazed. They're lying in bed—their usual Saturday morning routine—with coffee mugs on the side tables and newspapers spread around them, staining the white sheets inky gray. *Le Devoir* for her, the *Gazette* for him.

A referendum date has been set for October 30, which will decide once and for all whether or not Quebec will separate from Canada. James and Véronique are both giddy, for completely different reasons. They each think their side is going to win, and they're damn excited.

"Promise me you won't let politics get in the way of us?" he says.

"Why would I?" she says. "As long as you're not a poor loser, we'll be fine."

She moved into his place when her lease was up in July, and so far it's been harmonious. They chose his apartment because it's on a better street—the lovely Ste. Famille, with its narrow road and leafy canopy of trees. It's also a lot bigger. He occupies the top two floors of a gray-brick triplex with large bay windows, two large bedrooms—they use one as a shared office— two bathrooms, and a spacious, renovated kitchen that has a dishwasher. The fact that James also lives in the Plateau has made the transition that much easier for her. She can still get her groceries at Quatre Frères on St. Laurent and get her bagels from Fairmount. They keep joking that if they survive the referendum, they'll be together forever.

"What does your little nationalist newspaper say about it?" he says. "Surely even the *Le Devoir* can't spin these poll results."

Véronique slips out of bed. "Don't worry about our side," she says, putting a plaid shirt over her white T-shirt. She has a good feeling about this referendum. After a decade of failed constitutional talks, the French are more pissed off with Canada than ever, and with a new charismatic leader at the helm, she's certain they can win.

"I predict a 70–30 victory for the No side," he says.

She grabs a pair of his socks from the floor and puts them on her bare feet. "It's freezing in here. You want toast?"

"Bagel."

She leaves him in bed and pads downstairs to the kitchen. She's happy here. James offered to let her paint the place light blue—it used to be beige with brown trim. Now it has a softer, more feminine vibe. Their stuff has merged seamlessly—all of their books lined up together on his Ikea Billy shelves, her candle-holders and plants with his art and family heirlooms, a new rug. Her couch is in their office, and they use her antique wrought iron bed. Previously, James slept on a mattress on the floor. She gave away her hand-me-down dishes and pots to the Salvation Army; his are all brand-new, a housewarming gift from his mother. Somehow, it works. More importantly, *they* work. She's felt more like herself in the last couple of months than she has in a long time.

She still grieves for Pierre. It's been almost a year and a half since the accident, which sometimes feels like forever and other times like it was yesterday. You don't lose someone close to you and bounce back within a few months. She has enough common sense to know that grief is deep and savage, will ebb and flow throughout her lifetime, but there are days lately when she can think about him and it doesn't feel like a knife in her heart.

Getting out of her apartment was a start. She also quit Stan's. After Pierre died, she couldn't face going back. She would always remember her parents showing up there and announcing that he was dead.

She's still smuggling, though much less frequently. She reached a truce with James. She does one run a month to Billy's Marina and makes all her deliveries with Marc. She doesn't transport alone anymore. There were a lot of negotiations and ultimatums—not just with James, but also with Uncle Camil. She never told Camil about Callahan, but she did make it clear she would never go back to Ottawa. Camil wanted to know why, but all she said was she didn't trust him, it was too far, and she preferred to stay in Quebec.

Camil was pissed off. Callahan is one of his best distributers. He pressured her for months about it, but she kept refusing. She also told him she wanted Marc to start doing the transports with her, as a precaution. He agreed, figuring it was a good idea to train Marc anyway. Marc had already started smuggling the year before. Camil brought him in right away to replace

Pierre. He even asked Véronique to teach him English. Marc is a smart kid, a hell of a lot steadier and more reliable than Pierre was. He's the one who used to pick Pierre up out of the snowbanks when Pierre would pass out drunk at the end of a night of partying. She misses Pierre, but she feels a lot safer with Marc, even if he is only seventeen.

She sells mostly weed and booze—her uncle pays sixty bucks for a case of twelve bottles of Rikaloff vodka on the reservation, and she sells each bottle for twelve to fifteen bucks, depending on the customer. It's pretty lucrative, given it's really just an add-on to supplement the weed. Her uncle always says, "Even smugglers need to upsell."

She's still selling CDs, too, which is booming. She doesn't even need to work at Stan's to do it. Roger has a partner inside the warehouse now, and they've been able to double their inventory. All Véronique has to do is pick up the CDs at the locker and distribute them.

James thinks she's only smuggling booze. He doesn't know about the weed, and he assumes the CD thing ended when she quit Stan's. Although he doesn't like her smuggling at all—hates it, in fact—it was either accept it for the time being or lose her. She made her case around family loyalty and her obligation to her grieving uncle, and agreed to cut back to once a month—which frankly hasn't had any impact on her revenue—and to extricate herself when Marc was fully trained. That was over a year ago and she's not quite ready to walk away yet. The money is too good, and although she loves her free time, it's really more about her *freedom*. Meaning she's free to live her life on her own terms, apart from society's underpaid, undervalued cogs and minions.

She did have to make one other concession to get James off her back, and that was to go back to school. She quit after high school, not bothering to go on to university. Originally, she was going to take a year off and decide what to do, but when the offer came to smuggle cigarettes, she was relieved. University could wait, she figured, if she ever went at all. But the more she thinks about it now—and having made this promise to James—she thinks it's not such a bad idea. Fidel Castro and Karl Marx studied law in university, and Che Guevara went to medical school to become a physician. School may be an institution, but she's well aware it's one that breeds great revolutionaries.

She's twenty-five now. Without a degree, her options will be limited in a new independent Quebec. She wants to be part of the change. She doesn't want to just passively watch it unfold. More and more often lately, she imagines being able to say to her future children: *I was there when we voted to separate. I helped build this country.* She wants to leave her mark, just as her father yearned to leave his. She's even considered the possibility that she might be able to do it without breaking the law.

She applied to the political science program at a couple of local universities and has been taking night courses over the past year to make up some missing credits. This seems to have appeased James, and in return, he's adopted a "don't ask, don't tell" policy around her smuggling. If all goes well, she'll start college next September.

The Callahan incident is locked in a mental vault. Elodie said, "You can't bury something that's still alive." That may be so, but she's sure as hell trying. The memory may not be buried, but it's shoved somewhere out of the way. For the most part, she's feeling optimistic. Living with James in this beautiful, sun-filled apartment feels like a new beginning. She signed up to volunteer for the referendum's Yes campaign, which has made her father delirious with pride. Yesterday he called to tell her to do one hour a week of basic cleaning at the campaign office. "Don't wait for them to ask you," he told her. "Just do it. Pick up a broom and sweep. Empty the garbage cans. Clean the toilets. Even our party leader used to clean the toilets with us at the RIN headquarters."

"I know, Dad."

"Just don't wait to be asked. The campaign staff and the other volunteers will respect you. Parizeau might even notice you. Also, if you can bring in a vacuum and your own supplies, do it. It may not seem important, but it is. Trust me."

"Why don't you volunteer with me and you can clean the toilets?" she said.

He laughed, but didn't offer to join her. The first meeting is today.

She removes two bagels from the double toaster, smothers them with butter and cream cheese, and returns to their bedroom on the second floor.

James moans with pleasure when she enters the bed.

"Is that for me or the bagels?" she says.

"Both."

They eat bagels in bed, their legs entwined, sesame seeds spilling onto the sheets around them.

"Would your father be disappointed in you?" she asks him, out of the blue. "That you're going to vote No?"

She knows Gabriel was a separatist. Nowhere else do those two little words—Yes and No—say more about a person politically than in Montreal.

"Probably," James says. "But I have a mind of my own. He would have respected my choice."

The phone rings and James answers. "It's your uncle," he says, frowning.

Véronique gets out of bed and takes the call in the hallway. She can hear James sighing as she closes the bedroom door behind her.

"Véro?" Camil barks.

"Is everything okay?"

"It's frosh week in Ottawa," he says. "It starts Monday. I need you and Marc to do a delivery."

"*Mon'onc*—"

"I didn't push last year because it was so soon after Pierre, but we can't walk away from all that money. Those kids spend like crazy, especially this week."

"No."

"Véronique, please. Why are you being so irrational?"

"Send Marc. He doesn't need me."

"Of course he needs you. He's never met Callahan."

"So what? I'd never met him either the first time I went."

"Marc doesn't speak English."

"He can get by."

"No, he can't! Not in Ontario. Can't you do it this one time for me? Introduce him to Callahan?"

"No. I do plenty for you, *mon'onc*."

"And you make good money for it."

"I'm trying to get out of this, not get deeper in. I'm not doing any more universities."

"You don't care at all about the money?"

"We make plenty of money," she says impatiently. "I have to go. I'll see you next weekend."

She hangs up, not even waiting for him to say goodbye. James is grinning when she gets back into bed.

The Yes campaign office is in Parizeau's Outremont riding, a pleasant walk up her old street to Parc Avenue, and then onto bustling Bernard Street. She passes clusters of brunchers, enjoying their eggs and cappuccinos on patios, knowing these are the last rays of Indian summer.

Coming through the door of the second-floor office above the Cinq Saisons supermarket, Véronique is warmly welcomed by an older woman, about fifty, wearing a yellow T-shirt with bold blue writing: OUI ET ÇA DEVIENT POSSIBLE.

Yes and it becomes possible.

Véronique is given a name tag to stick on her shirt. She can see right away that she's one of the youngest volunteers, along with one other twenty-something guy. The other volunteers, about two dozen of them, are older; old enough to still vividly remember the loss of the 1980 referendum. This one is their redemption, as it is her parents'. The woman in the yellow T-shirt asks them to sit down on plastic folding chairs that have been set up haphazardly around the room. She remembers similar chairs, pea soup green, from her grandparents' apartment in the seventies.

"*Yes and it becomes possible!*" the woman bellows, startling Véronique.

Everyone applauds enthusiastically, a couple of people whistle. "My name is Céline, and I'm one of the campaign workers for the Outremont riding. Welcome!"

More clapping.

"There's coffee and donuts by the bathroom," Céline says, and Véronique turns toward the back of the room, where an abundant display of Dunkin' Donuts is laid out between two decrepit coffee dispensers, probably relics from the 1980 campaign. She notices the young guy is watching her—youth latching onto youth, a life preserver in a sea of the middle-aged. She smiles. He tips his head. He's got long hair parted in the middle, hippie-style. He's thin and pale, wears glasses. His sweater is ratty, unraveling at the neck and sleeves. She feels a certain solidarity with him, a guy his age who's also here on a Saturday to volunteer for a cause she herself is so passionate about. Go separatists!

"There are so many ways to help out," Céline is saying. "You can do whatever you're comfortable with, no one is here to force you to do anything. I'm going to read off a list of jobs—"

She looks down at her clipboard. "Everybody's favorite, the block walk," she announces to a roar of groans. "You walk around different neighborhoods, knock on doors, and leave a door hanger if no one is home. If someone is home, you engage in conversation. We'll give you scripts for the phone bank and the block walks. Feel free to ad-lib. The script is just a recommendation.

"Then we have the phone bank," she continues. "This is pretty straightforward. You just go down a list making cold calls. If you're good with numbers, there's data entry. We need people to log all our donations. Accuracy is very important, so if you're dyslexic, pick another job."

Everyone laughs.

"For those of you with cars, we need people to deliver lawn signs. We're going to get lots of calls from people who want signs, and we also want to reach out to potential supporters with prime property for our biggest signs—residential or retail corners, key streets. Just make sure you wear comfortable shoes! And if none of that appeals to you, you can distribute handouts or clean the office. No one here is above cleaning. We're all working toward the same goal: sovereignty!"

More cheering and applause.

"For those of you who were involved in the 1980 campaign," Céline says, her voice rising and cracking, "this is *our* time! And for those of you too young to remember"—she gazes directly at Véronique—"may you never have to suffer the disappointment we suffered fifteen years ago."

The volunteers are on their feet now, applauding and whistling like it's a pep rally. Even Véronique is standing, spellbound, clapping with these strangers with whom she already feels the deepest kinship.

"We're going to train you today in all the jobs," Céline says. "But to really be effective, we need you to show up on a regular basis. We need to be able to count on all of you to help us win this one!"

Véronique offers to start by delivering lawn signs and handing out campaign material at the colleges and universities. Her mandate is to engage Montreal's youth—the students, the dropouts, the slackers, the workers. "You're looking for the ambivalent ones," Céline tells her. "No need to waste precious time on die-hard separatists. We're looking for the people on the fence, the ones who aren't sure. That's where you can be most effective. Your job is to convince them they will have the brightest future in an independent Quebec. Master of our own domain and all that."

Véronique nods. Her partner is the young guy. His

name is Louis. They discuss their strategy over maple donuts and watery coffee. "I have a car," he tells her. "I can pick you up if you like. We can start with the signs. What days are good for you?"

"Any day," she says.

"Me, too. I work nights."

They decide on next Friday. Before they leave, Céline hands them each a yellow T-shirt with the Yes campaign slogan—YES AND IT BECOMES POSSIBLE!

Finally, after a long day of training, they set off for home, little soldiers of the revolution.

When she gets back to the apartment, weary and exhilarated, James is at his laptop, typing away. She kisses the back of his neck.

"Hey. How was it?" he asks her, pulling her onto his lap.

"Amazing. There was this feeling of excitement in the room," she says. "This energy and camaraderie. I totally get what my dad must have felt back in the sixties."

"Please don't kidnap anyone."

"I can't promise," she jokes. "What're you working on?"

"A twenty-five-year commemorative piece about the October Crisis."

She groans.

"The anniversary is coming up next month."

"Yes. I know."

"I'm doing a four-part series, and I need to ask you a favor," he says, taking her hands. She knows exactly what he's going to ask, and she glares at him, waiting.

"Let me talk to your dad," he says.

She gets up off his lap, annoyed.

"Please?" He tips his head, looking up at her with pleading eyes. "Just ask him if I can interview him. I know it's for an English wire, and it will probably be printed in the *Gazette*—among other Anglo papers— but think about it, V. He'd get to tell his story to the people who need to hear it the most: the English. The separatists already know why he did what he did. They're already sympathetic to him. The English don't understand. *I* don't understand, and I'm French Canadian. Your father is still perceived as a villain. I just want him to tell his side of things."

She's quiet, listening.

"And yes, this would be really good for my career, too," he adds. "I'm not going to pretend it wouldn't be. An interview with one of the original FLQ members? I've wanted to do this for a long time. Will you at least ask him?"

"I don't want you to paint him as a monster."

"I wouldn't. I'm going to be objective."

"Objective," she mutters. "Like you're objective about the situation with the Duplessis orphans? Or the separatists?"

"The October Crisis story will be in your father's own words. I will present his version of events as objectively as I can."

"That's what scares me," she says.

"Please, *mon amour*?"

Maybe because she's still on a high from her day at the Yes campaign, or maybe because she believes James, that it could be an opportunity for her father to finally explain his side of the story, that James could be the one to exonerate him after all these years of silence . . .

"I'll talk to him," she says.

"Really? Are you serious?" He kisses her face, his lips running up and down the side of her hairline, her jaw, her neck. "You sure?"

"I said I would talk to him. Don't get your hopes up."

21

"It's a paradoxical case," the appellate judge says to the gallery. "Both the plaintiffs and the defendants desperately want to be heard. One claims injustice, the other seeks to defend their actions and point of view. The court has already determined that a class action suit is not the best way forward for a complex matter such as this one. There does remain the inalienable right of each plaintiff to pursue individual recourse, but this task, to my mind, is next to impossible."

Elodie's body is rigid, bracing against the blow of another disappointment.

"I think we've reached the end of our judicial limits here," the judge concludes. "While I do respect your right to address the court, I believe this is not the appropriate venue to resolve this issue."

Outside the Palais de Justice, Elodie gropes around in her purse in search of a cigarette. Her hands are shaking.

"Elo!" Véronique calls after her. "Wait!"

"I'm sorry," Elodie says, lighting her cigarette. She sucks on it to calm herself down, expels a breath, and takes another drag. "I couldn't stay in there another second. The judge didn't even consider our appeal!"

"I know."

"What if no judge ever will? Are we stupid to think we might get justice in any of the courts?"

"No, of course not. That judge was awful," Véronique says. "But it's not over."

"He didn't even *consider* our appeal," Elodie repeats, pacing in front of the building.

There are no cameras here today, just another quiet loss. The public is far more interested in the referendum these days than in the ongoing misfortunes of the Duplessis orphans.

"Why don't we go out for lunch?" Véronique suggests.

"I'm not hungry."

"Come on," she insists. "Let's go to Old Montreal and walk around like tourists."

Reluctantly, Elodie lets Véronique lead her by the

hand along Rue Notre Dame. "What do you want to hang around a middle-aged woman like me for?"

"I guess I've got a middle-aged soul," Véronique says, and they both laugh.

They turn onto Place Jacques Cartier, which is full of people milling around the artisans' tents. "My mom and I used to come here and get our caricatures done," Véronique says. "I'd always send mine to my dad instead of real pictures."

"I'm sure even your caricature was pretty."

"Let's get one together."

"A caricature? Of *me*? What do I need that for?"

"It's a fun souvenir. Come on."

Once again, Elodie lets herself be pulled through the square, weaving through all the tourists, until Véronique stops at an orange-tented booth wallpapered in caricatures of famous people—President Clinton, Madonna, Jacques Parizeau. A sign above Barbra Streisand's face says: 5 MINUTES—$10.

They sit side by side on two stools while the artist sketches quietly, his head tipped to one side, his lips parted slightly in concentration. His hand moves like a conductor's, flicks and strokes and flourishes, and when he's done, he rips the page from the easel and proudly holds it up for them to see.

They both burst out laughing at how ridiculous it

is—Véronique with her messy hair, nose piercing, and doll's face; Elodie with the long, droopy features of a basset hound. Véronique pays the artist and gives Elodie the sketch.

"He made me look so sad," Elodie says, studying her exaggeratedly forlorn eyes in the drawing.

"It's just a caricature," Véronique says. "It's supposed to be exaggerated."

They decide to have lunch at La Grande Terrasse, a tourist spot in the center of the square. They sit beneath the red awning on the heated terrace, reveling in the fall weather. They order burgers and beer. The beer arrives in frosted mugs, just the way Elodie likes it.

"You know what pisses me off?" Elodie says. "When the judge said the court is not the 'appropriate venue' for resolving this issue. Where the hell *is* the appropriate venue then?"

"You have other options, you know."

"Like?"

"He said you could seek individual recourse."

"What does that even mean?"

"You can sue privately."

"With what money?"

"Maybe you could find a lawyer who would do it for a percentage of the damages."

Elodie moves the French fries around on her plate.

"There are other ways to get justice," Véronique says. "You could confront the nuns who abused you."

"Isn't it obvious after the past couple of years that the nuns don't think they did anything wrong?"

"What about the doctor who sent you to St. Nazarius? You know where he lives."

"We already picketed in front of his house. He wasn't even there. He went into hiding."

"He can't hide forever," Véronique says. "Stake out his house. Make him listen to what he did to you."

"He knows what he did to me," she says, remembering how cold a man he was, how aloof he'd been when he interviewed her. "It's been all over the news. Bruno even wrote a book about it."

"He doesn't know *your* story, Elodie. It would be cathartic for you to tell him."

"I don't know, Véro. You have to understand, when you're a bastard, people from his generation think you're subhuman. In their eyes, we're all worthless. They don't think they did anything wrong treating us the way they did."

"Don't you want to ask him why he made up that false diagnosis?" Véronique persists. "*What was in it for him?* Did he know what he was sentencing you to? Doesn't some part of you need to know?"

Yes. No. Of course she wants to know, almost as much as she doesn't. "I'm not sure I'm brave enough."

"Yes, you are," Véronique says. "You're the bravest goddamn person I know."

Maybe Véronique's right. She's come this far. Maybe she should continue to attack from all sides.

After lunch, they stroll through Old Montreal while Véronique tells her about her volunteer work for the Yes campaign, her new friend Louis, and her courses at school. The levity of the afternoon is a gift.

They stop at a souvenir shop on Rue St. Amable, and Véronique buys Elodie a blue-and-white key chain that says TABARNAK. They continue on past the train tracks to the Old Port, where they lean over the guardrail and watch the boats in the harbor.

"What's that ugly building?" Elodie asks, pointing across the water. "It looks like St. Nazarius."

"Silo 5. Boats used to transport grains into this port. It closed last year."

"What are they going to do with it now?"

"Who knows? Condos, probably."

"Sometimes it's hard for me to believe I grew up in this city," Elodie says, gazing out at the St. Lawrence River. "I had no idea it was so beautiful, that this river was always flowing. Boats were coming and going, tourists were walking along these cobblestone streets eating ice cream cones and getting caricatures. I had no idea anything existed outside that place."

"Well, you're in the world now, my friend."

By the time Elodie arrives at the deli for her night shift, the sky is dark and her mood is brighter for having let Véronique distract her all afternoon. The caricature is tucked inside her purse, and the TABARNAK key chain is already hanging from her keys.

She changes into her uniform and pours herself a cup of coffee. She's working with Rachel today, Lenny's grand-niece. Rachel goes to McGill University and only works part-time. She has an attitude, like she's better than everyone else, or at least better than Elodie, even though she's only nineteen. Elodie will only speak with her in French, to remind her who has seniority.

"Are you voting Yes?" Rachel asks her as soon as Elodie emerges from the back room.

"I'm not voting."

"How can you not vote?" Rachel says, indignant. "Don't you realize how important this referendum is?"

"I'm not sure Quebec should separate."

"That's exactly why you have to vote NO!"

"But I respect the people who think it's for the best."

"Elodie, seriously? That can't be your reason for not voting?"

How can Elodie explain to this brat that even though she is a forty-five-year-old Quebec-born woman, she does not feel qualified to vote in such an important referendum? She doesn't understand enough about either side's motivations to cast her vote. She doesn't even get the full implication of what separation would mean, and she's too embarrassed to ask.

Besides, she's not invested in any outcome. She doesn't consider herself to be a proper citizen of the province. These language squabbles have never mattered to Elodie. In fact, caring about this sort of thing has always struck her as a luxury.

"My dad says the economy will collapse if there's a separation," Rachel says. "You don't seriously want Quebec to break away from Canada, do you? Forget keeping your job. This deli won't survive."

A customer walks in then, and Elodie is relieved when he starts heading toward her section. He's old and frail, leaning heavily on a cane as he shuffles over to a booth. He's wearing a Red Sox baseball cap, which is not unusual in Montreal. He settles into the booth with some difficulty and looks up, presumably in search of a waitress. They make eye contact.

Elodie approaches him, hands him a menu. "Can I get you a drink?" she asks him. She knows to start off in English when she sees a Boston cap. No Montrealer would ever be caught dead in one.

"My God," the man says.

"Are you okay?" she asks. He looks unwell, pale and weak.

"I . . . My God. I don't . . ." He shakes his head, removes his glasses, which are fogging up. She can see he's crying. "It's *you*."

She's blank. Doesn't recognize him.

"Elodie. Like *Melody* without the *M*."

She nods, glances down at her name tag.

"You're still here."

This sort of thing happens when you've worked at the same place for more than two decades. She has no idea who he is, but she tries not to be rude about it. "Twenty-five years," she says. "They give me a free smoked meat sandwich on my anniversary." Her standard joke.

"I'm Dennis," he says.

Dennis? It means nothing to her at first. Dennis. Dennis. Her mind is churning. And then it comes to her. "*Mon Dieu*," she breathes. "It can't . . . Dennis?"

He's bobbing his head, wiping his eyes. "We met right before I left for basic training."

Elodie calls out to Rachel that she's taking a break.

"You just started your shift," Rachel mutters.

Elodie ignores her and sits down opposite Dennis, trying to steady her breathing. "I didn't recognize you," she says. "I'm sorry." All she can think is, *Are we this old?*

He can't be much older than forty-five, but he looks closer to sixty-five. Drawn, feeble. He removes his cap and sets it down beside the napkin dispenser. He's completely bald. His cheeks are sunken, off-white. She remembers the boy with the clear blue eyes, round pink cheeks, impeccable white teeth, and buzz cut. How cruel time is, she thinks.

"I'm dying," he says, as nonchalant as if he's just asked her to pass the ketchup. "Stage 4 soft-tissue sarcoma."

Elodie winces out loud, not meaning to.

"My job in Vietnam was loading herbicides onto airplanes and choppers," he says. "You ever hear of Agent Orange?"

"No."

"They don't know for sure that's what caused my cancer," he says. "But I do."

"My mother's father died of cancer, probably from pesticide," she tells him, in her terrible English. "He had a seed store."

Dennis nods sadly. "They stopped using Agent Orange in '71, but only after I'd been handling it for most of my tour."

"I'm sorry." She doesn't know what else to say.

"Hey, the way I look at it, I should have died in 'Nam. God gave me an extra twenty-five-year bonus."

"How do you still believe in God?"

"I didn't for a long time after I got back from Vietnam. But eventually, after my daughters were born, I started to believe again. My wife's been dragging me to church for twenty years. I guess it's rubbed off."

"How many daughter you have?"

"Four."

"Four." She smiles, genuinely happy for him. "What are their names?"

"Katy, Finn, Jennifer, and Denise. All redheads."

"There's so much I want to ask you," she says. "I don't know where to start."

"Ask. Now's your chance."

"What's your full name?"

"Dennis Finbar Duffy."

"And your wife?"

"Suzanne. She's back at the hotel. I had to beg her to let me walk the few blocks over here by myself."

"Why you came back here now?" she asks him, trying to keep her emotions in check as the memories of that weekend come flooding back. Memories of his kindness, his playfulness, the tender way he took her virginity. The gift he gave her. Nancy.

"I've been back once before," he says. "I brought the whole family. Must have been spring of '84 because we came to see Boston play Montreal in the playoffs. We lost. Ended up getting swept that series. I brought them here to the deli for smoked meat, but you weren't here. I didn't expect you to be."

"Did you tell them about me?"

"Are you kidding? No. But I've thought about you many times, especially during my tour. When I first got back, I thought about coming to see you."

"Why didn't you?"

"I just never got around to it. And then I met Suzanne. I guess I didn't want to ruin my memory of our experience together, you know?"

She nods.

"It was such a magical weekend," he says. "I didn't want to discover that we actually had nothing in common. We probably would have tried to have a long-distance relationship and it would have fallen apart, as they do. It would have been too disappointing."

"I know exactly what you mean."

"Instead, I have this perfect memory of a beautiful French Canadian girl. It's really special to me."

He doesn't know how special, she thinks.

"It was the last time I was . . . *myself.*"

"What do you mean?"

"I was never the same obnoxious, carefree kid again," he says. "The guy you met that weekend? He didn't come back from 'Nam. Which is kind of why I came back here today. This was the last place I got to be that kid."

"And for a Montreal smoked meat sandwich."

"That, too," he says, chuckling. "It's good to see this place again, relive that memory. Never in a million years did I expect to find you here." He shakes his head, incredulous. "If this isn't one of God's little miracles, I don't know what is."

"How long you have to live?" she asks him.

"Not more than two or three months. Maybe weeks even."

She was better off believing he'd died over there.

"I've had a really good life, Elodie. I promise."

She wipes her nose with a napkin from the dispenser.

"Have *you?*" he asks her. "Had a good life?"

She looks up at him. For a split second, she almost tells him about Nancy. But then she thinks about Nancy in all this, about how painful it would be for her to discover her father didn't die in Vietnam after all, but that he's dying now. What if he passes away before she ever gets a chance to meet him?

"Yes," she answers. "I've had a very good life."

"I'm glad," he says, smiling. He still has the nice white teeth and freckles. "Any kids?"

"One daughter," she tells him, leaving it there. Maybe it's the wrong decision to keep it from him, but it feels like the only way to protect Nancy. Besides, he's already got four girls; he doesn't need another.

"How about that smoked meat?" he says. "I've stopped treatment. My appetite is coming back."

22

On Friday, Véronique meets Louis at the corner of Pine and St. Laurent and slides into his red Pontiac Acadian. It smells of weed, French fries, and a faint masking odor of pine-scented air freshener. There's marijuana shake on the floor at her feet, several crumpled McDonald's bags on the back seat, and Black Sabbath is blaring from the tinny car stereo.

"The signs are in my trunk," he says. "You got the addresses?"

She can barely hear him above Ozzy Osbourne belting out "Sweet Leaf." "Here," she says, pulling out the list Céline emailed her. "The first house is a corner lot on Ninth and Bélanger in Rosemont."

"La Petite Patrie," he says, pulling out onto Pine Avenue. "*On y'va!*"

He roars north on St. Laurent, past shops and restaurants and a sprinkling of offices on the top floors of old buildings. Through one window, she observes a row of heads perched over their computers. The poor sheep, stuck in an office all day. She experiences a sudden surge of joy in the realization that she will never be one of them.

After three or four houses in the East End, they get a good rhythm going. Louis sticks the H-wire stand into the grass and Véronique slides the sign onto the frame. It's still warm for autumn, and they work quickly and efficiently under the September sun. Louis sings while he works, everything from Gilles Vigneault's nationalist anthem, "Gens du Pays," to the old French Canadian folk songs their grandparents used to sing. He sings in a deep, old-timey voice, and Véronique finds herself laughing along for a good part of the day, occasionally joining in when she knows the words.

Every now and then, someone passing by gives them a thumbs-up or shouts out, "*Quebec libre!*" An elderly woman even comes out of her house to hand them homemade banana bread wrapped in tinfoil. "You two give me hope for Quebec's youth," she tells them, shaking their hands. "I admire your commitment."

As the sky turns pink behind them and the air cools

down to a more seasonal temperature, they decide to grab a beer at Bar Bernard, a dark tavern on the outskirts of the Plateau.

"I used to live above this place," Louis tells her once they're seated. "Every weekend I'd have to listen to their shitty cover band until three o'clock in the morning. It was like they were playing in my bedroom. Their last song of the night was always 'The End,' by the Doors."

"Where do you live now?"

"A few blocks north. It's a shithole, but at least it's not above a bar. You?"

"The Plateau. On Ste. Famille."

"Nice street," he comments. "And you don't work, you said?"

She realizes he must see her as some kind of spoiled princess, someone whose daddy probably pays her rent on one of the prettiest streets in the Plateau. "I work," she says. "I just have extremely flexible hours."

"What do you do?"

"I'm a bookkeeper."

He looks impressed.

"I'm going back to school in the fall to study polisci." Even as she says it, she likes the sound of it more and more. "What about you? I assume you're interested in politics?"

"No, I'm interested in Quebec becoming an independent country, that's all."

"That's politics."

Louis shrugs. "I just want a better life for myself. My interest in this referendum is purely selfish."

"I don't think it's selfish to want a better life."

"Do you remember the '80 referendum?" he asks her.

"I do. I was only ten, but I remember how divisive it was."

"I was thirteen," he says. "My parents were fanatic separatists. They volunteered for the Yes campaign; we had a sign bigger than our house on the front lawn. They brought me to the Paul Sauvé Arena to watch the results come in with all the Yes supporters. I remember when it was official that we'd lost and Lévesque started singing 'Gens du Pays,' I looked up at my mom and dad and they were both bawling. I'd never seen my dad cry before. He was heartbroken."

Louis crushes his cigarette in the ashtray and lights another. His poutine is untouched.

"You said they *were* fanatic separatists?"

"My dad died of lung cancer in '89," he says. "My mom is still alive. She'll vote Yes, but she doesn't care about it the way she did fifteen years ago. She lost her fight. The goddamn English crushed her spirit."

Louis is angry—she can tell from spending just one

day with him. James also lost his father, but his pain is more diffused, expresses itself primarily as sadness. Louis is more like her father; their past pain is stored as resentment and blame, festering below the surface until it's eventually expelled in bitter rants or, in her father's case, violence.

"My father is Léo Fortin," she says, catching him by surprise.

"Your dad is *the* Léo Fortin?" he cries. "October Crisis Léo Fortin?"

She nods silently, savoring his pleasure.

"You're Léo Fortin's daughter?"

"I am."

"*Tabarnak!*" he cries, incredulous. After a long string of profanity, he says, "I have to meet him."

"Sure," she says, smiling. "Anytime."

"What are you doing tonight?" he asks her, and she realizes she hasn't mentioned James yet.

"My boyfriend and I have plans," she fibs. She's actually driving up to Ste. Barbe tonight.

"Oh, right. No problem," he says, looking embarrassed.

They split the bill and leave the bar. It's dark when they get outside. "I had a great day," he says.

"Me, too."

The lake is perfectly still tonight, the air warm and windless as she steers the boat toward her uncle's dock. Next time she makes a run to the reservation, it will be much colder, the water rougher, moodier. The weather changes dramatically from September to October, so she's enjoying the last sweet breaths of summer.

She looks back at Marc, who's calmly scanning the lake. The gun is clenched between his legs, his broad shoulders pressed against the boat. She feels safe with Marc on lookout. He's remarkably confident for his age, always poised and steady. He's well-spoken, bright. Billy and Tug took to him right away. They're friendlier with him than they ever were with Pierre. Véronique suspects they never trusted Pierre.

She also enjoys his company when they're making deliveries. Sometimes they have to drive a couple of hours there and back, and the time passes much more quickly with Marc. He has a great sense of humor, doesn't take himself too seriously. It worries her that Camil is grooming him to take over the drug-smuggling operation, which will eventually include cocaine. Camil's been talking about it for years. Weed and booze are small-time. The cigarettes were one thing—lucrative but with far less severe consequences—but the big money is in coke. She doesn't want Marc to waste his life selling drugs. She feels motherly toward him. He could be anything—a lawyer, an entrepreneur, a great leader. He has that sort of mind, as well as tremendous likeability.

James always says to her, "You're better than this life." It always offends her, but that's exactly how she feels about Marc. She would be devastated if he wound up in jail, or like Pierre.

When she pulls up to her uncle's, Marc hops out and ties the boat to the dock. Camil appears, and they start unloading the crates of booze and packages of weed. Nothing has changed since the contraband-cigarette days. They work in silence, quick and steadfast, grave. It takes them about half an hour to get everything inside the boathouse. Camil won't look at Véronique, hasn't uttered a word to her all night. He's still furious with her, punishing her because she won't go to Ottawa.

When they're finished, he locks up and starts heading back to the house without saying goodbye.

"He's giving me the silent treatment now?" she says to Marc.

"He has no one to send to Ottawa. He's upset."

"Are you?"

"Upset with you?" He shrugs. "No. I don't get why you won't, but you must have your reasons."

"I do."

He throws his arm over her shoulder, and they walk down to the lake. He's about a foot taller than she, and she practically has to lift her arm over her head to reach his shoulder.

"You want to swim?" he asks her. "Water's pretty warm."

"I'm not in the mood," she says, sitting down cross-legged on the dock. She'd like to be on her way home, but she's sleeping here tonight so they can head out first thing in the morning. They've got deliveries all day, from Repentigny to Trois-Rivières and then back via Sorel. It's going to be a long day.

Marc undresses down to his boxers and dives in, his body lean and straight, piercing the water with barely a splash. When he pops up, he lets out a whoop. "That's fucking cold!" he says, hoisting himself onto the dock.

He dresses quickly, putting his hoodie on and then his jeans. "It feels good, though," he says, and his eyes are twinkling in the moonlight, his lashes wet and long. *He's too good for this life.*

"Let's go for a beer," he says. "I'm not in the mood for Camil's sulking."

"Me neither," she says, getting up.

They drive over to Brasserie Olympique in Coteau-du-Lac, which is full of kids about Marc's age. He knows them all. He walks in like a pied piper, greeting everyone, kissing the cheeks of swoony girls. They sit down near the pool tables, and within minutes, the waitress—an older woman with dyed-purple hair—delivers a pitcher of draft and two glasses, and asks him if he wants any food.

"I'll have spaghetti," he says. "I'm starving."

The waitress rumples his hair affectionately and disappears. Marc pours them each a beer. He chugs his down in one gulp. When he notices Véronique's stunned expression, he says, "Smuggling makes me thirsty. All that stress and tension on the boat? This helps me relax."

"You feel stressed on the boat?"

"Of course."

"It doesn't show."

"Doesn't mean I'm not shitting my pants."

He pours himself another glass. "So why won't you do the Ottawa runs anymore?" he asks her. "I know there's a reason."

"I don't like the college students," she tells him. "They're entitled assholes. The last time I was there—"

"What?"

"I just got a bad feeling."

"From who? Callahan?"

"How do you know about Callahan?"

"From my dad. I know he's one of our best guys."

Véronique finishes her beer, and Mark fills her up again.

"What we do is dangerous," she says. "Really fucking dangerous."

"Yeah, and?"

Véronique doesn't elaborate.

"Pierre was high and he was speeding," Marc says. "We would never do that."

"I'm just saying. Some aspects are more dangerous than others, and they're not in our control."

"You're telling me a bunch of college morons in Ontario are more dangerous than the bandits on the lake or the guys on the res selling us drugs?"

"I'm just saying, we deal with a lot of really shady people. We don't know them. We don't know what they're capable of."

He's looking at her with a funny expression. She finishes her beer and this time replenishes her own glass. It does help take the edge off. "Do you ever think about doing something else?" she asks him.

"You mean like a real job?"

"Yeah. A real job." She hates herself for sounding like James, but it's different with Marc. He's so damn young. She's had this gnawing sense of responsibility for him lately, a protectiveness that seems to be getting louder the more time she spends with him. He's never had a mother. Maybe Véronique is the one who needs to step up and be that person in his life.

"Why?"

"You're a smart kid," she says. "Really smart."

"So are you."

"I'm not a kid."

"You were about my age when you started. And now you're rich."

"I have savings, yes, but this isn't sustainable, Marc." A direct quote from James.

"Why not?"

"It's too dangerous. You'll probably wind up in jail. Most dealers do. When I started, we were just smuggling cigarettes. It was always supposed to be a short-term thing. I haven't told your dad yet, but my plan is to stop completely by next summer and go back to school in the fall."

"Wow. Your boyfriend has really rubbed off on you."

"I make my own decisions."

The waitress comes back with Marc's spaghetti and another pitcher. Véronique notices the first one is already empty, and she realizes she's quite tipsy.

"I'm not going to school," Marc says, as though it's the most absurd thing he's ever heard. "I hated school. Besides, we're doing a service for people who can't afford to pay for that shit."

"So your plan is to become a full-time coke dealer? Because that's your dad's plan."

"My plan is to make as much money as I can."

"Until you're arrested. Or shot."

"*Câlice*, Véronique. That's pretty dark."

"That's the kind of thing that happens." *This story has no happy ending.*

"I'm not going to get shot. Nobody is."

"I used to think that way, too," she says. "That no one would ever get hurt—least of all me. It was just smokes. Just weed. Just CDs."

"What happened to you in Ottawa?" he asks her, stabbing his fork into a pile of noodles and twirling.

"I just got caught off guard," she admits. "I trusted someone I shouldn't have." The beer has gone straight to her head, loosened her tongue.

"Who?"

"It doesn't matter who."

"Callahan? What did he do?"

"I'm not saying who it was."

"Whoever it was, did he rip you off? You should tell my dad, Véro."

"He didn't rip me off." She's staring down into her glass. The draft beer smells vinegary, like a dirty tap faucet. A wave of nausea rushes over her.

"You okay, Véro?"

"You can't tell your father," she says, looking up at him. "I mean it. He'll do something stupid and I don't want that on my conscience."

"I won't," he promises. "Tell me what he did."

"He tried to rape me," she blurts. "My guard was down. I managed to get away, but . . . that's why I'll never go back."

Marc is quiet. His cheeks are flushed, and his free hand is clenched in a fist. She reaches for it and squeezes. "I'm okay," she says. "I'm just telling you this to make a point. We don't know the people we're dealing with, even when we think we do. Some of them are really bad people. One of them tried to rape me. Another one might just as easily shoot you for your weed."

"You're just going to let Callahan get away with it?" Marc says, his eyes darker than usual.

"I never said it was Callahan. I've got a couple of guys in Ottawa—one in the ByWard Market, one at Ottawa U."

Marc pushes his plate away and drinks more beer.

"Will you think about what I've said?" she asks him. "About maybe finding something legitimate to do with your life? You could do anything, you know."

Marc nods, humoring her. His mood has changed. She hopes she hasn't made a terrible mistake.

23

"Tell me, what's going on?" James asks Véronique, lowering the radio. They're in the car on their way to her parents' place. She's been short with him all day.

She's staring out the window. Outside, the street is a kaleidoscope of red, yellow, and orange. There's nothing like autumn in Montreal, he thinks, rolling down the window to let some of that crisp air into the car. "V?" he says, glancing at her.

"I just want you and my dad to like each other." Not looking at him.

"I do like him. I'm not sure how he feels about me."

"You don't respect him, though."

Because he's a murderer.

"I shouldn't have arranged this interview," she says.

"Is that why you're so irritable? Don't you trust me to be fair and open-minded?"

She shrugs.

"I really want to hear his side, V. I really do. I want to understand his motivation and his beliefs. That's why I want to write this piece."

She turns to face him, trying to read his expression.

"Just give us both some time," he says. "We don't know each other yet. And let's face it, it's complicated."

She lets out a little grunt of exasperation.

"It'll be fine," he says, touching her leg. He loves her. He can see himself spending the rest of his life with her, which is why he *wants* to like her parents. She's convinced that her father was the victim of an unfair system that set him up to fail, but Léo has never apologized for Laporte's death. James wants to be able to explain to his readers how he rationalizes that. Hell, he wants to know for himself.

Maybe today will be the day Léo Fortin expresses remorse. Maybe James—his possible future son-in-law—is the one to whom he will finally repent. What a coup that would be for James, being the first reporter to elicit an apology from the FLQ. The story would be picked up everywhere. It could be a game-changer.

Lisette greets them at the door wearing jeans, an Esprit sweatshirt, and slippers. "I made meatballs," she says, hugging Véronique and kissing James on either cheek. He can smell the tobacco in her hair. "It's just about ready," she tells them. "You and Léo can talk after we eat."

"Sounds good," James says. "I'm starving."

Léo is waiting for them in the small kitchen, already seated at the table with a beer. Lisette has laid out a can of Kraft parmesan cheese, a stack of white bread, margarine, garlic powder, and chili flakes. His mother would be mortified. She has four food pet peeves: cheese that doesn't need to be refrigerated, white bread, margarine, and garlic powder. ("Why use powder when you can crush up the real thing?")

James makes a mental note to keep them apart for as long as possible.

"Smells delicious," he says, sitting down.

Léo is watching him.

"How are you, Léo?" James reaches across the table to shake his hand.

"Looking forward to telling you my life story."

"I'm looking forward to hearing it."

Véronique smiles, looking a little more relaxed.

Lisette serves the meatballs, which, in spite of the garlic powder, taste pretty good.

"Maybe you'll understand my daughter better after you hear my story," Léo says, stabbing two meatballs with his fork. "How's the volunteering, Véro?"

"Great," she says, lighting up. "I've met some cool people. I think I've actually convinced a few students at UQAM to vote Yes."

"Good. Keep at it until you convert them all."

James makes a point of staying quiet. He knows they don't want to hear what he has to say about the referendum, and he's determined not to get off on the wrong foot tonight.

"Has she converted you to our side yet?" Léo asks him.

"Not yet," James responds, forcing a smile.

"His mother is English," Véronique says, by way of explanation.

"*Half* English," James corrects.

"Half is enough," Léo mutters. "If you're half English, you're not *pure laine.*"

James grits his teeth, shovels bread in his mouth to keep from saying something he'll regret later.

"Was your father a separatist?" Lisette asks him.

"He was," James answers. "He was very involved with his union at Vickers. He was a nationalist, for sure. Voted Yes in 1980. My parents were not on the same page about politics."

"And yet you're against it," Léo says. "You're a mama's boy, I guess?"

"I have my own opinions about it," James says, trying to keep his voice light. "I think separation would be terrible for our economy. The PQ is misleading you about what will happen if we separate, or they're at least asking you to bury your heads and vote Yes and then deal with the fallout."

"It can't be worse than it is now."

"Are you kidding?" he says, already forgetting to keep his mouth shut. "It sure as hell can. And it will."

"Spoken like someone who grew up in a nice country estate, got a college education, and now has a white-collar job at an English newspaper."

James is tapping his foot under the table. *Don't take the bait. Don't take the bait.* He looks over at Véronique, waiting for her to jump in.

"James's parents were proof that you can love someone and still disagree on politics," Véronique says. "I respect him, even though he's wrong."

They all laugh, even James.

"Maybe I can still change his mind before October thirtieth," Véronique says.

After dessert—a warm *pouding chômeur* right out of the oven, simmering with butter and brown sugar—James and Léo leave the women in the kitchen and settle in the living room. Léo's got a beer and James a cup of coffee. He's driving, which he has to remind them numerous times.

"So," Léo says, reclining in his La-Z-Boy. "What do you want to know?"

"Everything," James says, resting his small tape recorder on the coffee table. "Start from the beginning."

"That means starting at the *real* beginning," Léo says. "Long before 1970. I'm talking about a couple hundred years before the Quiet Revolution, so that you have some context."

James nods, eager to hear whatever Léo has to say.

"Here's a little history lesson for you," Léo begins, his tone lofty, patronizing. "After the British conquered the French in 1760, Quebec's economy switched into the hands of the English. English became the language of business, with the Anglophones filling all the highest positions in the province—management, white collar, civil service. The French were completely marginalized, which is pretty much how it stayed for the next *two hundred* years."

"I'm fully in agreement with you on that."

"Once a system like that is in place," Léo continues, "the dominant language only gets stronger. Can you imagine the Goliath we were up against? A two-hundred-year-old system designed to keep the French at the very lowest echelon of society? The Bank of Canada didn't even print bilingual money when it was first created in the thirties. Why? Because the federal government consistently refused to acknowledge Canada as a bilingual country."

"But that wasn't entirely the fault of the English," James interrupts. "The Roman Catholic Church oversaw education in the province. The French were trained to farm and pray, and not much else. They were poorly educated. That's why they couldn't get ahead."

"I never said our only problem was the English," Léo says. "They became a symbol of what was wrong with the province, but it was never just a struggle over language. It's always been a class struggle. The Duplessis government certainly kept us stuck in a world that revolved around rural life and religion so that we could never forge ahead and gain any ground, not until the Quiet Revolution."

James nods, appreciating Léo's knowledge on the subject.

"Still, the Quebec government operated almost entirely in English. Do you begin to see the picture?

Everywhere we turned in *our own province*, we were subjugated, belittled, marginalized, oppressed. Quebec belongs to the French. When we finally started to resist in the sixties, we had our work cut out for us. We were trying to change two centuries of oppression. You think we stood a chance without being willing to go to extremes? We never wanted to hurt anyone. We only ever wanted change for our people."

"I can appreciate that," James says. "But does it justify murder?"

"You're jumping too far ahead," Léo says. "All we wanted was a fair shot at getting off the production lines and into the professional and managerial jobs that the English had taken over. This was the society into which I was born and raised."

"Understood," James says, settling in for a long and lively conversation. He can see why Léo Fortin was so revered back in the day. He's not just some bandwagon fanatic. Imagine what he could have accomplished if he hadn't gone down the path he did.

PART II
October 1970

OCTOBER

I will join my burning companions whose struggle
breaks and shares the bread of our common lot
in the quicksand huddles of grief

we will make you, Land of Quebec
a bed of resurrections
and a thousand lightning metamorphoses
of our leavens from which the future shall rise
and of our wills which will concede nothing
men shall hear your pulse beating through history
this is us winding through the October autumn
the russet sound of roe-deer in the sunlight
this is our future, clear and committed

—GASTON MIRON, TRANSLATION BY D. J. JONES
AND MARC PLOURDE

24

The sky through the small window of their second-floor apartment has quietly turned dark, a languid, moonless blanket over the city. Fall has crept up on them over the last couple of weeks. Léo can't believe it's already October. Noticing the sudden absence of daylight in the room, he reaches over and turns on a lamp. The apartment is messy, neglected—empty bottles and overflowing ashtrays on the coffee table, pizza boxes stacked on the floor. An earlier version of their manifesto, with Léo's notes scribbled across every page, is strewn at his feet. The radio is tuned to CKAC, and they're listening to that very manifesto being read on the air.

"'The Liberation Front of Quebec is a group of Quebec workers who are determined to use every means possible to ensure that the people of Quebec take control of their own destiny. We want total independence . . .'"

They're known as the FLQ: three letters that inspire terror, confusion, pandemonium. There are multiple cells of the FLQ, each one acting on its own, communicating through a network of supporters, under one unifying mission. Last night, one of the other cells kidnapped a British diplomat, James Cross, and as a result, the FLQ is finally getting some serious attention. Which is why their manifesto is getting some airtime tonight.

Léo stubs out his cigarette and immediately rolls another one. He looks over at the other four guys. They're all serious, dead quiet. The room is a fog of smoke and nervous energy. *It's happening.* Goddamn it, it's finally happening.

"'Workers of Quebec, take back what belongs to you! Your jobs, your determination, your liberty. Make your own revolution in your neighborhoods, in your places of work. Only you are able to build a free society.'"

They're asking for what they believe they're owed, especially in light of what's been done to their people over the years. They want the release of two dozen political prisoners—among them some of their friends—enough gold to live off, safe transport to Cuba, and the broadcast of their manifesto. But Léo is a skeptic. He doesn't think the government will cave to all their demands. More will have to be done, this time by *their* cell. Léo is ready to do whatever it takes. He's been ready for a long time.

Léo grew up in a dirt-floor apartment in the East End. His father was a foreman at the CN factory, and his mother was a presser at a textile factory. She suffered crippling back pain, the result of having to stand hunched over a pressing table for ten hours a day. Léo stopped school at grade six so he could start working at CN, joining his father as slave labor for the English upper class.

He met Lisette in 1966, when they were nineteen. She was pretty and vibrant, and had also dropped out of school at a young age. He thought she was above cleaning houses for rich Anglos, but with no education, neither of them had ever had any choices.

At that time, Léo was already involved with a political group that had deep French Canadian, working-class roots. These were *his people.* (He used those words with great reverence, speaking of them in a way that elevated their plight to something noble. His mother's mangled back was not pitiful but heroic, their lack of education valorous.) To that point, his group's efforts had been mainly symbolic. Everything that had happened so far in Quebec—specifically the bombings that had killed five people in as many years, gaining some notoriety for the cause—had been the work of the FLQ, a much more radical group.

Léo felt sidelined and ineffectual until a turning point in the summer of 1968. At the St. Jean Baptiste Day parade that summer, a riot erupted between the separatists and the cops, and Léo wound up in jail for throwing a broken bottle at a mounted police-man's head. He got a taste for violence—he called it "action"—and it made him feel purposeful, so he left his group and joined the FLQ. His politics quickly flamed into fanaticism; he was involved in the bomb-ings at Dominion Square, the Montreal Chamber of Commerce, and Eaton's department store. Everything he did was with the clarity of focus that comes from living by your convictions and being willing to go to any lengths. He never wanted to hurt another human being—he wasn't a monster—but the alternative was the status quo, and that was no longer acceptable.

When the radio announcer finishes reading the mani-festo, Léo turns it off and they all sit in silence for a while. He's a little drunk and he can't remember the last time he slept. He downs his beer, fingers wrapped tightly around the bottle neck, smoke wafting from the collection of cigarettes in the ashtray. He's aware of Lisette watching him from the kitchen. She looks nervous. He looks away.

"They've broadcast the manifesto on the radio," one of the guys says. "Let's see what else they offer."

The next night, October 8, the manifesto is read on television, another attempt to placate the FLQ without really giving them anything meaningful. The news anchor reads in a somber tone, reflective, he says, of the mood of the province. When he finishes, Léo stands up, even more pissed off.

"They're not taking us seriously," he fumes. "They're not doing enough. The only reason they broadcast the manifesto on TV is because they think it's so idiotic it's actually going to discredit us."

"They're so goddamn privileged, they have no idea what kind of support we have in this province from our own people."

"This is a rejection of our demands," Léo states, pacing around the room. "Trust me, they won't offer anything else. They're stalling. The other cell is going to start backing down on these demands one by one. The government is still in total control here."

"It's still early," Bernard says. "Let's see what happens tomorrow."

But nothing happens the next day, just more stone-walling. On October 10, at five thirty in the evening, the justice minister holds a press conference on *Téléjournal*.

Jérôme Choquette represents everything Léo despises about politicians—the perfectly coiffed hair, the buttoned-up suit and tie, the pompous gesticulations, the steady regurgitation of bullshit.

"As a concession to save the life of Mr. James Cross," Choquette says, facing a frenzy of flashbulbs and microphones, "the federal government has informed me that they will offer safe passage out of the country for the *kidnappers only*, but *not* for the twenty-three prisoners in question."

"Arrogant shit!"

"To be clear," Choquette continues, "the federal government will *not* release any of the political prisoners mentioned in the FLQ communiqué, since they are not political prisoners at all, as the FLQ would have you believe. They are convicted terrorists charged with murder and attempted murder in numerous bombings." He pauses and looks directly into the camera—right at Léo—with a smug grin. "The FLQ's demands are preposterous and far-fetched, and there will be no further negotiations."

"Screw them," Léo cries, turning off the TV, not even waiting until the end of the speech. "So that's it then." He takes a long, deep drag from the nub of his homemade cigarette. "They'd rather let the diplomat die than address our 'poor people' problems."

"Léo's right," Paul says. They're all still camped out on Léo's couch—Paul, Jacques, Bernard, Francis—where they've been for days, waiting for something to happen. Now it looks like they're going to have to *make* something happen.

"We need to do what we talked about," Francis says. "Something that will show them we're serious. They don't think the FLQ will follow through with any of these threats. And frankly, the other cell might not."

"We need to hit them harder," Léo concurs, his entire body throbbing with adrenaline. "Another kidnapping. We need to show them our manifesto wasn't just theoretical bullshit," he says. "It's time to walk the walk. We need to show the people that they don't have to settle for welfare and unemployment. This is our obligation to them."

"I have to put the baby down," Lisette murmurs, rushing from the room.

Léo waits a few minutes and then follows after her.

"You're leaving us," she says.

He nods gravely.

"Are you sure you have to do this? What about Véronique?"

"She's six months old. She won't even know I'm gone."

"I will."

"We've come too far to stop now," he says. "I want to show our people that progress is possible, that we can use our pain and poverty and triumph over it. You know I was always meant to do this. Remember where we come from, Lise. I don't want our daughter to ever know that life."

Lisette nods solemnly. He lifts her chin and kisses her hard on the mouth.

"I don't know when I'll be back."

"Léo, why does it have to be you? Can't you leave this to the others? You're a father now."

"All the more reason for me to do this," he says. "So that Véronique has a better life than we did."

Lisette lights a cigarette from the pack she keeps in her bedside drawer. She smokes Du Mauriers, never hand-rolled like the men. "I hate being sidelined like this," she says. "Trapped in the apartment by myself."

"I need you here."

"I used to contribute. Bonnie and Clyde, remember? Now I'm just a fetcher of beer and sandwiches. Waiting around."

"Your job is being a mother to our daughter."

There's a tumult of noise outside the bedroom—the

men collecting their things, finishing their beer, plotting and strategizing in adrenaline-charged voices.

"I have to go," he says softly. He stands up, wipes away her tears with his fingertips. "I'll be in touch as soon as I can. I love you."

She doesn't respond, doesn't even look up.

The next day, they drive in silence all the way to the South Shore. No music, no conversation. Jacques is driving; Bernard is next to him in the passenger seat. Léo is squeezed into the back with Paul and Francis, staring out the window like he'll never see the trees or the sky or the outside world again. His muscles are taut, his breath shallow. In front of him, he can see Bernard's neck vein pulsing.

The six p.m. deadline to meet their demands has officially come and gone. Earlier, they went out and bought wigs and fake moustaches. Bernard is dressed like a hippie now, the rest of them as businessmen in trench coats and fedoras, wire-rimmed glasses and moustaches. If they weren't all so goddamn scared, it would be funny.

They chose Pierre Laporte, the labor minister, mostly at random from a list of politicians. He makes sense because he's the one directly responsible for the exploitation of the Québécois. He also happens to live in St. Lambert, just over the Jacques Cartier Bridge in Montreal's South Shore, which is very convenient. They looked him up in the phone book, and he was listed, like any ordinary person. Léo called his house, and the wife answered, said he was home but not available. Just like that. Léo and the guys were stupefied. It seemed impossible they would be so careless. She may as well have invited them over for tea.

They waited until six p.m. for the press conference, quietly hoping they wouldn't have to go through with the plan. For all Léo's bravado, it's not his first choice to kidnap someone and put his own life in jeopardy. But the deadline passed and Léo is a man of his word.

He gazes out at the St. Lawrence River as they cross the bridge, wondering if he'll ever see his wife and daughter again. He feels completely alone, even though his four closest friends are right here with him. It's a strange feeling, being on the cusp of committing a crime of this scope. It's a hell of a lot more terrifying than bombing an empty building.

Kidnapping a man is different. It's using a human being as a bargaining chip. Léo is not doing this lightly. He's gone over it again and again, but he justifies it by reminding himself that the people in power—the people who have *always* been in power—have even less regard for human life than the FLQ. Haven't they shown their indifference for far too long? They've never had any regard for his life.

"Maybe they'll change their minds," he says, his gaze still transfixed to the river as they cross into the South Shore.

"You think the government is going to change its mind and release our guys?" Bernard laughs, craning his neck to look back at Léo. "Come on, man. Get serious."

"Let's see what happens when we kidnap another one of theirs," Francis says. Léo is suddenly aware of how young he is, how young they all are.

"So we know what we're doing?" Paul asks.

"We get inside his house and hold him there until the police surround us," Léo says. "Just like we planned. The media and the reporters will show up, and that's when we'll start negotiating with them. The cops won't have to look for us anymore. We'll be right there in front of them."

The guys all nod, and then fall silent. *If only it goes that smoothly*, Léo thinks.

When they reach St. Lambert, Bernard follows the streets he took earlier today on a practice run. It's a short drive from the bridge to Pierre Laporte's house. When they turn onto Robitaille Street, Bernard gasps. "Holy shit. That's him."

"Where?"

"Jesus Christ," Jacques says. "He's playing football with someone in the middle of the goddamn street."

"Now what?"

"We grab him and throw him in the car," Léo says, thinking fast.

"And then what?"

"We'll take him to the house in St. Hubert," he says, sounding more confident than he feels. "Move *fast*."

They all reach for their guns and fling open their cars doors. It's surreal. Léo isn't in his body anymore. "Just get him inside the goddamn car as quickly as possible."

Jacques barely comes to a full stop as Bernard and Paul jump out of the Chevrolet, followed by Francis and Léo. Laporte is in the middle of the street, tossing a football with a teenage boy.

Léo raises his machine gun, and the others follow. Nothing was really planned, so they're all going on instinct. The teenage boy notices them and starts to approach, but Léo turns his machine gun on him. "Don't fucking move!" he screams.

The kid stops, terrified. Bernard points his gun at Laporte as Paul grabs him by the arms, drags him to the car, and throws him down on the floor of the back seat. The others pile in, and Paul grinds his knee into Laporte's back to keep him from getting up.

"Go!" Léo cries, and Jacques speeds off, screeching around the corner. Léo pulls the scarf from around his neck and blindfolds Laporte.

After a few minutes of silence, the shock breaks and they all explode. Swearing and yelling, releasing tension. They light smokes. "We did it! Goddamn it, we did it."

Laporte doesn't say a word, doesn't try to move or escape.

"You're going to drop me off in a few blocks," Léo tells Jacques. "I'll deliver the communiqué and then join you at the house tomorrow."

Léo has scribbled a short note claiming responsibility for the kidnapping, and now he has to get it to the media without getting caught.

"What do we do with him when we get there?" Paul asks him.

"Go in through the garage. Keep him blindfolded and handcuff him to one of the beds. Leave him like that until I get there."

"Do we feed him?"

"Yeah, you fucking feed him. We're not trying to kill him."

Léo takes off his disguise, shoving it all on the floor at his feet, close to Laporte's face. After a few blocks, Léo gets out of the car and starts walking. He's nervous as shit, but tries to look casual. He needs to get across the Jacques Cartier Bridge and back to the city before the cops discover Laporte's been kidnapped and close down access to the bridge in both directions. He flags down a taxi on Victoria Avenue and jumps in. "Downtown," he says calmly. "Queen Mary."

The driver nods, not in any rush. He's eating a hot dog. "You in a hurry?"

"Not at all," Léo says, smiling. Inside, he's panicking. His armpits are soaking wet; his heart is racing. He lights a smoke, then another. Chain-smokes the entire way back to the city.

The first thing he needs to do is get a message to the cell that kidnapped James Cross. There has to be at least some level of coordination between them; otherwise the whole thing will come off looking haphazard and amateur—exactly what the government expects of them.

He gets out of the cab and heads up Queen Mary to see a guy named Antoine, the liaison between all the cells. Léo pounds on the door, desperately wanting to get inside and out of sight. A guy answers—a hippie in bell-bottoms with a guitar slung across his chest.

"Antoine?"

The guy nods.

"I'm with the Chénier cell," Léo says. "I need a safe house."

Antoine lets him in, offers him a beer.

"I need to get in touch with the Liberation cell," Léo says, gratefully accepting the beer and dumping half of it down his throat in one gulp. He doesn't say a word about the kidnapping.

"I don't know how to get in touch with them," Antoine says. "They call me when they need to."

Léo collapses onto a pile of pillows on the floor, a makeshift couch in the cramped bachelor apartment. He needs a new plan.

"I can give them a message for you," Antoine offers, strumming his guitar. He's got a joint smoldering in an ashtray. "They'll call here at some point."

"I've got to go somewhere right now," Léo tells him. "But can I come back here and crash for the night?"

"Absolutely, man."

Léo takes a couple of tokes off the joint and lifts himself off the floor. "I'll be back later," he says, and heads off.

He takes the bus to the East End. He tucks the communiqué between the pages of a phone book, and calls CKAC. Whoever answers the phone is tasked with passing along the message. "The FLQ is responsible for the kidnapping of Pierre Laporte," Léo says. "A communiqué has been left in a phone booth at the corner of Tenth and Beaubien."

Back at Antoine's apartment, it's already all over the news. "Check this out, man," Antoine says. "Another kidnapping!"

He joins Antoine in front of the TV. "The FLQ did it again! They don't even know which cell it was."

Léo looks at him. Says nothing.

He splits before the sun comes up, hopping on a bus to the South Shore. It's early, but the city is already buzzing with the news—on the radio, in the papers, on the street. *I'm the guy who kidnapped Laporte.* Imagine if these people knew? He's at the center of this incredible event that's on everyone's minds and tongues, this thing that has immobilized the city. It gives him a feeling of omnipotence, an inflated sense of responsibility.

He arrives at the white-frame bungalow on Armstrong, a dead-end street surrounded by open fields, close enough in proximity to the St. Hubert airport that you can hear the planes landing and taking off. He's relieved to find the street completely deserted. He was half expecting the place to be surrounded by cops. He enters through the garage, eager to catch up with the guys. He can hear the radio as soon as he sets foot inside. The guys look relieved to see him.

"Jacques is with Laporte," Francis says, reading his mind. "Keeping guard."

"What's happening?" Léo asks.

The guys seem in decent spirits. Léo is relieved. The operation went smoothly; nothing terrible has happened yet.

"They just interrupted with a special bulletin," Paul says. "They got our communiqué. They know we're threatening to kill Laporte if our demands aren't met by ten tonight."

Léo nods, sits down on a plastic folding chair. "Where's Laporte?"

"Bedroom at the end of the hall."

"What have you said to him?"

"Just that he's been kidnapped by the Front de Libération du Quebec, and that he'll be freed if the government meets our demands."

"How was he last night?"

"I'm sure scared shitless," Bernard says. "But he was pretty calm. No violent outburst or anything, no scream-ing. Didn't even ask questions. We've got the radio on in there with him. He knows everything that's going on."

"How've you been treating him?"

"Fine. Fine. We've been giving him canned spa-ghetti. There's no other food. Just some cans of Chef Boyardee."

Léo gets up. He wants to see Laporte with his own eyes. He heads down the hall, apprehensive. *This is real. This is happening.* His heart is hammering in his chest.

He opens the door. Jacques is sitting in a chair, smoking. The radio is on. Laporte is flat on his back, blindfolded and handcuffed. He's lying very still, waiting. Waiting to find out if he will live or die, if he'll ever see his family again. That kid he was playing football with was his nephew. It's all over the news. Seventeen years old.

Standing over him now, Léo has to shove down a surge of guilt. To imprison another human being like this—a father, a husband, a son—requires a tremendous amount of compartmentalization. He has to stay focused on the cause. It's not easy. "This isn't personal," he says, and Laporte turns his head toward Léo's voice. He doesn't say anything.

"When's the last time he ate?" Léo asks Jacques.

"Last night."

"Give him another can of spaghetti. And a smoke, if he wants."

Léo leaves the room, struggling with his conscience. It's going to be a long day, waiting around for Premier Bourassa to respond. They need to write more communiqués. Instructions and updates need to be delivered regularly.

They write the next couple of communiqués at the table in the living room. Léo makes the decision to send Paul to deliver all of them. Paul will be the only one allowed to leave the house. It's a random decision, but Léo thinks it's better if the same guy comes and goes, so as not to arouse suspicion. Paul doesn't wear a disguise. None of them are on any wanted list; their pictures haven't been published anywhere. For now, they're all still anonymous.

After Paul leaves, Léo wanders down the hall, peering into the other bedroom. There's a makeshift bookcase, made from milk crates, full of books, which immediately draws Léo into the room. He doesn't know the guy who rents this house, only that he drives a taxi.

Léo grabs a book by Pierre Vallières, sits down on the bed, and turns to his favorite page: *It is by force . . . that we will be free. The sooner we arm ourselves with our courage and with our rifles, the sooner our liberation from slavery will make us equal . . . It is because I cannot bear to be a slave that I joined the FLQ.*

Léo smiles, inspired. *The Quebec revolution will not stop.*

He gets up off the bed and returns to Laporte's room. He signals for Jacques to leave them alone.

"You know Premier Bourassa," Léo says. "You think he'll negotiate to save your life?"

"I do," Laporte says, surprising Léo. "I think the government will meet your demands. I can help."

"How?"

"Robert is my friend," Laporte says. "He'll negotiate for my release. I believe that."

"I hope you're right."

Laporte tries to sit up, leaning back on his elbows. "Could I write him a letter?" he asks. "I think I can persuade him. If I could just send him a personal note, in my words."

Léo thinks it over. What's the harm if it helps get them what they want? He leaves the room and runs it by the guys. Everyone agrees it can't hurt. Léo grabs some paper, a pen. They all pile into Laporte's room. Léo removes the handcuffs, and Laporte stretches his arms above his head. "Thank you," he says, soft-spoken.

Léo feels sorry for the guy. He's just a regular middle-aged man, thinning brown hair, a thick awning of bushy eyebrows above the blindfold, mild-mannered. The problem is he's one of *them*. Léo has to keep reminding himself of that. Human being or politician— it's one or the other, not both.

"Should I dictate it to you?" Laporte asks.

Léo hands him the paper and pen, a book to write on. "You can write it with the blindfold on," he says. "We'll just make sure we approve what you say."

Laporte nods, grateful. Starts to write as best he can without being able to see his own words on the page.

> *My dear Robert,*
>
> *I feel like I am writing the most important letter I have ever written. For the time being, I am in perfect health, and I am treated well, even courteously.*
> *In short, the power to decide over my life is in your hands. You know how my personal situation deserves to draw attention. I had two brothers, both are now dead. I remain alone as the head of a large family that comprises my mother, my sisters, my own wife, and my children . . . My death would create for them irreparable grief, and you know the ties that bind the members of my family . . .*
> *You have the power of life and death over me, I depend on you and I thank you for it.*

Léo has a hard time reading the letter. He doesn't want to know any of this, doesn't want to see Laporte in this light. No man should have to plead for his life like this, have his vulnerability made so public. This letter will likely be printed in all the papers and read on every TV and radio station before the day is done.

Paul takes the letter, along with a new communiqué threatening to execute Laporte if their demands are not met, and heads off to the city to get it to CKAC. They've got a widespread, impenetrable network of friends and relatives helping them out, on which they now have to rely for all their communication with the media.

"I'm starving," Laporte says, with renewed energy. His spirits seem to have lifted. He seems more confident about his release, optimistic even. "Anything but canned spaghetti. Please."

"We've got no more money," Bernard says.

"I've got money," Laporte offers. "In my pocket. Take it. Get something for all of us. Real food."

The guys all look at one another. Bernard pulls a twenty out of Laporte's pocket.

"Order something," Léo instructs. For the first time since they grabbed Laporte on Robitaille Street, Léo is feeling confident they did the right thing. If the twenty-three political prisoners are freed and the kidnappers are given safe transport out of the country, then everything they've done will have been worthwhile.

The government's response to Laporte's letter is a vague, inscrutable statement delivered by Bourassa on TV later that night: "We have chosen individual and collective justice."

"What the hell does that mean?" Léo shouts.

He storms back to Laporte's room, where Laporte is listening to the same news conference on the radio. "I thought he was your friend?"

"Give him time," Laporte says, still blindfolded on the bed. "I understand it to mean he's willing to negotiate, and that he's choosing to save my life."

"'Individual and collective justice'?" Léo repeats. "That doesn't mean anything. It's empty words."

In the forty-eight hours that follow, nothing happens. No offers are made, no demands met, just a lot of back-and-forth between the FLQ's and the government's lawyers.

"It was all a goddamn stall tactic," Francis says. "That whole speech was just the government buying time. They were never going to negotiate with us."

"Laporte was so sure they would," Bernard says. "Those guys in the Liberal government are his friends. He's one of them, for Christ's sake. How could they not do everything in their power to save his life?"

"There's something none of us took into account," Léo says, taking a long drag off his cigarette. "The federal government."

Léo suddenly jumps up from his chair and starts walking around the room, processing the situation as he moves. "Laporte wasn't wrong about the Quebec government," he says. "His mistake was in not realizing how much power the federal government has over this province. Think about it. The one to blame here is Trudeau, the goddamn prime minister of Canada. He's the one who won't negotiate with us, he's the hard line."

"Léo's right," Francis says. "Laporte's friends in the cabinet would accept our demands in a heartbeat, but they're just lackeys and ass-kissers to their federal master."

"So now what?"

"We wait some more," Léo says. "Let's see if the lawyers can reach an agreement."

Just before midnight, another news bulletin. The lawyers have reached a standstill, and all negotiations have stopped. The government won't budge, not even to save Laporte's life.

Léo barges into Laporte's room, throwing open the door. "They're not accepting any of our demands!" he says, incredulous.

Laporte lies motionless, silent. He doesn't even react. He looks like a man who has lost all hope.

Returning to the living room, where the others are hunched over the radio, Léo says, "Laporte's given up."

Jacques silences him with a wave of his hand. "Trudeau is talking."

Léo circulates around the room, agitated. He pulls back the curtain and peers outside. It's deserted. He's starting to get paranoid. On the radio, Trudeau is responding to an English journalist about the criticism he's faced for sending military troops to Ottawa. Léo understands enough English to get the gist of his typically arrogant remarks.

"There are a lot of bleeding hearts around who just don't like to see people with helmets and guns," Trudeau is saying. "All I can say is, go on and bleed, but it's more important to keep law and order in society than to be worried about weak-kneed people."

"This prick doesn't back down," Jacques mutters.

"Our society must take every means at its disposal to defend itself!" the prime minister states.

"At what cost?" the reporter asks him. "How far would you go?"

"Well, just watch me."

Léo turns to the others, shaking with anger. "He's going to let Laporte die."

"Or he doesn't think we'll actually do it."

"Will we?" Francis asks. "Execute him?"

"If we do, it'll be because of Trudeau's ego."

Everyone is quiet.

"Look, it's still too soon for this conversation," Léo says. "However it ends, the government is going to have to deal with its own conscience. After today, they'll have blood on their hands. They'll be as guilty of murder as we are."

The only bright spot in an otherwise bleak day is news of a rally at the Paul Sauvé Arena, where three thousand students have come together to support the FLQ. The guys listen to the rally on the radio, heartened by the cheering crowd, their boisterous validation.

"The people are on our side," Léo says, his exuberance returning. "They're on our side."

"We're a more powerful force than they thought."

Proving that to be true, an offer from the government is made on the heels of the student rally: the release of five FLQ prisoners and safe passage out of Canada for the kidnappers.

"No way," Bernard says. "They release all twenty-three prisoners or Laporte dies."

"I agree," Léo says, his heart in his throat.

They don't respond to Bourassa's offer. It's an insult.

Léo finally falls asleep, comforted by the knowledge that his people are behind him.

"Léo, wake up."

Léo stirs, opens his eyes. He sits up, not recognizing the room. *Where is he? Where's Lisette?* He realizes he hasn't slept properly since the kidnapping, not more than an occasional restless catnap. This time he was really out.

"Léo," Bernard says, "Paul's back."

Léo shakes himself awake. Lights a cigarette. Paul never came back after delivering Laporte's letter two days ago. He was beginning to think they were all screwed. "Where was he?"

"He was tailed by two undercover cops on his way back to the South Shore. He figured it out and went over to one of the safe houses. He finally managed to sneak out in disguise and walk back here. He lost the cops."

"But they know Paul is involved."

"They do, but they didn't arrest him. They were obviously hoping he'd lead them to us."

The walls are starting to close in.

"Another thing, Léo. Trudeau invoked the War Measures Act early this morning."

Léo isn't entirely surprised. Yesterday, the army was called in and troops flooded the city. The guys watched it all unfold from their window. Their house is right next to the St. Hubert military base, so when the army was deployed, the trucks rolled past them for hours on their way to Montreal.

But the War Measures Act is something else. The police will be able to arrest and hold whomever they want, for however long they want. Trudeau is digging in his heels.

His first thought is of Lisette. He hasn't spoken to her since the day of the kidnapping. He can't call her now. The cops are probably watching her, tapping her parents' phone. He stumbles out of bed and takes a piss. He walks past the other guys, who are all dozing in the living room—including Paul, to Léo's great relief—and goes to the kitchen. They've been using Laporte's money for staples—coffee, beer, smokes. He pours some coffee into a used Styrofoam cup and turns on the kitchen radio.

On CKAC, the news is grim. The army has invaded Montreal, and the streets are filled with soldiers, their machine guns poised to fire at whatever provocation Trudeau has deemed appropriate. Hundreds of arrests have been made, and citizens are being stripped of their civil liberties all across the province.

He wakes the others and they convene around the coffee table.

"Now what?" Francis says. "We're screwed."

"We're not screwed," Léo says, putting on a calm facade. "They didn't arrest Paul, which is good for us. It means they don't have anything solid yet."

They all know Paul could have led the cops straight here, and that it's probably only a matter of time, but he sees it as his responsibility to keep up morale.

"Léo, you heard the news. They're rounding people up all over the city, trying to find *us*. Anyone who's ever supported nationalism is being held for questioning."

"They're throwing innocent people in jail just because they *can*. Orders of the government."

"It's a free-for-all. They arrested Pauline Julien."

"The singer?"

"She wouldn't sing for the queen a few years ago, remember? Now she's in jail for it!"

"We can't panic now," Léo says, concealing his own growing anxiety. Even as he reassures them, he feels sick. What if Lisette's been arrested and she's locked up somewhere? She has a record.

All of a sudden a loud crash from the other end of the house interrupts their conversation. They look at one another.

"Laporte!"

They all jump up and run down the hall in a panic, realizing how lackadaisical they've been about keeping an eye on him. They stopped guarding him around the clock after day one. Someone checks on him sporadically, but there hasn't been a sentry at the door. They almost never touch the guns.

When they get to his room, they find Laporte on the floor. There are shards of glass all over the floor, blood on his wrist and upper body, and the window above his bed has been smashed.

"He tried to escape," Paul says.

"His cuffs are off."

Laporte isn't moving. He's breathing, but not moving. As far as Léo can figure, he got free of his handcuffs and must have thrown himself into the window. The glass shattered, but it was too high for him to get out. Instead, he cut his wrist and chest. Strangely, he's still wearing the blindfold. If he had just removed it, he would have had a much better chance of escaping.

"He left the blindfold on," Francis says, as though Laporte isn't in the room.

"He's not in his right mind," Léo says. "Let's bring him into the living room. Do we have any bandages?"

They half drag, half carry him to the living room, where they sit him down on a chair. Léo removes the blindfold. It doesn't seem to matter anymore. Laporte doesn't even look at them. His head drops to his chest. He's slumped over, practically catatonic.

Jacques does his best to bandage Laporte's wounds. He uses some tape and the blindfold, some bandages they found in the bathroom. They clean him up, try to comfort him, but his body is completely limp.

"We're going to take you to the hospital soon," Léo tells him, without really thinking it through. Laporte doesn't react.

"Maybe we should let him go?" Jacques says.

Léo doesn't know what to do. Seeing another man this way, so hopeless and despondent, makes him feel genuinely sorry for the guy. It's like he knows it's over. He must have heard the declaration of the War Measures Act on his radio and he knows it's his death sentence. His friends and colleagues have all abandoned him; they've sent a clear message by not meeting the kidnappers' demands: *Your life is worthless to us. We choose to keep our power.* No wonder he's given up.

"He needs to go to the hospital," Bernard says. "He's bleeding through the bandages."

They're talking about him like he's not here. In a way, he's not. He's somewhere else—mentally, emotionally checked out.

"We can't take him to the goddamn hospital!"

"What then? Kill him?"

They all fall silent. Léo is up pacing now. He can't bring himself to look at Laporte. Panic is setting in for all of them.

"Maybe we should just let him go," Léo says, surprising them.

"After everything we've done?" Jacques cries. "We'll go to jail and we'll have accomplished nothing. The government wins. The politicians win. The English win. The rich win. It's always the same."

"I hate the thought of that, too."

"So we kill him. Is that what you're saying?"

"I don't know what the hell I'm saying."

There was no plan for this. No plan at all, really. It all sort of unfolded, one impulsive decision after another. For a while, it looked like it would all work out. Can Léo take a human life? Can he murder another man, even if it is for the cause? He's not a killer.

"He's suffering, man. Look at him."

Léo finally looks over at Laporte. He's pitiful and clearly in a lot of pain. "His life is in our hands," Francis says, and all Léo can think is he doesn't want this terrible burden anymore.

We could let him walk right out that door to freedom, back to his family, and it would be over.

"Let's just let him go then," Paul says. "We'll blindfold him and dump him somewhere. We'll have time to get away."

"And go where?" They're all moving around the room, circling Laporte's chair.

"We're forgetting why we did this in the first place," Bernard says. "We're letting him unnerve us, derail us from our purpose."

"Bernard's right," Léo says. "This isn't about the FLQ. This is about our *people*. We did this for them. Do we value this guy's life more than *theirs*? Look what the government is doing to our friends and family, man. Locking them up. Interrogating them like they're criminals. And we're going to put this politician's life before *them*? The government had a choice to save him. This is on them."

"If we let him go, we lose all our ground," Jacques agrees. "We did this for Quebec independence, remember?"

"Everything we've ever done has been to get more power for the workers in this province. Guess what? *We're* the goddamn workers! *We're* the people! *We're* the ones they keep exploiting." Bernard points to Laporte, inflamed. "This guy? He's part of it. Let's not forget that. He's one of the ones who forced us into this. He's just a casualty of our struggle."

"He's also a father and a husband and a brother."

Léo says this, thinking about the letter Laporte wrote. Thinking about his own baby girl.

"So you choose his life over ours?"

"Of course not," Léo responds. "We're all in this together."

"If we're not all on the same page, if we're not all one hundred percent in agreement, we don't do anything."

The other guys nod, wrestling with their consciences. There is not one among them who is more comfortable with the idea of killing a man. It was never supposed to happen, even as they wrote out their threats of execution.

"This is the moment of truth," Léo says, feeling the return of his resolve. "How far are we willing to go? Was it all bravado, or did we mean what we wrote in our manifesto?"

After a long silence, Paul says, "We swore we weren't going to give in this time. Why should we be the ones to cave?"

They all turn once again to stare at Laporte. Spiritually, he's already dead. He knows they're going to kill him, even though they don't even know it yet. Or maybe they do.

"The deadlines have all passed and they've responded with the War Measures Act. They've played their card. We're out of options."

"We either let him go or we kill him. That's it. We have to decide right now."

The tension in the room is untenable. *A human life. A human life.*

"I think we know what we have to do."

Léo goes to the kitchen and opens a window. It faces an empty field. He breathes deeply. His hands are shaking. He desperately needs to speak to Lisette, but he knows what she'll say.

Throwing homemade bombs into empty buildings is more of a theoretical exercise. They were destroying property, not lives. That's what they told themselves anyway. But to stand face-to-face with another human being and kill him in cold blood, this is something Lisette would never condone.

Release him. Kill him. Release him. Kill him.

Hours pass while they debate late into the night. The sun rises; someone makes coffee. They chain-smoke. The radio drones on in the background. Democracy is out the window. Léo hates that the government has put them in this spot.

Laporte still isn't moving. They keep checking his pulse to make sure he's alive. "Let's just put him out of his misery," Bernard says. "He's already gone. Look at him."

"I agree. If we let him go, we're acknowledging their

authority and accepting that this is how it's always going to be. We can't do that."

Francis gets up and leaves the room. When he returns, his eyes are red, swollen. Léo has no judgment about that. He loves him for it. He wants to cry himself.

"We have to kill him," Jacques says, his voice breaking.

The others nod. The room is heavy. Léo's chest hurts. *I'm going to end a human life, and I'll have to live with that forever.*

"Who's going to do it?"

Nothing feels real anymore. Léo is no longer in his body.

"Remember, this is *their* fault," one of the guys says. "They could have saved him."

PART III
1995—1997

25

September 1995

"It happened very fast," Léo says, his eyes welling. "We made the decision and we acted. After we did it, we were all numb, in shock."

James hasn't moved or breathed in hours. Hasn't touched his coffee or asked a single question.

"All I remember thinking is how fragile life is."

James cringes. Sure, life is fragile when you choke the last breath out of someone. "Who did it?" he asks Léo. "I know he was choked with his chain. But who actually did it? None of you has ever said."

"We all did it."

"That's not possible," James argues. "There's been speculation that Paul wasn't even there when Laporte was murdered, and also rumors that he confessed on tape to strangling him. Why keep the details to yourself after all these years? You're a free man."

"It was all of us together," Léo insists. "I don't remember the details, who did what. We were all there. We all acted together."

James sighs. Why doesn't he just come clean? Either take credit for himself or set Véronique free of the burden she carries of having a murderer for a father. If he didn't actually do it, why not exonerate himself? Why won't any of them tell the truth after all this time?

"It wasn't an accident," Léo says. "I can tell you that. The media thought maybe it was, or that's the story they told to make us look incompetent. But we made the decision to kill him and we did. Sometimes I can't believe we did it. I couldn't believe it then, I still can't. But it happened."

"What was it like? Watching another man die?"

"You're numb. I was . . . It's impossible to describe. It's surreal. You have to shut a part of yourself down. You act on instinct. We just kept moving after we did it. We had to keep moving, stay busy, so we wouldn't think about what we'd done. We weren't violent guys."

James has to suppress his anger. He tries not to react, bites his tongue.

"Anyway, that's it," Léo continues. "We wrapped his body in a blanket. We carried him out. We were gentle with him. I don't know why. Guilt, I guess. It wasn't personal. We put the body in the trunk of the Chevrolet, and one of the guys drove to the airport and left the car there. We took off to the Townships. We had a friend in the country. We hid in the crawl space of his farmhouse until they found us."

"In a tunnel, I read?"

Léo nods. "I've never talked about this to anyone before," he says. "Not a word.

"Why now?"

"For my daughter. She asked me to."

"That's it?"

Léo shrugs. "Maybe part of me hopes to make people understand why we did it."

"Do you regret it? Or at least how it turned out?"

"I don't regret any of it," he says. "I acted on my convictions. It was a tough decision, but it was sincere."

"Not a youthful transgression?"

"What we did was for our people—the workers, the exploited, the long-suffering French slaves in Quebec. It was for a cause I still believe in today. You're too young to really understand. You'll never know what it was like for us back then."

"So you'd do it again?"

"I would," he responds, not missing a beat. "We may have been idealists, but we were not misguided."

"You don't regret going to prison?" James presses. "Missing out on your daughter's life?"

"I didn't enjoy prison," he says sharply. "They strip you of all your dignity. They systematically destroy your spirit. You've never seen poor treatment until you've been inside a jail. They treated us like we were animals. Obviously I would have rather watched my daughter grow up, but I did what I had to do."

"Was it worth it?"

"Ask me after the referendum."

"I've seen the footage of your arrest," James says. "You looked into the camera and said you'd done it for Véronique."

"I did."

"You mean you killed Pierre Laporte for her?"

"No, of course not that."

"What then?"

"The political act. It was for her and her generation—for all of you—so you'd have a better future. Violence happened to be a part of it."

"*Part of it?* A man lost his life."

"It was necessary. The federal government forced our hand. Laporte was a casualty of war."

"But there was no war."

"There was indeed a war, M. Phénix. Your father knew it. It's sad that you don't."

"How do you think Véronique feels about what you did?"

"You'll have to ask her."

"Looking back with the perspective of twenty-five years, do you think you advanced the cause enough to warrant the murder of an innocent man?"

"I think so," he says. "The October Crisis paved the way for the Parti Québécois victory in '76 and the '80 referendum, and now this referendum. It had to start somewhere."

"A lot of separatists would disagree that the FLQ had anything to do with the PQ's success."

"Sure they would, because it's easy to distance yourself from the dirty work, even though you benefitted from it. The ones who denounced us, you don't think they were secretly overjoyed about what we accomplished for them? Someone had to break ground. Violence was required."

"You don't sound at all remorseful."

"Remorse is complicated. Why don't you ask your former prime minister Pierre Trudeau if he's remorseful? He is as much to blame for Laporte's death as we are, if not more."

"You can't be serious," James says, shaking his head in frustration. He *wants* Léo to feel remorseful, to say he's sorry for what he did. For personal reasons—not just for this story—he needs Léo to be a decent human being.

"Trudeau could have saved Laporte's life!" Léo shouts, his face turning dark red. "He just had to meet our very reasonable demands. Instead, he called in the troops and declared war. He sentenced that man to death. You don't think he bears *any* responsibility?"

"He was just trying to protect the people," James says. "The FLQ was a threat to society."

"Trudeau was protecting his pride. Nothing else."

James takes a breath. Gives Léo a minute to calm down.

"So, what's next for Léo Fortin?"

"Everything depends on this referendum result."

"Your old friend from the RIN recently said it would be a very dangerous situation if the Anglos and "the ethnics" hold back the will of the Francophone majority. Was he threatening more violence?"

"I don't know what he meant by that."

"Your daughter is a passionate supporter of Quebec independence," James says. "Would you advocate violence for her if the outcome doesn't go your way?"

"Not if it means she winds up in jail. Jail is the worst place on earth."

"Worse than a coffin?"

"I think so."

"You still haven't said how you killed him."

Léo is quiet.

"Was it like they said?" James presses. "You choked him with the cross around his neck?"

Still nothing.

"Was it you, Léo? Or was it one of the others?"

"We acted as one."

He sees now where Véronique gets her stubbornness. The Fortins are nothing if not dogged.

26

Nancy steps off the bus onto Union Street, pink-cheeked and smiling. She's got her backpack slung over her shoulder. Elodie waves, her heart filling at the sight of her girl. Nancy spots her and rushes over. She drops her backpack on the ground and hugs her mother.

"Let me look at you," Elodie says, pulling away slightly but still holding onto her.

She's tall and lanky, wearing high-waisted jeans and Doc Martens, just like Véronique wears. Her hair, once blond, has darkened to a warm nut brown. She has traces of all of them in her features—Gabriel, Maggie, Elodie, and, she sees now, Dennis. The Irish coloring, a splatter of freckles on pale skin, bright blue eyes, red lowlights in her hair. "You're so beautiful," Elodie murmurs, tugging Nancy back into her arms. "I've missed you."

"Me, too," she says.

"I'm glad you came."

"How could I not? My flight was only ninety-nine dollars."

A couple of Canadian airlines offered huge discounts to fly Canadians to Montreal for today's Unity Rally. The flood of support from Canadians outside the province is supposed to show how much they care about Quebec and hopefully persuade Quebeckers to vote No in Monday's referendum. It's yet to be determined if this last-minute "love-in" will sway the province's undecided voters.

The polls are showing it's neck and neck, with Yes slightly ahead. It could go either way. Unlike 1980, when the No side was the clear front-runner, this referendum is going to be dangerously close. Even three days away, no one knows what's going to happen. The overriding sentiment everywhere in the country seems to be one of grave tension, a looming dread that Canada may be days away from separation. Even Elodie has found herself swept up in referendum fever—watching coverage on the news, discussing it with her friends. Everyone has an opinion. Elodie is going to vote No.

In the end, it was Nancy who swayed her. It means a lot to her, keeping the country together. She's worried about the economy if Quebec separates; worried about her future, Elodie's future. Nancy said to her one night over the phone, "You're voting No, right, M'ma?"

"I'm not sure," Elodie responded, afraid to admit she wasn't planning to vote.

"What do you mean you're not sure? If Quebec separates, I'll never be able to come home."

"Why not?"

"I won't be able to build a life in the midst of all that political and economic chaos," Nancy said. "I certainly won't start a family there, not with everything so uncertain. Canada is going to cut Quebec off and let them fend for themselves, that's what the federal government is saying. Quebec can't survive without federal support. Why would I ever come back to that?"

Come back? Build her life here?

Elodie was stunned. She had resigned herself to Nancy staying out east, making a life for herself in New Brunswick. Nancy seems to have a different plan.

It was that simple for her. Having made her decision, Elodie was immediately committed to it. Now, when she watches the news and it's reported that the Yes side is gaining momentum, she feels anxious. She wants Nancy to come home for good.

"How are you?" Nancy asks her as they set off for the rally. "Anything new?"

Elodie doesn't mention what's been going on with the Duplessis orphans. There haven't been any significant wins or positive developments, so why bother? Old habits. The only other news she has is about Nancy's father, Dennis. His return to Elodie's life was so fleeting and surreal she still sometimes questions whether it really happened. They talked for more than an hour that day, sitting across from each other in that booth, until she could see that his pain and discomfort were becoming unbearable. When it was time for him to leave, they hugged goodbye as though they'd known each other their whole lives—and in some ways they have—and then he left. They didn't exchange numbers or pretend they would ever see each other again.

As much as she hates keeping this secret from Nancy, she doesn't have the heart to tell her that her father survived Vietnam but only has a few months left to live. It seems less cruel to say nothing.

"Tell me what's new with you," Elodie says, looping her arm in Nancy's, the way she does with Véronique.

"I'm still working at Sears, and I've been taking English classes in Shediac."

"Are you seeing anyone?"

"No, Bouctouche is too small."

"They still have boys, though."

"None I like. Anyway, I'm not looking for a boy-friend. Your generation is so codependent."

"What's that?"

"The way you all think a woman needs a man to be okay."

"I don't have a man. I never did."

"So why do you care if I have one?"

"Because I want you to have someone to take care of you. It's easier."

"That makes no sense," Nancy says. "It's old-fashioned."

"Look at your grandparents. Maggie and Gabriel were so happy together. They were best friends, and they took care of each other. That's what I want for you."

"Why didn't you want it for yourself?"

"I didn't know how to be in a relationship," Elodie admits.

Nancy stops and turns to face her. "Well, you do now," she says. "And you're good at it."

Elodie touches her daughter's cheek, but Nancy—not one to linger in sentimentality—turns around and says, "Can you unzip my bag? I made a sign for the rally."

Elodie unzips the backpack and pulls out a small

sign on white cardboard. It says NEW BRUNSWICK LOVES QUEBEC!

Nancy holds it above her head as they join the crowd, which is slowly forming a parade in the middle of the street en route to Place du Canada. The morning sun is bright white, glinting off the downtown high-rises. The air is mild except for a gusting wind—a reminder that winter is on the horizon. They quickly find themselves swept up in a throng of patriots, waving their No banners and homemade signs. UNITED WE STAND, DIVIDED WE GET OUR BUTTS KICKED. MY CANADA INCLUDES QUEBEC. VOTE NO SO WE DON'T BECOME THE 51ST STATE! TORONTO LOVES QUEBEC! PLEASE DON'T GO!

Elodie reaches for Nancy's hand, not wanting to lose her in the crowd. She hates big crowds. She's already feeling unsettled. People are chanting as they approach Place du Canada. "*Ca-na-da! Ca-na-da! Ca-na-da!*" A man walking beside them has a red maple leaf painted on his cheek; he's pumping his fist in the air as he chants. All around them, VOTE NO stickers are plastered across foreheads; some people are wrapped in red-and-white Canadian flags, others in Quebec's blue-and-white fleurs-de-lis. An airplane passes overhead, trailing a banner that says STRONG, PROUD & FREE in French and English.

Elodie is starting to feel emotional. "I never knew people cared this much."

When they reach their meeting place at the statue of John A. Macdonald, the square is absolutely mobbed. People are perched on the statues of Macdonald and Laurier like pigeons, hoping for a better view. A massive Canadian flag is surfing its way over the crowd, which is probably in the tens of thousands by now. Everyone is belting out the national anthem in French, loud and proud.

Elodie spots Stephanie standing on the monument above the crowd, waving a maple leaf and a fleur-de-lis flag. James and Maggie are waving them over, two dots in a sea of red and blue flags.

When they're all together, James hoists Nancy up onto the monument so she can have a better view of the rally. Nancy and Stephanie coolly acknowledge each other.

"Can you believe this turnout?" Maggie asks her, attempting an embrace. "There must be fifty thousand people here."

The hug is a little too long and tight for Elodie's comfort. She has trouble looking Maggie in the eyes. There's an awkwardness between them that didn't used to be there, at least not since the early days.

"I've never seen an Anglophone waving a Quebec flag before," Elodie says, turning to James.

"And you never will again," he responds, taking a picture of someone wearing a T-shirt with the slogan ON T'AIME QUEBEC. He's got the camera around his neck and a tape recorder in his hand.

"You're here as a reporter?" Elodie asks him.

"And as a No supporter."

"I guess Véronique isn't here?"

James laughs out loud at the question. "No, she's not. She's as far away as she could get."

"I hope you guys will be okay regardless of how it turns out."

"Of course we will," he says. "It's just politics."

It seems like it's much more than just politics to Véronique, but Elodie doesn't say so. "What happened with your story about her father and the October Crisis?" she asks. "I looked for it on the anniversary of Laporte's murder."

"My editor decided to hold it," James says. "He didn't think the timing was right with the referendum looming. He felt it would be too divisive. It'll run some time in November."

He takes a few more pictures of the expanding crowd, scribbles some notes on a small pad. He turns to a guy in a Vancouver Canucks sweatshirt. "Why did you come today?" he asks, in perfect English.

"I had to," the guy says, choking up. "I love Canada. I love Quebec. I just needed to be here. If we can convince just one Quebecker that we care about this province, it'll be worth it."

The crush of people is starting to make Elodie claustrophobic. The RCMP officers are setting up metal railings near the stage. A woman is already giving a speech up there. "Our French and English duality," she blusters from the podium, "is what makes Canadians so special and so different from our dynamic neighbor, the United States of America! This duality is *why* we want to stay together!"

The crowd is going wild. Elodie glances up at Nancy, who's on her tiptoes on the statue of John A. Macdonald, cheering louder than anyone else. Elodie loves her spirit. She's always had it, this unwavering exuberance for life. Elodie did right by her, shielding her from her past. Maybe she gets some of it from Dennis, too, the same kind of loyalty and patriotism that leads a young man to enlist in an unwinnable war.

A couple of guys carrying flags from Yellowknife jostle past, accidentally shoving Elodie into the people in front of her. They apologize and shake her hand, and when she mutters something back to them in French, they say, "We love Quebec! We love you!"

Elodie is not faring well in the mob, though. She wants to escape, can't take her eyes off the empty streets just beyond the square. She doesn't want to disappoint Nancy. Leaving early to be by herself is exactly the sort of thing she hates to do, but her heart is galloping, her throat starting to constrict.

"You okay?" James asks her, just as the prime minister takes the stage.

"I think I'm going to head home."

"Chrétien is about to give his speech. This is such a historic day, El—"

She ignores him and reaches for Nancy's ankle. Nancy looks down at her from her perch on the statue. "I'm going to go," Elodie calls up to her. "I'll meet you at home later, okay?"

"You're leaving now? Why?"

"Too many people," she says. "You can tell me about it when you get home."

Nancy nods, understanding, but Elodie doesn't miss the shadow of disappointment across her face.

As Elodie pushes her way through the crowd, she can hear the prime minister rousing the people: *Quebec is our home, but Canada is our country!*

The crowd starts to thin out at Mountain Street, so she turns and flees the downtown core. She decides to walk home. The weather is holding up and she's starting to calm down, breathe easier. The fresh air feels good on her face, in her bones. She inhales deeply, enjoying the breeze. She just wants to feel like herself again.

In the distance, she can still hear the echo of the prime minister's promises: "We will make the changes that are needed so that Canada can move into the twenty-first century united from sea to sea!"

27

"How was your propaganda rally?"

James spins around to find Véronique standing in the doorway of their bedroom. She cut her hair the other day. It's shorter now, falls just below her ears in a bob. Her roots have grown out, too, so her hair is more natural than usual—soft brown, slightly wavy. She wears no makeup, no jewelry other than a small diamond in her nose. Her beauty still startles him when she walks into a room.

"Shit, I didn't even hear you," he says. "I'm just filing my story about the rally."

"How was it?"

"Pretty incredible," he says, breaking into a grin. "You should have come with me. It was pretty memorable. It might even have swayed you to see all the support from across the country—"

"It's too little too late," she says. "If the Yes side wasn't ahead in the polls, there wouldn't have been a rally today."

"It's basically tied in the polls."

"Canadians don't give a shit about Quebec, James. The real message of today was *Don't leave us because we love Canada* exactly *the way it is.* It's not because they love Quebec."

"Does it matter, V?" he says. "They came, they showed their support, and it was pretty amazing. I'm a cynical guy, especially when it comes to politics, but I was moved today. A lot of people were. You just had the feeling you were witnessing something really momentous, history-making."

"That's touching."

"What did you do today?" he asks her, not in the mood to fight.

"Louis and I were campaigning at the colleges all day."

"Campaigning?"

"Talking to students. What should I call it?"

"You're spending a lot of time with him."

"Please don't do that," she says.

"What?"

"Be the jealous boyfriend. He's a friend. And he's downstairs, so let's not do this."

"Louis is here?"

"Yes. Would you like to meet him?"

James's high from today's rally is rapidly fading. In spite of what he keeps telling everyone—*it's just politics, we're fine*—his relationship with Véronique has become strained in the last couple of weeks.

"Let me just send this in," he says. "I'll be down in a minute."

Véronique turns and leaves the room. He sends the rally piece to Damian, aware that his mood has crumbled. He was looking forward to hanging out with Véronique tonight, renting a movie and ordering food, just the two of them. Now he's got to make small talk with her separatist friend.

Downstairs, Louis and Véronique are sitting at either end of the couch, facing each other. Louis is smoking; she's laughing. Right away, James is irritated. They never smoke in the apartment. Véronique has given Louis an empty Coke can from their recycling bin to use as an ashtray.

Louis gets up as James comes into the room and extends his hand. They shake. James manages a smile but makes a point of glaring at the cigarette perched on the lip of the Coke can.

"Good to meet you," Louis says.

James nods and sits down in the armchair closest to Véronique, sizing up Louis. He's a kid, like Véronique; still very much into grunge, with long dirty hair and a torn plaid shirt open to reveal a black Soundgarden T-shirt. Crooked teeth, yellow fingertips, acne scars along his cheekbones. He's not ugly, though, and James has to wonder if Véronique could fall for a guy like Louis. He's her age, with a similar background and a common purpose.

"Véronique mentioned you were at the rally today."

"I was covering it for work," James says, not sure why he feels the need to pretend he wouldn't have gone otherwise. He would have.

"We had our own rally of two," Louis says, smiling privately at Véronique. They both laugh.

"Oh, yeah?" James says, tensing. "I thought you were at the college campuses today."

"We were, but we went for a little bike ride in the East End."

"We were riding around with the fleur-de-lis," she elaborates.

James imagines them on a bicycle together, her arms around his waist, flying their Quebec flag.

"A reporter from *La Presse* took our picture."

"It'll probably be in the paper tomorrow," she adds, finishing Louis's thought.

"We called it a Yes rally of two," Louis says, grinning. "And we didn't take any money from the federal government to show our support either."

"You do realize the federal government has a stake in this referendum," James says.

"How so?" Louis asks. "Canada has nothing to do with our referendum. The private businesses outside Quebec that subsidized the rally are in violation of the international right of people to self-determination."

"The entire referendum is *about* Canada," James says. "The word *Canada* is literally in the referendum question on the ballot."

"Canadians should have no right to interfere in our decision about separation."

"How would you feel if the rest of Canada held a referendum about whether to kick Quebec out of the confederation?" James asks him. "And then they told Quebeckers that they had no say in the vote because it didn't involve them?"

"I'd be thrilled if Canada wanted to kick us out of the confederation."

"You're missing the point." *Asshole.*

"Look," Louis says. "Your government has been speeding up the citizenship process for immigrants in order to increase No votes, and it also paid for today's love-in, which is against the referendum law's spending limits."

"*My* government? We still have the same government."

"Not for much longer," Louis says. "The No side blew a ten-point lead and is now seven points behind the Yes side. Wake up, brother."

"I'm starving," Véronique interrupts. "Should I order a pizza?"

James is fuming but doesn't want to let on. Doesn't want to come off as jealous or petty. Louis is smart, and that bothers him. It doesn't help that he feels old around the two of them, like he's the only grown-up in the room. "I'm going to head over to St. Laurent and grab a beer," he says, getting to his feet. "I've been looking forward to one all day."

"Should we all go?" Véronique says.

"No, no. You guys order pizza and hang out here," he says, a little too nonchalant to be credible. "I won't be late."

He doesn't give her time to argue. He hopes he's coming off indifferent, but inside he's raging. He can't stand that arrogant imbecile spouting off about international law. Riding a bicycle with *his* girlfriend and laughing with her at their stupid inside jokes. Smoking in *his* apartment.

"Later, man," Louis says.

James walks over to Bifteck, stewing. First thing

he does is order a snakebite—a shot of whiskey with lime—and a pitcher of beer to chase it. It's still early and the bar is completely empty. James heads to the back room to shoot some pool by himself. He sets up the balls, breaks. He goes on a run, wishing Véronique were here. Regretting how he handled himself with Louis. He behaved exactly the way he knows she would hate him to behave—argumentative and contentious, huffing off by himself like a martyr.

Maybe they're laughing about it right now, smoking and sharing a pizza. Why didn't he see this coming? The minute she started hanging around Louis—delivering signs, "campaigning"—he should have been on his guard. Véronique is beautiful; there's no way Louis isn't attracted to her. He's probably in love with her, biding his time until she dumps her middle-aged, federalist boyfriend.

Oh, how Léo would welcome Louis into the family! What more could he ask for in a son-in-law? Surely this has to have crossed Véronique's mind. It's what happened to his mother. Maggie loved Gabriel, but she married her first husband, Roland, to please her father. Her father was the reason she never told Gabriel she was pregnant with Elodie. It wasn't about being poor; it was always about her father's approval. Why should Véronique be any different?

He can hear his own father's words as he leans over the pool table and takes his final shot, sinking the black ball in the corner pocket. *Whatever you do, don't let her get away. I let your mother go because I was too proud and self-righteous, and I almost didn't get her back.*

Proud and self-righteous, those were Gabriel's words, uttered hundreds of times over the course of James's life, always in reference to how close he came to losing Maggie. He always said it was only when he finally set aside his enormous ego and showed up on her doorstep, begging her to take him back, that he made things right.

James orders another snakebite, downs it at the bar, and then returns to the back room to set up another game of solitary pool. He's already feeling a little drunk and sorry for himself. Wondering what Véronique and Louis are doing back at his goddamn apartment.

"You winning?"

He turns around and there she is. His heart speeds up a bit, but he doesn't want her to know how happy he is to see her. *Proud and self-righteous.* He can hear Gabriel's voice in his head.

She's so beautiful. Even now, it makes him feel so vulnerable, like she has all the leverage.

28

"Where's Louis?" James asks her, leaning on his pool cue. She can tell he's trying to act blasé, but he looks worried.

"He left."

"Oh."

James turns back to the pool table.

"You're jealous of Louis?" she asks him.

"Yeah. I am."

She smiles.

"You've spent every day of the last month with him," James says, wiping chalk off his hands onto his jeans. "He's probably in love with you."

"Probably."

"I'm serious."

"And I'm in love with you," she says. "He's not my type."

"Isn't he?"

"No. Why? Because we're the same age?"

"He's a separatist."

"That doesn't make him my type," she says. "You think I want to sleep with every separatist in the province?"

"No, just Louis."

"Well, I don't."

"I'm sure your father would love him."

"I'm sure he would," Véronique says. "But he's not *my* type. You're my type."

"We've been arguing a lot lately," he points out. "And every time I turn around, you're with Louis."

"The referendum will be over soon. We're both tense. The whole province is tense."

"I love you," he says.

She reaches out to touch his chin. "You've got chalk here," she tells him, rubbing it off with her thumb.

"Will you marry me?"

"What?"

"I'm serious," he says. "Obviously, this is not how I imagined proposing—in this shithole with blue chalk all over my face—but you're the one for me, V. I can re-propose later with a ring and everything. I've got my grandmother's wedding ring."

"I don't care about a ring."

He drops to one knee, takes her hand. "Véronique Fortin, will you marry me?"

She strokes his hair and tosses her head back, laughing. "Of course I'll marry you."

"Let's do it tomorrow," he says, standing up. "Let's go to the courthouse—"

"No. No way. We're not rushing to get married two days before the referendum."

"Screw the referendum."

"What are you afraid of?" she asks him. "I'm not going anywhere."

His expression is uncertain; he doesn't quite believe her.

"I'll marry you after Quebec wins its independence," she says. "And then we'll raise little Quebec citizens."

"And if you lose on Monday?"

"I'll marry you anyway," she says, kissing him. "I promise, win or lose, I'm not going anywhere. Now rack 'em up and let's play."

James goes over to the other end of the table and grabs the triangle. She starts rolling the balls to him, and he arranges them inside the triangle for the break.

Her cell phone rings. She signals for James to give her a minute. His face falls. The only people who call on her cell phone besides him are Camil, Marc, and Louis—none of whom he can stand. She can tell he's pissed.

"Véro? It's Marc. Can you talk?"

"What is it? I'm in a bar. It's hard to hear."

"My dad has a new distributor in Ottawa," he says. "He wants to know if you'd be willing to go back."

"Who is it?"

"The nephew of one of Camil's Hells Angels friends from Howick. He's in his second year at Carleton. He lives in the residence. He's super keen. I'll be with you. There's nothing to worry about with this guy."

"I don't know if I want to get involved with that whole scene again."

"Think about the money, cousin. Think how much you can make and save up before you go back to school."

"Let me think about it."

"Also, Callahan is dead."

The words land like a brick to the solar plexus. She stops breathing.

"Véro?"

"How do you know?"

"My dad's been trying to reach him for a while," Marc explains. "Callahan's father finally answered."

It can't be true. It can't be true.

"How?" she asks, trying to calm down. Her hands are shaking so hard the phone is wobbling against her ear.

"He overdosed."

She doesn't believe him. She hangs up and leans against the pool table to stay upright.

"What is it, V?" James's voice sounds far away, but he's right beside her. "What is it? What happened, V? Are your parents okay?"

She doesn't answer. She can't. Her uncle did this—she's sure of it—or he hired someone to do it. Not just as payback for what Callahan did to Véronique, but to clear the path for a new distributor so that Véronique would return and make him more money.

Maybe Callahan did OD, she tells herself. *It's possible.* Still. The timing. It's too much of a coincidence.

"What's wrong?" James is asking, shaking her shoulders. "Talk to me."

"Callahan overdosed."

"Shit. Is he dead?"

"Yes."

Without a word, James pulls her against his chest and holds her there. He doesn't say anything, which is a relief.

29

October 30, 1995

The polls close at eight p.m., in about half an hour. Véronique looks over at Louis. His expression is serious, in spite of the blue and white fleurs-de-lis painted on his cheeks with Halloween makeup. He's wearing the Quebec flag as a cape, just like her father did at the rally for Charles de Gaulle and the St. Jean parade in the sixties. There's a photo of Léo in the family album looking much like Louis tonight.

Véronique's been holding her breath all day. She hasn't spoken to James since they voted this morning. They were both somber through breakfast, then on their way to the polling station. They didn't fight, but there wasn't the usual light banter between them either, no affection or tenderness. James went straight to work afterwards. He'll be covering the results at the Metropolis nightclub tonight, temporary home of the No headquarters.

Véronique went to see her parents in the afternoon. The mood at their house was equally tense. They'd already started drinking. There's so much riding on tonight, she worries another failure will be too much for them.

She found her mother unloading groceries in the kitchen—bags of potato chips, nuts, plastic trays of party sandwiches, veggies, onion dip. Lisette chain-smoked while she bustled around, opening and closing the fridge, the pantry.

"I think we're going to win tonight," Véronique said, helping to put away the food.

"I hope so," Lisette said, sipping from her beer. "We're expecting half the neighborhood."

"We're still ahead in the polls. That's a good sign."

"We're not ahead. It's 50–50. I'd feel better if we had more of a lead."

"The No side has blown a twenty-point lead in the polls in less than a month. The momentum is on our side."

"I can't face a déjà vu of 1980."

"My generation will make the difference this time," Véronique assured her. "Trust me, *we* want our own country."

Léo came in from sweeping the leaves then. "What about your boyfriend?" he said, full of nervous energy. "Where's he watching tonight?"

"The No headquarters."

Her father pulled up a chair and straddled it. "Véro, what does that tell you?"

"It tells me we disagree about this referendum."

"It's more than the referendum you don't agree on," he said, his face right up close to hers. "You don't agree on separation, or the future of this province. For that matter, you don't agree on the *past*. Our beliefs are at the heart of who we are, Véro. I spent more than a decade in prison for those beliefs. We didn't raise you to wind up with some federalist traitor."

"He'll adapt to an independent Quebec. Things won't always be this intense."

"He disagrees with everything you stand for. He works for the enemy, Véro. Christ, he *is* the enemy!"

"James is not the enemy," she responded.

"He's sure as hell not on your side."

Inside the Palais des Congrès, the lights dim and the crowd roars to life. Bernard Derome, the news anchor from Radio-Canada, appears above them on the jumbotron TV, where *Le Téléjournal* is being broadcast live.

"Here come the results," Louis says, staring up at the screen.

Véronique wishes James were here. She wouldn't admit it to her father this afternoon, but she hates that he's at Metropolis right now. It would be so much easier if they were in sync on this.

The first results show the Yes side in the lead. Everyone in the audience erupts. Véronique grabs Louis's shirtsleeve in her excitement. In the first half hour, the Yes side surges to a 57 percent lead. The atmosphere is charged, the noise deafening. No one can hear Derome above all the chanting. When the jumbotron suddenly cuts to the silent, grim-faced crowd at the No headquarters, everyone inside the Palais des Congrés goes wild.

Véronique catches a snippet of what Derome is saying on TV: "The rest of Canada is stunned right now."

Everyone is on their feet, singing, "*Na, na, na, na, hey, hey, hey, goodbye!*"

The Yes vote continues to climb. "Is this really happening?" she says to Louis.

"We just need the Montreal votes," he says, knowing, as everyone in this arena knows, that Montreal will determine the outcome of the referendum. As they wait, a nervous tension settles over the crowd. Time slows, causing a perceptible mood shift. Ever so slowly, the gap between Yes and No begins to close.

"We may only win by a single percentage point," Louis says.

"It would still be a win."

On the jumbotron, a young separatist is being interviewed. "Sovereignty is a deep conviction for my generation," she says. "Whatever the result is tonight, people across Canada have to understand that for us, our country *is* Quebec, and that will never change."

An hour later, the results are dead even. The crowd has gone quiet. Véronique can hear the sound of nervous gum chewing behind her. Everyone is transfixed to the jumbotron, where scenes from the No headquarters are unfolding above them; people there are cheering and singing "O Canada" as they watch the No side creep up to tie the Yes side for the first time all night.

Véronique swallows a lump in her throat. She imagines James in that crowd, singing "O Canada."

"It's not over yet," Louis says, seeing the look on her face. But she can feel it slipping away.

At ten, the No side officially takes the lead. All around her, shock and confusion.

"Nationalism is not done in Quebec," a separatist is telling a reporter on TV. "The people of Quebec will continue the battle for recognition."

The final results come in at ten twenty p.m., declaring a marginal win for the No side. It's over.

"For the second time in fifteen years," Derome announces, "a majority of Quebec voters have rejected the idea that Quebec should become a sovereign country, and have chosen for Quebec to stay in Canada. It's a narrow victory, but a victory nonetheless."

Véronique looks around the arena. People are stunned, shaking their heads in disbelief. Some are crying into their hands or on the shoulders of their neighbors. Louis is crying beside her, his tears smudging the blue and white fleurs-de-lis on his cheeks. She thinks about her parents.

"It always ends this way for us," Louis says, wiping his face.

"Let's get out of here." She can't stand the idea of being here for the political postmortem, the speeches and concessions, the false optimism. *Next time!* Parizeau will say. *Next time!* Bouchard will say.

This was their time and they failed. By less than half a percentage point, they failed.

She follows Louis out of the arena, keeping her head down. Outside, a crowd of frustrated Yes supporters is collecting in the street, their disappointment already turning to anger. It's mostly young people; the older ones are still inside, grieving with their politicians. Louis grabs a case of beer at one of the *dépanneurs* and cracks a bottle open for each of them.

They start moving west with the crowd. Véronique realizes, after a few blocks, that the mob is heading toward Metropolis. No one had to give the order or let everyone else know the plan. They all just instinctively knew to go and find the No voters.

Louis is waving his Quebec flag in the air. Someone throws an empty beer bottle into a storefront on Ste. Catherine Street, and it feels satisfying to watch it shatter. Véronique finishes her beer and throws her bottle into an alley. "*C'est pas fini!*" she screams. *It's not finished.*

The horde is swelling as more people spill out of the Palais des Congrès. Metropolis is only a ten-minute walk. *Here we come*, Véronique thinks.

Within blocks of the No headquarters, the two sides eventually come face-to-face on Ste. Catherine Street— the Yes side angry and grieving, the No side celebratory and gloating. Her people are yelling, "Quebec! Quebec!"

The other side: "Canada! Canada!"

She whips another bottle into the sky. Someone else

throws one at a storefront, and she watches the glass shatter. She wonders briefly if the owner of the store voted Yes or No—she hopes No—and then moves on. *"Quebec libre! Quebec libre!"*

Someone hurls a rock into the oncoming No supporters. Véronique turns and realizes it was Louis. His face is pure hatred. "Don't hurt anyone!" she cries, and then loses him in the riot.

English people are screaming in her face. She screams back in French. Someone from her side rips a Canadian flag out of a No supporter's hands and lights it on fire. Everything is happening so fast. Bottles and rocks are flying back and forth, cars bursting into flames, store windows being smashed.

Véronique manages to throw her remaining bottles— full, exploding with beer—into the swarm of rioters before getting swallowed by the crowd. A helicopter flying overhead is the first sign of police. Soon, the street is full of them, lined up in riot gear, cordoning off the side streets, breaking up fights and making arrests.

She searches for Louis, but he's long gone, vanished in the fray. More than anything else, she feels betrayed. Not by Louis but by the province, the politicians, James. She thinks about her parents and Pierre and Uncle Camil; about Céline from the volunteer office and Louis's parents and Elodie. She thinks about everything they've all suffered by simple virtue of being poor and French, and she's overcome with frustration. She will probably never see Quebec separation in her lifetime. Her parents certainly won't.

She spots a brick from a nearby construction site, and without any hesitation or forethought she throws it at the rear windshield of a white Subaru with a McGill University sticker on the bumper. She watches the glass smash and lets out a primal scream. It feels good to smash things.

When two cops grab her from behind and push her to the ground, she isn't afraid. She remembers the stories her father used to tell her, and she makes her body go limp. The cops cuff her and struggle to get her to her feet; she's dead weight in their arms. They're screaming at her to stand up and cooperate.

"*Quebec belongs to us!*" she cries.

They drag her to the police van. Her jeans are torn, her knees bloody, her boot shredded from the pavement. She doesn't care anymore. She wants it out of her—the pain, the disappointment. The violence, she realizes, brings a reprieve from those feelings. Her father must have always known that. The straightforwardness of throwing bricks and destroying property is far more therapeutic than quiet complacence.

James keeps encouraging her to live by society's rules and work diligently in her pursuits. She tried. She volunteered for the Yes campaign; she stuck signs in the ground, cleaned toilets, and handed out flyers. Look where it got her. She refuses to accept tonight's loss. Her father had it right. She will smash and fight and rage until something changes.

When the cops finally manage to lock her inside the van, she folds over with her face in her lap and sobs. After a few minutes, she feels a hand on her lower back, consoling her. She lifts her head. It's a woman, not much older than she, with a swollen bottom lip. "It's not over," the woman says, through her own tears. "We'll win the next one."

30

James is staring at his cell phone, waiting for it to ring. It's ten in the morning. Twenty-four hours since he's seen or heard from Véronique. He's been calling her all night—he bought her the new Nokia cell phone in August, mainly as a safety precaution—but he hasn't been able to reach her. After what happened with Callahan, it makes him feel better to know she can always call him, no matter where she is or what's going on. But she made no use of her phone last night, and she's obviously turned it off today. He hasn't heard from her since they parted ways at the polling station yesterday morning—not even to let him know she's okay. He's left her at least twenty messages since the referendum ended.

The truth is he's not really worried she's in danger;

he's worried she's with Louis. And he's furious. He's been trying to watch the news to distract himself. It's been hour after hour of referendum coverage, panels, and political analyses. The Yes side's now infamous concession speech, in which their drunk and defeated leader blamed the Jews and the "ethnic" vote for the loss, has been playing in a loop on every channel. If James weren't so damn frantic about Véronique, he'd be enjoying every minute of it.

Every so often he gets up and goes to the window to watch the street for her. He called her parents' place last night at around eleven, but hung up as soon as Léo answered. He didn't want to worry them, also didn't want them to know he had no idea where she was. They'd know right away something was wrong. He didn't want to give Léo that satisfaction.

The TV is still droning. James is half listening to some panel on CBC while staring down at his cell phone. "We were all extremely anxious and nervous last night," some pundit is saying. "If the Yes side had won, we were going to be in a lot of trouble this morning. All my instincts told me that no one had a clue what we were going to end up with today."

James absently changes the channel over to a French station for a different take. "The No side winning such a narrow victory has caused a great deal of tension in this province," a French commentator is saying. "There is a lot of bitterness today."

James tries Véronique's cell phone again, more to keep busy than out of any real hope she'll answer. She doesn't. Just as he's about to try her parents again, the front door opens, keys jangling from the vestibule. He jumps up and rushes to greet her in the foyer. "Where have you been?" he says. "I've been calling you all night!"

She looks disheveled, tired.

"Were you with Louis?" he asks her.

"Let me inside, James."

"Did you spend the night at his place? Did you sleep with him to punish me?"

"I was in jail!" she screams.

"Jail? Were you in the riot?"

"Yes."

"V—"

"Just leave me alone."

"What happened? Are you okay? Why didn't you call me to come bail you out?"

"I called my dad."

"I would have come."

"I couldn't face you," she says, heading for the kitchen. She goes to the fridge, pulls out the pitcher of filtered water, and drinks straight from the pitcher.

"Tell me what happened."

"I was arrested."

"And?"

"I'm exhausted. I just want to shower and go to bed. I don't want to get into this now."

"Get into this?" he says, annoyed. "I've been up all night waiting for you. Do you know how worried I was? And you don't want to talk about it?"

"It was a terrible night," she says. "I was angry and I got caught up in the riot and I was arrested. Oh, and we lost the referendum."

"I know how much you're hurting—"

"No, you don't!" she cries. "You won. *You always win!*"

"Don't lump me in with whomever it is you're blaming," he says. "I'm as French as you are."

"You're nothing like me," she says. "You voted No. You work for an English corporation. You're the reason we lost. *You're* the reason Quebec will never be independent."

"Baby, I'm not the enemy.'"

She shakes her head. "'They have French names, Quebec roots, Quebec diplomas, Quebec parents . . . but they have disavowed us. They work for Masters who scorn us. This fear they have that we will be on our own in here—'"

"All right, V, enough with the nationalist poetry. It's just politics."

She looks at him. *Through him.* Her face is hard.

"Look," he says, "it was so close. Things are going to change now for the better. Quebec has sent a very clear message to the rest of the country."

"Nothing will change," she says. "We didn't want to just send a message."

He attempts to pull her into his arms, but she pushes him away.

"I know you're upset, but it's just a goddamn referendum. It wasn't the first and it won't be the last."

"To *you* it was just a referendum."

"We have a good life together, V. Certainly not the life of poverty and hardship you've been commiserating about for the last few months. You're young, you're going back to school, we're getting married. You have a lifetime ahead of you to achieve whatever it is you want, including Quebec independence."

"My parents don't."

"No, they don't. But they'll move on. They did before."

She slides past him to go upstairs. He follows her.

"Louis keeps asking me how we manage to make our relationship work when we both want different things."

"I'm sure he does," James flares. "Maybe you should be with him. Is that what you want?"

"This isn't about Louis," she says, reaching the second floor, her back still to him.

"Isn't it?" he says. "Isn't that what you're really trying to tell me? That you and I don't belong together because I'm not a separatist?"

"I don't know."

"My father grew up poor!" James reminds her. "He was a farmer and a factory worker. You and I are not so different. Stop beating that drum."

"And your mother inherited a successful business from her English father and that's what lifted you all out of poverty. Don't you see that? Don't you get it?"

She goes into their bedroom and collapses on the bed. He stands in the doorway, fuming. "I'm not going to beg you to stay," he tells her. "It's not my fault you lost. I don't represent all of the No voters in the province. I'm just one vote. Your side lost the referendum. So what? It would have been an epic disaster if the Yes side had won anyway."

She sits up. "I'm going to shower."

"You're pissed off at me because I want to keep Canada in one piece," he says. "I can't keep apologizing for that, V. If you want to be with someone like Louis and make your daddy proud, maybe you should go."

He turns to leave the room.

"Where are you going?" she calls after him. "To get drunk and shoot pool by yourself?"

He stops in the doorway.

"It's nine o'clock in the morning," she says.

He turns back to face her. "Don't you see how crazy you're being?"

"I'm upset!"

"I know you're upset," he says, lowering his voice. "I get it, but I can't keep being your punching bag."

She doesn't say anything.

"Either we're solid, or our relationship is contingent on . . . what? Me becoming a separatist?"

"I just wish we were on the same side."

"I am on your side," he says, approaching the bed. "I'm the one who's always on your side. *Always.* You're talking like a victim, V, and you're better than that. You're better than Louis, better than the choices your father made."

He waits for her to blow up again, but she doesn't. She's staring at the floor. Poor thing. Her jeans are torn; there are dark circles under her eyes. He hadn't even noticed. "Are you okay?" he asks her. "Were you hurt last night?"

"Can we not talk about it right now? Will you just shower with me?"

He hesitates a moment. A difficult offer to refuse, but he can't let it be this easy for her.

"Please?" she says, looking up at him with her big eyes.

He nods, goes over to the bed.

"I have to go to court," she says.

"Tell me what happened."

"I smashed a car with a brick."

"That's pretty badass."

"I'm going to have a record."

"What were you thinking?"

"I wasn't," she says. "I was so angry."

"Was Louis arrested with you?"

"No. I lost him in the crowd before the cops showed up."

"He doesn't know you spent the night in jail?"

"No."

James feels some satisfaction knowing she didn't call Louis. He holds his hands out to her. She lets him pull her to her feet, and they go into the bathroom together. He takes off her clothes. There are dark purple bruises on her arms, probably where the cops grabbed her. He doesn't ask about them. He just kisses them.

She guides his head to her breasts and shivers when his tongue finds them. At the same time she's unzipping his jeans and their clothes fall to the floor. He turns her around and bends her forward over the tub. They don't even make it into the shower. The sex is a little rough, a little angry. They're both still smarting, for their own reasons. The tension between them isn't fully resolved. It makes for good sex, but James knows they're not finished with this conversation. Maybe they never will be.

31

November 1995

Elodie pulls up in front of the house on Terrace Groulx. There's a large OUI sign on the front lawn, Christmas lights strewn around the railing. It's just after four in the afternoon, but the sky is already dusky violet and quickly darkening. Outside, she pulls her hood over her head and looks up at the house. She has no idea what she's going to do if he's there. One minute she was home, rereading parts of Bruno's memoir. Next thing she knew, she was on the Champlain Bridge headed for the Townships.

Standing at the foot of Dr. Duceppe's front walk now, she can hardly remember what she thought might come of such a confrontation. She approaches the house. She can see there's a light on inside through the curtains of the picture window. She closes her eyes and presses her finger to the doorbell. *Let him not be home. Let him not be home.* Her heart is pounding. She can hear muffled voices inside. A woman. *Let him not be home.*

The door opens. She freezes.

"Can I help you?" he says, without warmth. *It's him.*

Forty years later, she is standing in front of the man who blithely sentenced her to life in hell. He must be in his seventies now, but the essence of him is unchanged; he's still intimidating, with an edge of brusqueness in his tone and cold eyes. His hair is white, with the same Clark Gable moustache trimmed exactly as it was back then, in two perfectly symmetrical spear tips with a clean-shaven Cupid's bow. He's wearing bifocals and his teeth have yellowed, but otherwise, he looks remarkably the same.

He's watching her, obviously not recognizing her. Time stands still. She's five years old again, trying to find her voice. "My—my name is Elodie."

He nods impatiently, waiting for more. Her name means nothing to him. She means nothing to him.

"Elodie . . . de Ste. Sulpice," she stammers.

Recognition slowly lights his eyes. She senses his discomfort. He seems to shrink back from her. "Do I know you?"

"Elodie de Ste. Sulpice," she says, with more confidence. "I was an orphan at Ste. Sulpice in 1955."

He shakes his head, dismissing her. "I'm sorry, I don't—"

"This is my file," she says, shoving it at him. "You were the one who diagnosed me mentally retarded." She opens the file and points to his signature at the bottom of the page. "That's your name, right there."

"I saw so many children," he mutters. "It's late—"

"I just want a few minutes of your time," she says. "I just want to ask you some questions. Please? I just need answers."

"I'm sorry," he says, attempting to close the door.

She holds up her hand. "Please? Isn't it the very least you can do? Just talk to me for a few minutes? Help me to understand."

"I'm sorry."

"*Let her in, Guillaume.*"

A woman's voice, behind him. Dr. Duceppe turns, startled.

"Let her in," Mme. Duceppe repeats.

He hesitates a moment and then holds open the door with an audible sigh. Elodie steps inside the vestibule. The house is already decorated for Christmas—a tree twinkling from the corner of the living room, a garland hanging from the fireplace. The wife collects fancy dolls, which are displayed all over the place—creepy little girls wearing fur stoles and hand muffs. There's a round table beside the couch, on which a Nativity scene is spread out over a fur-trimmed emerald green velvet tablecloth. A musical snow globe of Santa and Mrs. Claus is playing "Deck the Halls." Elodie doesn't know where to look.

"Would you like a cup of coffee? Some *sucre-à-crème?*"

Dr. Duceppe shoots his wife an irritated look.

"No thank you," Elodie says.

"Can I take your coat?"

"No."

"Sit, please," Mme. Duceppe says.

Elodie removes a needlepoint cushion of a reindeer from one of the press-back chairs facing the couch and sits down. Not knowing what to do with the cushion, she places it on her lap, resting her hands on the reindeer's face.

"Guillaume, do you want coffee?" his wife asks him.

He shakes his head and she bustles off, but not before giving Elodie an unmistakable look of sympathy.

"I'm not sure how I can help," Dr. Duceppe says, taking a seat on the couch. "It was a very long time ago."

"Why did you do it?" Elodie asks him, holding up her file. "Why did you sign this?"

Dr. Duceppe is silent.

"I wasn't mentally deficient in any way," she says. "I didn't know what a wallet was. Or keys. *How could I?* I'd never seen any before. I was only five! And from that you determined I belonged in an insane asylum?"

"It was much more complicated than that."

"How could it be?" Elodie says, her file shaking in her hands. "I was a normal little girl. You ruined my life—"

"No," he interrupts. "Duplessis ruined your life. You have to understand, our hands were tied. Duplessis gave the order. The nuns told us what to do. If it hadn't been me signing your assessment, it would have been another doctor. You were going to wind up in an institution no matter what. There was nowhere else for all of you to go."

She can feel tears coming, but she wills them back.

"The orphanages were terribly overcrowded," he explains. "They were filled well beyond capacity. There simply weren't enough of them to house all the illegitimate children in the province, let alone enough money. There was nowhere for all of you to go but to the hospitals. I told myself you would all be better off there than on the street. That's what it came down to."

"You knew the nuns and the provincial government would get more money for mental patients than for orphans," she says, unbuttoning her coat. The room is hot; her face feels flushed. "You knew and you just went along."

"Of course," he admits. "We all knew. Everyone knew. But what could we do? The order came directly from Premier Duplessis. Quebec was basically a theocracy back then. The church ran just about every institution in the province, and in return, Duplessis helped the church impose its traditions on every aspect of Quebec society. It was quid pro quo, and it was impenetrable. Those of us in the College of Physicians—we were just puppets. We did what we were told. We asked no questions."

"You turned a blind eye," Elodie accuses. "You had an obligation to uphold the standards of all the psychiatrists in the province. Your obligation was to protect *us*!"

"My sin was following orders and staying silent, yes. But what choice did I have back then? I couldn't disobey the most powerful man in the province. Or the church, for that matter. To whom should I have reported what was happening? Duplessis himself? The police, who were also under his thumb? *My* priest? There was nowhere to turn with my doubts."

"You had to know where you were sending us."

"No," he says, shaking his head. "I never knew about the mistreatment in the hospitals."

"That can't be true," she says. "If you'd ever set foot on any of those wards—which of course you must have done hundreds of times—you would have seen with your own eyes."

"Mam'selle Sulpice," he says, "we had no choice but to transfer all those children to mental hospitals. As a practical reality, there was no alternative. Not only were the orphanages overcrowded, but the hospitals were understaffed and in desperate need of labor."

"*Cheap* labor. Which we provided."

"Yes. In those days the nuns believed they had the right to judge and punish illegitimate children for the sins of their parents. It was the morality of the times. Given your circumstances, you were considered fortunate to be housed and cared for *anywhere*."

"Cared for?" Elodie cries, standing up. "We would have been better off in the street!"

"Well. As for what went on behind the walls of those hospitals," he says, "we knew implicitly not to infringe on any practices or decisions made by hospital management. That was the church's domain, certainly not within the purview of the doctors."

"It's always the same excuse. The doctors blame the church, the church blames the doctors—"

"I only did what the nuns told me to do."

"Most of the children you misdiagnosed are illiterate, uneducated, and living on welfare now. I did okay for myself. I found my family. But my friend Francine has brain damage from all the drugs she was given. She can't work. And my best friend from Ste. Sulpice is dead. She overdosed in her twenties."

Elodie pauses long enough to notice Mme. Duceppe standing in the doorway, looking horrified. Elodie takes a breath and sits back down, this time on the reindeer cushion.

Dr. Duceppe lowers his head.

"Do you remember me at all?" Elodie asks him.

He shakes his head, still looking at the floor. "Truthfully," he says, "I don't remember doing any proper exams at all. Not really. It was more like paperwork, bureaucracy."

"Do you even feel guilty about what you did?"

"I don't like to think about it," he says. "At the time, back in the fifties, I thought I was doing the right thing by trying to keep a roof over your heads. But when you all started showing up outside my house, picketing and protesting . . ." He returns his gaze to the floor. "I've questioned my actions many times."

"*Questioned?*"

"Yes, questioned whether I could have done something different. Something more noble." He looks up at her again. "And the answer is no. There was nothing else I could have done. Not then. But to answer your question, do I feel remorse now? Yes, I do. I'm a good Catholic. I'd have to be a monster not to feel terrible about what happened to you all, or not to feel guilty about my hand in your suffering."

"You knew we weren't at all mentally deficient when you diagnosed us, didn't you?"

"I do remember the smaller orphanages like Ste. Sulpice," he admits. "I did think the children seemed normal and well-adjusted, in some cases quite bright. Happy, even."

"I was happy," she says. "Until the day you came."

"Understandably," he murmurs.

"I'd like you to put that in writing."

"I beg your pardon?"

"I would like you to write a letter saying that you falsely diagnosed me on the orders of the nuns and the Duplessis government, even though you knew I was not mentally deficient."

"I don't understand what that will accomplish."

"Having it in writing will bring me some peace of mind."

She did not come here with the intention of forcing him to write a confession letter or an apology; the idea did not occur to her until just now. But having asked for it, she will not leave here without it.

"What will you do with it?" he asks nervously. Not a monster, but a coward.

"I don't know yet. Probably just keep it in the drawer beside my bed, to remind myself every day that I'm not crazy, and I never was."

"He'll do it," Mme. Duceppe intervenes, stepping into the room with a pen and a notepad. She hands it to her husband, glaring at him. Dr. Duceppe takes the pen. Elodie can't help thinking about the last time they sat across from each other, him with his pen and pad, jotting down notes, barely looking at her; and Elodie, completely naïve and trusting, her fate—unbeknownst to her—about to be sealed by the stroke of his pen.

"What do you want me to say?" he asks her.

"The truth."

He bows his head over the page and begins to write. A strand of white hair flops over his eye. His brows furrow in concentration, a snowy ledge across his forehead. Elodie watches him write. Anxious about reading it. She isn't sure what she'll do with it yet, possibly just leave it in her drawer, read it whenever her self-confidence is waning. Or maybe she'll present it in court one day—proof of the falsification of her records. She makes a mental note to discuss it with Bruno.

"You said you were five?" he confirms, head still bent.

"Yes."

"And you go by Elodie de Ste. Sulpice?"

"Elodie Phénix," she clarifies. "I took back my parents' name."

He looks up, smiles. "Well, that's wonderful." When he's finished writing, he rests the pen on the coffee table. "I wish I could do more," he says, handing her the letter.

"It's too late for that," she says, standing up and taking it from him. She reads it right in front of him.

I am writing this letter to acknowledge a grave moral mistake I made in the early years of my career in psychiatry. In 1955, I was tasked with examining a number of children at the Ste. Sulpice Orphanage in Farnham, Quebec, in order to diagnose their mental health. Under direct orders from the Grey Nuns, immediately following Premier Duplessis's reclassification of the province's orphanages into psychiatric institutions, I personally diagnosed a number of seemingly healthy children as mentally deficient. My reports were entirely false.

What stood out to me during those interviews at Ste. Sulpice was that the girls—ranging in age from five to fourteen—were generally bright and of sound mind. In other words, they were normal and frankly educable. While the level of their education to that point lagged somewhat behind the provincial standard, this was no doubt the result of having been institutionalized since birth. The orphans I examined were indeed sheltered and unworldly, but not one of them was mentally deficient.

One of those orphans was Elodie Phénix. She showed up on my doorstep this evening with her medical records in hand and asked me why I had signed a false diagnosis of mental deficiency. Mlle. Phénix is a grown woman of forty-five now. She is well-spoken, intelligent, resilient, and courageous. She couldn't be farther from the diagnosis I gave her forty years ago. To my great shame, the only answer I could offer her was my own cowardice in the face of the Catholic Church and the Duplessis regime.

I eschewed my responsibility as a psychiatrist in favor of towing the line. As such, I was complicit in the crimes against humanity that were committed against these innocent children. I feel deep shame for what I did, and on behalf of all the doctors like myself who were a discredit to the profession, I am deeply sorry. To Mlle. Phénix and all the others like her, I apologize for my part in your suffering.

Sincerely,
Dr. Guillaume Duceppe

She thanks him. She does not forgive him.

"I am sorry," he says, getting to his feet.

She turns away, not wanting him to see her eyes.

"Good luck," Mme. Duceppe tells her.

Outside, Elodie quickly lights a cigarette to settle her nerves. She gets inside her car and cranks up the heat. She unfolds the letter and reads it again, and again, and again.

She lowers her head onto the steering wheel and cries for little Claire, who could not count past ten.

32

The October Crisis Remembered
by an FLQ Killer

By J. G. Phénix, Special to the Canadian News Association

"It wasn't about the FLQ. It wasn't even about the FLQ versus the government. It was about the people. We did what we did for all the exploited Québécois who struggled and suffered and got nowhere," recalls Léo Fortin, one of the five FLQ members responsible for the murder of Labour Minister Pierre Laporte in October 1970.

"The government has blood on its hands, too," Fortin claims, twenty-five years later. "They sacrificed the life of one of their own to show us they had all the power. The War Measures Act was Laporte's death sentence. It was *the politicians* who did that to him—not us."

In spite of Fortin's assessment, he was convicted of murder in 1971 and sentenced to life in prison. He served eleven years for the crime. Still, in Fortin's eyes, the real victims of the 1970 October Crisis were the working-class Québécois, not the man who lies buried at Notre Dame des Neiges Cemetery, nor the family he left behind.

"The stories they put out about the FLQ were all propaganda," Fortin claims. "We weren't the villains they made us out to be. They had a choice to negotiate with us and save the life of their colleague, or to dig in their heels and throw Laporte to the wolves. We all know how it turned out."

After all these years, Fortin is still trying to convince himself that the *real* villains of the October Crisis were the politicians Pierre Trudeau and Robert Bourassa, the "arrogant, power-hungry" prime minister and his "lackey," the provincial premier. Fortin accepts no responsibility for the killing, nor has he ever expressed remorse.

Véronique stops reading and rips the entire paper to shreds, which she lets fall to the kitchen floor. No wonder James wouldn't show her the article before he filed it; he's a coward. Every newspaper in the country has picked it up, too, including the French ones.

This is her fault. Her father trusted her, and she trusted James. She's had her doubts about their compatibility over the years, but she never doubted *him*. If anything, she thought *her* choices would be their undoing. She never imagined he would use her this way, exploiting her trust to gain access to her father. And for what? For a goddamn story. *The* story.

How did she not see this coming? He was always willing to sacrifice their relationship for his own personal ambition. Léo warned her the night of the referendum. "He's sure as hell not on your side," he said.

James should never have been the one to write that article. She grabs a box of garbage bags from the kitchen and goes upstairs to pack. *Screw him*, she thinks, throwing open their closet. She starts pulling her clothes off the hangers, shoving them into a garbage bag. Her sweaters and jeans from the two bottom shelves, her socks and underwear from her two drawers—all of it goes into the garbage bags. James hired one of those organizing companies to redo the closet with fancy built-ins. It cost him a small fortune, but all their stuff fit perfectly. He can have it all to himself.

She clears out the bathroom, haphazardly dumping everything that's hers into one of the bags—hair dryer, toothbrush, cosmetics, shampoo, tampons, her favorite white towels that they bought together at the Bay. Brown for him, white for her. Back in the bedroom, she strips the bed. The sheets are hers. She's not leaving them. Into a garbage bag they go, with her goose-down duvet and pillow. She'll send for her wrought iron bed when she's settled somewhere. At the moment, she has no idea where that will be.

She'll have to stay with her parents for a little while—she doesn't have much choice right now—but she's determined to be in her own place as soon as possible. She decides all this as she's rushing from room to room, collecting her things, filling garbage bags, tossing James's shit out of her way.

When all the bags containing her life are piled in the vestibule, she calls Louis and asks him if he can pick her up. Her car's been parked at her parents' since she moved in with James. There's no parking on his street and she doesn't need it much now that she doesn't smuggle cigarettes. But she's not quite ready to call her parents. It's still too raw, and she's embarrassed to face her father. Louis doesn't ask questions. She likes that about him.

She sits down on one of the garbage bags to wait.

Wipes her eyes. They were going to drive up to the Laurentians this weekend and chop down their own Christmas tree. They'd also talked about going snowboarding at Mt. Sutton over the holiday. They were going to stay with his mother in Cowansville, spend a quiet New Year's Eve in the Townships, maybe at a B&B. Véronique was really looking forward to it. Instead, another loss. She forces herself to stop crying. Better to stay angry and strong.

Just as she has that thought, the door swings open and James appears.

"Hey, babe," he says, noticing the garbage bags. "What's going on? You cleaning stuff out?"

"Yeah, everything I own."

He looks confused. He steps around the garbage bags and dumps his coat on the banister. "What are you doing?"

"Leaving."

"Leaving *me*?"

"Yes."

"Why? What's going on?"

"I read your article about my dad."

"V—" A shadow of guilt in his eyes.

"Don't bother. There's nothing you can say. Nothing."

"V, just listen to me—"

"Fuck you!" she cries, standing up. "You called him an FLQ killer in the headline!"

"I didn't write that headline," he defends. "Damian did. Editors write the headlines, not the reporters."

She laughs, disgusted.

"V, please calm down. Let's talk about it, okay?"

"It reads like an opinion piece, and you've certainly made your opinion of my father very clear. Not just to me but to the entire country. Do you realize how humiliating this is for my family?"

"He did *murder* someone, V. And he *is* remorseless, by his own admission. Isn't that more humiliating for you than my stupid article?"

"You're an asshole," she says. "A selfish, calculating asshole."

"All I did was relay the facts," he says. "I told the truth."

"*Your* truth."

"*The* truth. Véronique. I basically recorded his story as he told it to me. If you don't like the article, it's because you don't like seeing the truth in print."

"You shouldn't have written it at all!" she screams, ignoring the possibility that James may be right about her father.

"I'm a journalist."

"Oh, for Christ's sake," she mutters. "Here we go again with your code of ethics."

"It's better than living by the criminal code."

"What wouldn't you do for a story?"

"Break the law."

"Oh, so you'd break my heart, but not the law," she says. "See, I'm the opposite. I'd break the law in a heartbeat, but never deliberately hurt someone I love. That's *my* code."

"Your code is fucked up."

"You used me!" she screams. "You manipulated me into letting you interview my dad. You deceived all of us, pretending you were going to let him tell his story in his own words. You swore you would be objective. Isn't that also part of your goddamn code?"

"I simply wrote his story as he told it to me."

"You should have fought Damian on the headline."

"I have no say in that."

"Our principles will never align," she says, feeling suddenly very clear and calm. "You betrayed me."

"The way you talk about principles and morals. What about your job and your family history?"

She laughs softly, hurt but not entirely surprised. She's always known this is where he stands. "My father is never going to forgive me."

"*I* wrote the story," James says. "You had nothing to do with it."

"Are you kidding me? I'm the one who promised him you would be fair. I convinced him to talk to you!"

"You don't have to move out over this, V."

"You just don't get it. You put your career before me. And let's face it, you have no respect for me or my family. You never did."

"I think you're the most brilliant woman I've—"

"Save it. You've been trying to change me since day one. You can't stand how I earn my living, you're embarrassed by what I do."

"You earn your living selling drugs," he reminds her. "So yes, it embarrasses me. I would like the woman I love to actually live up to her potential."

"See? You don't accept me for who I am."

"You don't know who you are," he counters. "You're not a criminal like your father. That's who you *think* you are. It's who you try to be, maybe for his approval or I don't know what. But you've got it backwards. *I'm* the one who actually sees who you really are, what you could be. You're too scared to try something different."

"It's a nice speech, but it doesn't change anything."

"Being a criminal isn't hereditary, you know. It's not like you're predisposed to it. You have choices."

"It's in my blood," she says. "I am what I am. At least I'm not an opportunist."

"Your principles are so twisted."

"Louis respects my principles."

The moment she utters Louis's name, she regrets it. It was never her intention to pit James against another man. She sees her mistake at once.

"Ah, Louis," he says, seizing the opportunity to exonerate himself and avoid taking any responsibility for what he's done. "So that's what this is about. You're just using my article as an excuse to be with Louis."

"I don't want to be with Louis," she says, exhausted. She checks the street for Louis's car through the window.

"You brought him up."

"As an example of someone who understands *why* my father did what he did," she says, silently berating herself for having given James a scapegoat. She's made it far too easy for him to deflect culpability. "Louis is a friend, that's it. But if you want to tell yourself he's the reason why I'm leaving you, I don't give a shit anymore. Blame Louis. He's convenient. That way you don't have to look at yourself or what you did."

On cue, she sees Louis pull up in front of their apartment.

"Whether you believe me or not," she says, "I'm

leaving you because you've never stopped trying to make me into someone I'm not."

"That's Léo talking."

"Maybe so," she concedes. "It doesn't matter, though, because what you did was unforgivable. You shouldn't have written the article. Period. You exploited my love for you and you broke my heart. Tell yourself whatever you like. You're the one who has to live with yourself."

With that, she grabs two garbage bags and throws open the front door. Louis is coming up the steps toward her. He sees the garbage bags, immediately reads the situation. "Let me take those," he says, and she hands them to him and he takes them to his car and tosses them in the back seat.

"There's more," she says.

James is standing in the doorway, looking smug. "So it's not about Louis," he says.

She ignores him, grabs two more garbage bags.

"Let me help you with those," James says, dripping with sarcasm. He reaches for one of her bags and throws it out the front door.

"Stop it!" she cries.

Louis is behind her. "Hey, man," he says to James. "You don't have to do that."

"Stay out of this."

Véronique holds her arm out and gently pushes Louis back. "It's okay," she says. "Can you just wait in the car?"

Louis hesitates.

"You didn't waste a minute swooping over here to rescue her, did you?" James shouts.

"She called me for a ride, man."

Véronique turns to Louis. "Please," she says. "Wait in the car."

"Have you been fucking him all along?" James wants to know.

"*You* did this," she says, pushing past him to collect the rest of her things.

He's on her heels, following her up the front steps. "Just tell me. Have you slept with him?"

"No!" she cries. "My God, no! Is it so hard for you to believe that this is all on you? The moment you made the decision to publish your stupid article, we were finished."

She grabs the last of the garbage bags and drags them out the door. "I'll send my parents back for the rest of my things," she says. "I want my bed back."

She feels stupid for saying that. It's just an old wrought iron bed she found at an antique shop for a hundred bucks. The place had dozens of them, but damned if she's going to let him sleep in it with his future girlfriends.

"Take care of her!" James calls out to Louis. "Best of luck to you both!"

He slams the door on her back, and she has to fight hard not to cry. She still loves him. This would be so much easier if she didn't.

She won't make this mistake again.

She slides into the front seat beside Louis, slams the car door. All her bags are crammed into the trunk and the back seat. They can't even see out the back window.

"Where to?" he says.

"I have nowhere to go."

"Your parents'?"

"I can't face Léo."

"Let's go back to my apartment and figure it out," he says.

She nods, leans her head against the window, and lets him take her to his place. She doesn't really care, as long as it's not back to her parents in Verdun.

Louis lives in a honey-colored brick building on Jules Verne, north of the Jean Talon Market. He rents the basement apartment, which has two bedrooms and one small window that's level with the street. There's a kitchenette with just enough room for a small table, and a couch facing the TV in the main room. The second bedroom is more of a storage closet—there's a rolled-up futon in the corner, Louis's bike, some boxes, dumbbells and weights. "You work out?" she says.

"Can't you tell?" He holds up a bony arm and makes a muscle.

She's not in the mood to laugh.

"You want a Coke?" he asks her.

"Have you got any beer?"

"Absolutely."

He goes to the fridge and returns with two 50s. "You want to smoke a joint?"

"Sure," she says. Perfect.

Louis lights one up and passes it to her. He doesn't ask her questions or try to get her to talk, doesn't say anything to fill the air. He just lets her be, which she appreciates. He puts on some music, and they pass the joint back and forth. Her anger starts to feel hazy and far away. She leans her head back against the couch.

"This is my father's favorite album," she says, staring up at the ceiling.

"Oh, yeah? He likes Pink Floyd?"

"He was in prison when *The Wall* came out. It was one of the first albums he bought when he got out."

She sings a couple of verses, not even a little self-conscious in front of Louis. "The first time he listened to it, he said, 'I can't believe I've lived without this all these years.'"

At the time, Véronique wasn't sure whether he'd meant that particular album or music in general. "It was one of the things he hated most about prison," she says. "No music."

"I can't even imagine."

"He's never going to forgive me."

"Of course he will. You're his kid."

Her cell phone rings and she jumps. She stares at it for a few seconds, not sure what to do. She looks up at Louis for guidance, but he just shrugs.

She flips open the phone and makes an effort to sound straight. "*Allo?*"

"Véro?"

"Daddy?"

"I called your apartment," Léo says. "The *crosseur* told me you moved out."

"I'm sorry, Daddy."

"You have nothing to be sorry for," Léo says. "How could you have known he'd do that to us?"

"He promised me it would be objective."

"We both believed him, and he screwed us. But you're the one I'm worried about."

"I'm fine. I just feel so terrible."

"You did the right thing by leaving him," Léo says. "He's not one of us, Véro. He never was. He's worse than an Anglo. He's a goddamn traitor."

Véronique starts to cry.

"He doesn't deserve your tears," Léo tells her. "He doesn't deserve *you*."

But I love him, she thinks. She would never say that to her father; it's hard enough to admit to herself. She's aware of Louis watching her, and she wipes her eyes. "I know," says. Her mouth is so dry it's difficult to get the words out.

"Why don't you move back home for a while?"

The idea of moving back in with them—sleeping in her old single bed in her childhood room, eating meals with them every night, watching her father get drunk to *Hockey Night in Canada* every Saturday—fills her with dread. "I can't think about that right now," she says. "I'm going to crash here tonight."

She looks at Louis to make sure it's okay, and he nods emphatically.

"Just take care of yourself," Léo says. "Don't feel bad about me. I should have known better. I let my guard down."

"You did it for me," she reminds him.

"No, *mon amour.* I did it for me. I let my ego get in the way."

"I'm sorry, P'pa."

"Me, too. He's not one of us, Véro. Don't ever forget that."

33

July 1996

The moment the waitress leads him through the arched door to the garden terrace, James regrets his choice. Café Santropol was Véronique's favorite brunch spot, with its jungle of greenery, creaky wood floors, and three-decker sandwiches. What was he thinking meeting a blind date here, his first date since Véronique left him?

He's been hearing a lot of *It's time to move on* from the people in his life—his mother, his sisters, his colleagues. Everyone has an opinion about how long it should take to get over the love of your life. It was the same after his father died. People are only comfortable with a certain amount of grieving; beyond that, it makes them uneasy.

Getting over someone you love—someone you thought you'd spend the rest of your life with—is its own kind of grieving. Véronique is gone for good. She didn't even indulge him in any post-breakup contact. Didn't give him the opportunity to grovel or stalk her or try to win her back. She just got rid of her cell phone and disappeared from his life. He never heard from her again.

Elodie is still in touch with her. They've stayed close, but Elodie won't give James Véronique's new number. She's too loyal.

Not long after Véronique dumped him, he went over to Elodie's, trying to track Véronique down. He'd been drinking, was desperate to see her. "I just want to tell her I love her," he pleaded with Elodie.

"Did you drive here like this?" she asked him, letting him inside.

"I'm fine."

"James, you can't do that."

"Just give me her number. Please, Elo."

Elodie sat him on the couch and sat down across from him on the recliner. She lit a cigarette and stared at him through a cloud of smoke.

"Why are you looking at me like that?" he muttered.

Elodie didn't say anything, just kept watching him through that veil of smoke.

"You think I fucked up."

"You hurt her very badly," she said. "She trusted you, James, and you put your ambitions before her."

"Not just my ambitions," he argued, "my integrity. Her father is a murderer! I had to tell the truth."

"Did you?"

"I'm a journalist."

"Stop lying to yourself, James. You didn't have to write that story. It was calculating and you know it. You exploited them."

"I admit it was a good opportunity for my career," he said. "It was a story I'd always wanted to write. Why should I have to apologize for that?"

"Knowing you would lose her, would you do it again?"

"No," he said without even having to think about it. "Of course not."

"It wasn't worth it then, was it? Getting your big story."

"You sound like Véronique."

"I happen to agree with her."

James slumped down, sinking deeper into the couch. "I guess I knew she'd be angry, but I thought I could handle it. I thought I could get her to see my side. I really didn't think she'd leave me."

"If you thought you could 'handle' Véronique, then you don't know her as well as you thought you did."

A few months later, Elodie broke the news that Véronique was living with Louis.

"Living with him like they're roommates?" James asked, deluding himself.

Elodie shook her head. She was quiet, her face pained.

"Are you sure?" he said. "She probably didn't want to move back in with her parents."

"They're a couple," Elodie said.

"Since when?"

"I don't know. She's been living there since she moved out of your place."

"Why didn't you tell me?"

"What for? You were in no place to hear it."

"And now?"

"You need to move on. She's not coming back to you."

"That asshole. He was just waiting for us to break up."

"*You* caused the breakup," Elodie reminded him. "Not Louis, not Véronique. It was your fault."

James huffed off, feeling betrayed by his own sister. He still blamed Véronique for overreacting. Her leaving, he told himself, was just a cowardly way of ending a relationship she knew would never work. The way she rebounded into Louis's arms confirmed that.

He didn't speak to Elodie for a couple of weeks after that, but Elodie isn't a person you can stay mad at for long. Besides, all she did was put him in his place. She told him the truth.

It's taken him a long time to digest that truth and admit he never should have written the article about Léo, He's come to realize, during the contemplative nursing of his broken heart, that it was always a conflict of interest. Somewhere along the way, distracted by ambition, he convinced himself he was entitled to have his big story. He didn't even consider that Véronique would be the collateral damage. Or if he did, he dismissed it, thinking he could clean up the mess and manage her after it was done. It was a profound lapse in judgment that has cost him the woman he loves.

It was his editor, Damian, who arranged this blind date. The woman is Damian's wife's younger cousin. Her name is Sarah Abney. She's thirty-one, a gym teacher at one of the private schools downtown, lives in Westmount. As Anglo as they come, his father would have said. He's seen her picture and has to admit she's pretty cute. Fit, blond, preppy—about as far away from Véronique as he could get. It's been almost nine months without Véronique, without any woman. There was the brief thing with the bartender at Laïka, but he doesn't really count that. No feelings were involved on either side.

And so he agreed to meet Sarah Abney, a blond WASP who will never remind him of Véronique. Which is a good thing. Damian cautioned, "Keep an open mind."

He just wishes he hadn't chosen Café Santropol. Even the smell of the place—a comingling of growing plants and coffee—makes him sad. This was their Sunday place. Véronique always had an espresso milkshake and the Coin Saint-Urbain sandwich with ham. She'd eat half and save the rest for Monday's lunch.

"James?"

He looks up, discovers an attractive blonde staring down at him. "Sarah?" He gets up, shakes her hand. She's prettier in person.

"Sorry I'm late."

"No, I'm early," he says, comfortable in English. "I live around the corner."

"Oh, nice. I love this area."

They sit down, navigating the unavoidable awkwardness of the first few minutes. She crosses her legs to the side of the table, and he can't help glancing at them, suntanned and muscular. She's wearing white

Bermuda shorts and a heather-gray tank top, very little makeup. Her eyes are green, her nose freckled.

"This place is adorable," she says, looking around.

"You've never been?"

"No. I don't usually get much farther east than my school, which is on Simpson. I probably should, though. I'm completely out of touch with the Plateau scene."

"You're not missing anything," he assures her. She doesn't look like she belongs on the Plateau; she belongs on a tennis court.

"Damian tells me you're one of his best reporters," she says.

"Does he? He tells me you're his favorite wife's cousin."

She laughs, opens her menu. "What's good?"

"I always have the chicken salad. The Duluth is pretty good, too."

"Pears and caramelized onions?" She shakes her head, crinkles her nose. "I prefer meat on my sandwich. How's the roast beef?"

He's starting to relax. She's cute. *Keep an open mind, James.* He's been single almost a year; he's thirty-five and wants a family at some point. Véronique has moved on—why shouldn't he?

The waitress comes by and takes their orders. Sarah

orders the espresso milkshake, which feels like a good omen.

"So, should we just get straight to the ex conversation?" she says, folding her arms on the table and leaning closer to him.

"The ex conversation?"

"Your ex, my ex. Damian told me you're coming off a bad breakup, as am I."

"Ah. The ex conversation."

She nods, waiting for something from him.

"My girlfriend and I split up about eight or nine months ago," he says. "You?"

"Just over a year. It's taken me this long to brave going out on a date."

"Same."

"It hasn't even been a year for you," she says, sounding a little dubious about his readiness.

"We weren't compatible," James says. Which isn't exactly true. They were incredibly compatible in almost all ways.

"Damian told me you wrote an article that pissed her off," she says. "He said that's why she left you."

"Ouch. Okay. Thank you, Damian."

"Don't blame Damian. I asked him to tell me everything about you before I agreed to the date."

"And you still wanted to meet me?"

"At least you didn't cheat on her."

"No. I just wrote a very unflattering article about her father."

"The FLQ guy who murdered Pierre Laporte."

"Yes."

"You're a journalist, though. Isn't that your job?"

He's starting to like her more and more. "Yes, it is," he says, perking up. "But I shouldn't have written it. I should have put her feelings first, I guess."

"He murdered someone. How were you supposed to portray him? As a hero?"

"I guess I wasn't supposed to portray him at all. I should have recognized the conflict of interest."

"From a career standpoint, I can imagine it was exciting to get that interview."

"It was," he admits. "But she thinks I used her to get it."

"Did you?"

The question catches him off guard. He remembers back at the beginning, when he showed up on Véronique's doorstep. Yes, he was looking for a story, for access to her father, but he fell in love with her. He loved her right from the start. He still does. He would never have written that goddamn article if he'd known he was going to lose her. "No," he says. "I didn't use her. Not for a second."

"Did you mislead her?"

James looks up with relief when the waitress shows up with their food and interrupts their conversation. Sarah asks for extra mayonnaise. James asks for a Coke.

"I didn't realize we'd get so deep into this territory on our first date," he says when the waitress leaves. The giant sandwich on his plate looks unmanageable; he's lost his appetite.

"We could talk about the weather and our hobbies and where we went to school," she says. "I take a pottery class at the Visual Arts Centre."

"Funny."

"I'm almost thirty-two," she says, turning serious. "I wasted five years in a relationship with a guy who was cheating on me the entire time."

"And you didn't know?"

"Of course not. He was a personal trainer, so he was always at some client's house. I trusted him. I had no idea he was sleeping with most of them until one of them showed up at our apartment. Pregnant."

"Shit."

"We were planning our wedding," she says. "We were going to have it at his family's farm in North Hatley."

"Damian didn't tell me any of that."

"He probably didn't want to scare you off."

"I guess we're both still a little traumatized."

"I've done a lot of soul-searching over the past year," she says, twirling a gold bracelet around her wrist. "I've asked myself many times, why did I choose someone like him? How could I have been so clueless? Because even though I didn't know, I must have *known*. Like, on some level, you have to know. That's what my therapist says. I'm just grateful I found out before we got married."

James is quiet. He's also done his fair share of soul-searching. In his case, he was the perpetrator, not the victim. He wonders if Véronique has been asking herself the same questions as Sarah. *Why did I choose someone like him? How could I have been so clueless?*

"Anyway," Sarah says, "all that is to say, I don't want to be in a rebound relationship. I don't have the time or the energy. I need to get that out right up front."

James isn't sure what to say.

"And if you're not quite ready," she continues, smearing mayonnaise on her bread, "or if you're not fully over your ex, I'd rather know now."

He thought Véronique was straightforward, but Sarah is on a whole other level. She's mature, confident. He respects that. He's also a little scared of her.

"What are you thinking?" she asks him.

"I don't really know what to say. I'm a bit intimidated, to be honest."

"Intimidated how?"

"By your straight-up lack of bullshit."

She laughs and takes the first bite of her roast beef sandwich. She struggles with a rogue piece of lettuce, has to use her finger to get it in her mouth. When she's done, there are two dots of mayonnaise in the corners of her mouth. She dabs at them with her napkin, never taking her eyes off him. "Is that a bad thing?" she asks him.

"No, it's not," he says. "Not at all."

After lunch, they step outside onto Duluth Avenue and linger a moment in the bright July sunshine. James is feeling good, his spirits high. "Want to head over to the mountain?" he asks her, not wanting to go back to his apartment alone. Sundays are the worst. "We can check out the scene at the Tam-Tams." *Check out the scene?* Did he just say that?

"What are the Tam-Tams?"

He turns to her with a look of exaggerated shock. "You've never been to the Tam-Tams? And you call yourself a Montrealer?"

"I told you I never come to the Plateau."

He takes her hand, emboldened by their earlier conversation, and leads her toward Parc du Mont Royal. The thought crosses his mind that they could potentially run into Véronique. They used to come here together on Sunday afternoons. They'd get high and lie around in the sun. She always knew people. She liked the whole vibe. If he's honest, he's kind of hoping to see her, especially since he's with Sarah.

When they get there, the vast green space surrounding the Cartier monument on the eastern edge of the park is already packed with sunbathers, picnickers, hacky-sack players, people dancing to the beat of the bongo drums. At the center of the spectacle is the drum circle. Shirtless men, women in bikini tops, tourists, children—it's a beautiful convergence of hippie and grunge, with the smell of weed hanging thick in the summer air.

"It's like Woodstock," Sarah says, taking it all in.

It's so crowded, people are spilling onto Mont Royal and Pine Avenue, across the street into Parc Jeanne-Mance. There's barely enough space to sit, but they manage to stake out a small patch of open grass, facing the drum circle. "I feel like a tourist," she says, applying fresh lip gloss.

James looks around, scoping out the crowd. Searching for Véronique. He'd know her body from any angle—front, back, sideways. The thought of seeing her here with Louis, holding hands or lying with her head on his lap, the way she used to with James, makes his stomach churn.

"Who're you looking for?" Sarah asks him. *She knows.*

"Just people-watching," he responds, caught.

"Were you hoping your ex would be here?" She has a way of asking questions that makes him feel guilty regardless of the answer.

"No," he says, fibbing. "I wasn't hoping. But it's possible she might be."

"Was she the type to dance in the drum circle?"

"Absolutely not. And neither am I."

"That's good," she says. "I was a bit worried."

He laughs, feels more at ease.

"Your face is getting red," she tells him.

"So are your shoulders." He touches one of them, and her skin is hot under his fingertips.

"Maybe we should go."

"Oh. Sure." Disappointed.

"I was thinking we could go back to your place."

Less disappointed.

"I'm not much of a game player," she confesses.

"It's kind of a relief," he says, feeling a twinge of guilt.

"So. Your place?"

"Yes. Absolutely," he says. *Do I have condoms?* He tries to remember. *Yes.* There's a stash left over from the bartender at Laïka.

As they head back through the park, James scans the crowd discreetly for Véronique. He doesn't see her, which is probably for the best.

He rolls onto his side and slips out of bed, not wanting to disturb Sarah. He squints at his watch, trying to make out the time. It's just after two in the morning. They had screwed all afternoon, ordered in Szechuan for dinner, screwed some more. She fell asleep about an hour ago; he hasn't been able to.

Sex with Sarah was like screwing your best friend, the one you've secretly always wanted to screw. There was no awkwardness; it was familiar, compatible. When he came, he was overwhelmed with emotion. He's not sure why, but he definitely got choked up. Maybe he's finally over Véronique, or at least realizing it's possible to experience that kind of intense connection with someone else.

He tiptoes into the bathroom and guzzles water from the tap. Pees, brushes his teeth. When he crawls back into bed, Sarah reaches for him. "Where am I?" she says, turning to face him, smiling in the dark.

"You're still in my bed," he says. "Twelve hours and counting."

"Best blind date ever."

"Thank you, Damian."

"Don't tell him I slept with you. My cousin is a prude."

"He's my editor," James says. "I would never."

She rests her leg across his body, and he rubs it. She has fantastic legs. Not as long as Véronique's, but hard and well-defined. She mentioned something about step class. She rolls on top of him.

"Goddamn, you've got stamina," he murmurs.

"You make me horny," she says, her blond hair tickling his chin. She leans in to kiss him, and just as they're about to go another round, his cell phone rings. They both turn to look at it.

"This can't be good," he says, reaching for it. Sarah slides off him and pulls on her tank top. She sits cross-legged, facing him.

"*Allo?*"

"James?"

"Damian? What's going on?"

"Is he checking up on me?" Sarah whispers.

"A firebomb just went off at that new coffee shop on Greene Avenue."

"Shit. Any injuries?"

"No. There was no one around, but someone found a note in a phone booth nearby."

"Signed by who?"

"The French-Language Protection Brigade? Something about a linguistic cleansing."

"Shit."

"It was a crude Molotov cocktail," Damian explains. "Turpentine in a beer bottle. They threw it at the window of the Perfect Cup."

"English name?"

"That's the assumption. The window didn't even break. The thing exploded on the sidewalk, and the fire petered out in the drizzle. The cops are still there."

"Do they have a suspect?"

"Not that I know of."

"I'm on my way," James says, already scrambling out of bed.

"What's wrong?" Sarah asks him, looking frightened. "Where are you going?"

"A firebomb just went off in Westmount," he says, pulling on his jeans.

"Where?"

"Greene Avenue."

Sarah follows him out of bed, starts getting dressed.

"You don't have to leave," he tells her. "You can stay. We can have breakfast when I get back."

"I'm coming with you," she says.

"Really?"

"That's just a few blocks from my place."

James's mind is reeling. Could this be a brand-new generation of post-referendum radicals? A rebirth of nationalistic violence? His heart is racing as he flies down the stairs, exhilarated. Sarah is right behind him. He's not sure how he feels about her coming along. This is his work. He doesn't want to have to worry about her while he's in the zone.

Outside, the air is muggy and moist. He locks the door behind them. *The political chaos is starting again,* he thinks, probably happier than he should be.

34

September 1996

Elodie pulls up in front of Maggie's store on Rue Principale, and the first thing she notices is the name change. The store is no longer called Semences Supérieures/Superior Seeds; the new sign says CENTRE DE JARDINAGE COWANSVILLE GARDEN CENTER. Staring up at it, Elodie is reminded how estranged she's become from her mother since joining the Duplessis orphans. Maggie never even mentioned she was changing the name of the business. It would have been a big decision, given that her father founded Superior Seeds more than sixty years ago. Maggie has always resisted making major changes, right down to the back wall of antique wooden seed drawers that have been there since the thirties. James and Stephanie have been telling her for years to modernize, but Maggie always says she doesn't want to lose the charm of her father's original shop and turn it into another version of Canadian Tire or Home Depot.

Elodie gets out of the car with some trepidation. Maggie isn't expecting her. Their last conversation was a rather stilted one about her plans for Thanksgiving. "You're coming, right?" Maggie said. "James is bringing his new girlfriend."

"I was thinking of going out east to see Nancy."

"Oh."

"I'm not sure yet," Elodie said, ambivalent.

She has no interest in meeting James's new girlfriend, an English woman from Westmount who teaches at a private all-girls school. Elodie couldn't possibly have less in common with her.

"Can't Nancy come to us?" Maggie suggested. "So we can all be together?"

"She won't want to. She works on weekends."

Maggie was quiet, obviously hurt. Elodie doesn't mean to hurt her, but she's still processing all this anger that's coming up. She needs time.

The store will be closing soon. Maggie will send her employees home and beg Elodie to come home with her for dinner, to catch up over a bottle of wine and sleep over. Elodie used to fantasize about moments like that with her mother, and for a long time after they were reunited, she used to cherish them. These days, it's like they're starting over from scratch.

She hesitates a moment outside the door, on which Maggie has stenciled: OPEN YEAR-ROUND, 6 DAYS A WEEK, WITH THE EXCEPTION OF NEW YEAR'S DAY, EASTER, AND CHRISTMAS DAY. The bell jingles as she enters. The store smells earthy and moist, with a strong scent of sweet peas. Nothing much has changed inside. It's still homey and overflowing with houseplants and planters, outdoor accessories, tools, garden-care products, and the old wooden seed drawers still labeled in Maggie's father's handwriting. There are homemade signs with arrows pointing to THE LARGEST SELECTION OF ANNUALS, PE-RENNIALS, BULBS, AND SPECIALTY PLANTS IN THE AREA and sandwich-style chalkboards advertising terrarium workshops and orchid workshops. An antique pine table in the center of the store is piled with gardening books and candles, gift cards and handcrafted vases. "We don't just serve farmers anymore," Maggie said when she started adding gift items and offering workshops. "The retail landscape is changing," she explained. "I'm competing with box stores now."

Elodie doesn't really understand her mother's excitement over such things. To Elodie, it's all just work. A middle-aged man behind the counter looks up and smiles. He's new. Elodie doesn't recognize him. "Can I help you?" he asks, setting aside a pile of invoices.

"I'm here to see Maggie," she says.

"Elo!" Maggie cries, emerging from her office. "Luc, this is my daughter, Elodie." Maggie rushes over to Elodie and pulls her into her arms. She smells of soil. "What are you doing here, *mon amour*? This is the best surprise!"

Maggie is still beautiful. She's over sixty and yet her hair is as black and soft as it was when they first met. She colors the roots, but it never gets dry or wiry. Her skin is barely lined, her teeth all her own. She looks more like Elodie's sister than her mother, but then Elodie is the opposite. She looks older than she is. Feels much older, too. The aches and pains from all the old injuries are getting worse every year.

"You'll come for dinner and sleep over? Why didn't you tell me you were coming? I would have bought groceries."

"I can't sleep over," Elodie says. "I have to work tomorrow, but we can have dinner. We can go to Kentucky Fried Chicken. You don't have to cook."

"We're not going to Kentucky Fried Chicken," Maggie says. "I have leftover shepherd's pie in the fridge. Steph is back at school, so it'll be just the two of us. Okay?"

"Okay."

"Is something wrong?"

Elodie shrugs.

"Are you sick?"

"No. It's nothing like that."

Maggie looks relieved. "I have to help Luc with the closing," she says. "I'm still training him."

"It's fine. I can meet you at home."

Maggie squeezes her hand before turning away and disappearing inside her office.

Stepping into her parents' house always feels like a homecoming. This is the place where she first met them, where they welcomed her into their lives. She will forever associate its smells and design features and mementos with her very first experience of belonging. It was here that she celebrated her first Christmas, had her first Easter egg hunt, her first birthday cake with candles that she got to blow out. Even though she was already in her twenties, they tried to give her all the things they would have given her had she grown up with them. They used to pretend it was all for Nancy, but Elodie knew everything was meant for her. She wasn't even embarrassed scavenging the house for Laura Secord chocolate bunnies or having her own patchwork stocking on Christmas morning. Maggie made her one out of red and green gingham remnants, with her name embroidered at the top. It hung on the mantel alongside James's and Stephanie's, as though she'd always been there.

She passes by the framed picture of Gabriel on the refurbished antique dry sink in the foyer and stops to look at it. He's on his boat, holding up his fishing rod with a perch hanging by its mouth. The photo was taken the summer before he died. He looks so happy. She misses Gabriel. If he were alive, she can't imagine being angry with him the way she is with Maggie all the time. Loving Gabriel always felt less complicated.

The house feels more and more like Maggie's now. There's a little less Gabriel every time she visits. His things are surreptitiously vanishing. It's only Maggie's knickknacks that remain, her coats and shoes, the smell of all the meals she's cooked for the week mixed with her lavender sachets; the piles of her papers and catalogues, her gardening and self-help books strewn on various surfaces. Elodie has to look hard for Gabriel these days, the way she once searched for Easter treasures in all the house's hidden places.

In the kitchen, she lights a smoke and turns on the oven. May as well warm up the shepherd's pie. She reaches for the lopsided ceramic ashtray Stephanie made years ago in art class. Even as she flicks her ashes into it, she experiences that familiar prickle of jealousy. *Stop feeling sorry for yourself—it's just a goddamn ashtray.*

She makes coffee, shoves the casserole dish into the oven, and sets the table. When she's done, she sits down at the table to wait for Maggie. When she finally hears the front door open, she stares down into the ashtray and realizes she's smoked six cigarettes, one after the other. The timer on the oven starts to buzz just as Maggie enters the kitchen. "Oh, good, you've already warmed it up," Maggie says. "I'm starving."

She makes a move to stand, but Maggie waves her hand. "Sit," she says, putting on oven mitts and removing the shepherd's pie. She sets it down in the center of the table and then grabs a bottle of Pepsi from the fridge. "Ketchup?"

"Please."

"Should I defrost a baguette?"

"I'm fine," Elodie says.

Maggie joins her at the table and smiles. "This is nice."

Elodie doesn't say anything.

"Remember when I taught you how to make shepherd's pie?"

There was a time when they spent every Sunday together, cooking in Maggie's kitchen. Maggie tried to teach her everything she knew, from the basics—spaghetti, roast chicken, stew—to the traditional family dishes like *tourtière* and pea soup. Elodie was a total failure at cooking. Even Maggie finally had to concede that it was more an innate lack of talent than a lack of training. But they had fun.

"Remember I left you alone for fifteen minutes and you mashed the ground beef with the electric mixer instead of mashing the potatoes?"

"When Gabriel came home, there was ground beef all over the ceiling and the walls."

"And in your hair, too."

They both laugh.

"Maybe we should start again."

"No way," Elodie says. "I'm no good at cooking. Besides, I don't really enjoy it."

"What about a trip together?" Maggie suggests, always strategizing how she can make it up to Elodie. "It would be good for us to spend some time together again. What about somewhere warm?"

"It's warm here."

"Now it is," Maggie says. "But in two months it won't be. Wouldn't a trip be nice? I'm sure you could use it. You've had a tough year."

Elodie mashes her shepherd's pie with a fork until it's a thick paste.

"We had so much fun when we went to Vermont for your fortieth," Maggie goes on. "I could book that bed-and-breakfast in Woodstock again."

"I prefer to be home."

"I thought you loved it there."

"I'm not in the same place right now."

"What place do you have to be in to go on holiday?"

"I have to want to spend time with you."

Maggie's eyes immediately fill with tears. She sets down her fork and gets up from the table, turning her back to Elodie. "Ever since you found the Duplessis orphans, you've been pulling away from me."

"A lot of stuff has resurfaced."

"Maybe that's not such a good thing," Maggie says. "You just keep getting angrier. You're stuck in your anger. After so many good years, all of a sudden, you don't want me in your life anymore."

"Of course I want you in my life."

"It doesn't feel that way." Maggie rips a strip of paper towel from the roll next to the sink and blows her nose.

"Why didn't you marry Gabriel and raise me together?" Elodie asks, needing to hear it again. "You loved each other."

Maggie goes to the fridge and removes a bottle of

white wine plugged with tinfoil. She pours herself a glass. "I was fifteen," she says, sitting down. "I was terrified to get married and lose my family. It was 1950, and they were prepared to disown me. What else could I do?"

She reaches for one of Elodie's cigarettes and puts it between her lips. "I feel like we've had this exact same conversation a thousand times," she says wearily, the cigarette bobbing as she speaks. She lights it and expels a cloud of smoke with her eyes closed. "Obviously you don't believe I was as powerless as I was."

"It's just that I know how much Gabriel loved you when you got pregnant with me. I know he wanted to marry you. Why didn't you just tell him you were pregnant?"

"I wish I had, Elo. You know that. But I wasn't ready. Not at fifteen." Maggie gulps her wine, puffs her cigarette. "I never felt like I had a choice. I guess I wasn't brave enough."

"I accepted that at one point."

"And now?"

"I don't know. The more invested I am with the Duplessis orphans, the more conflicted I feel."

"But you are getting somewhere," Maggie says. "You got an apology from the doctor."

"His letter helped a bit," Elodie admits. "But not the way an apology from the nuns would, or some kind of financial compensation. Money would help."

"Would it?"

"Hell yes. My back problems are so bad I won't be able to work soon. Then what?"

Maggie looks away.

"I'm angry," she says. "But maybe that's not a bad thing. Maybe the anger has to come up so I can get stronger. And I *do* feel stronger."

"I guess it's my job to bear the brunt of it," Maggie says, resigned.

Elodie can't tell if she's mad or merely stating a fact. "I don't want to be angry with you," Elodie tells her. "You're the one I love the most. I want it to be how it used to be between us as much as you do, before the Duplessis orphans. But right now, this is where I am."

Maggie reaches for Elodie's hand and holds it across the table. Neither of them has touched their supper. "What can I do?"

"Let me be."

Maggie doesn't say anything. She releases Elodie's hand, and the effort seems to leak out of her like air. She just sits there smoking, staring out at nothing. After a while, she says, "What did you come here to tell me?" Suddenly remembering there was some reason for the visit.

"They're tearing down St. Nazarius Hospital next spring."

"Thank God," Maggie says, brightening. "I hope that old bitch Sister Ignatia goes down with it."

"I want to go and see it before it's demolished."

"Do you think that's a good idea?"

"I need to go," Elodie says. "And I want you to come with me."

"Because you need my support or because you want me to see how bad it is?"

The answer is both, but Elodie doesn't answer the question.

35

January 1997

"Put these on," Louis says, handing her a pair of rubber gloves. "Don't handle anything without them."

She takes the gloves and puts them on.

"We don't want to leave any fingerprints."

She fills the wine bottle halfway to the top with a mixture of gasoline and motor oil. Louis says adding motor oil will make the fire burn bigger and longer. "Leave some empty space at the top," he says. "That way it'll fill with gas fumes and be even more explosive."

He's learned a lot since his first botched attempt to firebomb the coffee shop in Westmount. For that one, he used a beer bottle and turpentine with no motor oil.

There was no impact whatsoever; it didn't even crack the glass. Véronique finishes pouring and shows Louis.

"That's good," he says. "Now the fuse."

She works diligently, intensely focused. There was a brief moment in time, under the influence of James, when she thought she might try a more conventional life—school, a regular job, marriage. All the things that bring social acceptance. But people don't change. She didn't. James couldn't.

Her relationship with Louis turned sexual a few weeks after she moved in with him. She started out in his spare bedroom, which was just easier than finding a new place or moving back home. One night, Louis made a move. Véronique acquiesced, not with great enthusiasm but with resignation. Why not? They were good friends, he understood her, they were basically on the same page about life. Mostly, it was the easy thing. She doesn't love him. A lot of the time, she doesn't even like him, but they have in common their politics, their backgrounds, and their resentments.

She's not working, not even smuggling. She hasn't been able to face Marc or her uncle since she found out Callahan is dead. She's opted to disappear rather than have to confront the possibility that one of them killed Callahan. She knows her uncle is capable of it. It's in his DNA. The men in her family kill people, which is a strange and disturbing knowledge to carry around. The last thing she ever wanted was to bear the responsibility for yet another death. She still sees her father's face in black and white, screaming into the TV camera with wild eyes and hands cuffed behind his back. *I did it for my baby girl! So she grows up in a better world than I did!*

She's been having this recurring nightmare lately. In it, Pierre Laporte, her cousin Pierre, and Callahan are all lined up on their knees, pleading with her for their lives. She's standing above them, shotgun in hand, emotionless. James is there, too, watching her. The look on his face is pure disgust as he realizes she is a killer, just like the men in her family.

Louis is also unemployed, currently living off a combination of employment insurance and Véronique's savings. He was laid off from his job shortly after the referendum and now spends most of his time plotting and writing pamphlets for the French-Language Protection Brigade—an organization he started and of which he and Véronique are the only members. So far, recruitment has been slow. At first he didn't tell her about his plans for the Perfect Cup chain; didn't mention it until it was on the news. And then all he said was, "That was me."

She turned to him, stunned. "Are you serious?"

He nodded, grinning. He looked pleased with himself. He told her he'd built the bomb in his brother's garage.

"What's the matter with you?" she cried. "Are you insane?"

"I'm fed up. It's time to do something."

She stood up from the couch and looked down on him, horrified. "Do you want to wind up in jail?"

"I don't really care."

"You should talk to my father about that," she said, her voice rising. "It's not some great achievement, you know. You won't be a hero. My father is a nobody, and Quebec still hasn't won its independence. It was absolute hell for nothing."

Louis shrugged. His indifference made her want to smack him, or leave him. She never intended to live her mother's life—the life of a criminal's sidekick, the Bonnie to his Clyde. She left Louis's apartment that day without another word and went home to her parents' place for a few days.

Two things happened that changed everything. First, her father lost his job. His company brought in a new CEO from Toronto and swiftly laid off a third of its workers—mostly the older guys. When her father came home that afternoon, she could see the light had gone out of his eyes. Whatever spark he'd had left was now extinguished. He didn't even have his anger. Véronique stayed a few more days—only because she was still furious with Louis—but eventually she couldn't stand her parents' misery any longer. They were both drinking heavily—Léo slumped in front of the TV, Lisette staring at the kitchen wall or locked in her bedroom. Véronique had to get out. She asked Elodie if she could spend a couple of nights with her, and Elodie said yes, of course, she was genuinely happy to have her.

On her first night at Elodie's, they went for dinner at a greasy spoon called Paul Patates. "This is where I had my very first hot dog and Pepsi," Elodie said, sitting down on one of the spinning vinyl stools. They both spun themselves around like little kids, giggling as they twirled, and then ordered two *steamés* with fries and Pepsis. "My roommate Marie-Claude brought me here."

Elodie smiled, remembering. "Can you imagine going seventeen years without a Pepsi?" Elodie said, closing her mouth, still self-conscious about where her back teeth had been pulled out by one of the nuns.

"Are you still in touch with Marie-Claude?"

"Oh, no. After I had Nancy, she didn't want anything to do with me."

"That's awful."

"I understood why," Elodie said. "After everything we'd been through as illegitimate children, she couldn't forgive me for bringing another one of us into the world. I couldn't really blame her. She was kind enough to let me stay with her until Nancy was born, and then she was there with me at the hospital when I gave birth. She's the one who gave me the pep talk when I wouldn't even hold Nancy."

"But then she just abandoned you?"

"I had Nancy, so I didn't really mind. I didn't actually like Marie-Claude very much. It was circumstances that brought us together. She helped me a lot and I needed her, and I'll always be grateful. But I didn't especially like her."

The waitress set their food down on the counter, and when Véronique bit into her hot dog, she closed her eyes and tried to imagine what it would have tasted like for the very first time at seventeen years old, freshly released from the asylum. It must have been exquisite—the soft, warm bun and globs of sweet ketchup oozing out the corners of her mouth. She felt her spirits beginning to lift for the first time in a long time. Seeing the world through Elodie's eyes never fails to bring her back to life's simple pleasures—a perfect hot dog, a spinning vinyl stool in a greasy spoon. Elodie has become her beacon of humility.

"I have to tell you something," Elodie said, her voice turning solemn.

"What's wrong? Is it the lawsuit?" All Véronique could think was, *Not something else. Please, not another terrible thing.*

"James has a girlfriend," Elodie told her. "She's moved in with him."

Véronique hadn't seen it coming. Certainly, it wasn't the kind of bad news she was expecting. It was no tragedy, not as bad as an illness or more legal disappointments for Elodie. And yet as soon as Elodie said it, the air went out of the room. She felt a puncture in her chest. *Living with a new girlfriend already?* She couldn't keep the shock or disappointment from her face. Elodie could see it at once, and Véronique was embarrassed that he'd already moved on and that she still cared.

"She's English," Elodie said. "She teaches at a private girls' school."

Véronique wanted to ask if the girlfriend was pretty, if she was intelligent. Most of all, was James really in love with her? But she didn't ask. She pretended not to be too bothered about it. Elodie offered no other information about her, not even a name. "You okay?" Elodie asked. "You're with Louis now."

Véronique nodded, but her living with Louis was not the same thing. She's not in love with Louis; it's just a matter of convenience, laziness. For James to have met someone and asked her to move in with him, he must be in love. "Do you like her?" Véronique finally asked.

"Not as much as I like you."

A few days later, when Véronique finally returned to Louis's apartment, something was different about her. She was angrier than before. Knowing that James had moved on with an English woman was the final thing that untethered her from whatever path she had been on that might have led to anything good. She didn't care anymore. She withdrew from the night course she was taking and began to channel her considerable time, energy, and anger into what has lately become her mission: the French-Language Protection Brigade.

"We're going to tie a knot right here for the fuse," Louis explains. "It has to fit in the opening of the bottle, about an inch from the top."

She ties the gauze in a knot and shoves it inside the bottle.

"It should reach the gasoline," he says. "Good. Now turn the bottle upside down. The knot should hold."

It was her idea for this attack. She wanted to go after a business with ties to Ontario, vengeance for her father being laid off. Screw the rich Toronto Anglos invading her city and expunging the working-class French like exterminators. *Screw them all.* So she chose a British clothing chain with its head office and flagship store in Toronto. Louis was pleased with the idea. She didn't have to do any convincing.

"Now put the duct tape here to make the opening more airtight." He watches her work. They're both calm, focused. "Seal it in the garbage bag so it doesn't smell like gasoline."

She looks up at him and he smiles at her. "You're doing good," he says. "Your dad would be proud."

She isn't so sure about that. After Louis bombed the Perfect Cup, she told her father what he'd done. She was probably looking for his approval, or trying to cheer him up. He was impressed with Louis, but he said, "Whatever you do, stay the hell out of jail."

She remembers visiting her father at the Cowansville Penitentiary when she was about six. He'd just lost his first appeal and was now facing the reality of his life sentence. They were sitting across from him at a table in the visitors' room. Lisette was crying. "What are we supposed to do now?" she asked him. "It's a life sentence, Léo!"

"My lawyer is not giving up," he said. "It won't be life, I promise you."

"Why did you do it, Léo? *Why?*"

"Do what?" Véronique interrupted.

"The lawyers are going to file another appeal," Léo said. "They don't know which one of us actually did it. We still have a chance to get out of this."

"Did what?" Véronique repeated.

Neither of them answered her. Lisette leaned across the table and lowered her voice. "Léo, if you didn't do it, please, please, I'm begging you, tell your lawyer. It's not too late. Now's the time to be loyal to *us*." She looked over at Véronique, and then back at him. "Just tell the truth if it wasn't you, Léo. *Please.*"

Léo turned to Véronique without acknowledging his wife's pleas, and reached for her small hands. "This is the worst place on earth," he told her. "I'd give anything to come home with you, but I have my principles, Véro. It's all I have. Hopefully, one day you'll understand."

She still thinks about that day and wonders if there is a line beyond which the stakes are too high and one's principles must be abandoned. She can't help feeling like she's standing at that line, and she's about to have her answer. To this point, crime has always been a means to an end for her, a practical way to earn a living. But something has always been missing—a higher purpose, a calling. Her father had that. He spoke of his people with tears in his eyes. He was driven by a sense of profound righteousness; a belief so cellular, so primal, he was willing to give up his freedom for it. Now it falls to her to pick up where he left off. It's no longer enough to whine and complain about wanting an independent Quebec, or to stew in self-pity without backing up that desire with meaningful action. Like her father before her, Véronique now sees clearly that the only meaningful action left to take will have to include violence. She learned from Léo to do whatever is needed to achieve the goal. She's found all other paths to this point ineffectual.

Louis carefully tucks both bombs into his backpack and zips it up. "Let's type something up," he says. "You want to write the communiqué?"

She nods wordlessly and goes to retrieve some paper.

We are fighting for the independence of Quebec. We always will be, until we succeed. When you don't have a country, you feel like a refugee in your own land. You are an outcast, displaced by intruders who have all the money and power. If we are ever going to become a nation, it must begin with the pure laine French Canadians and the restoration of this province to its Mother Tongue. In the aftermath of the failed referendum—a loss ensured by the greedy English minority and the inept and disconnected politicians—we must revive the revolution by whatever means necessary. It must begin with protecting our precious French language. This was our grandparents' cause. It was our parents' cause. Today, it must be our cause so that it need not be our children's. Our campaign of violence is just beginning . . .

"Wow," Louis says. "You're a hell of a writer."
Véronique smiles, feeling strangely exhilarated.

36

February 1997

"James? Can you open the wine for me?" Sarah calls upstairs to him from the kitchen. "My hands are covered in raw chicken!"

James looks up from his laptop, his shoulders tensing. "Give me a minute!" he responds. He just wants to finish this chapter before her friends show up for the dinner party he did not want her to have. He finally started his book about Elodie's life—*Born in Sin: The True Life Story of a Duplessis Orphan*—and he's eager to keep writing.

"Babe? I need that wine opened!"

James slaps the laptop shut and goes downstairs. Sarah's got her hands inside one of the chicken breasts, stuffing it with what looks like fruit salad. Her cookbook is open to a recipe for roast chicken breast with apple and nutmeg stuffing. His mother would be horrified. Fruit doesn't belong in a stuffing, and stuffing has no place after the holidays. He opens the bottle of white wine and hangs there for a moment. "Anything else?"

"Would you mind adding a generous splash to the gravy? It's simmering on the stove."

"You made the gravy *before* roasting the chicken?"

He's no chef, but he's watched his mother make gravy many times and knows it's supposed to be made in the roasting pan from all the juice and fat and scrapings. That's gravy 101.

"I always do it this way," Sarah says. "I use canned chicken broth and then I just dump the pan juices in when the breasts are done. It saves a lot of time and I get way more gravy."

James eyes the two empty soup cans with chagrin, thinking this is not how the French make gravy. Canned soup? It's a goddamn sacrilege.

"Since you're down here," she says, "do you mind peeling the carrots?"

"I'm working on my book. I'd like to get my chapter done before your friends show up."

Sarah purses her lips, the way she does when she's not getting her way. He's noticed this is a very effective tactic and soon finds himself scouring the top drawer for the peeler. He finds her hurt silences far more intolerable than the screaming matches he used to have with Véronique. Sarah's passive-aggressive sulking causes this strange, uncomfortable combination of feelings inside him—guilt and shame and confusion. It's easier just to please her.

"I told you Courtney and Will are engaged, right? Tonight is sort of an engagement celebration for them."

"You mentioned it."

"They've been together for three years. It's a good thing he proposed. She was about to leave him."

James looks up from the ribbons of carrot on his cutting board. Three years doesn't seem like a very long time to be dating. Is this a message for him? They haven't even been together a year, so he should still be safe. Sarah smothers the bird with vegetable oil and then adds salt and pepper, poultry seasoning, garlic powder. His mother wouldn't be caught dead using garlic powder. Sarah washes her hands three times with dish soap and shoves the pan into the oven.

"We have about an hour before we need to get ready," she says, coming up behind him and wrapping her arms around his waist.

"Great. I'll try to finish my chapter."

"That's not what I meant."

He stops peeling the carrots and turns to face her. "What did you mean?" he asks, kissing her neck.

"Let's go upstairs."

"Let's stay right here."

"The kitchen is a mess," she says. "Let's go upstairs."

Easier just to go along with her before he loses his erection. He follows her upstairs, and they fall onto the bed together. He never gets tired of her body. She works hard to stay fit, and he appreciates all the work that goes into it. She's always smooth and buff and fresh-scented. Sarah cares about things like fitness, manicures and pedicures, flossing, professional waxing, strict moisturizing regimes. Véronique didn't give a shit about that stuff. Not that one way is better than the other; it's just different.

When he attempts to pull Sarah on top—the only way she can come—she puts a hand on his chest to stop him. "Do you mind if I'm on the bottom?" she says. "My lower back is spasming."

When he finishes, she pretends to orgasm at the same time, which doesn't really bother him. He collapses on top of her, flattening her into the mattress.

"I love you," she says, and he can feel her heart beating against his rib cage.

"I love you, too."

He thinks he means it. He really does. He keeps a mental list of all Sarah's pros and cons, and there are definitely more pros. He kept no such list about Véronique. Had he ever thought to, it would have been all pros and one glaring con: she was a criminal. Sarah's are minor by comparison, a collection of innocuous quirks and idiosyncrasies that run the spectrum from perfectionistic to slightly controlling. On the good column, she's a teacher; she loves children; she takes great care of herself, loves to cook for him, shares his political views—or doesn't have any at all—and, of course, she has those legs.

"I'm going to shower," she says.

"I'll finish my chapter."

Sarah rolls out from under him and swings her legs over the bed. "You don't really have time," she says. "I'm going to need you to set the table, choose some music."

He almost says, *I didn't want to have this goddamn party.* "Sure."

Sarah has known the same group of friends since seventh grade. She went to an elite, private all-girls school called Miss Edgar's and Miss Cramp's, much like the school where she currently teaches. It's situated on bucolic Mt. Pleasant Avenue, cloistered among the oak and chestnut trees of Westmount. So fond are Sarah's memories of this era, she actually brought James to see it one afternoon when they were visiting her parents. Her friends' names are Courtney, Carrie, Alexandra, and Wendy. Their husbands and boyfriends are Will, Beckett, Gavin, and Ryan, all from good Irish or Scottish stock. James speaks English with them, but feels outnumbered.

"Listen, I'm all for scientific advancement," Sarah is saying, "but cloning? There's something really creepy about that."

"I agree," says Beckett, named after the Irish novelist. "Cloning is not something humans should be experimenting with."

"First it's a sheep, then it's the child you designed and manufactured."

"I don't think that's an inevitability," says Courtney. Or is it Carrie? James gets them mixed up. They both have chin-length white-blond hair, layered and straightened like Jennifer Aniston's.

"This is just the beginning," Beckett says. "Dolly has opened the door to all kinds of dangerous genetic engineering."

James reaches for the champagne and makes a tour around the table, refilling all the empty glasses. They already toasted the newly engaged couple. Everyone clapped, and the guys said things to Will like *It's about time!* and *Welcome to the club, bro.*

One of the girls leaned over and said to Sarah, loud enough for the rest of them to hear, "You're next, Sass." Their nickname for her is Sassy.

"How hilarious was *Friends* this week?" Alexandra says. She's the only one with dark hair. A real beauty.

"Oh, my God, when Ross is at the Lamaze class? Gav and I were hysterical."

Sarah gets up and starts clearing away the main course. *Thank God,* James thinks. They've been lingering over dinner for more than two hours. "James? Give me a hand?"

Obediently, he starts collecting the baby blue china dinner plates Sarah's mother gave her when she moved in with him. They were her grandmother's. He follows her into the kitchen and starts loading the plates into the dishwasher.

"No!" she cries. "Those don't go in there. We have to hand-wash them, babe. Leave it for now."

She runs the tap, filling the roasting pan with hot water and soap, and leaves it there to soak. "Should I serve dessert now or wait till later?"

"It's almost ten thirty."

Sarah sighs, not sure what to do. Dessert now or later? When James feels the familiar vibration of his pager on his hip, he almost cries out with joy. "I'm getting paged."

"On a Saturday?"

"I'll just check in with Damian and see what's going on."

Sarah purses her lips and reaches for the oven mitts. She's got a pie warming in the oven. "Smells delicious," he says, and leaves her pouting in the kitchen.

Upstairs, he closes the bedroom door and sits down heavily on the bed. Exhales, calls Damian.

"You watching the news?"

"No. What's going on?"

"Another bomb just went off."

James was beginning to wonder if there would be another one. These things rarely occur in isolation. "Where?"

"That clothing store across from the Bay. Camden Threads."

"Any damage?"

"Definitely more damage than the last one. This one was much more powerful."

"Anyone injured?"

"I don't think so. The store was closed, but there were people on the street. I'm in Ste. Adele, so I can't get there myself."

"Do they know who did it?"

"No idea. Someone identified a guy taking off down the street after tossing the Molotov cocktail through the window. If it's the same guy, he's getting bolder."

"I'm on my way," James says.

He grabs his tape recorder and heads back downstairs to break the news to Sarah. He finds her standing at the head of the table, slicing into her pie. "Babe, would you mind putting on a new CD?" she asks him. "It's gotten a little somber in here."

"I've got to head out."

Sarah stops what she's doing and looks up at him. "Are you serious? On Saturday night?"

"Another bomb went off downtown."

The friends look at each other nervously. They're old enough to remember the October Crisis. They would have been little kids, but they would know about the bombs that were detonated in mailboxes all over Westmount.

"Ali, would you finish serving the pie?" Sarah says. "James, can I speak to you?"

Reluctantly, he joins her in the kitchen.

"Do you really have to go?" she asks him.

"Yes, I really have to go."

"Can't Damian go?"

"He's in Ste. Adele. Besides, I'm the Quebec Affairs guy."

"You *want* to go!" she accuses.

"Yes," he says. "Of course I do. It's my job."

She folds her arms across her chest and glares at him. "There's no one else who can go?" she says. "We have people over."

"They've been here for hours. Dinner is over."

"That's not the point."

"You're right. The point is there's a breaking story on my beat and I have to go."

"It's not just tonight," she says, dropping her voice to a whisper. "This is a pattern."

"A pattern?"

"You care more about work than you do about our relationship."

"We're not going to do this now," he says, shutting her down. "I have to go."

"You're barely present with me," she says, her eyes welling up. "Even tonight, you've been disconnected, distracted. You'd rather be anywhere than here with me. You work late all the time. I mean, who stays at the office until two o'clock in the morning, James? You're not a surgeon, for God's sake! And when you are here, you're locked in the bedroom writing."

"It's an important story."

"Which one?"

"All of them."

"Maybe I should have paid more attention to how things ended with you and Véronique."

"What's that supposed to mean?"

"You chose your career over her. Isn't that right?"

"That's low."

"It's true, though, isn't it? You would do anything for a story."

James turns to leave.

"All this time I thought you loved her more than you love me," Sarah shouts after him, "but it's work you love most. It's getting your *story!*"

37

Elodie stares straight ahead at the colorless sky, sucking quietly on a cigarette. If not for the steady inhalations, she wouldn't be breathing at all. She hasn't seen this place in almost thirty years, and she dares not turn her head to look. She's parked across the street, which feels safer than pulling into the parking lot. A strong gust of wind causes the car to shudder. It's minus thirty-five with the windchill, and they can feel the draft through the windows.

"We don't have to do this," Maggie says, breaking the silence.

"Yes, we do." It's taken her a few months to get up the nerve to come, but she's here now and determined to face the demons before it's too late.

"They're already preparing to demolish," Maggie says.

Slowly, Elodie turns. There are several bulldozers and excavators parked in the lot. The building, fittingly set against a backdrop of somber gray sky, stripped trees, and a wrathful wind, is remarkably unchanged since that night she arrived in 1957. The name, Hôpital St. Nazarius, carved in stone beneath the center spire, has a visceral effect on her. She lifts her eyes, gazing up at the top floor. Somewhere behind those white-trimmed dormer windows, she lived on Ward B.

"Maybe this is enough," Maggie says gently. "You don't have to go inside."

Elodie turns to face her mother, anger pulsing in her temples. "I want *you* to see it," she says.

Maggie shrinks back. "It's you I'm worried about."

"I grew up here. I'll be fine."

Elodie opens the window a crack, flicks her cigarette outside, and reaches for another in her purse.

"You're smoking too much," Maggie says.

Elodie looks at her, saying nothing. Maggie turns away and stares quietly out the window. Elodie lights her cigarette with the car lighter and leans her head back against the seat. Her heartbeat is uneven, fast. So many unpleasant memories are churning close to the surface. What the hell did she expect, coming back here? She's an adult now—independent, safe, free—but she feels as small and defenseless as she did back then. "Okay," she says, putting the car in drive and turning onto the road that leads to St. Nazarius. "Let's get it over with."

The parking lot is empty except for some construction trucks. She parks at the front entrance to avoid the cold, holds her breath, and opens the door. Outside, Maggie takes her hand, and they walk slowly toward the front steps. She learned early on at St. Nazarius to detach from what was going on around her. As she approaches the hospital now, her scalp tingles, and she has the familiar sensation of her mind floating away.

She pushes on the doors, half expecting them to be locked. The hospital was closed down years ago, so she's a little surprised when the doors swing open. Maggie turns to her, her expression vague, and they step inside to find a handful of workers milling around—two contractors by the abandoned information desk, an electrician on a ladder. Otherwise, it's deserted. Wires are hanging from the ceiling. The lights are off, but there's enough natural light from the windows that they can see. They both remember exactly how to get to the psychiatric pavilion, which is accessible via a long corridor off the main building. The walk there feels endless. They pass the turnoff for the boys' wing—Wards E to H—and climb the stairs to the sixth floor of the girls' wing.

At the sixth floor, Elodie begins to feel light-headed. She hasn't eaten today—didn't have an appetite this morning—and now, between the chain-smoking and the six flights of stairs, her lungs are aching.

"Are you okay?" Maggie asks her, looking worried. "You're very pale."

"I'm out of shape."

"Is that all it is?"

Elodie nods, dismissing her mother's concern, and exits the stairwell into the girls' psychiatric wing. Maggie goes straight to the intake desk. "This is where she told us you were dead," she says. "She cost us twelve years together. To my dying day, I will never understand how someone could be so sadistic."

Elodie doesn't say anything.

"*I'm* the one she was trying to punish," Maggie says. "*I'm* the one who sinned, not you."

Elodie walks toward the sign for Ward B, and Maggie follows. "This was the dormitory," she says, opening the door into a huge, empty room. The walls are still beige with yellow undertones, completely bare except for some water stains and nails where the crosses used to hang above the metal cots. The floors are light brown linoleum with flecks of darker brown. There are six barred windows overlooking the other pavilions, an endless vista of concrete merging with sky.

"There were sixty beds lined up in here," she explains. "With no space in between. I tripped over a stray boot one night on my way to the bathroom and knocked over a lamp. Sister Ignatia punished me with an ice bath."

She points to the corner of the room. "There was a creepy statue of Jesus on the cross over there, always watching over us."

Maggie quietly takes it all in.

"My bed was right here," she says, standing in the spot that once lined up perfectly with the fourth window and an unobstructed view of Jesus. So much is coming back to her. The pills they gave her every night and the wild, hazy dreams that ensued; the constant lethargy and boredom; the nighttime silence of their shared terror. "The bathroom is over there," she says, leading her mother across the room.

Maggie gasps as they enter. The claw-foot white tubs are lined up in a row, rotting and rusted. The floor is checked linoleum in shades of brown, the ceiling a map of water stains, cracks, exposed pipes. Above each tub are crudely built wooden cubbies for soap and shampoo, towel and nightgown. She turns to the mirror, staring at the woman she's become. *You survived*, she tells herself.

She pictures her current bathroom, with its floral plastic shower curtain and purple tub mat, its spotless modern toilet and gleaming white built-in acrylic bathtub, and she can't believe how far she's come.

"It's like out of a horror movie," Maggie murmurs.

"You have to go through the bathroom to get to the Big Room," Elodie tells her as they make their way to the common area, where she must have spent thousands of hours sitting in a rocking chair, staring emptily at the wall.

"My God," she says, pointing to a lone wooden rocking chair left behind in the corner. She goes over to it and crouches down to look underneath the seat.

"What are you doing?" Maggie asks her.

"There were numbers under each one," Elodie says. "Look!" She flips it over easily—it's small, the size of a child's desk chair—and shows Maggie the spray-painted number. "Forty-three."

She stands back up, leaving the rocking chair upside down. "I'll never forget the first time I set foot in here," she says. "Talk about a horror movie. There were all these girls rocking back and forth in these rocking chairs—dozens of them, staring out at nothing like zombies. They all had the same haircut, the same creepy stare. And that sound, the squeaking of the chairs."

Maggie looks past her, out the window.

"I always used to check what number rocking chair I had," Elodie says. "And I would count them all. It was something to do while I sat here. When we weren't working, it's all we did. We sat in those goddamn rocking chairs, listening to the pipes rattle. There were no books, no toys, no games. We weren't allowed to talk to each other or to play or laugh. There was nothing to do but vegetate. This is where I really started to lose my mind. I thought I would die in here."

Maggie moves to hug her, but Elodie steps back, guarded. "You know I was transferred here exactly forty years ago?"

Maggie nods, silent.

Elodie feels a twinge of guilt. Isn't this what she wanted? For Maggie to see with her own eyes the hell to which she condemned Elodie? That was the whole point of bringing her here today. And yet all she feels is a sickening hollowness. There's no gratification in seeing her mother suffer like this.

"I shouldn't have made you come here with me," she says, realizing with some disappointment that if revenge is to bring any sort of mollification, it will have to be directed at the people who actually deserve it. Maggie was an impetuous teenager, at worst guilty of poor judgment. She was careless with her sexuality, but what teenager isn't?

"It's not your fault I wound up in here," Elodie finally concedes, meaning it. "It's Duplessis's fault."

Maggie sighs, not seeming to take any satisfaction in being let off the hook.

"Let's go," Elodie says, wanting to get as far away as possible. Maggie looks visibly relieved as they walk back toward the stairwell in silence.

"M'ma?"

"Hm?"

"I think I need to find Sister Ignatia." As soon as she says it out loud, she knows that no victory in the courts or written apology or sum of money will bring the kind of vindication she longs for. Those things would be welcome, but any meaningful sense of relief or closure will have to come from confronting the woman who all but destroyed her life.

Maggie looks at her. "I'd murder her if I saw her now."

"I don't mean right now, I'm not ready yet." Elodie says. "But someday."

38

Anti-English Separatist Group Claims Responsibility
for Clothing Store Bombing

By J. G. Phénix, Special to the Canadian News Association

The radical-fringe nationalist group that bombed
the Perfect Cup coffee shop several months ago has
claimed responsibility for Saturday's firebombing
of Camden Threads, a UK-based clothing chain in
Montreal. The French-Language Protection Brigade
sent a communiqué to the *Gazette* on Monday, saying
it was behind the attack, which caused extensive
damage to the store but no injuries. In the communiqué, the group blamed the "greedy English minority and the inept and disconnected politicians" for

the referendum loss, and promised more violence to come.

"Your ex-boyfriend must be salivating," Louis says. "We've given him great material for his little column."

"Let me see that."

He hands Véronique today's *La Presse*, and she reads it with a sinking heart.

"Imagine if he knew it was you who wrote that!" Louis laughs.

She doesn't laugh with him. James would be ashamed of her. She can picture his reaction—disappointment, revulsion. Not that he had any respect for her to begin with.

"Why do you look so bummed?" Louis asks her. "You're actually doing something. You're taking a stand and making a difference. What the hell is he doing? Writing stories on the sideline, impugning us for having the goddamn balls to fight for what we believe in."

"I know."

"Do you?"

She doesn't say anything.

"You still love him."

She has no interest in explaining how she feels about

James to Louis. Of course she still loves him. She also hates him. Can't stand the thought of how superior he'd act if she were ever to get caught.

"Did you tell your father?" Louis asks her.

"Are you kidding me? He'd lose his shit."

"He'll be proud of us."

"He doesn't want me in jail. He'll be pissed."

"So tell him I did it on my own."

Véronique has come to realize that Louis is every bit as opportunistic as James was. He wants to impress Léo as desperately as James wanted to publicly tear him down. And Véronique is always their means to an end. She glances back down at the newspaper and finishes reading.

Montreal urban-community police have increased security patrols in the downtown core, and are treating the group's communiqué with "extreme seriousness."

"We don't want another October Crisis on our hands," said Commander Jean-Luc Dumas at a press conference yesterday. "Most importantly, we don't want anyone getting hurt."

According to Commander Dumas, the communiqué makes clear that this second gasoline bombing in seven months is a direct response to last October's referendum loss, and that the target was chosen specifically because of its English name.

"This will certainly have an impact on other businesses with English-language trademark names," Dumas said. "The priority right now is to stop this from happening again."

Véronique tosses the paper onto the coffee table, which is littered with rolling paper, tobacco and marijuana shake, and Louis's silver Zippo. "I know who we can target next," she says, looking up at Louis.

"What about going old-school," he says, not waiting to hear her out. "Mailboxes in Westmount."

"That's stupid."

"What were you thinking?"

She pushes the paper at him with her foot. "The Canadian News Agency."

Louis smiles.

"They're based out of Toronto."

"And James."

She shrugs.

"It's genius," he says.

"And *I* want to do it."

"I don't know about that."

"I'm doing it. It has to be me."

"It's dangerous."

She laughs. "I build them with you, Louis. I smuggled cigarettes. I'm used to danger."

Louis smiles in a way that suggests he's proud of her. Or turned on. Probably both.

"Obviously I'll do it in the middle of the night," she says. "When no one is there. I don't want to kill him."

"Just destroy the building."

"Something like that."

"We have to wait, though," Louis says, reaching for his rolling paper and tobacco.

"Why?"

"It's too soon," he says. "You read the article. They've increased security everywhere."

"Around stores in the downtown core," she points out. "The CNA is in Old Montreal."

"It's too soon. There will be cops everywhere. We have to lay low for a few months."

"A few months?"

She's disappointed. She wants to do this now, while she's fired up. She doesn't want to lose her nerve or her purpose.

"A few months at least," he says, rolling a cigarette. "We want them to forget about us. Get rid of the extra security. Trust me. We wait."

Véronique nods. She will have to keep her anger sharpened and buffed until the time is right. Louis runs his tongue along the edge of the rolling paper and puts the cigarette in his mouth. She leans across the table and lights it with his Zippo.

They wait out the months, restless and bored. Spring comes late, lazily thawing the city at the tail end of March, but then delivering an unexpected blizzard at the beginning of April. For a day or two, a blanket of pristine snow buries the streets, lawns, roofs, and tree canopies; winter boots and parkas are retrieved with great discouragement, ice scrapers and snowplows reappear, and then, just as quickly, it's over. April drags, gray and wet, until the first scilla wildflowers spring up on Mont Royal, dotting the park with purple. The air warms up, the bicycles come out, the birds resume singing from their fire escapes and telephone wires. Véronique and Louis drift along, waiting.

Louis is still unemployed. He spends his days getting high, getting angry. He lives off his meager unemployment checks, taking handouts from Véronique whenever possible. All she has going on are the stolen CDs. She's earning much less than she used to, but she also cares less about money than she ever did. There are other things more important now.

By the time July rolls around, the weather turns and the heat becomes oppressive. They don't have air-conditioning, so the apartment is stuffy and humid. Véronique grows irritable. She spends long afternoons in bed, lying in her bra and panties in the dark, with a fan blowing stale air at her. When the heat becomes unbearable, she has a cold shower and then returns to bed. She doesn't feel like doing anything; she's just going through the motions, biding time.

One afternoon, Louis brings her a Dairy Queen Oreo Blizzard. It's the first thing she's felt like eating since the heat wave kicked in. He asks for a kiss in exchange, and she obliges.

"You still want to go after the CNA?" he says, sitting down on the mattress.

She looks up from her Blizzard and nods. "Of course."

"I biked around down there today."

"You were in Old Montreal?"

"St. Antoine Street was pretty deserted. It's far enough away from the tourists to be pretty isolated, especially if we do it on a weekend night during the construction holidays."

Véronique slides her legs off the bed. "That's next week."

He nods. Véronique experiences a surge of adrenaline. "I'm ready," she says.

"I'll make a list of everything we need."

After the decision is made, they move quickly. They build two Molotov cocktails—one for backup—exactly like the one they made for Camden Threads. Véronique is becoming quite proficient at it, a new skill to add to her criminal repertoire. The Canadian News Agency occupies the main floor of an old stone building one block east of the *Gazette* building. It has a large storefront window, which will make it easy for her to hit from street level. Louis got hold of a map and has circled where he's going to be parked on Rue Montfort. She's to detonate the bomb and then take off down Rue Ste. Cécile toward their car. They're doing it on Sunday night, halfway through the two-week construction holiday, when the city will most likely be deserted.

On the day of the planned bombing, Véronique wakes early and goes out for a walk. The heat has broken, and the air is slightly cooler, more pleasant. It's the twentieth of July. Her spirits are high, though she's not without some anxiety. She decides to head down to her old neighborhood, a good long walk to keep her body moving, her mind engaged. She puts on her Discman and walks at a good clip, all the way to Café Santropol, where she orders an espresso milkshake to go.

She starts walking toward Mont Royal, her tank top clinging to her back. The park is practically empty, with the exception of a few joggers and dog-walkers.

She sits down on the grass, legs extended, and squints up at the sun. She wipes her forehead, which is beaded with sweat, and presses her ice-cold drink to it to cool down. She feels the tickle of the grass blades against her thighs, an ant skittering along her shin. She's been cooped up in that damn apartment for so long, she's forgotten how soothing nature can be, how tender and welcoming. She used to appreciate it more in the country, when she would hang out by the lake in Ste. Barbe. It seems like such a long time ago, those days with Pierre and Marc.

She makes an effort now to pay attention to the sun on her back, the hermit thrush singing in the woods around the park, the wet-dog smell of trillium in the air. She has a strong sense of this moment being the calm before the storm.

I'm going to bomb James's office tonight. A dull ache settles in her chest. Her heartbeat suddenly feels irregular, like an out-of-tune instrument. How will he react when he gets the call? Will he be excited? He always loves a good story, especially something like a political bombing. Or will he be afraid? Pissed off? Will this one be too close to home?

She doesn't think he'll suspect her. Why would he? She's not worried about getting caught. Their plan is well thought out, almost foolproof if she executes it properly. What she needs to do is stay focused on her anger: the way she felt the night of the referendum, when the final votes were in and they had lost. The way she felt when the cops handcuffed her, threw her into the police van, and slammed the door in her face. The way she felt when her father was fired, when Elodie's lawsuits were quashed in court, when she read the article James wrote about her father and realized the love of her life had betrayed her for a story.

If she can hang on to the anger, she has no doubt her bomb will detonate according to plan. Her mood begins to darken. The birdsongs and dewy summer smells are suddenly edged out of her consciousness, sidelined by a resurgence of old grudges. *He deserves it*, she thinks. *They all do.*

He's probably engaged by now—Elodie hasn't mentioned it, but maybe she wouldn't say—and that thought, the thought of James marrying another woman, is the most enraging of all.

She sleeps for the rest of the day, blinds drawn, fan rattling beside her. It's not quite so hot anymore, but she's gotten into the habit of falling asleep to the whir of the blades. She wakes up briefly to smoke a joint and heat up a leftover empanada for dinner, and then returns to bed. It's the only thing she can think to do to make the day pass. Finally, at one in the morning, the alarm goes off.

She rolls onto her side and faces Louis. He's already awake, smoking in the dark.

"You ready?" he asks her.

"Yes."

"You sure you want to do this? Because I can do it."

"It was my idea."

"It'll still get done."

"I want to."

He exhales a stream of smoke, which rises and disperses into a white haze above her head. "I need you to be careful," he says, running his hand through her hair.

"I'm not going to get caught."

"That's not what I'm worried about."

"You're worried I'm going to blow myself up?"

"It's happened before," he says. "The shoe factory bombing in '66."

"Yes, yes. I know. That's not going to happen to me. He was just a kid."

When Louis doesn't say anything, she reaches for his hand. "I can do this."

"I know," he says. "I'm still going to worry about you until you're safe in the car."

They dress in the dark. She puts on black jeans, a

hoodie, her Docs. She retrieves the backpack from the closet. By the time they leave the apartment, it's almost two. Outside, the air is cool, even for the end of July. The streets are empty, which is a good omen.

They drive to Old Montreal in silence. Louis doesn't even turn on the radio. The only sound in the car is the sporadic *tick-tick* of the turn signal. Véronique stares outside, visualizing herself throwing the bomb into the window, the way an athlete might visualize her performance before a big sporting event.

When Louis finally turns off St. Jacques Street and pulls the car into the parking lot on Montfort, Véronique has that same feeling she had the first time she smuggled cigarettes—the lurch of adrenaline, racing heart, and mix of terror and excitement in her stomach. *This is no different*, she tells herself. *You've done far more dangerous things before, with far less at stake.*

Louis parks in the far corner of the lot, secluded beneath a canopy of trees. "I'll be right here," he tells her, interrupting her silent pep talk.

She nods.

"I could still do it," he says. "You don't have to prove anything."

"I'm not doing this to prove anything," she responds. "I'm doing this because I want to. I *have* to."

"I get it," he says, leaning over and kissing her on the mouth.

She pulls away and reaches around for the backpack. The bottles clang around in there, reminding her of when she was a teenager and used to sneak beer out of the house in her schoolbag. One time, her father caught her. He stopped her at the door and pulled a ten-dollar bill out of his wallet. "Go to the *dépanneur* and buy your own beer," he said. "You don't steal from your parents."

She opens the car door and slings the backpack over her shoulder.

"Be careful," Louis says. "Do it exactly how I showed you. Once it's lit, you've got to throw it fast and hard. As hard as you can, or it won't detonate."

"I know, Louis. We've been over it a hundred times."

"You've got your cell phone?"

She nods and slams the car door. Her heart is pounding in her throat. *It's just like smuggling*, she tells herself, taking slow, deep breaths.

She walks up St. Jacques, not passing a single person along the way. The bottles rattle against her back. It's a perfect part of town for a bombing—no nightlife, very few businesses. As she gets closer to St. Antoine Street, she realizes she could also bomb the *Gazette* building. She's got the two bombs in her bag and the buildings are side by side. Certainly, the double bombing of two major English news agencies would make even more of a statement for their fledgling group.

She feels a rush of energy as she contemplates it. Imagine the coverage, the attention it would garner. The *Gazette* and the CNA in one night. People would wake up to the news, and a sweep of shock would paralyze the city. Just like the FLQ days.

As she's about to turn the corner, she peers into the doorways and alleys on both sides of the street. *Always look for homeless people*, Louis cautioned. *They hide in plain sight, they see things.*

There's no one. She looks behind her. No one. She swallows and turns onto St. Antoine, where the CNA building sits on the corner. She scans up and down the street, inside the doorways, looking for a flash of movement, a sign of life.

She stands in front of the CNA's window, which is dark behind the closed industrial blinds, and remembers all the times she met James here, in this very spot, picking him up from work. They would walk the few blocks over to St. Paul, the hub of the most bustling part of Old Montreal, grab dinner and drinks, or play pool and catch each other up on the day. She'd been happy with him, which fuels her even more now. He gave her something she'd never had before—a sense of groundedness and stability—and then he blindsided her, taking it all away just as she was beginning to get used to it, to like it even. She will never forgive him for that.

She glances around one more time, and then, confident she's alone, slips the backpack off one shoulder so it's hanging off the other. Her fingers are trembling as she unzips it. Her body is turned away from the window as she digs down into the bag.

She stops a moment to catch her breath. She's afraid. More afraid than she thought she'd be; more afraid than when she used to drive the boat in the pitch black of night, surrounded by potential armed bandits lurking on the lake. *You can do this.*

Moving more quickly now, her fingers enclose the neck of the bottle. It's cold in her hand. *Bomb,* she has to tell herself. *This is a bomb.* She feels strangely detached.

What am *I doing?*

She quickly dismisses the question, which seems to have pushed its way up from some unfamiliar, unwelcome place inside her. She takes a second to recall the night of the referendum—the police, the beating, the paddy wagon, the jail cell, the despair, the hopelessness—and renews her determination.

Throw the goddamn bomb and get out of here.

A noise from behind startles her and she freezes. Keys jangling. A lock turning and clicking into place. She lets go of the Molotov cocktail, and it slips safely back to the bottom of her backpack. She moves stealthily to zip up the backpack and secure it on her back, both straps around her shoulders, and then turns around.

Even in the dark, with his back to her, she knows it's him. Two o'clock in the morning and here he is, like a mirage. She could run, pray he doesn't recognize her taking off down the street.

He tugs on the door handle to make sure it's locked, and then, before she can muster the wherewithal to flee, he turns around and their eyes lock.

"Véronique?"

She doesn't move. She can't. Her feet are cemented to the sidewalk.

"V? What the hell?" He comes toward her. "What are you doing here?" he asks her. "How did you know I'd be here?" *Is his tone hopeful?*

She doesn't say anything. Can't find her voice to speak. Can he see that her whole body is shaking?

"Did Sarah tell you I was here?" he asks her.

Sarah.

"Véronique, what's going on? What's wrong?" He

takes another step toward her and she backs up. "V, why are you acting so strange? Say something."

What can she say? In all the scenarios she played out with Louis, not one of them included bumping into James outside his office.

"V, it's two o'clock in the morning. What are you doing here?"

What the hell are you *doing here?* she almost screams.

She has to remind herself she hasn't done anything wrong. She has not been caught. He doesn't know there are two bombs in her bag. He probably assumes she's just here to talk.

"V? Why are you here?" he asks again, softening his tone, speaking to her like she's a lost child.

"It was a mistake," she manages, her voice coming out small and strange. The bombs feel heavy on her back, weighing her down. What if he can smell the gasoline?

"Do you want to talk, V?"

It slowly begins to sink in. Had she arrived ten minutes earlier, she would have killed him. James would be dead.

"What was a mistake?" he presses.

"Coming here."

"Why did you?"

She shakes her head.

"V, what's wrong?"

"I have to go," she says, crossing the street, backing away from him.

"Véronique, wait!"

She ignores him, turns, and quickens her pace. Going in the opposite direction of where Louis is parked. *I almost killed James.* That's all she can think about right now.

"Do you need a lift?" he calls after her.

She's jogging now, aware only of the sound of the bottles rattling, her boots hitting pavement, her breath coming in short, loud puffs. The smell of gasoline is burning her nostrils. She's worried the rags will slip out and the gasoline will spill in her bag.

When she's a few blocks away and she's sure James hasn't followed her, she slows down. She's heading west now, toward Griffintown. She keeps walking. *Don't stop, don't stop.*

What if he got in his car and decided to follow her? She spins around, looking for his car. Doesn't see him. Whatever she does, she can't go back to Louis.

She pulls her phone out of the zippered pouch of the backpack and tries to call him. Her hands are trembling so violently, she keeps punching the wrong numbers. "*Tabarnak*," she mutters, on the verge of tears. She stops walking and takes a deep breath, tries again.

"*Allo.*"

"Louis?"

"Did you do it?"

"He was there!" she cries, her voice tipping on hysteria.

"Who was there?"

"James! I was about to throw the bomb and then he came out of the building—"

"At two o'clock in the morning?"

"Yes."

"So you didn't do it?"

It takes Véronique a few seconds to comprehend the question. "Are you serious?"

He doesn't answer.

"Louis. I'm not a murderer."

"Of course not," he says. "I guess we can't do the CNA tonight."

"No, we can't do it tonight. We can't do it *ever*. He'll know it's me!"

"We can hit another target then. I've got a list. But we should do it right now—"

"I almost just killed my ex-boyfriend!" she cries. "I'm a little messed up."

"Just come back and we'll talk about it. Where are you?"

"I'm walking. I need to clear my head. I'll meet you at home."

"Walking where?"

"It doesn't matter. Just go home."

Louis sighs, and she can hear the disappointment in that sigh. He wants to bomb something. He doesn't care what.

"Louis," she says, "would you have done it? If James had walked out of the building and you'd been the one there with the bomb?"

"Of course not."

She isn't sure she believes him. There's a part of her that thinks he would have done it. He's out for destruction tonight. She's not even certain it has anything to do with their cause anymore. His anger feels like a separate thing: a dark, self-sufficient entity that would exist with or without the French-Language Protection Brigade.

She does not want to become like him. And yet, even as she has that thought, she realizes it's already true. It is exactly who she's become.

She follows Notre Dame Street to Mountain Street, and then turns onto Rue du Séminaire, which she knows will take her straight to the Lachine Canal.

She's walking with purpose now; she has a plan. *Just get to the water.*

As her legs carry her forward, the same refrain reverberates in her head: *You almost killed James. You almost killed the man you love.*

She wipes tears off her face. The smell of gasoline is in her hair, her clothes. What's happened to her? Did she really mean to turn out exactly like her father? Maybe that was always her goal.

She wonders if young Léo was like Louis—blowing shit up and destroying lives out of pure rage. What if Léo's cause was never a noble channel for his political anger, but merely an excuse to wreak havoc on the world and unload his own shame and self-loathing?

When she reaches the water, the first thing she does is rip the backpack off and drop it on the ground. She stares bleakly out across the flowing canal at the old red brick metallurgy factory. It's after three. Her phone vibrates. Louis must be wondering where she is.

She ignores him. Bends down to unzip the backpack and takes out the two bombs. She removes the rags, which are soaked in gasoline, and tosses them into the water. She watches as they get carried off toward the St. Lawrence River. Funny she should find herself here now, throwing the empty bottles into the canal rather than into the Canadian News Agency's front window.

Going back to Louis's apartment is not an option. Being with him equally so. She knows it's over. She's very close to Elodie's apartment, so she walks along the pedestrian path in the direction of Pointe St. Charles, about fifteen minutes away. The smell of gasoline is still making her sick, so she pitches her backpack into the woods, getting rid of it once and for all.

Véronique waits until morning on Elodie's front steps. As the sky begins to lighten, a palette of diffused yellows, oranges, and pinks fans out from the most glorious tangerine sun. It seems to open up above her as it rises, like the palm of a hand, releasing a flood of golden light. She barely hears the door open behind her.

"Véronique?"

She turns around and Elodie is standing in the doorway, wearing a white nightgown with an eyelet trim. "What are you doing here?"

"Watching the sunrise."

Elodie sits down beside her, and they survey the pastel horizon together.

"You're up early," Véronique says.

"I never sleep past sunrise. It's my favorite time of day."

"It's peaceful."

"It is," Elodie says. "I put some coffee on. Should I bring you a cup?"

"Yes. Please. Black."

Elodie returns a few minutes later with two mugs of coffee. She hands one to Véronique and sits back down on the concrete step. "You smell like gasoline," she says, lighting a cigarette. "What's going on?"

Véronique lowers her eyes. *I almost killed your brother.*

"And what are you doing on my doorstep at five o'clock in the morning?"

"I did something last night," Véronique says, not meeting Elodie's gaze. "Well, I almost did something." She takes a sip of coffee. It's strong, hearty. "Louis and I, we built a gasoline bomb."

Elodie swears under her breath.

"I was supposed to detonate it last night, but . . ."

Her voice trails off. She can't tell Elodie the truth about what happened. She can't bear the thought of not being forgiven by her. "I couldn't go through with it," she says.

"Thank God."

"We weren't going to hurt anybody."

"What were you going to bomb?"

"It doesn't matter. An English business."

"You mean you and Louis . . . ? The clothing store and the coffee shop?"

Véronique nods.

"Holy shit," Elodie says, taking a long haul off her cigarette. "This was Louis's idea, I assume?"

"Sort of. He started it with the coffee shop, but I wanted to do it, too. I helped him build the clothing store bomb."

"Why?"

"I'm just so tired of losing," Véronique says. "We just can't ever seem to get ahead."

"There are other ways to fight."

"Like?"

"I don't know. I just don't think violence is the answer. I don't think it satisfies the way you think it will."

"How do you know?"

"It didn't work for your father, did it?"

"Your way doesn't work either," Véronique points out. "You've been fighting in the courts for years, and where's it gotten you? You've been patient, tireless. And for what, Elo? Your criminal suit was dismissed, your civil suit is still languishing. You've never had any acknowledgment from the nuns or the government, let alone an apology. You haven't received a penny."

"And what should I have done instead? Bombed a church or a hospital?"

"Maybe. You might feel better."

"I don't think so."

"Why not?"

"I grew up with more violence than I ever care to witness again."

"Well, that's you, Elodie. You're a better person than I am."

Elodie reaches out with her free hand to cup Véronique under the chin. "That's not true," she says, her tone imploring. "Do you hear me? This may be who Louis is—maybe even your father—but it's not who *you are*."

39

July 1997

When his alarm goes off in the morning, James quickly slaps it off and checks to make sure Sarah is still asleep. He's not in the mood for another conversation about how late he's been working or how much time he's been spending on the book. He got home at around three in the morning and did his damn best not to wake her. He grabbed a beer from the kitchen and drank it standing at the counter to calm his nerves. Upstairs, he stripped down to his boxers and quietly slipped into bed.

"It's almost three," Sarah said, her voice shooting out of the dark, startling him.

"I finished the first part of my book tonight."

She didn't say anything. Her back was to him. He

didn't mention seeing Véronique. Sarah must have told her where to find him, but she didn't say anything about it. He didn't probe.

"I'm sorry it's so late," he murmured.

Silence.

He rolled over, turning away from her. Still reeling from the shock of seeing Véronique.

Sarah let out a soft whimper. He looked over, and her back was quivering. She was crying. He knew that she wanted to be held and reassured. He didn't move, though, just pretended to sleep.

He showers and dresses quickly, tiptoeing around the room. Downstairs, he chugs orange juice from the carton and scribbles a note for Sarah: *Gone to Cowansville to see my mom. Back tomorrow.*

In the car, he leaves a message for Damian. *Working from home today.* And then he takes off, eager to get his manuscript into his mother's hands, and to get away from Sarah.

He thinks about Véronique the entire drive. How she looked, how she smelled (faintly of gasoline?). The moment he saw her standing there, he wanted to pull her into his arms. Let's be honest, he wanted to take her into the alley and have sex with her against the side of the building.

Beyond that, he still wants to rescue her. She looked scared, agitated. She was withholding something—he could tell immediately. He wondered if it had to do with Louis. She took off before he could ask.

Does she miss him? Want him back? His head is swimming with unanswered questions. Should he call her?

He stops at one of the stands on the side of Route 139 and picks up two dozen ears of corn. It's the end of July—not quite peak season, but they'll be good enough. He tosses the paper bags into the passenger seat, missing his father. He always feels like a traitor, buying corn from another farm. Gabriel's was the best in the region, his pride and joy.

James decides to stop at the cemetery.

"*Salut*, Pa," he says, sitting down on the ground in front of Gabriel's headstone. The sun feels good on his bare arms, the back of his neck. The air is filled with the scent of peonies, one of his mother's favorites. What would his father say to him right now?

Don't settle. Love is too goddamn precious.

His father believed in that kind of once-in-a-lifetime love. He liked the idea of having a soul mate. He'd found his, after all. It made him sentimental.

Not everyone is so fortunate. Then again, James *did* find the love of his life, but he screwed her over and lost her to a total loser, so it's not really misfortune so much as egregious buffoonery. They probably wouldn't have made it anyway. You can't love someone without accepting who they are. Maybe the person you want to change that much isn't really the person for you.

Which leaves him with Sarah, who has always felt to him like the consolation prize. Maybe it doesn't have to be so black and white. Maybe there's another woman out there for him. Still, he hasn't been free of Véronique for a single moment since he saw her last night. She's infiltrated his head, his body. And she's not happy either—that was obvious. She was there last night for a reason. Why? What was that expression in her eyes? *What do I do, Pa?*

A plea. A prayer.

When he gets to his mother's house, he finds Stephanie at the kitchen table with a mug of tea and a bowl of strawberries. She's wearing a T-shirt and nothing else, her hair in a messy knot on top of her head. She still looks about eighteen, nothing close to her actual age, which is twenty-six. Maybe all older brothers feel that way about their baby sisters. Or maybe it's because she still acts like a teenager—living at home, working for her mom, partying with friends on the weekend. *Aimless.*

"What're you doing here on a Monday?" she asks him.

"I finished the first part of my manuscript," he says, placing it on the table. "I want Mom to read it."

"*Born in Sin*," she reads, her lips stained red. "Congratulations. Has Elodie read it?"

"No. First I need Mom to make sure it's okay."

"Do you think it'll get published?"

"I don't know. I'm still at the beginning. I've only written up to where Mom gave her away."

"Mom didn't give her away," Stephanie says defensively. "Our grandfather did."

"You know what I mean."

"I don't get why you want to tell Elodie's life story. Isn't it going to be horribly depressing?"

"It's an important story," he says. "It has to be told, and I want to be the one to do it."

"But she's your sister," Stephanie says. "It's not like she's a stranger. We already know enough about what she went through. Why put yourself through that?"

"Because it's my job."

"And you're fine with the whole world knowing our family history?" she says. "Mom's fine with it?"

"The 'whole world' is a stretch," he says, pouring himself a cup of coffee from the pot his mother must have put on this morning. It's still warm. "And yes,

Mom wants Elodie's story out there as much as Elodie and I do."

"Well, for the record, I don't."

"Noted."

Stephanie pops a strawberry in her mouth. "Where's Sarah?" she asks him.

"Home."

"Why didn't she come today?"

"She had plans," he says irritably. "We don't have to do everything together, do we?"

"It was just a question."

"Why aren't you at work?" he asks her.

"Monday's my day off."

"Mom lets you have a day off?"

"Sunday and Monday. I had to campaign for two days off in a row."

"Let's go to Douglass Beach," he says, suddenly inspired. "We haven't been in years."

"I don't know."

"Come on. It's gorgeous out. You could use some sun."

She frowns, examining her arms. She is quite pale; it looks as though she hasn't been outdoors all summer. She probably hasn't. She's always been a homebody, preferring TV to nature.

"Go put on a bathing suit," he tells her. "We're going."

Maggie is waiting for them at the kitchen table when they get back. "You guys are burnt to a crisp!" she says. "Where have you been?"

"Douglass Beach."

"Did you use sunscreen?"

James's manuscript pages are stacked in a neat pile on the table in front of Maggie. "I'm done with the first part," he tells her. "I want you to read it."

"It has the makings of a masterpiece, James. The writing is exquisite."

"You've already read it?"

"I just finished."

He sits down at the table.

"I'm going to shower," Stephanie says, disappearing.

"James," Maggie says, "it's excellent."

"Really? You're okay with the material?"

"Of course. It's all true. It has to be told."

"Anything you'd change?"

"I made some notes," she says. "But it's very poignant. The hard part will be Elodie's story."

"I've already started interviewing her," he says. "And I've got your notes, the first draft of your memoir. She also showed me her scrapbook."

"That scrapbook." Maggie sighs. "It's hard to go through."

"She's documented everything in there."

"I know. And her drawings. I've never gotten over them."

"I've had a few sleepless nights since I started," he admits. "But I think the timing is right for this."

"I have no doubt you'll find a publisher."

"If she can't get justice in the courts, I can at least help her get some with this book."

"I hope those nuns are still alive to read it," Maggie says, handing him the manuscript. "Your cheeks are flaming red, James. You have to be more careful in the sun."

"Steph seems to be floundering. What's she going to do with her life? Live here with you forever?"

"Tell me about it," Maggie says, getting up and going to the fridge. "I made lasagna. Where's Sarah? Didn't she come with you?"

"No."

Maggie turns around, gives him a concerned motherly look. "How is she?"

"Good."

Her eyes narrow.

"What?"

"It's strange to watch your children living your life."

"What do you mean?"

"Sarah. She's your Roland."

"Oh, please," he says dismissively. Roland was his mother's first husband. A decent guy, a banker. Not the love of her life.

"Listen, a lot of people marry their Roland or their Sarah and they're perfectly happy," she says, preheating the oven. "It's not a bad thing to marry someone reliable and solid. Lust wears off anyway."

"You weren't happy with reliable and solid."

"No, I wasn't."

"I saw Véronique last night," he confesses.

"You did? Where?"

"She showed up outside my office at two o'clock in the morning."

"How did she know you'd be there?"

"Sarah must have told her, I guess. But Sarah didn't mention it. I don't know."

"What did she want?"

"She wouldn't say. She looked . . . kind of out of her mind. Not herself. She was agitated."

"Drugs?"

"Maybe."

He'd considered this, of course. She was selling them, last he heard. How big of a leap is it to become a user?

"Why don't you call her?" Maggie says. "She's made the first move."

"I didn't get a sense she was happy to see me last night. It was like I'd caught her off guard or something. Maybe she was just out in Old Montreal and it was a coincidence."

"That's ridiculous."

"I don't know. She looked so distraught. Maybe I should stay away."

"Your father came back for me."

"But I'm the one who hurt *her*, M'ma. She's never going to forgive me for what I did."

"I thought the same thing about your father," Maggie reminds him. "But he forgave me for doing far worse than you've done. I gave away his daughter."

Later, he goes out onto the front porch to check in with Sarah. She doesn't answer. His spirits are low. It's muggy tonight, and he's got a headache from too much sun. The mosquitoes are out in full force and he slaps one dead on his forearm, leaving a smudge of blood. He's still thinking about Véronique.

He calls Elodie. "Véronique came to see me last night," he blurts.

"What do you mean she came to see you? Where?"

"At work," he says. "I was there till about two in the

morning. When I got outside, she was standing in front of my building."

He's almost positive he can hear a sharp intake of breath on the other end of the line. "Elo? I need her number. She obviously wants to talk."

"James, I don't think it's a good idea."

"Please, sis. I need to speak to her. We ended so badly."

"She doesn't want to speak to you, James."

"How do you know? She came to see me."

"Because she's *here*."

James paces up and down the length of the porch. "What did she say? She told you she doesn't want to see me?"

"She didn't mention you."

"Then why was she at my office last night?"

"Leave it alone," Elodie says.

"How did she know I'd be working late? Did she speak to Sarah? Elo, is she okay?"

"I don't know if she's okay," Elodie says, sounding upset. "I don't think so."

"Is it Louis?"

"She's not herself. That's all I can tell you."

"Is it drugs?"

"You need to forget last night," Elodie says, dropping her voice to a whisper. "For *your own good*. She's in a bad place and it's not about you and you can't fix it."

"I was moving on," he says. "But when I saw her last night . . ."

"She shouldn't have been there."

"Why are you being so cryptic? I want to come over. I can be there in an hour and a half."

"That's a mistake," Elodie tells him. "She's still with Louis. They're together. You're reading too much into last night and you shouldn't."

Before he can answer, Maggie sticks her head outside and says, "Supper's on the table."

James is bone-tired. He grunts a brusque goodbye to Elodie and hangs up.

"Who was that?" Maggie asks him. "Did you call Véronique?"

"No," he says, not elaborating.

He follows his mother inside, the screen door slapping shut behind him. He can smell the lasagna from the kitchen, and he remembers how famished he is.

Maggie scoops a massive helping onto his plate. Stephanie pours them each a glass of milk. Gabriel used to love a glass of milk with spaghetti and lasagna; now it's tradition. Only Elodie thinks it's disgusting. "Oh, M'ma," he moans, inhaling a forkful before she's even sitting down. "This is delicious."

"Does Sarah cook?"

"Not like this. No one cooks like you."

She tousles his hair and bends down to kiss the top of his head. "My boy," she murmurs, her lips against his hair.

"What about me?" Stephanie says.

Maggie goes around the table and kisses Stephanie on her damp hair. "I see you every day," she teases. "I'd like to see you a bit less."

They laugh, and James feels a little better. The melodrama of moments ago begins to recede.

I'm better without V.

It's the first glimmer of lucidity he's had since last night. He has no idea why she showed up outside his work. In the end, it doesn't really matter. There is something fundamentally broken between them, irreparable. He knows that. He doesn't want to go backwards, doesn't want to join her in that bad place. His heart just hasn't quite gotten there yet.

"Leave it alone," Elodie said, echoing his own inner wisdom. He's lost his way before, but his pragmatism always leads him home.

"Pass me the bread," Stephanie says, and James rips off a piece of baguette and tosses it across the table.

"Should we open a bottle of wine?" Maggie says.

"Have we ever said no?"

Maggie jumps up and goes to the pantry.

"One glass and I'm going to pass out," Stephanie says. "I got *so* much sun today. Look at me."

Her chest and arms are an angry purplish red. Her face is puffy. She's definitely worse off than James, whose complexion is more olive and tends to burn less.

"That's going to blister tomorrow," Maggie says, retrieving a bottle of Chianti. "You have to be more careful in the sun these days."

James and Stephanie look at each other. Maggie sets three glasses on the table and pours the wine. James can hardly wait to crawl into his old bed tonight. Between the sun and the wine, he's going to sleep hard.

Maggie holds up her glass in a toast. "To my children," she says, flushed and ebullient. "And to your book, James. It's going to be big."

As the warm wine slides down his throat, James feels suddenly expansive. A surge of energy, a tingle of inspiration. Maggie's validation has reinvigorated him; he can't wait to get back to writing.

40

Véronique hears Elodie hang up the phone in the kitchen, but several minutes pass before she returns to the living room. She waits with a terrible feeling of dread. When Elodie finally emerges, her eyes are red and swollen.

"That was James, wasn't it?" Véronique says, knowing it by the expression on Elodie's face.

Elodie sits down beside her. "Were you going to bomb the Canadian News Agency?" she asks her.

Véronique lowers her eyes.

"Oh, Véronique. You could have hurt James."

And it's those words, spoken so plainly and without acrimony by her closest friend, that finally shatter her trance of disassociation. She breaks down. Elodie takes her in her arms, giving her permission to let go.

Something primal begins to move through her body, a force that is dark and ferocious, excruciating. She cries. Forgetting herself, she lets it out, this beast that has fed on her pain for so long. Elodie holds onto her, rocking gently.

"I didn't know he'd be there," Véronique sobs. "What if I'd killed him?"

"You didn't." Elodie says. "That's not who you are. You haven't been yourself for a long time."

"What if it is? What if it is who I am?"

"No," Elodie states, earnest and unequivocal. "I *know* you."

Véronique looks up, searching Elodie's face. "I don't deserve your kindness," she says. "I almost killed your brother."

"You deserve it the most," Elodie tells her. "You're hurting."

"Did you tell James?"

"No. And I won't. He doesn't need to know."

"I'm sorry, Elo."

"I know you are."

"I should go."

"Where?"

"I don't know," she says, pulling away. "I don't blame you if you don't want anything to do with me anymore."

"I love you like a daughter," Elodie says. "I just need some time."

"I understand."

"And you need help."

"Help," Véronique repeats, a little dazed.

Louis is thumping around the apartment when she walks in. "Where have you been?" he wants to know. His ashtray is overflowing. The place smells rancid. How has she never noticed before?

"Were you with him?" he asks her.

"With *James*?" She laughs out loud. "Yeah, I almost blew the shit out of him and then we spent the night together."

"I didn't know what to think. We had a plan and then you vanished. I've been calling you all night."

"I don't want to do this anymore."

"I never said you had to do it in the first place! You're the one who wanted to do it. It was *your* idea!"

"I know. And now I'm done."

"I agree, it was too close," he says. "From now on, you can just write the communiqués."

"I don't want to do any of it anymore."

Louis sighs. "Don't lose your nerve now," he says. "We're making a difference."

"Are we? How?"

"We have their attention."

How stupid he sounds. How deluded.

"How about a mosque or a synagogue next?" he says, and she realizes that somewhere along the way, it stopped being about the cause for him. He doesn't represent the real French anymore, doesn't care about the working-class struggle. He's a self-hating, marginalized misfit. Louis will keep doing what he's doing until he gets caught. Eventually, he's going to kill someone and wind up in jail, and she wants no part of it.

"We've lost our way," she says, deflated.

Louis laughs at her. "Who have you been speaking to? Your orphan friend?"

"I'm done."

"What about the Brigade?"

"You don't give a shit about the Brigade," she says. "You're not doing any of this for Quebec, or for independence."

"Of course I am. Why the hell else would I be doing it?"

"Hatred."

"Sure, that's part of it. I hate the English. I hate the rich. That's what motivates me. You hate them, too, or have you forgotten?"

"You don't know me."

"I think I do."

"Then I don't know you."

"Sure you do," he says. "I'm exactly like your father."

She packs her things in garbage bags—again—and calls her father to pick her up. Leaving Louis is one of the easiest decisions she's ever made.

"I liked Louis," her father says, stuffing the last garbage bag in his trunk.

Véronique doesn't respond. They drive most of the way home in silence. As they turn the corner onto their street, Véronique says, "I hate your legacy."

"Heh?"

"I don't want to relive your life anymore."

"No one asked you to," Léo says. "You've made your own choices."

"Not really. It's always overshadowed my life. I can't escape it."

"What are you talking about?"

"Being the daughter of Léo Fortin. The infamous FLQ murderer."

"You can thank your ex-boyfriend for dredging it up again," he says. "Don't blame me for that."

"That's not the point. The point is what you did. You killed someone."

"What I did," he says, pulling up in front of their house. "I did for you."

"Stop saying that. It's bullshit! You did it because you're a criminal, plain and simple. The cause was just an excuse."

Léo stops the car in front of the house and faces her, his neck red and splotched, his eyes black. "I did what I did so you would have a better life."

"But I *didn't* have a better life!"

"You should never be afraid to fight for what you believe in," he says. "This is how the world changes, Véronique. It's how slavery was abolished. It's how the Nazis were stopped."

"You can't compare our situation in Quebec to slavery or Nazi Germany, for Christ's sake!"

"You weren't alive in the forties and fifties. You have no idea what it was like. Things changed because guys like me *fought*."

"We weren't at war," she says. "Pierre Laporte was not at war with you. He never signed up for combat. He was just playing football outside his house."

"You don't get it," Léo mutters. "Which proves you *have* had a better life."

Véronique gets out, dragging two garbage bags from the back seat. "Violence isn't the way," she says. "The

FLQ is not the reason things improved in Quebec. Things improved because of the Quiet Revolution, the PQ, Bill 101 . . . Not because you blew up mailboxes and kidnapped a politician."

Léo dumps her garbage bags on the sidewalk and slams the trunk. "You don't know that," he says, leaving her stuff there and heading to the house.

"I know it cost me my father for the first twelve years of my life!" she screams after him.

She hauls the bags inside by herself.

"What the hell is this?" Lisette wants to know, standing in the vestibule, staring at all the bags.

"I'm moving back home for a while."

"Why? What happened with Louis?"

"I left."

"Why? I thought you were so good together."

She finds her father at the CD player, already with a can of beer and a cigarette. He's got a Deep Purple CD in his hand, about to put it on.

"Do you feel any remorse?" she asks him, coming between him and the stereo. "Are you sorry for killing him? I've always wanted to know."

"I'm sorry a man had to die, but—"

"He *didn't* have to die, though."

"I only ever wanted you to grow up in a world where you were in charge of your own destiny."

"Stop laying his murder at my feet," she cries, still blocking his access to the CD player. "I never wanted that burden. I was a baby, completely innocent. You justified killing a man in *my* name, which you had no right to do, and your reputation has hovered over me ever since."

"Stop being so dramatic, Véronique."

"You took a man's life. He was a father, like you. A husband, a son. You did the most monstrous thing a human can do."

"It was heroic!"

Véronique wants to slap him, scream, smash something to shake him up. She understands James's frustration now. The stakes were never high enough in Quebec to justify murder. Why could she never admit that to herself? Why can't her father, even now, after twenty-seven years?

"I'm as passionate about Quebec's independence as you are," she says, hands on her hips. "But I have a line."

"There can't be a line!"

"That's the lie you tell yourself," she says. "I believed it my whole life. I *wanted* to believe it, but it's just a big lie. It's the myth of Léo Fortin. You know what I think? I think it's possible to fight for change but not lose yourself in violence and anger and hatred. That's who *I* want to be."

"Good luck, Gandhi," he says, and heads for the kitchen, forgetting about the CD. She goes after him, waits behind him while he gets another beer.

"I don't know how you've lived with yourself all these years," she says, relieved to finally unleash the truth. She's never had the guts to question or confront him before; she's been far too invested in protecting his story, propelling his myth. They all have. "How do you live with yourself, Daddy? I need to know."

"Leave me alone, Véro."

She's got him cornered now. "Tell me!"

"It wasn't me!" he blurts, throwing the Deep Purple CD across the room in a rage. It hits the wall above the table, leaving a small dent. The case smashes on the floor and the disc slides out. "I wasn't there when they killed Laporte, okay? Now you know the goddamn truth."

He shoves Véronique aside and flees the kitchen. She follows him. Lisette is standing in the middle of the room, stunned. Her hand is over her mouth. She looks like she might fall over. *She never knew.* "What did you say, Léo?"

"*I said it wasn't me,*" he repeats, raising his voice. "I wasn't even there!"

"What do you mean? You weren't even *where*?"

"I wasn't at the house when they killed him. I was out delivering the last communiqué."

A soft gasp from Lisette. The color is completely gone from her face.

"The plan was in motion," Léo explains. "We had already decided to go through with it. Someone had to deliver the communiqué, and I wanted to speak to you, Lisette. I knew it was ending. I knew I'd be going to jail."

"*Tabarnak*, Léo!"

"I needed to hear your voice, Lise! And . . . I couldn't . . . I didn't have the balls to kill the guy. I was too weak. I was so ashamed."

"*Ashamed?*"

"I was their leader!" he cries, wiping tears from his eyes. "I was the instigator from the beginning. They looked up to me. But when it came down to it, when the shit really hit the fan and we had to act, I couldn't even stand by and watch."

Véronique has a million questions, but nothing comes out of her mouth. She watches silently as her father cries with regret over *not* having killed a man.

"None of the guys judged me or resented me for not being there," he continues. "They understood. I was the only one with a wife and a kid. When I got back, Laporte's body was already in the trunk."

"You made everything else up?" Lisette whispers, her tone pure disbelief. She's still standing in the middle of the room—all three of them are—looking shell-shocked.

"They told me what happened," Léo says. "All the details."

"So you *chose* to go to jail for my entire childhood, even though you weren't guilty?" Véronique clarifies, the reality of her father's confession beginning to crystallize.

Léo doesn't answer. He's looking down at his feet, sobbing quietly.

"I'm trying to understand," Véronique says. "You were so ashamed of *not* being able to murder Laporte that you actually pretended you were a murderer to save face? You abandoned me and Mom because you were embarrassed?"

"I was a coward!" he cries. "After everything I'd done for the cause, what was I going to do? Admit I hadn't been there? Turn on my friends? Testify against them? That's not who I am."

"You chose them over your own family."

"I was as guilty as they were, Véro. Don't you see? I was always guilty. I may as well have been there."

"But you weren't! And if you had spoken up, you could have been home with us all along. You didn't need to go to prison. You let yourself get sentenced to life. You chose being some kind of FLQ hero over *me*. Over fatherhood."

"I chose my honor and my beliefs," he says, punching his heart with his fist. "Those boys did what *I* had set in motion. I was just as guilty as if I'd choked Laporte myself. I never had a choice but to go down with them."

"The court wouldn't have seen it that way."

"I wouldn't have been able to live with myself. The lawyers would have forced me to turn on them. The story had to be that we had all done it together, that we were all guilty. And I don't regret it. I only regret that I left them to do the dirty work, that I wasn't there for them when it counted."

"Weren't there for *them*?" Lisette says.

"Lise—"

"No more," she says, and leaves the room. They hear her bedroom door close and then faint sobs through the thin walls.

"What you thought was cowardice, normal people would have seen as humanity," Véronique tells him.

"You'll never understand," Léo says, collapsing into his recliner. He lights another smoke and closes his eyes.

Véronique is standing over him. He looks pathetic to her all of a sudden, slumped over in his chair, tired and defeated. "You don't give me enough credit," she tells him. "I understand more than you think."

She takes the metro to Sherbrooke station with no real plan other than a desire to be back in her old neighborhood. It's a short walk to Ste. Famille, to the apartment she shared with James, but she avoids going anywhere near it. Last thing she wants is to run into him again, lurking outside his place. Instead, she strolls aimlessly up St. Laurent for a while, eventually stopping at the Parc du Portugal on the corner of Marie-Anne. She remembers when the city fixed up the park—refurbished the shabby gazebo, added the mosaic tiles to make it look more Portuguese. She was living up the street on St. Urbain at the time. She always thought it looked more like a Chinese pagoda.

She sits down on the steps of the gazebo. She can hardly believe how much has happened in the last twenty-four hours. She hasn't slept since yesterday. Was it only last night that she almost blew up the Canadian News Agency? Since then, she has left Louis for good and discovered that her father didn't actually kill Pierre Laporte. What she thought she knew about herself, her family, her entire world, has been annihilated. Now what?

PART IV
1999–2001

41

March 1999

"Turn on the radio!" Elodie calls from the kitchen. "Radio-Canada!" She hangs up the phone on Huguette and rushes out to where Nancy is fiddling with Elodie's stereo. "Hurry!" she barks.

"What's going on?" Nancy asks her. She's staying with Elodie until she finds a job and can afford her own place.

"Bouchard made a surprise announcement in the National Assembly today," Elodie says. "Apparently he apologized and made some offer to compensate us."

"How much?"

"I have no idea, we weren't even consulted about this." She nervously lights a cigarette. "It's on the news now. Turn it up."

"We can't undo the past," Premier Bouchard is saying in a clip. "But we can apologize to the Duplessis orphans and do our best to ease their lot in life."

"Premier Bouchard did make clear that the government has no legal responsibility for what happened to the orphans," the reporter says. "He doesn't blame the nuns who ran the psychiatric institutions either. He says they took on a burden that no one else wanted."

"We have to put what happened to these orphans in context," Bouchard says. "Back then, illegitimate children were regarded as deviants of society. We will be setting aside a three million dollar fund to help the orphans reintegrate into society, but there will be no public inquiry and no charges laid against the church."

Elodie jumps up and turns off the radio. "Three million dollars for three thousand of us?"

"That's a thousand dollars each."

"*A thousand dollars each?* A thousand dollars for everything they did to us?"

The phone starts ringing. It'll be Huguette, or Francine, or Bruno. She picks up.

"A thousand dollars!" Huguette cries. "A thousand dollars to compensate for all our suffering!"

"It's humiliating."

"I don't want my goddamn birth certificate!" Huguette goes on. "I want money! I want an apology from the church!"

"Their offer is meaningless," Elodie says. "Bruno won't accept it."

"So it's over."

"It's not over."

"How can you say that? You heard Bouchard. We were a burden no one else wanted. 'Deviants of society.' There won't be a public inquiry. It's over."

"This is still progress, Huguette. Think where we started in '92. We're not where we want to be yet, but we're making inroads."

She's not sure she believes her own words. She feels as discouraged as her friend, but someone has to keep the spark lit.

As soon as she hangs up, the phone rings again. All of them will call at some point, ranting, venting. Another moment of shared disappointment. She ignores it.

"You're not going to answer?"

"No."

Nancy quietly unplugs the phone. "At least Bouchard apologized," she says. "That's something."

Elodie glares at her. "Please don't tell me I should be happy about this."

"You just said yourself it's progress."

"I said that for Huguette's sake."

"Maybe it's time to give up, M'ma," Nancy says delicately. "How much more disappointment can you stand? It's been almost *seven years*."

"A lot more. I'm tougher than I thought I was."

"I miss my mother."

"You *have* your mother," Elodie says. "*I'm right here*."

"Are you?"

"This means more to me than I can explain, Nance."

"But it's taken over your life, your identity—"

"I may still identify as an orphan, but I don't equate that with being a victim anymore. I equate it with being a *survivor*. I made that doctor write me an apology letter. I went back to St. Nazarius with my mother. I've protested and will keep protesting until I get justice and am properly compensated. Until then, I will not stop."

They started picketing at the Quebec College of Physicians on René Lévesque Boulevard in the morning, marched over to Bouchard's office to publicly reject his offer, and then on to the Notre Dame Basilica, where they're now gathered outside the Archbishop of Montreal's office. Cardinal Turcotte was quoted in the papers this week saying, "The Duplessis orphans do not deserve an apology. We don't have time to waste on that. To apologize is to recognize one's guilt. The whole thing has been sensationalized."

There are a couple hundred orphans huddled in the rain, carrying their signs, chanting in unison as they've done on so many different occasions. Francine, Huguette, and a few others are wearing straitjackets; some of them have blue duct tape over their mouths. Elodie's sign says, WHERE IS YOUR COMPASSION, CARDINAL TURCOTTE?

In spite of the rain, in spite of this most recent setback with Bouchard, Elodie and her friends are in good spirits. There's a buoyancy among them today, a renewed sense of enthusiasm, mostly due to all the support they're getting from the public. People driving by have been honking and waving; passersby have been giving them the thumbs-up, telling them not to give up. In today's paper, a poll shows that 71 percent of Quebeckers think the church owes them an apology. One reporter even referred to them as "Bouchard's orphans."

They've also got the Quebec ombudsman on their side. Ever since Premier Bouchard's surprise announcement, the ombudsman has been speaking out all over the news, condemning the offer as unfair and degrading. In one interview, he said he was shocked by Cardinal Turcotte's lack of compassion, charity, and justice, especially since Turcotte himself worked at Mont Providence in 1954, the year it was converted into a mental hospital. It's the most validated Elodie has felt since Dr. Duceppe wrote her the apology letter.

Today, Francine is passing around a flask that she's been keeping under her straitjacket. "We may as well have some fun out here in the rain."

There's such an easy camaraderie between them all. They've become like family over the years. They laugh together as much as they cry, which is a miracle, considering what binds them.

A loud honk from a car on Notre Dame gets their attention. "*Courage!*" a woman yells from the open window of the passenger seat. "Justice for the Duplessis orphans!"

"*Merci!*" Francine yells back. She's already a little drunk. She may be in too good of a mood. "I never told anyone this," she says, "but I still sleep on my back with my arms folded across my chest. I got so used to sleeping in a straitjacket at Mont Providence."

The Radio-Canada van pulls up in front of the church, and a TV reporter Elodie recognizes gets out. Huguette gently nudges her forward. Elodie has become their unlikely media spokesperson.

"What's the reason for today's protest?" the reporter asks her, thrusting the microphone under her chin.

"We're here because we want an apology from the church," Elodie says. "Their refusal to apologize to us is outrageous. Everywhere else in Canada, institutional abuse against children has been repaired. Quebec has always wanted to be a distinct society? Well, now it is. A distinct society of injustice!"

"A spokesperson for Cardinal Turcotte is arguing that a blanket accusation against the entire Catholic Church is not founded," the reporter says. "They claim there are only a few isolated incidents. What do you say to that?"

Elodie gestures behind her, where at least two hundred orphans are marching up and down the sidewalk. "Does this look like a few isolated incidents to you? Even the government acknowledges there are at least three thousand of us, and we're just the ones who survived."

"The church is doing damage control!" one of the guys shouts from behind her, waving a sign that says TORTURE RAPE STRAITJACKETS.

"Cardinal Turcotte maintains that the orphans were not exploited or abused," the reporter says, "and that you would have been homeless if the nuns hadn't taken you in."

"You know, the pope has apologized for the Inquisition and the Crusades," Elodie responds, "but the

Archbishop of Montreal won't even apologize to us for something that happened just a few decades ago in his own province. It's a national scandal."

"Why the tape and straitjackets?"

"Because we're still being muzzled. Because we want a public inquiry."

"What's next for the Duplessis orphans?"

"You see this rain falling?" Elodie says. "This rain represents all our tears. We've shed a lot of tears in our lives, and I vow to you, we're not going to stop protesting until we get what we're asking for from the government and the church."

When Elodie gets home, she's still in a good mood. She's enjoying having the public on her side for a change, and it feels as though her voice is being heard more than ever before. Best of all, there was laughter.

Nancy is on the couch, watching her favorite game show, *Piment Fort*. Elodie goes straight to the kitchen without speaking to her. She's not mad, but there's still some tension between them. She grabs a box of Kraft Dinner from the pantry and a beer from the fridge. Fills a pot with water and turns on the stove.

"Did you see this?" Nancy says, startling her.

Elodie turns from the stove. Nancy hands her the *Journal de Montreal.*

"More bad news?"

"There's an article about two researchers who say the Quebec government and the Catholic Church made a huge profit by falsely certifying the orphans as mentally ill in the fifties."

"We already knew that. Why is this news?"

"I mean they get specific," Nancy says. "They make a conservative estimate that by today's standards, the church got about seventy million dollars in subsidies."

"*Seventy million?*"

"And the government saved thirty-seven million dollars *per orphanage*," Nancy says. "How many were converted into mental hospitals?"

"All of the Catholic ones, I believe." Elodie leans against the counter. "I knew they made money, but I had no idea it was that much."

"And Bouchard had the nerve to offer you a thousand bucks each. It's disgusting."

Elodie reads the article, livid. Seeing that number in print somehow makes it more horrific, more malevolent. "At least now I know what my life was worth," she says.

What a stroke of genius it was, that decision to profit off society's most defenseless citizens. An order given from on high, a few thousand records doctored, a little harmless collusion, and the money began rolling in. Millions and millions of dollars, no strings attached, no foreseeable consequences other than the sacrifice of a few thousand illegitimate children. "Of course the nuns are arguing it's all made up," Elodie says, crumpling the newspaper and dumping the box of macaroni into the boiling water. "Why the hell else would they have turned us into mental patients if not for the money?"

"The point is, it's in the news," Nancy says. "You guys have been in the news every day. It's becoming a movement. People are outraged."

A movement. Elodie likes the sound of that. "It *is* a movement, isn't it?"

"Yes. And you're leading it, M'ma. This article is a good thing," Nancy assures her. "It's going to add fuel to the fire. Even more people will be on your side."

Elodie considers this. Maybe the surfacing of all these damning details will bolster their position, give them some leverage.

The phone rings. Nancy hands it to her.

"I saw you on TV today," Maggie says. "You looked good, Elo. Your cheeks were rosy. You were so confident and well-spoken. I'm proud of you."

"Do you think we might be making some progress?" she asks her mother. "I was so discouraged after Bouchard's shitty offer."

"There's momentum, for sure. You're getting a lot of media attention."

"It's about time. We've been at it long enough."

"Keep it up, *cocotte*."

When she hangs up, she removes the noodles from the stove, drains the water in the sink, and adds the orange powdered cheese, not bothering with milk or margarine. She uses a wooden spoon to stir it, and then eats a mouthful straight from the spoon. She loves macaroni and cheese.

Nancy grabs two bowls from the cupboard, and Elodie fills them both. They eat standing up.

"I've been thinking a lot about what you said to me the other day," Nancy says.

"You have?"

"Your past makes me uncomfortable," she admits. "It makes me feel helpless. Like, I wish *I* was enough to make you happy."

"But you do make me happy. You don't even know how much. My work with the Duplessis orphans doesn't undermine the joy you bring to my life. But it does give me a sense of power I've never felt before."

"I want to be a good daughter to you, M'ma. But I don't always know how."

"I only ever wanted you to be free and untroubled and happy. And you are those things. You *are*!"

Nancy's eyes fill with tears, and Elodie takes her in her arms. "I know it hasn't been easy for you," Elodie says.

"I just don't want you to be in pain," Nancy sniffles. "I know that's selfish—"

"No," Elodie says, holding onto her. "Of course you don't want to see your mother suffering."

"Will things ever go back to the way they were before the Duplessis orphans?"

"I don't think they can," Elodie says. "Not anymore. But I believe they can be better."

"How?"

"For one thing, I'm going to be more honest with you. From now on, I won't always act like everything is fine when it's not. That doesn't mean I'm going to burden you with all my crap, but there's definitely room for more authenticity between us."

Nancy nods and steps back from her mother's embrace. She puts her bowl of Kraft Dinner in the sink.

"I have to tell you something," Elodie says, suddenly moved to rid herself of all her secrets. She doesn't want any more unnecessary barriers in her life, certainly not between her and her daughter. "Let's sit," she says, leading Nancy by the hand to the kitchen table.

"Should I be scared?"

Elodie takes a cigarette from the pack she keeps

in the wicker fruit basket. "This is hard to say," she begins, feeling a weight pushing on her chest.

Nancy looks wary.

"I need to tell you something about your father, Nance."

Typical Nancy—her expression doesn't change, not even a flinch.

"He showed up one day at the deli."

"When?"

Elodie braces herself. "Four years ago. Right before the referendum."

Nancy is quiet.

"I'm sorry I didn't tell you sooner," Elodie says. "He was dying, Nance. He only had a few months to live at most. He had cancer. I made the decision to protect you from meeting him and then losing him right away. Maybe it was the wrong decision, looking back."

Nancy remains silent.

"Obviously he didn't know about you," Elodie explains. "And I didn't think it would be fair to tell him in the last weeks of his life."

Elodie gets up and tears off a piece of paper from her grocery list pad. She sits back down at the table and scribbles something on the paper. "I'm sorry I kept it from you," she says. "I didn't think I had a choice, for both your sakes. I really believed in my heart it would be cruel to introduce you to him and then have him die on you."

"That must have been a hard decision for you."

"Would you have wanted to meet him?" Elodie asks her. "Was I wrong?"

"Of course I would have wanted to meet him," she says. "He may not have wanted to meet me, though. I get that you were thinking about him, too. Especially since he was dying. It would have been a lot to take in."

"I'm sorry," Elodie says again. "Maybe I should have given you both a choice."

"Why was he at the deli?" she wants to know. "He was from Boston, right? Was he there to see you?"

"No, he was surprised to see me," Elodie says. "He enjoyed Montreal. He used to visit with his family."

"His family?"

"You have sisters, Nance."

Nancy's eyes widen. A flicker of emotion in her face.

"Here," Elodie says, handing Nancy the piece of paper.

"Katy, Finn, Jennifer, and Denise Duffy. Four of them?"

"Four redheads, like him. His name was Dennis Finbar Duffy. You'll probably find them in Boston, if you decide you want to."

"Of course I do," Nancy says. Elodie can't tell if she's happy or angry, but she's always been like that.

They sit like that for a while, Elodie smoking quietly, Nancy staring down at the names on that piece of paper.

"Say something," Elodie finally says.

"I don't know what to say."

"Are you angry with me?"

"No."

"Would you like to go to Boston?"

"Would you come with me?" Nancy asks her, and Elodie is struck by her vulnerability.

"Yes," Elodie says. "Of course. I want to meet your sisters."

42

April 1999

Véronique is sitting on the dock, staring out at the lake that once belonged to her and Pierre. That's how she used to feel about it, back when they were smuggling. Like they owned it. Maybe that's how you're supposed to feel about the world in your twenties.

Pierre has been gone exactly five years today. A sad coincidence, given today is her father's wake. Lisette wanted to have it here in Ste. Barbe, where people could be outside if the house got too crowded. It's been a parade of separatists, nationalists, and ex-FLQ members drunkenly singing "Gens du Pays" and reminiscing about the old days. A couple of journalists tried to crash the party. Léo would have loved it. It would have made him feel important, beloved. Maybe he was.

Véronique finishes her beer and tucks her face into her scarf to protect it from the wind. She misses Léo. It doesn't matter that she's been away for almost two years; she misses knowing he's here. Sitting in his recliner, nattering about something, listening to his music. She misses knowing he's in the world. Even when he was in jail, he was there.

What a void it leaves, the death of a parent. She'd been angry with him leading up to his stroke; their relationship had been tenuous over the last couple of years, but there was comfort in knowing he was waiting for her at home. She'd come to take it for granted, having a father; thought, with the hubris of youth, that she had the luxury of deciding when she would whole-heartedly forgive him.

A gust of wind kicks up, spraying her with a mist of water. The lake is rough, choppy. She can viscerally remember how it felt to be out riding in wind like this, the boat banging against the waves like they were formed of concrete. Pierre shouting from the back, *"Câlice, mon queue!"*

Inside of five years, the three men she's loved most in her life are gone. The heartbreak feels untenable today under the dim gray sky and battering wind.

"Véro?"

She turns. Marc is there, shivering in a thin K-Way

jacket. He joins her at the edge of the dock, not saying anything for a long time. At some point she feels his arm around her shoulders, heavy and strong, a log of solid muscle.

"What now?" he asks her.

"I'm going to stay," she says. "I can't leave my mom."

"You know you always have a job if you want it," he says. "Camil needs more people."

"No."

He doesn't push. She wishes Marc would get out of this life. The last thing she wants is to lose him to an arrest or a gunshot. But he's flush from selling drugs, just bought a house and has a baby on the way. She knows he'll never give it up. He was born for it.

She once thought she was born for it, too, but the people in her life helped her to see otherwise. It took a long time, a lot of catastrophic choices, but she would never go back now.

"I have a plan," she tells Marc. "I know what I want to do next."

When she gets back up to the house, she sees Elodie standing in the middle of the room by herself. They haven't seen each other since the morning Véronique showed up on her doorstep, having just narrowly escaped detonating a bomb outside of James's office. "Elo?"

"I hope it's okay that I came," she says, turning to Véronique. "I read about your father, and there was a notice about today's wake—"

"I'm so happy you're here," she says, practically falling into Elodie's arms. "You don't know how good it is to see you."

"I think I do."

They look each other over, teary and relieved to be together again. "You look good, Elo. Really."

"So do you, Véro."

"I've wanted to call you so many times."

"I wish you would have."

"I've been away, traveling."

"Tell me everything you've been doing for the past two years."

"I went to Europe in the fall of '97. I visited Buda-pest first, then Prague, Berlin, Amsterdam. I ended up in Paris and just stayed there. I had nothing to come home to."

"Did you work over there?"

"I worked at a bookstore in the Marais. Mostly I just read. I read everything I could get my hands on. I met someone and moved in with him. And then Léo had the stroke, so I came back. He died while I was home."

"So you're staying?"

"I can't leave my mother."

"I'm sorry, V. And the man you left in Paris?"

"He's still there. He owns the bookstore where I worked."

"Do you love him?"

"I do. Just not enough to stay in Paris." *Not the way I loved James.* "He's not about to leave his store and move to Montreal for me either. It ended by default."

"Maybe when your mother is back on her feet, you can go back to Paris."

"I belong here," she says. "Montreal is home."

"I'm glad," Elodie says. "I miss you."

"I miss you, too, Elo. I've wanted to reach out so many times, but . . ."

"Why didn't you?"

Véronique shrugs. "Remorse. Embarrassment. I never said goodbye to you. I never even wrote."

"I understood why."

"What I did that night," she says. "The bomb—"

"But you *didn't* do it."

"I would have."

"You were in a dark place, Véro. That was never who you were, and I knew that. I never judged you. I just needed a little time."

"Did you ever tell James why I was at his office that night?"

"Of course not. He wanted to believe you were there because you still loved him."

"I did."

"I know," Elodie says, squeezing her hand. "I heard about Louis."

Louis was arrested throwing a Molotov cocktail into a sandwich shop in NDG. He got some notoriety when he was arrested, but his Language Brigade fizzled out and he was quickly forgotten. Véronique was in Europe at the time. She felt sad for him, but relieved it was over. He never mentioned her name to the police when he was questioned about the first couple of bombings. At least he was loyal to her. He's in jail now, sentenced to eight years. She has not been to see him. She probably won't go. She's still so ashamed of that episode in her life.

"Maybe this doesn't matter anymore," Elodie says, "but James is genuinely sorry he wrote that article about your father."

"It was a long time ago."

"You are the last person he ever wanted to hurt, Véronique."

"I know that now," she admits. "If I'm honest, I

really hoped that article could somehow change the past or justify what my father had done. I had all these silly expectations about how it could exonerate him. *I'm* the one who needed to be convinced he was a hero and not a murderer, so the truth in black and white was unbearable."

"Still, James didn't need to be the one to write it," Elodie says. "And he's been paying for it ever since."

"What do you mean?"

"He lost you. That's what I mean."

"You know it's funny, in a way," Véronique says. "It turns out Léo didn't even kill Pierre Laporte."

"He didn't?"

"He told me the truth before I went to Europe. He wasn't even *there* when it happened."

"Why did he let you think he had? Why did he let the world think that?"

"I guess he thought it was the more heroic version of himself."

"He was willing to go to jail for life?"

"That was Léo," she says. "He had his principles, they were just completely fucked up. James always used to say that."

"James will feel even worse."

"Léo wanted everyone to think he had done it. James was just doing his job."

"But you haven't come out and publicly cleared his name."

"Léo wouldn't have wanted that," Véronique says. "He spent his entire life committed to that lie. It was his legacy, his legend. It's not my place to tell his truth."

"That must have been quite a bombshell."

"It's partly why I went to Europe," she says. "I needed to get away from him, from Louis. From James."

"Did you reconcile with Léo before he died?"

"Sort of. I came home for Christmas last year with Féderic so he could meet my parents. We had a good time, but there was no formal truce between my father and me. He didn't apologize. We just sort of moved on. I went back to Paris a lot less angry."

Elodie touches Véronique's cheek in her warm, motherly way. "Maybe you can drop by the deli for lunch next week?"

"I'd love that. I haven't had a smoked meat sandwich in too long."

"James is still at CNA," Elodie mentions. "He's bureau chief now."

"I know. He's pretty well-known."

"He's not seeing anyone."

"Sarah didn't work out?"

"Sarah was never right for him."

"I see what you're doing here," Véronique says, "but I'm not ready. I'm still sorting things out with Féderic, and I have to get my life in order here. I'm starting over."

"Maybe it's selfish of me," Elodie says. "I'd just like two of my favorite people to be together, where you belong."

Later on, after all the guests have gone, Camil and Véronique cap off the night with shots of crème de menthe. Marc has gone home, and Lisette is in the kitchen washing dishes. The house is quiet except for the rattle of cutlery and clanging of plates being loaded into the dishwasher.

"Did Marc speak to you about coming back to work?" Camil asks her.

The den is blue with cigarette smoke. They're both drunk, heavy-lidded. "I'm not coming back to work for you," she tells him.

"I need you."

"I'm done, *mon'onc.* I can't."

"Do you know how much money we're making? What else are you going to do?"

"I have a plan," she says, emptying her shot glass.

Camil manages to get back on his feet and wobbles over to her. He refills her glass, then his. "To Léo!" he says, holding it up, exposing the faded blue tattoo of his wife's face on his forearm.

"To Léo."

They down the shots, and he pours them two more before sinking back in his recliner. She watches him from across the room as he watches her. He's got a mean stare. She wouldn't want to mess with him if she weren't his niece. This is what Marc will become one day, hardened and intimidating; a seasoned, lifetime criminal. Camil is the real deal, maybe more so than her father ever was.

He lights a cigarette, which he holds between his middle and pointing fingers, a quirk she always found strange. She would like to ask him if he killed Callahan. She's drunk enough; *he's* drunk enough. But part of her would rather not know.

He closes his eyes, lets out a long, low snore, and then jerks awake. "It was a good turnout today," he slurs, remembering the cigarette burning in his hand. "Your father would have been pleased."

Véronique nods, letting the syrupy crème de menthe slide down her throat; the sweet, mouthwashy taste is starting to nauseate her. Her uncle is watching her through half-closed eyes. "I had nothing to do with Callahan's death," he says. "If that's why you won't come back."

She doesn't respond.

"I swear, Véro. I would never kill one of my best customers."

That's the problem with a guy like Camil. You can never tell when he's lying.

43

June 30, 2001

Elodie is sitting very still. A hush has fallen over the room. Her hands are folded on her lap. She can feel them trembling against the fabric of her cotton dress. They've all said their piece. Bruno has spoken eloquently on their behalf. They're close. So very close. All that's left is to vote on the agreement, which was written by Bruno and their attorney: "For a Reconciliation with Justice."

Elodie is fifty-one years old. She's been at this almost ten years. The Duplessis orphans have their own headquarters now, here at the St. Pierre Centre on Rue Panet. There's a new premier of Quebec, and he's made the best offer they've had yet. The only offer worth considering.

Bruno, sitting at the front of the room, looks out at the assembly of Duplessis orphans, his peers, and says, "Are we in agreement then?"

One of the men, an outspoken critic of Bruno, leaps to his feet. "This decree is an insult!" he says, flushed with anger. "Where is the complete text of the offer from Premier Landry? You've made too many concessions in this agreement, Bruno."

"It's this or nothing," Bruno says calmly. "This is as far as the province will go, Robert."

"We wanted double this amount!" Robert rails. "In Article 10 of the original document, the wording stated specifically that the provincial government, the medical community, and the church would have to contribute to a compensation fund in the amount of fifty thousand dollars per orphan. Why is that article removed from this decree?"

"Because it was not agreed upon, Robert. They refused our counteroffer. It's this or nothing."

"But this doesn't go far enough! You've betrayed your principles, Bruno. Did you make a secret deal with them?"

"I made the necessary concessions to get you as much as you're ever going to get."

Someone else stands up and says to Robert, "We're getting old and we need the money before it's too late. We're at the end of the line. This is what we've wanted."

"It's a deal with the devil," Robert counters. "You're about to sign away the possibility of ever getting an apology from the church!"

"We were never going to get an apology from the church."

"Bruno, ten days ago you rejected Landry's offer. Now you're about to accept it with no significant changes! What's in it for you? What happened to 'I will never settle this case at a discount!'?"

"You're free to leave," Bruno says. "You and anyone else who isn't satisfied with this agreement can walk away right now. I suggest the rest of us vote."

Heads start bobbing. Everyone is growing restless. The room is airless.

Bruno reads the final paragraph of the decree. "'In witness whereof, the parties recognize having read all and each of the clauses of this agreement protocol and having accepted them, and have duly signed two copies as follows: The Duplessis Orphans Committee, signed by the President of the Committee—'"

Bruno pauses and looks up. The room is tension-filled and silent. Elodie's heart is pounding. A moustache of sweat has collected above her lip.

"All those in favor," he says solemnly.

One by one, from the back row to the front, they begin to raise their hands. Sitting nervously on folding chairs in a room similar to the one from their very first meeting, Elodie can feel the tension, a collective holding of breath. It seems like forever since that first meeting. Elodie can't even count how many protests she's marched in, how many letters she's written to politicians, how many disappointing days she's sat in court in the last decade. *Could it really be over?*

She raises her hand.

The prosecutor counts them all as Elodie looks around. She estimates about two hundred people are here today, representing the eleven hundred orphans across the province who qualify for compensation in this new agreement.

"And all those against," Bruno says.

A few hands shoot up in the air, Robert's first among them.

"The majority votes in favor," Bruno declares. "The decree is validated."

A deafening explosion of cheers and applause erupts in the room as Bruno signs the document.

Elodie hugs Huguette and then Francine.

"It's done."

"What am I going to do with my life now?" Elodie says, only half kidding.

"Live it," Francine says. "Spend your money."

Elodie will get about twenty thousand dollars—a base sum of ten, and another thousand dollars for every year she was wrongfully locked up. They will not get their apology from the Church, and they'll have to sign a waiver accepting that, in order to claim their money. There will be no public inquiry into any crimes against humanity, nor will any criminal charges be laid. But this will have to do. It's better than nothing. It's much better.

Outside, the sun is shining. The orphans burst through the exit door into the sunlight, like children being let out of school for the summer. The air is thick and humid. People are milling around the parking lot, hugging one another and high-fiving, celebrating. One woman is dancing for the CBC camera.

This is a victory, Elodie tells herself. Twenty thousand dollars is a lot of money for someone like her.

The media is everywhere. One of the familiar faces—a reporter for CKAC—approaches her. "What happened in there?" he asks her, offering the microphone. "There are a lot of happy faces out here."

"We've accepted the offer," Elodie tells him, shielding her eyes from the sun, "but with a very clear statement for the government: the offer is insufficient in many ways, but we're accepting it because we're getting old. We've been at this a long time, and it's time for us to move on."

"Insufficient how?"

"The church is getting off scot-free," she says. "We'd also hoped for double the amount of money, but we know it's this or nothing. At least this money gives us a chance to enjoy the last years of our lives."

"So you're happy with the settlement then?"

Elodie considers her answer. She adjusts the strap of her sundress, which has slipped off her shoulder. "Yes," she says, enjoying the warmth of the sun. "I'm happy in the way I've learned how to be happy in the world."

"Can you explain what you mean?"

She thinks about her past, what she's lived through in and out of the asylum, and shakes her head. "I'm not very good with words," she says, and smiles, knowing she doesn't need to explain anything anymore.

44

September 2001

The Residence of the Beatitudes is in a squat, two-story apartment complex on a dead-end street in Cartierville. The facade is beige brick with white aluminum windows and railings, set back on a barren plot of interlocked pavement. "This is a far cry from her life at the convent," Maggie says as they approach the building. "She probably thought she would live out the rest of her days at St. Nazarius."

When St. Nazarius Hospital was torn down, the adjacent convent had to be vacated, and the few dozen elderly nuns who still lived there had to be moved to assisted-living residences. More nuns from other convents will surely follow. As the decline of the Catholic religious orders continues, the convents are becoming more and more anachronistic. The future is uncertain for the Motherhouse in Shaughnessy Village, the convent of the Miséricorde downtown, and the Ursuline Monastery in Quebec City; all of them will soon be obsolete. Aging nuns throughout the province will have to be relocated and decisions made about what to do with all the empty buildings that once housed a powerful community of religious orders. The nuns who once ran all the hospitals, schools, and orphanages are vanishing, and in that, Elodie takes small comfort.

She recently read an article in the *Journal de Montreal* that said there are only about five thousand Catholic nuns left in the province, compared to ten times that when Elodie was growing up in St. Nazarius. Most of them are in their seventies and eighties, with no new novices on the horizon. Sister Ignatia is probably in her eighties now. One of Elodie's contacts from the Duplessis Orphans Committee, a friend of a friend of a friend, provided the address of the Residence of the Beatitudes, where Ignatia was sent to live out the rest of her miserable days.

"They used to run an empire in Quebec," Maggie says, looking outside at the grim building that is now home to the few remaining of them. "They've certainly come down in status."

The reception desk sits to the left of what appears to be a common room. There are a few elderly women watching TV, others staring at the walls. It reminds Elodie of the Big Room at St. Nazarius, which seems fitting.

"We're here to see Sister Ignatia," Elodie says to the woman at the front desk. She's holding a copy of James's book in her hands: *Born in Sin: The True Life Story of a Duplessis Orphan*, by J. G. Phénix. Her hands are shaking.

"Is she expecting you?"

"I was hoping to surprise her," Elodie says. "I knew her at St. Nazarius." She turns to Maggie and Nancy. "This is my mother and my daughter."

"Sister Ignatia will be happy to have visitors," the woman says, smiling warmly. "What's your name, dear?"

She wonders if Sister Ignatia will remember her. And if she does, will she even let her in?

"We'd like to surprise her if that's okay," Nancy says.

The receptionist looks them over—three generations of good Catholic women here to see one of their former caregivers—and doesn't even hesitate before calling up to Sister Ignatia.

"You have visitors, Sister. A friend from St. Naz-arius. A *friend*, Sister. From St. Nazarius."

Hanging up, she says, "Go on up. She's on the second floor. Room 7B."

They take the stairs up one flight. Elodie knocks on the door of 7B. Her heart is pushing against her chest, thumping wildly. The door opens, and she holds her breath, anticipating that monster from her past. But it's just an old woman, short and thick, stooped heavily over a walker. Not exactly frail, but certainly not threatening. She still looks like a bat with those small black eyes, wide-set on her broad face. She has jowls now, a sunken mouth. Her hair is a cloud of white, and she's wearing a navy blue knee-length skirt and white shirt instead of a habit. A heavy gold cross rests between her large sagging breasts.

Sister Ignatia appraises them, showing no trace of recognition.

"I was at St. Nazarius," Elodie says, her voice a tremor.

"Come in," Ignatia says, opening the door wider and stepping aside for them.

Elodie doesn't move, so shocked is she to have been invited in without any qualm or apprehension. She thought Sister Ignatia would have slammed the door in her face the moment she realized Elodie was an orphan and not a former colleague. Why would she just let her in?

Nancy gives Elodie a gentle push, and they file into the room, which is cramped and sad. Pea soup green walls, dingy sheer curtains, and a single bed with a bedspread of brown and green circles. A needlepoint cushion in the center of the bed is embroidered with a psalm: THIS IS THE DAY THE LORD HAS MADE, LET US REJOICE AND BE GLAD IN IT. A large crucifix hangs above the bed, a bronze Jesus gazing down on her while she sleeps. There's an old rocking chair, exactly like the ones at St. Nazarius—she probably stole it—and two brown vinyl armchairs squeezed into the corner, facing a small TV on the wall. The only other furniture in the room is a brown dresser adorned with an altar of candles, statuary, and framed pictures of Jesus.

Sister Ignatia painstakingly lowers herself into the rocking chair. Elodie and Maggie take the armchairs in the corner, with Nancy perched on one of the armrests.

"Do you remember me?" Elodie asks her.

"Were you a nurse, dear?"

"I was a patient from '57 to '67. My name is Elodie de Ste. Sulpice."

"What a pretty name. *Elodie.* That's a lily, isn't it? I used to love to garden."

Elodie doesn't know what to say.

"Did you say you were a nurse?"

"I was a patient on the psychiatric ward at St. Nazarius. You were in charge of my ward. Don't you remember me?"

"Yes, of course. You were a sweet girl. Very bright. You played the violin, didn't you?"

Elodie looks over at her mother. It's obvious to her now why Sister Ignatia agreed to see her. She has no recollection of the past.

"How are the others?" Sister Ignatia asks her. "I miss them. I wish they'd visit more often."

Elodie is thrown off guard. She's rehearsed her speech so many times in her mind, but never did she imagine giving it to a pathetic old woman with dementia. What a waste it is, after all the buildup. "You abused me and tortured me when I was there," Elodie tells her, studying that craggy face for some sign of lucidity. Trying to jog her memory. "Don't you remember?"

The old woman just stares at her with an empty, untroubled gaze. It's like the devil's been exorcized from her body by age and senility, and all that's left is the shell.

"You chained me to a metal bed frame and left me

there for days," Elodie continues, needing to say it anyway. "You told me my mother was *dead*."

"I cared for all my girls," Ignatia says, sounding genuinely confused. "Why would you say such things to me?"

"I don't believe you don't remember anything."

Sister Ignatia looks past her at Maggie and Nancy. "You two were there," she says to them. "Tell her how I cared for you. I cared for all my girls. I was outnumbered, but it didn't stop me from doing God's work." Her whole body is trembling as she defends herself, her eyes jumping from Maggie to Nancy to Elodie. An animal, cornered, with no idea why.

Everything Elodie had wanted to say now seems utterly futile. Sister Ignatia may as well be dead. There will be no contrition or acknowledgment from her, no apology or pleas for mercy. Her mind—that former crux of evil—is gone.

"We should go," she says softly.

Maggie and Nancy stand up. Maggie is crying into one of her vintage floral hankies. Nancy puts her arm around her grandmother, and Maggie rests her head on Nancy's shoulder. They lean on each other.

"I'm very happy for you," Sister Ignatia says. "I only wanted the best for all of you. You were always a sweet girl, Lily. And very bright."

When they get outside, the weather has turned muggy and the sun is bobbing between a smudge of clouds. The air feels heavy, like rain is coming.

They get inside the car. No one says anything. No postmortem is offered. Elodie fastens her seat belt and rolls down the window to let in the Indian summer air.

Finally, after starting the car and adjusting the air conditioner, Maggie breaks the silence. "Do you feel any sense of closure?" she asks Elodie.

Closure is a word that gets thrown around a lot these days, but she has no idea what it's supposed to feel like. She's had an apology from Dr. Duceppe, a financial settlement from the government, and a glimpse into Sister Ignatia's pitiful life. All those things have been marvelously healing, moments of great vindication. But *closure* implies something far more permanent. Her past will not be shuttered in one final grand gesture just because the government compensated her or because Sister Ignatia is going to die alone with her delusions and her framed pictures of Jesus.

"I feel relief," she says, glancing outside as a light rain begins to fall. "I feel like I've been chained to that bed my entire life, and now I'm suddenly free."

Maggie reaches over and touches her knee, and Nancy puts her arms around her from the back seat.

Elodie looks from one to the other, swelling with love for both of them. Love is her revenge, she realizes. And her life is filled with it today.

As Maggie pulls out onto the road, Elodie thinks about that slogan on Sister Ignatia's needlepoint cushion. *This is the day the Lord has made, let us rejoice and be glad in it.*

45

October 2001

Véronique steps up to the microphone and taps it to make sure it's on. There are about forty people waiting for the reading to get started. It's standing room only, with a pleasant din of conversation over which Véronique has to raise her voice. "Welcome to De Gournays," she begins. "I want to thank you all for coming out tonight to celebrate the one-year anniversary of this little bookstore."

Applause, whistles.

"I recognize so many faces tonight, which is what I'd always envisioned," she says. "A neighborhood bookshop where a community of like-minded people could come together and hang out. And I'm so honored to be hosting the book launch of one of my favorite local authors, Maryse Poile. She's here tonight to read an excerpt from her new book, *La Rue Castelnau*. Afterwards, Maryse will be signing books at the back of the store."

Véronique points to the table over by the Marie-Claire Blais section, where a few people are already waiting, copies of the book in hand. Maryse approaches the microphone, hugs Véronique, and sits down on a stool to read.

"Thank you, Véronique," she says, "for creating this very warm space for us to gather and celebrate our love of books."

Véronique is smiling so hard her upper cheek muscles are strained. Maryse starts to read as Véronique gazes out at the crowd, feeling quite pleased with herself. It's a better turnout than she anticipated. The reading is well received, and when it's over, the crowd moves to the table for the book signing.

There's already a queue snaking its way to the front door. She'll probably sell about fifty books tonight. She does a quick calculation. It's a good night. She stands beside Maryse to facilitate the signings, opening the books to the first page, sticking Post-its with people's names on them so the line moves more quickly. Lisette is standing by the cash register. Every time a sale gets rung through, she gives Véronique a thumbs-up. She's beaming, talking to everyone who buys a book. Véronique can read her lips from here. *My daughter owns this place.*

And then she spots James leaning discreetly against the bestseller shelf at the front of the store. Their eyes lock. He smiles. She hasn't seen him since that night outside the Canadian News Agency. Four years ago. It takes her a moment to catch her breath, steady her racing heart.

He must be at least forty, but he doesn't look it. He's still got that thick hair, with flecks of silver at his temples now. He seems confident and self-assured, a man who's forged a life for himself. He looks practically the same as he did almost ten years ago, when he showed up outside her apartment trying to get an interview. It was the summer of '92. He was doing a story on the October Crisis, absurdly introduced himself as J. G. Phénix. He was so self-important back then. She told him to get lost. She was probably already in love with him.

"This is for Pierrette."

Véronique turns back to the elderly woman standing in front of her; she's smiling eagerly, a little reverential. "It's P-i-e-r-r-e-t-t-e," she spells out.

Véronique has to pull her attention away from James. She writes *Pierrette* distractedly on the Post-it note for Maryse.

"I grew up on Rue Castelnau," the woman tells her.

Véronique nods and listens. *Stay in the moment,* she reminds herself. She sticks more Post-it notes, shakes hands, answers questions. Everyone has a story. People keep telling her how much they love her store.

When she looks up again, James is gone.

The place finally empties out at around nine. Lisette stays to help clean up the mess—half-empty trays of party sandwiches, plastic cups of white wine, crumpled napkins and biscotti crumbs on every surface.

"What a success," Lisette says, sweeping the floor. "Léo would have been so proud."

"Maybe," Véronique says, collecting the empty wine bottles.

"Just be proud."

"It's quite surreal," Véronique admits, looking around her store. She wonders if James was impressed. She hasn't stopped thinking about him all night. She was rattled when she first saw him across the room, and then disappointed after he left. Why would he show up only to leave before speaking to her? He looked damn good, too. She might feel a bit more ambivalent if he'd gained some weight and lost some hair. At least he knows about De Gournays. As a matter of pride, she wanted him to know.

Véronique sends her mother off with a few leftover bottles of beer and a box of party sandwiches. When she's alone, she fills a plastic cup with warm wine and goes behind the counter to close out the night's sales. As the cash drawer swings open, she notices a copy of James's book, *Born in Sin*, next to the till. It wasn't there before the event, which means he must have left it for her earlier. She was beginning to think she had hallucinated him.

She picks up the book and presses it to her chest, wishing he had stayed to talk. It's a beautifully written story—she wept at every page—and she would have liked to have told him that. There are so many things she would like to tell him.

She opens the book to the dedication page, where James has handwritten a note for her.

V,

"People who love as you do, with that plenitude and fire, always forget what others experience."

Thank you for loving me that way, and teaching me to love (you) that way. I'll always burn brighter for it.

J. G. Phénix.

She always loved how he called her V. He's the only one who ever did. To everyone else, she is Véro. She immediately recognizes the Marie-Claire Blais quote from one of her favorite books, *Le Loup.* She introduced James to Blais's writing in their early days together, and he came to love her books as much as Véronique did.

They're from different worlds, James and Véronique. When they were together, they had opposing ideologies and clashing political views. But she's older now and mature enough to understand that real love does not compromise itself for politics. Love doesn't judge or discriminate against conflicting opinions or ambitions; it does not divide or bully. Love is far more resilient than the average human being, forever indomitable in the face of frail egos and heavy chips on shoulders and stubborn, self-righteous pride. Love has nothing to prove; only humans do. This is what she would like to say to James: the love they had for each other did not fail. They are the ones who failed, at a time in their lives when they were still both inflexible and inept. Which makes her wonder if maybe it's not too late for them.

She reaches for her phone and dials his number. He answers on the first ring, and the sound of his voice makes her a little light-headed.

"J. G. Phénix?" she says.

"This is he." Knowing it's her, playing along.

"Thank you for the book."

"I know you own a bookstore," he says. "But just in case you hadn't read it . . ."

"I liked your inscription."

"I'm glad. I probably overthought it—"

"Blais has a new book," she says. "Have you read *Dans la Foudre et la Lumière*?"

"Obviously."

"And?"

"I thought it was better than *Soifs*."

"Oh," she says. "I didn't like it as much."

"I figured."

They never could agree on *Soifs*. "If ever you want to get together and discuss the new one—"

"I'm free now," he says.

She laughs.

"Are you still at your store?" he asks her.

"I am," she says, smiling. Going along with the moment.

She doesn't want to forget what happened between them any more than she wants the things she did—both misguided and worthwhile—to be forgotten. But maybe love is expansive enough to remember everything and still transcend it all.

Acknowledgments

First and foremost, thank you to my brilliant editor, Jennifer Barth. I am so grateful for your support and guidance. You are the one who so gently inquired if there might be a sequel to Elodie's story, and I am forever thankful that you encouraged me on that path. You gave me permission to finish the story that was twenty-plus years in the making.

A humongous thank-you to my greatest champion and cheerleader, my longtime agent and friend, Bev Slopen. Thank you for never, ever giving up. *Ever.* We've come a long way since that first meeting twenty-three years ago. Who knew where that little novel called *The Seed Man* would take us?

Another huge debt of gratitude to Billy Mernit, the guy who makes everything I write much, much better.

You are an extraordinary reader, editor, and mentor, with unmatched insight and vision. *Thank you.*

I feel truly blessed to have so many incredible people on my team. Birthing a book takes a village! To that end, I owe a huge thank-you to the most amazing marketing team ever: Irina Pintea, Cory Beatty and Katie Vincent (or as they're known worldwide, Cory & Katie), Leo Macdonald, and Sandra Leef. The past couple of years have been a wild ride. I can't wait to see what lies ahead.

The idea for this story was inspired by my own life experience growing up half-English and half-French in 1990s Montreal, and then working as a journalist at the time of the 1995 referendum. But much of the insight I gained into the emotional story of the Duplessis orphans came from Pauline Gill's book, *Les Enfants de Duplessis* (Quebec Loisirs Inc., 1991), the shocking and heartbreaking true story of Alice Quinton. I am deeply grateful to Alice Quinton for sharing her story with Pauline Gill, and for her candor, honesty, courage, and resilience.

I would also like to acknowledge Francis Simard and his book *Talking It Out: The October Crisis from Inside* (Guernica Editions, 1987). Simard's frank and brutally honest account of his involvement in the events of October 1970 were invaluable to my research and understanding of those events, beyond just the facts. Although this story was inspired by real events, my depiction of Léo's role in the October Crisis is purely fictional and the product of my imagination.

To my best friend and toughest editor, Miguel, I'm copying and pasting here for the sixth time: thank you for accompanying me to every reading and every festival and on every tour, for managing all my contracts, for saving all my publicity in a beautiful scrapbook, for picking up the kids and driving them all over the city and basically taking care of my entire life, so I can continue to be The Writer. I love you. Jessie and Luke, you bring all the joy.

Finally, thank you to my mom, Peggy, aka the real Maggie. It's been a bittersweet ride without you, but I know for certain that you're up there orchestrating every magical thing that has happened with and because of these books.

About the Author

JOANNA GOODMAN is the author of the bestselling novels *The Home for Unwanted Girls* and *The Finishing School*. Originally from Montreal, she now lives in Toronto with her husband and two children.

HARPER
LARGE PRINT

We hope you enjoyed reading
our new, comfortable print size and found it
an experience you would like to repeat.

Well – you're in luck!

Harper Large Print offers the finest in
fiction and nonfiction books in this same larger
print size and paperback format. Light and easy to read,
Harper Large Print paperbacks are for the book lovers
who want to see what they are reading without strain.

For a full listing of titles and
new releases to come, please visit our website:
www.hc.com

HARPER LARGE PRINT

SEEING IS BELIEVING!